HOUSE OF THE LOST

Also by Sarah Rayne

Ghost Song
The Death Chamber
Spider Light
Roots of Evil
A Dark Dividing
Tower of Silence

Visit www.sarahrayne.co.uk

HOUSE OF
THE LOST

Sarah Rayne

POCKET
BOOKS

LONDON • SYDNEY • NEW YORK • TORONTO

First published in Great Britain by Simon & Schuster UK Ltd, 2010
This edition published by Pocket Books UK, 2010
An imprint of Simon & Schuster UK Ltd
A CBS COMPANY

1 3 5 7 9 10 8 6 4 2

Simon & Schuster UK Ltd
1st Floor
222 Gray's Inn Road
London WC1X 8HB

www.simonandschuster.co.uk

Simon & Schuster Australia
Sydney

A CIP catalogue record for this book is available from the British Library

ISBN 978-1-84739-357-9

Printed in the UK by CPI Cox & Wyman, Reading, Berkshire RG1 8EX

ACKNOWLEDGEMENT

Grateful thanks are due to Hildegard and Ron Harman, who provided me with practical travel routes for Central and Eastern Europe during the writing of this book.

CHAPTER ONE

———◆◆◆———

Messrs Hewitt and Wellsbury
Solicitors and Notaries Public
Lincoln's Inn Fields
London

30 November 20—

Dear Mr Kendal

ESTATE OF CHARMERY KENDAL
(DECEASED)

Under the terms of Miss Kendal's will, the ownership of
the property known as Fenn House, Melbray, in the
County of Norfolk, passes to you.

You will appreciate that the shocking manner of Miss
Kendal's death delayed probate, but it has finally been
granted and so we are sending you the keys to Fenn House
by special courier, together with a copy of the transfer of
title.

Again, we offer our condolences for your cousin's dreadful and untimely death.

Yours sincerely

Hewitt and Wellsbury

Theo Kendal had never expected to see Fenn House again and he had certainly never expected to own it. He had not been to the place for a good ten years and if his cousin Charmery had not died, he would have continued to live in his own small north London house, churning out a novel a year, eking out his income with a little dilettante journalism and some radio scripts, and managing to forget for most of the time that Charmery had ever existed. But because she was dead he was driving into the wilds of Norfolk at the beginning of a cold grey December, along roads which a decade ago had been familiar but which now included a confusing bypass which sent him speeding in the wrong direction for half a dozen miles.

Melbray, when he finally reached it, had changed very little. Here was the high street with the tiny market square, a scattering of shops, the local pub and a doctor's surgery. It had been the local doctor who found Charmery's body; Theo had not met him but he had seen him being accosted by reporters on TV news bulletins after the inquest. The doctor had clearly disliked the attention; he had pushed the microphones away and walked off with his shoulders hunched and his coat collar turned up defensively. Theo, his emotions still in tatters over Charmery's death, had been grateful for the man's discretion.

A mile beyond the village was the turning to Fenn Lane. Once this turning had caused a lurch of delighted anticipation because it had meant the holiday was really beginning: long drowsy afternoons by the river with the sunlight glinting on it, pleasantly haphazard meals and lawn cricket played with whichever members of the family were around. It meant being with Charmery.

But there was no lurch of anticipation this afternoon, because four months ago someone had crept into the old boathouse where Theo and Charmery used to hide, and had forced Charmery into the water and held her below the surface with a boathook until she was dead. The local police, diligently reporting to Theo as Charmery's closest living relative, had explained that forensic reconstructions and investigations suggested the murderer had probably assumed the body would drift out into the Chet and be lost. Instead, it became wedged in the struts of the landing stage and was found three days later. A lot of the most useful evidence had been washed away, of course, but they had been able to perform DNA tests on the body – none had produced any results, however.

The police had questioned Theo, which he supposed was inevitable, given that he was the sole beneficiary of Charmery's will, and had asked him to provide an alibi, which he had not been able to do since he had been at home working. The various aunts and uncles and cousins whom he and Charmery shared had been questioned as well: a matter of trying to build up a picture of the victim's life, the police had said, which had not been well received. Nancy Kendal, a formidable unmarried aunt, said the questions were sheer impudence and she would write to the chief constable, but Theo's Great-uncle Frederick Francis Kendal – Guff to most people – said peaceably that the police had to look at all aspects of the situation.

Theo, driving down Fenn Lane four months later, with Charmery's killer still uncaught, did so with a degree of apprehension. For the first time, Fenn House struck him as vaguely sinister. The family, hearing Charmery had left the place to Theo, supposed he would sell it. It was all very well as a holiday house, they said; they had enjoyed all those summers there, and the autumn weekends and the Christmases, but surely no one would want to live there permanently? It might not be actually in the fen country, despite its name, but it was still one of Norfolk's remoter parts.

At first Theo had also thought he would sell it, probably without seeing it again, but Charmery's murder had churned up such a scalding array of emotions he had been unable to work for the past four months. Last week, receiving Fenn's keys from the solicitor's office, exhausted with staring at a blank computer screen and trying to write a book that refused to be written, he had made the decision to face the memories and the pain head on, and spend a couple of months living there. He was trusting to luck that the ghosts and the journalists would not realize he was in residence. Although he thought he could deal with the ghosts and he could certainly deal with the occasional reporter prowling around for fag ends of information about the Fenn House Drowning. In London, with the book barely a quarter written and the deadline for its delivery to his publishers looming alarmingly close, it had seemed a good idea, but with river mist creeping over the road and a cold dark house ahead, it was starting to feel like downright lunacy.

The car headlights picked out the tanglewood garden that had grown up round the house, then swept over the front of the house itself. Theo frowned, realizing he had not even asked the solicitors if the electricity was on. He had a vision of himself wandering through dim rooms by candlelight or oil lamp, wrapped in blankets to keep warm. Even in the fading light Fenn House looked dismal and somewhat neglected. Charmery's parents had always looked after it meticulously. 'Well, they had the money,' Theo's mother used to say. But they had been dead for more than five years and it looked as if there had not been as much money as everyone thought; even in this light Theo could see the missing roof tiles and peeling paintwork. For the last few miles he had been cherishing the idea that Charmery had bequeathed him the enchanted memories of their shared secret teens, but it was starting to look as if she had left him an expensive liability.

He unlocked the door and stepped inside and, as he did so, there was a curious sensation deep within his mind: a shutter-flash of something insistent and so startlingly real he stopped dead. It

4

imprinted itself vividly on his vision. It was the image of a young boy entering a shadowy and silent house, fearful of what might be waiting for him in the gathering dusk.

Entering the house at dusk was always difficult for Matthew, because even if the house seemed silent, he could never be sure who might be inside. His father had to have quiet to write his books; Matthew understood this. Father's work was important – books were very important and so were the newspapers for which Father sometimes wrote – so he was always careful not to disturb him. But there were times when the house became wrapped in a different quietness; a deep, frozen silence, which Matthew hated because it was as if the building was deliberately being very still and silent, like an animal trying to avoid being noticed by predators. Predators meant people who hunted and sometimes killed: Matthew knew that because Father liked him to know as many words as possible.

If he came home to find the house in this silent, frightened state it meant the cold-eyed men were there. Matthew did not know what went on between the men and his father, but after their visits Father often shut himself in his study for days and Wilma had to carry his meals in on trays, puffing a bit as she came up from the scullery because she was quite stout. Once when the men were there, Matthew listened outside the study door, his heart hammering with panic in case he was caught, but he did not hear anything because this was an old house with thick doors.

'Better not to hear anything at all,' Wilma always said about the men. 'Better to stay out of their way.'

For most of the time Matthew did so. Once he was in his bedroom at the top of the house with the door closed, he felt safer. He loved this room, because it was the place where he could escape into his own world. He had several of these worlds. Father once said it was the best thing ever to escape into worlds you made for yourself, but he meant the worlds he wrote about in his books. Matthew knew Father would like him to write books one day –

5

stories anyway – but he did not think he would. In any case, his father often seemed to find writing books quite hard. He wandered round the house with his hair in an untidy tumble because he could not be bothered to brush it, and swore at pieces of paper or angrily crumpled them into balls and threw them across the room.

Instead of writing stories Matthew would rather have the private worlds he drew in the sketchbooks he was given for Christmas and birthdays. Father explained that they did not have much money for presents, but Matthew thought drawing paper, coloured pencils and crayons were the best presents. For his ninth birthday he had a whole paintbox which was the loveliest thing he had ever been given in his whole life.

It would be wonderful if the pretend worlds could be real, so that if the cold-eyed men ever came into his bedroom they would not find him because he would have walked into one of the painted pictures like Alice vanishing into the looking-glass world. Father had read that story to him last year, saying it was not actually a fairytale but something called an allegory, in fact a number of allegories. That was interesting, wasn't it? Matthew had not known what an allegory was, but his father always expected him to understand lots of words and he had not wanted to disappoint him, so he had said politely it was very interesting indeed, then went away to make drawings of the playing cards who had chased Alice. When he said his prayers each night (his teachers said everyone should do this), he always added a prayer that one morning he would wake up to find one of his worlds really did exist and he was living in it.

The inside of Fenn House was as dingy as the outside.

The curious image that had printed itself on Theo's vision like a dark sunburst when he entered the house was no longer so vivid, but it had not entirely left him. He supposed it had been a result of eye strain due to the long drive, probably with a degree of emotion generated by returning to this house.

The musty desolation of the house was rather daunting, but the electricity was connected which was one mercy. Although, when Theo switched on the lights, he thought he would almost have preferred oil lamps and candles which might have softened the ominous look of the peeling wallpaper and damp patches under some of the windows.

He unloaded the boxes of provisions he had bought in Norwich and carried them through to the kitchen, distributing them in the larder and fridge. After this he took his suitcases upstairs, pausing outside the bedroom Charmery always had when they were children, sometimes sharing it with their younger cousin, Lesley, who loved coming to Fenn because of being with these two nearly grown-up cousins.

Dust lay thickly in Charmery's room and there were several faded oblongs on the walls where pictures had hung and been removed. But the old grandfather clock was still in its corner. It had originally been in the big, low-ceilinged sitting room, but as a child Charmery had fallen in love with the clock and persuaded her parents to carry it up to her bedroom. She liked to fall asleep listening to it, she said; it was like listening to Fenn's heart beating. The clock had to be wound every seven days or it stopped, and Charmery had always made a little ceremony of the winding. Every time she came to Fenn House she would race up the stairs to start it: she always insisted the holiday could not begin properly until the clock was ticking.

No one had wound the clock recently, though. The elaborate brass hands stood at some long-ago three o'clock, and there was dust across the face and the carved door. Theo found himself wondering if three o'clock was the hour Charmery had died.

He closed the door and went along to the bedroom he had always used. There was a view towards the river from this side of the house, and in the gathering dusk he could just make out the outline of St Luke's Convent. The convent's land did not exactly join up with Fenn House, but parts marched alongside here and there. On a quiet day – and most days in Melbray were quiet – you could hear the chapel bell. Nancy Kendal said it was intrusive, but Theo had always rather liked hearing the soft chimes. He stared at the crouching bulk of the convent for a moment, then closed the curtains and went back downstairs.

After several unsuccessful attempts he managed to fire up the central-heating system. It clanked protestingly and the pipes juddered alarmingly, but eventually it sent out a reasonable warmth and Theo began to feel more in touch with normality. He went into the dining room which he had not looked at yet, but in which he intended to work.

It was annoying to find, when he switched on the light, that the bulb had blown. Theo swore, but although the room was dim, the curtains framing the old-fashioned French windows were open and there was enough light for him to make a cautious way to a table lamp. He was halfway along the wall, skirting the shadowy shapes of furniture, when a face, the eyes looking straight into his, suddenly swam out of the shadows. Charmery.

Theo's heart gave a great leap and he felt as if he had been plunged into a vat of ice. For several seconds he could not move and could scarcely breathe for the sudden constriction round his chest. Charmery could not be here, she simply could *not*, not unless he was really going to accept Guff's premise of ghosts. He forced himself to reach for the lamp's switch and reassuring light sprang up.

It was not Charmery herself, of course, nor was it a ghost. It was a framed sketch of her, head and shoulders, almost life-size, done in a smudgy charcoal. In the uncertain light it had been disconcertingly lifelike. Theo had never seen it before and it must be fairly recent, because it was not the Charmery he had known: this was the teenage cousin finally grown-up. The tumble of copper-coloured hair did not show up in charcoal, of course, but the long narrow eyes with the thick dark lashes were there. The artist had given an impression of a low-cut gown of some kind so that the shoulders were bare and she was wearing what looked like a rather elaborate Victorian pendant, which Theo did not recognize.

The sketch did not seem to be signed, but Theo reached up to unhook it. Cobwebs floated down, ghost-strands from the past. He turned the picture over, to see if there was any signature or date on the back, but there was only a layer of dusty backing paper. Theo turned it round and studied it closely, noting the differences again. Hair and clothes were all unfamiliar, and the expression ... The expression was the most unfamiliar thing of all. Whoever had drawn this had caught a side of Charmery Theo had never seen. A softer side. Had something happened to her in those years he had not shared? Someone who had come into her life after he left it? There had been a series of lovers – the family had reported that with gleeful disapproval, of course – but towards the end had there been someone who had wrought this extraordinary change? Or had it been someone who had been going to give her the things Theo could not? Marriage, a child ... An old pain stirred – a pain that after ten years ought to have been safely buried under thick layers of scar tissue but which still had the power to claw painfully into his mind.

He went blindly out of the room.

After he had put together a makeshift meal and eaten it, he began to feel better. He carried his laptop into the dining room and set it down on the table. He could not decide whether to put Charmery's portrait completely out of sight, but to shut it in a drawer or cupboard seemed like shutting her in her coffin all over again. He had dreamed about Charmery's coffin for weeks after the funeral. It had been smothered in roses – two of the aunts had sent Charmian roses because originally she had been christened Charmian Marie, although Theo did not think anyone had ever called her that.

He surveyed the room, and thought he would work at the

dining table, facing the French windows. In those long-ago summers, these windows always stood open to the gardens; now they were closed and bolted and the gardens were wreathed in river mist.

Theo stood at the window for a moment, looking towards the smoky outline of the old boathouse. Charmery's death house. He would have to go inside it at some point, but he could not face it yet. He still had dreams of how her beautiful face must have looked when she was found there, bloated and grotesque, her hair matted with river weed. He frowned, pushed the image away with an effort, and switched on the laptop.

Reading the chapter he had been working on during the summer he was not knocked out by it, although neither was he disgusted. It was not mind-scaldingly brilliant; it would not set literary-award ceremonies alight or cause film directors to fall over their feet in their haste to offer six-figure sums for the film rights, but it was not bad. He could polish it and make it shine a bit.

He opened a new document, typed Chapter Five at the top, and plunged into the world he had been working to create. The main storyline centred on a young man trying to cope with the aftermath of his experiences in the Iraq war. Theo intended it to be modern and biting: a self-examination by the central character, with flash-backs to the war-torn Iraqi cities and a few excursions into the difficulties the character had with renewing his relationships.

'Don't neglect to put in a bit of bonking,' his agent had said on reading Theo's outline of the plot. 'I don't mean heaving and grunting. Classy bonking.'

'Can you have classy bonking?' Theo had demanded.

'I can,' said his agent, with the grin that made her look like a patrician cat.

It was four months since he had been able to write anything, and he had expected to find that re-entering the story with the nightmare-ridden ex-paratrooper and the searing bomb-explosion flashbacks and the classy bonking in deference to his irrepressible agent, would be difficult. What he had not expected, however, was for a whole new story to thrust its way into his mind and find its way onto the computer screen; nor had he expected to type several pages of this new and unknown story almost without realizing it.

But when he leaned back from the table-top and reached for his drink, there it was. A totally new plot, apparently told from the point of view of a child. A child who lived in a dark remote house, and who had some nameless menace threatening him. A child whose only escape was into imaginary worlds of his own creating.

CHAPTER TWO

———◆———

If one of Matthew's painted worlds ever did turn out to be real, he would like it to be the cool green-field one, with silvery rivers and nice houses with flower gardens. In that world, the people were rich and happy; they could go into the towns and buy whatever they wanted in the big shops. Very occasionally his father talked about a place like that, although Matthew did not know if it was somewhere Father had once lived, or just somewhere he had read about.

Occasionally Father went away for a night or two, returning with a sick white look, with dark shadows under his eyes. Wilma said it was nothing to worry about; it would be some business matter. 'Gentlemen have to deal with business matters, and he'll be back late tonight or early tomorrow. Best not to talk about it though, not to anyone.' She did not look up from the stove where she was cooking supper when she said this, but when she said it was best not to talk about it, her voice changed, and Matthew instantly began to worry that the place his father went to was the Black House.

The Black House was the most frightening place in the world. If anyone ever said its name, people looked uneasy and glanced over their shoulders as if afraid of being overheard. It stood a little way out of the village – it might be about half an hour's walk always supposing anyone had ever wanted to walk to it – and it was at the end of a narrow lane with thick old trees growing up all round it. You could not see it from the road, but Matthew could see it from his bedroom at the top of the house. The windows looked out across huge expanses of open countryside, and he could see the Black House, which was like a smudgy bruise on the horizon.

Sometimes he sat on the window seat before going to bed, resting his chin on his hand, staring at this horrid crouching silhouette, seeing the occasional light glinting in its depths, wondering what kind of people lived there and made those lights. The house got into his dreams occasionally, and he would find himself wandering through dreadful stone corridors with people locked away in cells, crying and beating on the bars to get out.

Matthew's friend Mara knew about the Black House and she knew about the cold-eyed men as well. She sometimes talked about the men when she and Matthew walked to school, speaking quietly, partly so no one would hear but also because her small brother walked to school with them and she did not want to frighten him.

Mara thought the cold-eyed men might live in the Black House but Matthew was not so sure. It was most likely empty, he said, trying not to remember the pinpoints of light he sometimes saw from his window.

'But there are gates,' said Mara, stubbornly. 'Huge gates with padlocks, and you wouldn't have gates and padlocks unless you had secrets to hide.'

'How do you know there are gates? I'll bet you've never even been there.'

'My grandmother said so. She's lived here all her life and she knows everything about this place. She says there are a lot of secrets here.'

'What kind of secrets?'

Mara glanced back at her brother and lowered her voice. 'Things people don't want to be known. Things about your father,' she said, and Matthew forgot about not letting Mara's brother hear them and stopped in the middle of the path and stared at her.

'What things about my father? What d'you mean?'

But Mara was already looking frightened and walked on very fast. Matthew almost had to run to keep up with her.

'It's only that people sometimes say things,' she said. 'That there's a secret. Only it's better not to talk about it, that's what they say.'

'A secret about my father?' Matthew's heart skipped a beat. It's about him going away and coming back looking ill and dark-eyed, he thought. That's what she means.

'I don't know anything,' said Mara, and pushed her small brother into the infants' part of the school building, then dived into the girls' cloakroom, banging the door.

Most of Mara's secrets came from her grandmother's stories and Matthew did not pay much attention to them, but he wanted to know what people said about his father so he shouted through the cloakroom door for her to come out and tell him. But she would not, and the bell went for lessons so in the end Matthew went off to his own classroom where it turned out to be the day for arithmetic which he hated.

When he got home his father was away on one of his mysterious trips. Things happened like that, Matthew had often noticed it. You talked about something or you remembered something, and there it was. But it wasn't until he was going up to his bedroom to do his homework that he realized the house was sliding down into its frozen silence. His heart gave a thump of fear, and although he tried to tell himself it was just the dark afternoon – it was November and bitterly cold – he knew, deep down, the men were here because the house's dark stillness was unmistakable. He ran

14

the rest of the way up the stairs and shut his bedroom door with a bang. Through the main window he could see the crouching shape of the Black House, dark and ugly and remote, but there was a little side window that looked down into the lane that led to this house. Summoning all his courage he looked out of this window and fear closed over him.

The men were here. They had driven along the lane and parked their big noisy car, and they were sitting in it looking at the house. The car had bulbous headlights like frog's eyes that would be able to swivel round and find you no matter where you hid. There were three men – they never came singly, there were usually three of them and quite often four. Matthew had the feeling they were talking to one another about what they would do and say when they got inside the house. As he watched, they got out and walked up to the door, their shoes rapping out on the ground like claws. They were always very smartly dressed. Wilma once said it was as well not to ask where they got the money to dress so smartly, then clapped a fat hand over her mouth as if to push the words back in before anyone could hear them.

The men hardly ever knocked because Wilma always heard their car pull up and panted up from the kitchen to let them in so they would not be kept waiting. Once she had not heard them and they had just walked in and gone across the hall and opened the study door without waiting to be invited. Matthew hated this. In the world he would one day escape to it would be possible to lock doors and not open them if you did not want to, no matter who knocked.

The men did not go into the study today, as if they knew Matthew's father was not there. They came up the stairs – up the first set of stairs and then up the little twisty stair that led to Matthew's own room. This had never happened before and Matthew turned to his bedroom door in panic, listening to the cloppety-clopping steps on the bare oak. It sounded as if there were two of them. They would not come in here of course: they would not even know he was in the house . . . They would know, though. They knew everything that went on and they would know what time school ended and how long it took the children to get back to their various homes.

He glanced round the room then darted across to the cupboard behind his bed and squeezed inside it. If the men opened the door they would just see a dark room with no one there and they might go away. It was not a proper cupboard, more a gap between the wall and the roof, and it was hot with a stuffy smell from the old wood. Matthew would normally be worried about spiders or beetles, but at the moment he would rather face a hundred spiders than the men. Would they come in here – *would* they? And if they did, what would they do?

The footsteps were coming along the landing and fear came up all over again. Matthew huddled as far back as possible, trying not to make any sound. Mara said if you prayed really hard God always helped you; Sister Teresa at school had told them that. So Matthew tried to pray in his head but the words jumbled themselves up and God could not have heard or not have understood, because the bedroom door was opening and the men were stepping inside.

They switched on the light – it came into the cupboard through the cracks in the cupboard door – and moved round the room. Matthew, hardly daring to breathe, thought they were looking at his books which were stacked on the windowsill and leafing through the drawings he had left on the table. Through the terror he was aware of a sudden surge of anger because how dared they look at his things, his most private paintings he did not show anyone, not even his father or Mara.

Without any warning the cupboard door was pulled open and one of the men stood looking down at him, starting to smile. This was the most frightening thing yet: Mara always said the men's smiles would be the worst part – they would have teeth like the jagged-edged saws Wilma's cousin used when he mended people's windowsills or roofs. The man's teeth were not like the jagged saw, but the smile was still frightening.

He said, 'Matthew.' He did not make it a question, he made it a statement as if he knew quite well who Matthew was. 'Come out of there. There's no need to hide. We aren't going to hurt you. We just want to talk to you.'

They stood in the centre of the room and although there were only two of them they seemed to fill up all the space.

They gestured to him to sit on the edge of the bed and talked to him. They did not shout or make their voices sharp in the way grown-ups and teachers at school sometimes did, but their voices were so cold that if you had been able to see their words, they would have looked like icicles, white and cold, with horrid sneering faces in the ice and long, dripping-icicle fingernails like pictures of Jack Frost.

At first Matthew did not understand what they wanted. Then he thought he sort of understood but he could not see the point. It sounded as if they wanted him to listen and watch everything that went on in the village and tell them about it every time they came to this house.

'Nothing much happens here,' he said. 'Hardly ever. Nothing worth telling. It's—' He had been going to say it was a boring place, but that might sound rude so he said, 'It's very quiet.' Greatly daring, he added, 'It's why my father likes living here. He likes to be quiet for his work.'

The men glanced at one another, then the one Matthew thought of as the leader said, 'We like quiet places as well, Matthew. But we need to know about the people who live here, you see. That's the law.'

Matthew did not really understand about laws, but he knew the men could march into houses without being asked and that they could rap out questions in their icicle-voices and people had to answer them.

'Most of all,' said the man, and now there was a tiny change in his voice, so tiny that Matthew thought if he had not been listening extra-specially hard he would not have noticed it, 'most of all we need to know about your father.'

When the man said this, Matthew realized they were not really interested in the village at all: they were only interested in his father. This was starting to be very scary indeed. Trying hard to keep his voice smooth and ordinary, he said, 'What do you mean? What do you need to know about him?'

'Oh, about his writing.'

'He writes books,' said Matthew, feeling on safer ground. 'He always says there isn't much to say about it. You just sit down and do it, that's what he says.'

'We know about the books. But he writes other things as well, doesn't he?' said the man and moved nearer. 'Things he sends to other countries.'

'Articles,' said the other one. 'You know what articles are, don't you, Matthew?'

'Um, things in newspapers. Yes, he writes stuff for newspapers sometimes.' It surely could not hurt to say this. It was something his father occasionally joked about, saying the newspaper work did not provide their bread and butter, but did provide a bit of jam to spread on the bread.

'It's the newspaper articles we're interested in,' said the first man.

'But you could read them, couldn't you?' said Matthew, puzzled. 'You'd just have to buy a newspaper. None of it's secret or anything.'

Secret. Neither of the men moved, but it was as if something invisible pounced triumphantly on the word.

'That's just it,' said the man. 'We think there might be secret things your father writes.'

'What kind of secret things?'

'Things that might not be printed in the newspapers. Things that aren't articles.'

'D'you mean letters? Stuff like that?'

'It might be letters, yes. Or even diaries. He goes away some-times, doesn't he? He's away now, isn't he?'

'It's just, um, business things he goes to,' said Matthew. 'I 'spect it's about his work.'

'Don't you know where he goes? Doesn't he tell you?'

'No.'

'Does he keep a book with appointments written in?'

'No.'

'We'd really like to know where he goes, Matthew,' said the man, 'on those trips he makes two or three times a year. It's quite important to us to know.'

'Why?' It came out quite bravely, even though Matthew was not feeling in the least bit brave.

The men looked at one another. Then the leader said, 'Do you know what a traitor is, Matthew?'

A traitor. The word dropped into the quiet room like a stone. Traitors were very bad people indeed. Matthew knew that because they had history at school on Wednesday afternoons, and the lessons told about traitors. Traitors were liars and cheats; they were sly and secretive and everyone hated them.

('There are lots of secrets,' Mara had said. 'Only it's better not to talk about it, that's what they say.')

In wars, enemies wanted to know where soldiers and armies would be so they could send their own soldiers sneaking in, so traitors were given money for finding this out and telling it to the enemies. But they were dangerous and wicked people and at times they even killed, which was the worst thing anyone could do in the whole world. These things were all very clear in Matthew's mind, but what was also clear was that terrible things were done to traitors if they were found out. They were put in prison and usually they were shot or had their heads cut off. Matthew sat on the edge of his bed and looked at the two men, who were watching him, and tried to imagine how it would be if his father were to

19

have his head chopped off or if he were propped up against a wall and shot through the heart.

At last he said, 'My father isn't a traitor. I know he isn't.'

'We don't think he is either, not really,' said the man, 'but some people do think it, that's the difficulty. Important people think it. So we have to make sure. We have to – to prove his innocence. Do you understand what that means? Yes, I thought you would, you're such an intelligent boy.'

'I'm sure you can help us,' said the second man. 'Let's see, you're nine years old, aren't you? You recently had a birthday, in fact. So I expect at nine, you can read and write pretty well.'

'Yes.'

'You could read what your father writes and tell us about it,' said the first man. 'And you could find out when he's next going to be away. Could you do that?'

'I'm not sure,' said Matthew, staring at him.

'I think you could. You'd have to do it without him knowing, of course.'

'Then once we knew for certain, we'd be able to – what's called "clear his name",' said the man, 'with the people who suspect him.'

'Haven't you asked him?' said Matthew. 'I 'spect he'd tell you where he goes. And he'd show you the things he writes. You'd know it was all right, then.'

'Oh, we've done that, of course,' said the second man at once. 'But your father is very clever, Matthew. He says he hardly ever goes away, but when he does it's to see people about his books and articles. But we aren't sure about it. And we can't be sure he isn't posting things off we don't know about.'

Posting things off. It provides 'jam to spread on the bread', his father had said, with the little sideways smile, sealing his articles into envelopes and going off to post them.

'So you see,' said the man, 'you'd be helping your father by doing this.'

A tiny voice was whispering inside Matthew's head that this was all wrong, these men did not want him to help his father and they did not want to prove his father's innocence. They wanted to prove that he really was a traitor. They *wanted* him to be a traitor.

He was trying to find a polite way of saying he could not do any of this and wondering if they would believe him if he said he was not allowed in the study or that it was locked when his father was out of the house, when the first man said, 'I expect you've got a lot of friends, a boy like you. I expect you're very fond of them, those friends. You'd want to help them all you could.'

'There are all kinds of ways of helping friends,' said the other one. 'One way is to make sure they stay safe.'

Their voices sounded different when they said this, and Matthew began to feel more frightened than ever. He had no idea how to reply, so he hunched a shoulder and stared determinedly through the window so he would not have to look at either of them.

'Well, Matthew?' said the leader after a moment, and although his voice was smiley and nice again, Matthew could still hear what he had said earlier: 'You'd want to help them . . . to make sure they stay safe.' Did they mean friends like Mara?

But if these men could say his father was a traitor, he would be taken away and put in prison – perhaps for years. Or he would die because they would shoot him or chop off his head.

'I won't do it,' said Matthew, looking the man straight in the eyes. And then, because his father said he must be polite to every-one no matter who they might be, he said again, 'I'm very sorry indeed, but I won't do it.'

He had expected them to return, but they did not, and after a while he began to think he might be safe. Life was ordinary again. Matthew went to school each day and Wilma cooked the meals, and his father worked in the study. Sometimes he went into the town to buy paper or ink, or post one of the large envelopes he said contained an article. If it was a Saturday Matthew could go

21

with him on these trips, which he liked because of seeing shops and people. It was quite a long journey to make, so they nearly always had lunch while they were out. Matthew liked this as well, because it was different and interesting.

It was on one of these trips that his father said, 'Matthew, I know there's something troubling you – I can sense there is – and I won't pry because everyone's allowed a few secrets. But I hope you know you can always talk to me about things. I'd never be shocked or upset by anything, and I might be able to make things right for you.' He paused, then said, 'Your mother could always make things right for people – it was a gift she had. I don't have her gift, but I can try.'

His father hardly ever mentioned Matthew's mother, but when he did it always sounded as if the words were being scraped out of some deep hurting place inside him. Matthew could not remember his mother at all, but he could not bear hearing this scraping pain in his father's voice. He had been drinking lemonade which was served in a frosty glass, and he kept his eyes on the glass so he would not have to see the pain in his father's eyes. 'There's nothing wrong,' he said in an awkward mumble. 'Well, only school things, I s'pose.'

'School things?' Was there a note of relief in his father's voice?

Matthew hunched a shoulder. 'Arithmetic.' He risked a glance at his father and saw his face break into the rare, sweet smile he loved, but which he sometimes found painful without understanding why.

'Oh God, figures,' said his father. 'I hated them at school, as well. I used to make up stories about how the figures were in a conspiracy – that's a plot – to confuse me. How the eight times table was in league with the fractions, and how the multiplication hid inside the square roots, waiting to pounce.' He laid his hand over his son's in a brief gesture of affection or sympathy, Matthew was not sure which. 'Boring arithmetic,' he said.

'Flummery and moonshine?' suggested Matthew hopefully,

because this was one of his father's expressions, and he liked saying it.

His father's smile broadened, but he said, 'Well, not exactly that, because you need to know about some of it. But there are other things in life as well as maths. Just do the best you can and I'll help you with your homework. Remember, figures aren't everyone's strength and you've got a lot of other strengths.' He withdrew his hand, as if embarrassed by his own display of emotion. 'Let's have some lunch,' he said. 'I see they've got chocolate pudding today.'

Matthew did not write stories about arithmetic like his father had done, but he drew pictures of all the figures laying plots, giving them secret faces and swirly cloaks like villains in stories, making them seem to be dodging in and out of the columns. He showed them to his father who laughed and said Matthew was a genius, and how about them trying to write a comic-cartoon strip together – like you saw in newspapers? He would write the stories and Matthew could illustrate them. They might try to sell the whole thing to a newspaper or a children's comic. This was a wonderful plan and what was even better was that his father thought Matthew's sketches were good enough.

'It will probably help the arithmetic as well,' said his father, smiling.

It helped with arithmetic, but it did not help with the cold-eyed men when they came to the house. Each evening, as Matthew drew his pictures or did homework or read a book, he waited for the house to plunge into its frozen state of fear that meant the bulbous-eyed car had driven up the lane. He listened almost all the time for the sounds of their footsteps outside the house.

CHAPTER THREE

———————◆◆◆———————

Each evening, as night fell, Theo found himself listening for the sounds of footsteps outside Fenn House.

He did not immediately realize he was doing this. When he did he was annoyed because he was used to living on his own and, although he had his fair share of writer's imagination, it did not normally prompt him to listen uneasily for prowlers the minute darkness descended. But then he had never stayed in Fenn House on his own and he had certainly never been at Melbray during a bleak Norfolk winter. And he had never, he thought uneasily, experienced anything quite like that insistent image that had scalded his mind when he arrived – the image of the boy frightened to enter the dark house.

He had been at Fenn for four days and had quelled some of the dusty dereliction, swiping at cobwebs and trundling the vacuum cleaner over a few of the rooms. Charmery would have laughed; she would have said, 'Theo, darling, how can you be bothered – why don't you just hire a cleaner?' But Theo did not have Charmery's careless attitude to money, and he did not want anyone disturbing his work. He had still not been down to the boat-house, though. He thought it was because he did not want to see it with the remnants of the police investigation strewn around; he wanted it to stay in his mind exactly as it had been all those years ago.

He had worked almost non-stop since he arrived. Once or twice he wondered vaguely what his agent and editor would say when they found out he was writing a totally different book to the one outlined in his current contract, and that it was a book so different from anything else he had written, it might not even be recognizable as a Theo Kendal novel. Still, providing he added a few scenes of classy bonking and injected a touch of humour here and there, his agent would be appeased even if his editor tore her hair in exasperation.

At intervals he went rather absently into the kitchen to make coffee or a sandwich or to heat tinned soup, eating it at the end of the dining table with the laptop in sight, unwilling to stay away from his boy for longer than necessary. Once or twice he paused to wonder where the boy's story was coming from, but it was tumbling onto the screen with such insistence he was almost afraid of questioning it too much in case it vanished. It did not vanish, though – if anything it grew stronger, and the boy's world gradually became so vivid that Fenn House and its rooms seemed dim and slightly unreal. If Theo half closed his eyes, he could see the house where the boy lived and the rather sparse bedroom at the top of the house beneath low eaves. It seemed to be a large but slightly shabby house. Like Fenn House? said a voice inside his head, but he rejected this at once because he refused to accept that this was some kind of lingering ghost from Fenn House's past. But it was a very similar house.

It was just about possible that the boy was some kind of mani-festation of Theo's own childhood: there were several parallels. Theo's early years had not been as dark and fearful as the boy's seemed to be, but they had been a bit mixed. There had been patches of unhappiness and times when he had not understood why people around him behaved oddly. His father had died in a car crash when he was four and his mother had been devastated: it was a bit of a family legend that when John Kendal died Petra had, as Nancy put it, gone to pieces for years. Theo could not remember his mother's in-pieces behaviour, nor could he really remember his father, but he could remember escaping into fantasy worlds of his own making, although in Theo's case the worlds had been the ones he wrote about. There had been compositions for school – My Holidays, My Pets, My Favourite Place – which had expanded, almost without him realizing, into short stories. He had been secretive about those early stories, scribbling diligently in an old exercise book in his bedroom for hours on end, spawning another little family legend that Petra's son was slightly odd, although what could you expect? poor fatherless child, without any brothers or sisters. Nancy and several of the older aunts had been thinly disapproving, but Guff, kindly and concerned, had invited the small Theo to stay with him at his own house. It was a rather precise, over-tidy house, because Guff himself was precise and over-tidy, but Theo had liked being there and he liked Guff, who had explained about his mother not being very well. 'She'll get better, though,' Guff said.

Petra had got better as Guff termed it, but she had become what Nancy called very flighty, travelling for long spells while Theo was away at school.

'Nancy thinks your mother's a bit of a tart,' Charmery said, years later, when they were at Fenn House for her ninth birthday celebrations.

'No, she isn't,' said Theo, furious and hurt.

'Is it a bad thing to be, a tart?'

'It would be if she was, but she's not. Nancy's jealous of her, that's all. But if you're going to call my mother a tart I'm not coming here again.'

'I'm sorry,' said Charmery, and Theo forgave her because she was only nine, which was too young to know what a tart was.

*

The boy in the story was called Matthew. Theo had written the best part of an entire chapter before he realized this. He had, in fact, been getting slightly cross at not knowing the boy's name, particularly when he knew so many other things about him. He knew what he liked to eat, and how he struggled with arithmetic, and he knew how, every morning, he met a small friend, a girl with whom he walked to school. The girl was a bit of a chatterbox but Theo's boy liked listening to her, because he was rather quiet himself. Theo knew all this, but he still did not know the boy's name, and he was starting to think it was a bit much of him to invade his life like this without providing a name.

And then, on the crest of this thought, as clear as lightning against a night sky, the name came scudding into his mind. Matthew.

Matthew. There was a moment when Theo thought – Matthew, yes, of course, that's who he is, I should have realized right away! He did not think he knew any Matthews but he liked the name. Matthew. Yes, it was exactly right. He pressed the Save key at the end of the scene where Matthew was drawing master-spy faces on his troublesome arithmetic lesson, and ended the paragraph with a description of how Matthew suddenly looked up from his drawing and listened for the footsteps. Matthew's bedroom curtains were open and for a moment Theo caught a fleeting glimpse of what lay beyond that window – there was a dark garden with an uneven brick wall, and on the horizon was the fearsome Black House which Matthew and the small school friend seemed to fear so much. But what else was beyond that wall? Was it the fields – those fields Theo himself saw from the windows of this house? Was it even possible that the Black House was St Luke's Convent? He got up to stare through the windows, but the flickering image had already vanished, and in any case it was too dark to see anything, so he closed the curtains, and went back to the table, switching on the small lamp, grateful for the warm pool of light it cast.

He had intended to close the chapter with Matthew's gradual

realization that the footsteps were approaching, which should make for a nicely tense ending. But the paragraph did not go that way and, instead, Theo found himself describing how there was someone Matthew feared even more than the men. This was the person who gave the men their orders. It was not another man who did this, though, it was a woman.

No one Matthew knew had ever seen this woman, but everyone knew how powerful she was. She was beautiful but evil and cruel, and if people did not do what she said, she had them thrown in prison. The younger children said she was like somebody from an old fairytale – the Snow Queen or the wicked stepmother – and if she caught you she would put you in a cage or bake you in the oven and eat you up. Matthew knew this was silly because people did not eat children, but all the same, he hoped he never met her.

Theo typed all this without pausing, then broke off to read it with growing puzzlement. He had not envisaged an evil beauty as being part of this strange story, and even if he had intended to create such a character he certainly would not have added that touch about the Snow Queen or the oven – it gave a Gothic flavour to the whole thing, and Theo's work had never been remotely Gothic. But he knew this female very well indeed; he even knew her name. She was called Annaleise.

He frowned, and returned to the footsteps. At one moment there was an ordinary quietness inside Matthew's house – Theo thought that for all the old timber creakings and sighings it was rather a silent house for most of the time – and then the next moment the footsteps began. At first they were faint and distant like a tap dripping or a thin drum skin softly vibrating, but then they grew louder and stronger. Matthew, seated at the ramshackle little desk in his bedroom, looked up, his eyes dilating with fear . . .

It was at this point Theo realized the sounds were no longer solely in his story – they were real sounds and were coming from just outside. He listened intently but there was nothing. You really are taking me over, Matthew, he thought, but as he prepared to go on typing the sounds came again. Soft light crunches – exactly as if someone was walking along the gravel path that wound down to the old boathouse. There could be no mistake: someone was outside. He pressed the Save key so the Snow Queen would not be lost, reached across to switch off the table lamp, and sat absolutely still in the faint glimmer from the monitor. The footsteps had stopped. Had the walker seen the light go out and paused? Perhaps it was an animal. A fox, maybe. It was then that a new sound sent prickles of fear scudding across his skin.

Someone tapped, very lightly, on the French window. Three light measured taps. Someone must be standing just outside them. Theo waited in the darkened room, aware of his heart thumping erratically. After a moment the tapping came a second time, lightly and eerily. Tap-tap-tap. Almost as if someone was tapping out Morse code. *Let-me-in.* Or was it, *Come-out-side.*

Theo stared at the curtained window, fighting for calm, trying to decide what to do. Was someone really standing there? Mightn't it be a branch brushing against the glass? There was even the possibility that it was a perfectly ordinary caller – it was only six p.m., for goodness' sake, Theo had heard St Luke's chime the hour. But there were no other houses in this lane, and would an innocent visitor really tap so furtively on a window? Wouldn't he or she go openly up to the front door and cheerfully ply the knocker?

It might be a prowling journalist, perhaps a local reporter, an embryo paparazzo who had kept an ear to the ground and learned that Theo had inherited the house and was spending the winter here. If that was the case, he would deal very sharply indeed with the prowler.

He got up slowly from the table, and walked cautiously across to the windows. A faint draught of cold night air came in from round the frames. Theo listened for a moment, then reached up to draw the curtains back.

29

A face – a pale face that looked as if it was framed in some kind of dark scarf or hood – was looking in at him.

Theo gasped and felt his heart leap into his throat, but in the same instant realized he was seeing his own reflection in the window. It was the thick glass that made it look slightly ghost-like and the darkness of the gardens beyond that had twisted the eerie hood-like shape round it.

Nothing moved in the darkness. The tapping must have been a branch or an animal or even just the wind. In any case, Theo was blowed if he was going to yomp through the unlit lonely gardens in search of an intruder – especially since he was living in a house whose owner had been recently murdered, with the murderer still at large. What he would do was make a careful check of all the locks and bolts in the house to make certain no one could get in, and keep his mobile phone near. He picked up the poker from the fireplace, just in case, and, switching the lamp back on, he set off.

Fenn House had started life as a relatively modest, rather old-fashioned house, but Charmery's parents had built on to it after buying it and the extension did not completely line up with the original structure, so there were several short, rather dim, passages linking the old to the new. The house was not entirely silent, in the way old houses never were entirely silent, but even though it was ten years since Theo had been at Fenn, its sounds were as familiar as ever. He had no idea what he would do if he really did encounter someone hiding in the house because although the poker made him feel reasonably brave, he was not sure if he could actually use it.

But Fenn's ground floor was innocent of intruders, and feeling slightly more confident, he crossed the hall to check the first floor. The stairs were wide and shallow, uncarpeted because Charmery's mother, Helen, had loved the mellow dark grain of the wood. They creaked loudly, as they always had, and halfway up they twisted round sharply, so there was a view through the balustrades to the upper landing. As Theo reached this twist, there was a blur of movement above him, as if someone had whisked out of sight into one of the bedrooms. He stood still, unsure whether it had been a trick of the light, his heart racing. Then he took a firmer grip on the poker and forced himself to go up the remaining stairs. When he reached the top, he looked very deliberately down the corridor.

Icy sweat slid between his shoulder blades. Standing at the far end of the corridor was a pale, bowed figure, its long hair heavy as if dripping wet, as if the figure had just been brought out of deep water . . . Theo, in the grip of horror, blinked several times before his sight adjusted to the dimness. It was not a ghost. The long window at the far end was slightly open at the top and the pale muslin drapes were stirring in the night wind. As he watched, a section of the flimsy fabric billowed out again.

He kicked his mind back into focus and began a systematic search of the bedrooms. They all had shrouded furniture, bare walls and oblong patches on the walls where pictures or mirrors had hung. There was no one hiding anywhere, although Theo was still glad he had brought the poker with him.

The only room he had still to check was Charmery's, and he was within two strides of the door when the creakings seemed to shift gear. He paused to listen, not exactly frightened, but puzzled. Perhaps the roof timbers were contracting in the night air, or perhaps the open window was rattling. The sounds were curiously rhythmic, but they were not loud enough for footsteps. He pushed open the door of Charmery's room and it was then that another sound came – a sound that sent his heartbeat skittering wildly.

The old clock – the clock that Charmery claimed was Fenn's heart, the clock that had not been wound since she died – had just chimed the half hour. The rhythmic sounds that had puzzled Theo a few minutes earlier had been the clock's measured ticking.

Someone had wound it up.

*

31

Theo came out of his frozen terror and half fell through the door into Charmery's room, with absolutely no idea what would be waiting for him. But there was nothing. Nothing moved and the room was exactly as it had been on his arrival, apart from the ticking clock. He stood in front of it, hearing the measured tick that had comforted Charmery every night, seeing that the minute hand was moving, slowly but perceptibly. He reached for the small gilt clasp that held the door in place and released it. The door opened with a small soft creak, revealing the brass mechanism. The pendulum with its circular copper striker, swung back and forth, regular and steady, like the good piece of Victorian machinery it was. Theo watched it for several minutes, then looked round the room. There was nowhere anyone could possibly hide in here – even the wardrobe was a small one, with a narrow hanging space and shelves taking up half its interior. He checked it anyway, then drew the heavy curtains back from the deep bay window. Nothing.

It was beyond all logic that an intruder would creep into the house for the sole purpose of starting up an old clock, but it was what seemed to have happened. He went back onto the landing and examined the window with the pale curtains. Was it possible that the faint gust of wind through that open window had somehow disturbed the clock's mechanism? Along eight feet of corridor and through a closed door? How about mice? Could a mouse have got inside the clock and nudged the pendulum?

Theo found a linen handkerchief in one of the tallboys, and tied it round the copper disc in order to muffle the chimes. He could cope – just about – with ghosts and intruders, but whether the ticking clock was due to an act of God or an errant wind, he did not think he could cope with it chiming the half hour through the entire night.

CHAPTER FOUR

———◆◆◆◆———

Theo had expected to lie awake, listening for sounds and rustlings. He had even considered whether he should take one of the mild sedatives prescribed to help him sleep after Charmery's death. 'Very low dose indeed,' his GP had said. But Theo preferred to be in charge of his own sleep and had hardly ever taken them. He thought he had better not risk being zonked by pills tonight in case there really was a prowler.

In the event, once in bed he fell asleep almost at once, not waking until half past seven the next morning. Sunlight came in through the curtains and if anything else had tapped on the windows or tinkered with clocks he had not heard it. Last night's bizarre happenings retreated to the vague, unreal status of a dream.

He was pouring a second cup of coffee and planning how he would unravel more of the intriguing world of Matthew and his Snow Queen, when the doorbell rang. As he unbolted the front door he remembered that hardly anyone knew he was here and experienced a jab of apprehension.

Standing outside was a small figure dressed in the modern version of nuns' robes: a plain navy coat, flat-heeled shoes, and a small veil like an old-fashioned district nurse. After the eerie incidents of last night, Theo was so relieved to find this unthreatening figure on the doorstep, that he held out his hand and said, 'Good morning! Do come in.'

She smiled a bit warily and said, 'Thank you very much. Just for a moment though – I don't want to intrude. You're Mr Theo Kendal, I think. I'm Sister Catherine from St Luke's.' As she stepped into the harlequin patches of sunlight inside the hall Theo saw she was younger than he had first thought – perhaps late twenties – and that she had clear grey eyes, fringed with black.

'I've mostly called to say welcome to Melbray,' she said as he opened the door to the dining room. 'You're the first member of the family to come down here since Miss Kendal's death, so I'm a kind of emissary to convey our belated condolences at what happened. We're all truly sorry and very shocked.'

'Thank you very much. Would you like some coffee? I made a large pot shortly after breakfast and it's still hot.'

He was surprised when she said, 'I'd love some if it's no trouble. Good coffee is one of the things I miss in the convent.'

Theo set the cups on a tray, and carried everything into the dining room. Catherine was standing at the French windows, looking into the gardens. 'It's a lovely old house, isn't it?' she said. 'I've often looked across at it from our grounds. I remember there used to be the most beautiful rose garden here – it was just visible.'

'It's still there, but only just.' Theo handed her the coffee. 'The gardens are a tanglewood and the house needs a lot of work; I'm not sure if I'm going to be able to deal with that.'

'Your cousin intended to update it, I think,' said Catherine, and Theo, who had been adding milk to his own coffee, looked up.

'Did you know my cousin?'

'I met her briefly a couple of times. You look surprised.'

'I don't really know what was going on in her life over the last few years. I didn't see much of her,' said Theo.

34

'But you spent holidays here with her? When you were both children?'

'Yes, we came here almost every summer and for the odd week here and there. Christmas, too, some years. You can't possibly remember those holidays, though. You're much too young. Sorry, I probably shouldn't say something like that to a nun.'

'Of course you can say it. And it's true I've only been at St Luke's for about nine years. I'm the baby of the convent.' She smiled, and Theo smiled back. 'But I know a bit about your family from the older nuns. Next-door neighbours, you know. I expect you've got good memories of this place. Childhood memories are so precious, aren't they?' Theo thought there was a faintly wistful note in her voice, but almost without pausing she said, 'I remember the Bursar saying your family have owned this house for years.'

'Nearly twenty,' said Theo. 'My uncle and aunt bought it as a kind of holiday retreat in the early 1990s, but they began to spend so much time here – and they liked holding open house for the family – that they extended it. They seemed to add a room each year – I think they virtually doubled the size of the original house in the end. Aunt Helen used to say it made it a nightmare to clean and heat.'

'Some of the older nuns met one or two of your family,' said Catherine. 'Mr Frederick Kendal, and also your mother, I think.'

Guff would have rather enjoyed trotting along the lane to St Luke's, and helping with charity events, although Theo was surprised to hear the nuns had met his mother. But before he could think how to respond, Catherine said, 'Actually, Mr Kendal, I have another reason for coming to see you. We wondered if you might have time to come along to St Luke's one of these days. Perhaps to give a talk to the patients. Do you do that kind of thing?'

'Well . . .'

'No pressure,' said Catherine and Theo had the impression she used the modernism carefully as if not sure she had got it right. 'We're more of a nursing home than an actual hospital. We specialize in bone injuries: severe compound fractures that need manipulation and physiotherapy or osteopathy. Most of the patients are in wheelchairs or beds a lot of the time, but they're not actually ill so they appreciate as many diversions as possible. I'm sure they'd love to meet such a distinguished writer.'

'Distinguished is stretching it a bit.'

'I don't think so. We borrowed your last book from the local library – we all read it in turn and it's very good indeed.'

It was nice that the nuns had been sufficiently interested to go to this trouble, but it was also slightly worrying, because Theo had allotted the central character of that book a rather robust appetite with the ladies and had described some of the various bedroom exploits fairly graphically. As if picking this up and almost as if she was finding his discomfiture amusing, Catherine said, 'We're really very worldly, you know.'

This time the smile narrowed her eyes, and Theo, who normally ran a mile from giving talks and lectures, smiled back, and said, 'Of course I'll come to talk to your patients. For about an hour?'

'That would be exactly right.'

'D'you want anything in particular touched on? Anything you think they'd like to hear about?'

'Well, just about writing books in general, I suppose,' said Sister Catherine. 'How you go about it, how you deal with research.'

'The whole process,' said Theo. 'Yes, I can do that.'

'Could you? Would one day next week be all right? You can phone us to arrange it – we're in the directory. Afternoons are a particularly good time, but I expect you're very busy so we'll fit in with whatever you can manage.'

'How about next Wednesday afternoon?' He had not been intending to make such a definite arrangement, but again the words were out before he realized.

'That would be lovely. Come about two o'clock if you can.

36

They'll be so pleased.' She hesitated, then said, 'I don't know the etiquette for this, but we'd be happy to pay a fee if that's customary.'

'No fee's needed,' said Theo at once.

'Well, thank you very much. Oh – is there anything special we should provide for you on the day?'

Theo thought for a moment, then said, 'A blackboard or white-board would be quite good if you have one. Or just an ordinary flipchart.'

'There's a flipchart in the library,' said Catherine. 'You can use that. There are twenty or so patients at the moment and most of them are reasonably mobile so you'll probably get a full house. Dr Innes will probably come along, as well.' There was a pause as if she expected a reaction to the name.

Theo said, 'Innes? The man who found my cousin's body?' Damn, he thought, why can't I say Charmery's name aloud?

'Yes. It was a dreadful shock for him – he admired her very much.' This was said quite ordinarily and openly, but Theo thought she glanced at him a bit warily. Had there been something between Charmery and the local GP?

Sister Catherine took her leave smoothly and easily. 'Thank you for the coffee, Mr Kendal.'

'I've enjoyed meeting you,' said Theo, accompanying her to the door.

'So have I. God bless.' It came out naturally and unself-consciously. Since Theo could not think of a suitable rejoinder he merely nodded and waited until she had walked back down the overgrown drive and into the lane beyond.

Rinsing the cups in the kitchen, he considered that remark about some of the nuns having known his mother. It was vaguely surprising, because Petra had never spent much time at Fenn House. She had certainly shared one or two of the Christmases there, but they had been brief holidays and no one had ventured much out of the house because Norfolk in winter was about the bleakest place imaginable. And during Theo's school years she had usually driven him to Melbray in July, stayed a night or two, then left him to it.

'Too many Kendals,' she always said, with the smile that Theo sometimes found painful although he had never quite known why. 'When I married your father I didn't realize I was marrying an entire clan, and I'm not very good at family gatherings. But you stay and riot with your cousins, darling, and I'll collect you well before term starts so we can have a bit of time together in London.'

She had always arrived at Melbray punctually to pick him up, usually with gifts for everyone. Guff, who was a regular visitor to Fenn, said happily that she lit up the house the minute she came in, but Nancy said sourly it was Petra currying approval as usual. 'Playing fairy godmother,' Nancy said. Nancy never seemed to come to Fenn because she enjoyed the house or the company of the family; she apparently came because the drains had packed up at her house, or because she wanted peace and quiet to work out next term's assignments for her sixth-formers, or she was recovering from flu.

They had all enjoyed the presents from Petra's travels, though. There were generally clothes for Charmery who said delightedly that no one had such exquisite taste as Aunt Petra, books for Lesley, who would seize them eagerly and vanish for hours on end, and unusual toys for Lesley's small twin brothers, whose birth had taken everyone by surprise, including Lesley's father. Charmery's mother and Lesley's would be presented with frivolous designer silk scarves or perfume, and there was vintage port or brandy for the men. Once Petra brought a pair of embroidered Turkish slippers with curved toes for Guff who trotted delightedly round the house in them, refusing to listen to Charmery's father, Desmond, saying he looked like an escapee from a harem.

Theo, Charmery and Lesley always stayed up later than usual when Petra was there. 'She turns it into an occasion,' said Lesley's father, rather wistfully. Lesley's father was Desmond's younger brother, and Theo often thought he seemed a bit over-shadowed by the genially successful Desmond, just as Lesley so often seemed over-shadowed by Charmery.

Charmery had loved those evenings; even from the age of nine or ten she flirted with Guff and any other uncles who were there, laughing and making a fuss of them, coaxing her father to let her have a sip of wine in water like French children and usually getting her way. Lesley, three years younger than Charmery, always sat quietly, listening to the conversation. 'Only speaking when she's spoken to,' had been Nancy's approving observation, and Petra had told Theo she sometimes wondered which century Nancy lived in because her outlook was positively Victorian at times. 'But then Helen and Desmond are Edwardian anyway,' she added. 'Nursery tea and children being allowed to eat with their parents, my God, it's archaic. D'you suppose they're really time travellers from about 1900?'

'I don't know, but there's a peculiar machine in the shrubbery, labelled, "Property of H. G. Wells",' said Theo, and was pleased when she smiled appreciatively and made a joke of her own about the Tardis parking in the cabbage patch.

Time machines or not, there had been something remarkably restful about Fenn House in those days. As Theo put the coffee cups away after Sister Catherine's visit, he was deep in the memories of those summer evenings round the big cherry-wood table in the dining room. There would be huge bowls of roses everywhere – Sister Catherine had been right about the rose garden. Helen had planted a rose called Charmian to mark Charmery's tenth birthday. 'Because it's clear no one's ever going to use the correct version of her name,' she said, 'so this is a reminder of it.'

The French windows would be wide open and people would be relaxed from the wine and the huge suppers that were served. Aunt Helen fussed about the food which was always perfectly all right –

it was a bit of a family joke, Aunt Helen's fussing – and Uncle Desmond became genial after a few drinks, exchanging bluff jokes with the other men, but doing so *sotto voce* if Nancy was there, because Nancy did not approve of coarseness. Guff listened to the jokes and always laughed, although Charmery said he probably did not understand half of them. Theo thought Charmery probably did not understand half of them either, but he did not say this.

Catherine got back to St Luke's shortly before twelve. Even at this time of year she enjoyed the walk along Boat Street. Old trees fringed the lane that wound up to Fenn House so that even with the branches bare the house was hidden from most people's view. Local legend said it had originally been built by a recluse who had wanted to hide from the world but had liked having the tributary to the Chet at the end of his garden. The Bursar was going to compile a history of the area on account of it having so many interesting fragments of gossipy lore. Catherine had been at St Luke's for nearly ten years and the Bursar had still not got any further than saying at intervals they really must get down to drafting some ideas. The murder of Charmery Kendal had daunted even the Bursar from putting pen to paper, although it had certainly added another layer to the legends.

Mr Kendal had been very polite and welcoming, and it had been companionable to sit drinking coffee with him. It was the kind of thing people in the outside world did all the time without so much as thinking about it, but for Catherine, who had entered the convent at eighteen, it was sufficiently unusual for it to occupy most of her thoughts as she walked back. It would not be occupying any of Theo Kendal's thoughts, of course; he would most likely have dismissed it as soon as she had gone, because he would be used to drinking coffee and stronger substances than coffee with all kinds of females. He was very nice-looking with that dark hair and those deep blue eyes. There had not seemed to be a wife or girlfriend in the picture, but there would surely be one somewhere. Catherine caught herself thinking that his wife or girlfriend would not wear a plain navy woollen dress with flat-heeled lace-ups; she would be smart and modern, with glossy, well-cut hair. This was a thought that was dangerously close to vanity, so she pushed it firmly away.

Morning coffee was over at St Luke's, and there was already a smell of food from the kitchens, which meant Sister Agnes, who was the convent's kitchener, was presiding over the midday meal. Today being Thursday it would be Irish stew with dumplings and big platters of accompanying vegetables.

Catherine hung up her coat and went along to see Reverend Mother, who was with the Bursar, both of them frowning over some accounts. Catherine thought they were rather pleased to be interrupted, although neither of them would have admitted it. They were certainly pleased to hear she had managed to arrange for Mr Kendal to talk to the patients. The Bursar said Catherine must remember to tell Dr Innes when he came in for his clinic day tomorrow. He would be interested to meet Mr Kendal.

'Yes, he will,' said Catherine, carefully making her voice bland.

Reverend Mother said they would make sure Sister Miriam, the convent's librarian, got a couple of Mr Kendal's books from the library van when it came round, and the Bursar said Sister Agnes must be asked to provide an extra-nice afternoon tea. Mr Kendal would be glad of a substantial tea after talking to them all.

Catherine remembered the empty wine bottle on the dining room table at Fenn House and thought, but did not say, that after facing the community of St Luke's, Mr Kendal would probably prefer a large drink.

CHAPTER FIVE

————◆◇◆————

As Theo went back to the dining room, he was smiling at the prospect of plunging back into Matthew's world. And as he switched on the laptop, that other house and its atmosphere were already closing round him.

Matthew's story seemed to be shifting focus and his small friend was insinuating herself more definitely into the plot. This was the girl who accompanied him to school each morning. She apparently lived in a small cottage, and each evening she liked to curl up by the fire with her back to the brick chimney breast. The firelight spun garnet and black shadows in the room, and an elderly lady sat in a rocking chair, her own shadow falling blurrily on the walls as she rocked and talked. The girl's grandmother? Yes, of course.

Theo typed all this, then stared at it in surprise, because he seemed to be going back into the land of fairytale once more. Small girls and grandmothers who rocked by fires, and views of thick trees through the window, suggesting the house was in the middle of an old forest . . . Once again he was aware of puzzlement as to where this was coming from.

The girl was swept along by the tales grandmother wove in

those fire lit nights. 'Tell more,' she said eagerly, leaning forward, her small face alight.

'They're only stories,' said the grandmother. 'Some of them written by clever men, but they're all stories made up out of people's minds, remember that, Mara.'

'But some bits might be real,' said Mara. 'You can't be absolutely sure, can you?' She leaned forward, her eager little face vivid in the firelight. 'Annaleise is real.'

Annaleise ... The shadows seemed to shiver at the sound of the name.

'Yes, Annaleise is real,' said the grandmother. 'You must keep out of her way, though, Mara. You must keep your brother out of her way, as well.'

'I do,' said Mara earnestly. 'I truly do. Tell me about Annaleise. Why does she come here?'

'To watch people. To listen to what they say. That's why you must always be very wary of her, Mara. She's not watching you, not at the moment, but one day she might.'

'Who is she watching?'

The old woman glanced round the room again, as if making sure no one could be hiding and listening. Very softly, she said, 'Your friend Matthew's father.'

Mara sat up very straight. 'How do you know that?'

'I listen to what's said. I know what happened in that family once, and I can guess why Annaleise sends the men to that house. Others might know as well – we have long memories hereabouts.' The shadows shivered again, but this time it was the movement of the rocking chair and of the old woman's head as she nodded to herself.

Mara leaned forward eagerly. 'What is he trying to keep secret?'

The grandmother paused, and then said, 'The truth about what happened to Matthew's mother. Elisabeth her name was.'

'But Matthew's mother died when he was a baby,' said Mara, puzzled.

43

'Did she? Are you sure about that?'

'It's what Matthew thinks,' said Mara after a moment.

'It's what Matthew was *told*,' said her grandmother, and again the shadows seemed to twist themselves into eager, listening shapes as if they, too, wanted to know about this. 'It's what his father wants everyone to believe.'

'But what happened to her? Where is she?'

'No one really knows what happened to her, and no one knows where she is, either, not now, not for sure. But—'

But people in this village have long memories.

The shrilling of an electric doorbell sliced through the silence, shattering Theo's concentration and sending the crimson shadows fleeing into the corners of the forest cottage. He swore, blinked at his surroundings, hit the Save key more or less automatically, then went across the hall to the front door.

'Mr Kendal? I'm Michael Innes – Dr Innes. I hope I'm not interrupting you, but I thought perhaps we should meet . . .'

The man who had found Charmery's body. He was recognizable from the TV news bulletins, although he was slightly older than he had seemed then – probably thirty-eight or forty – and he had a careful manner of speech, as if he considered every word before actually saying it. Theo thought he looked clever and slightly intense. He bade a mental farewell to finding out more about Mara and the forest cottage for the next hour, and said, 'Come into the dining room. I've been working there and it's probably the warmest place in the house at the moment.'

'I don't want to disturb you if you're absorbed in something,' said Innes, taking in the open laptop and the sheaf of notes on the dining table.

'You aren't disturbing me,' said Theo, not entirely truthfully, but wanting to talk to this man who, according to Sister Catherine, had 'admired' Charmery. Had he done more than just admire her? Was he the kind of man Charmery might have found attractive?

'Apart from anything else,' Innes said, taking one of the fireside

44

chairs Theo indicated, 'if you're here for any length of time you might like to know the whereabouts of the local medic.'

'I'm probably here for a couple of months,' said Theo, 'so it's nice to know there's help at hand. I'm fairly healthy at the moment, though.'

'Good. Actually,' said Innes, 'the real reason for coming is in case you want to talk to me about Charmery – I was the one who found her.'

'I know,' said Theo gently, as Innes' face suddenly became haggard and drawn.

'Mr Kendal—'

'Theo.'

'Theo, I'm supposed to be used to dead people and traumas and in the main I am, but when it's someone you know and when you aren't expecting . . .'

Theo said carefully, 'You'd have been fairly friendly with my cousin, I expect. In a small place like this where everyone knows everyone else . . .'

Innes appeared grateful for this tact. He said, 'I met her quite a few years ago – when I first came to Melbray. Only briefly, though. She lived in London most of the time, didn't she?'

'Yes, I think so. I think she liked to come to Fenn in the spring, though.'

'Yes, she once said that,' said Innes. 'And spring is lovely here. But this year she stayed much longer and I got to know her properly.'

And you fell for her, thought Theo. 'If there's anything you can tell me about her life – about what was going on in her life before she died . . . It's a long time since I last saw her, you see. I'd be interested in even the smallest detail.'

'The police asked me that,' said Innes. 'I couldn't help them much, though.'

'They asked all of us,' said Theo. 'They tried to build up a picture of her life, her friends, what she did for a living.'

'I remember she talked about some PR work she did last year for a small advertising agency,' said Innes. 'She made it sound fun – amusing.'

'She always made things sound fun and amusing,' said Theo. 'I think that's how she found life.'

'Yes. But there was nothing unusual about her while she was here,' said Innes. 'I'd seen her that weekend – she'd sprained her wrist a couple of days previously. Quite a bad sprain; she'd tripped over some stones in the garden and come in to the surgery. I checked there were no fractures, strapped her wrist up, then gave her a lift home – she couldn't really drive with the sprain. She asked me in for a drink. Surgery was over, so I accepted.'

And, thought Theo, perhaps the drink became two or three drinks, and perhaps the two of you ended up in bed.

'I left around half past seven that evening,' said Innes. 'She was perfectly all right. And then the next day . . .'

'The next day someone killed her,' said Theo softly, and felt a stab of pain at the thought that Charmery might have spent her last few hours making love to this unknown man. The only way to go, Theo darling, she would have said, with the smile that was half angelic, half mischievous.

'I phoned her the following evening but there was no reply,' said Innes. 'I had surgery the day after that, so it wasn't until the next day that I called at the house. I was passing on my way back from a clinic day at St Luke's, so I thought I'd look in to see how she was. There was no response when I knocked on the door, but her car was in the drive so I thought she might be in the garden. She liked the garden in summer, didn't she?'

'Yes, very much,' said Theo. He had no idea what Charmery's likes and dislikes had been for the last ten years, but he did not want Innes to know that. And Charmery had liked the garden in those long-ago summers.

'I remember she once showed me a rose bush in the garden here

– she said it was called Charmian and that Charmian was her real name,' said Innes.

'It was. My Aunt Helen – Charmery's mother – planted the rose bushes.'

'She seemed quite proud of them,' said Innes. 'And that,' he said, his face white and pinched, 'was the last time I saw her alive.'

'Tell me about finding her,' said Theo suddenly. 'I'd feel better if I knew exactly what you found. It can't be worse than all the things I've been visualizing.'

Innes nodded. 'I went round the side of the house and down through the garden,' he said. 'People say, after a tragedy, that they had a feeling something was wrong, don't they? I'm a man of science, Theo, a doctor, and I don't have feelings of that kind. But as I walked down to the boathouse that day, I had a very strong feeling of – this will sound impossibly melodramatic – but of something very dark close by.'

'And that's when you found her,' said Theo.

'Yes. I went into the boathouse – you'll know it very well, of course. It smelt of the river and it was very dim . . .'

It always did smell of the river, thought Theo, but the dimness was a good dimness, green and secret, with waterlight from the river rippling on the walls.

'She was wedged under the landing stage,' said Innes. 'Right underneath it, jammed against two of the main timber uprights supporting the platform. She had been there for at least two days and probably three.' He made a brief gesture with his hands. 'I saw my fair share of violent deaths – car crashes and accidents – when I was training. But since I came to Melbray – well, a country GP deals more with flu and eczema or chicken pox. There's my work at St Luke's clinic as well, but that's more orthopaedics and osteopathy – it's a branch of medicine I'm quite interested in. The nuns do a very good job with their patients.'

'I met one of them this morning,' said Theo. 'Sister Catherine. She seemed very dedicated to her work.'

47

'Yes, she's very good indeed,' said Innes. 'I don't think the restrictions of religious life come easily to her, though. I think she might be a bit of a rebel under that cool exterior.' He broke off, then said, 'I'm sorry, you want to hear about Charmery. Well, as I said, it looked as if she had been dead for at least two days, so ...' Again the abrupt gesture. 'There were post mortem changes,' he said. 'But she had been in the water all the time and creatures live in rivers – not just fish, but scavengers. Water rats ... There was erosion of the flesh, and the face was— It wasn't pleasant.'

'No longer recognizable,' said Theo, half to himself, and Innes said explosively, 'Oh God, her face was almost entirely gone and the eyes had been eaten—' He stopped and swallowed hard. 'I'm so sorry,' he said. 'I honestly didn't mean to say that.'

'It's all right,' said Theo, knowing it wasn't all right for either of them.

'The police surgeon concluded she had been held down in the water, probably with a boathook,' said Innes. 'She had lacerations on her shoulders where the hook had torn into her flesh. I don't think they ever found the boathook. I think they agreed it was probably thrown into the river after – after the killer finished.'

He stopped, and Theo, who was feeling slightly sick, but who was also feeling sorry for Michael Innes, said, 'Let me make you a cup of tea. Or something stronger if you'd prefer.'

'Tea would be welcome.' He looked up gratefully, and his eyes widened suddenly, as if he had seen something behind Theo's chair that startled him. Theo half-turned and realized it was the framed sketch of Charmery.

'It's a startling likeness, isn't it?' he said.

'I've never seen it before.' He seemed unable to take his eyes from the sketch.

'It looks quite a good drawing, although I've no idea when it was done or who the artist might be. It isn't signed or dated and there's nothing on the back – I looked. I thought I might get it appraised some time – I've got a cousin who's just finished studying art at the Slade – she might know how to go about it.'

'Lesley?'

'Yes. Did you know her?'

'No, but Charmery mentioned her,' said Innes, still staring at the sketch.

'It makes her look quite different, doesn't it?' said Theo, going out to make the tea. 'But then my cousin Charmery possessed a chameleon-like personality.'

'Able to be all things to all men,' said Innes, half to himself.

'Exactly.'

After Innes left, Theo did not attempt to reclaim Matthew, or Mara's forest cottage. Instead, he sat at the table, his chin resting on his hands, staring through the French windows.

Darkness was creeping across the garden, as if a veil was being drawn down slowly over it, and the small courtyard was already in shadow. In the old days they usually had breakfast there in the summer because it caught the morning sun. Charmery always wore a huge 1920s sunhat; it made her look like something from a soft-focus romantic film. But the wrought-iron table and chairs were covered in moss now, and the rose garden Helen had planted – the garden that had scented the air every summer – was choked with weeds and smothered in shadows.

Charmery had said summer twilight was deeply romantic – black-bat nights and poets entreating their ladies to come into gardens, she said. Moon rivers and the deep purple falling over sleepy garden walls. It was a secret time, she used to say, her long narrow eyes smiling. It was a time when no one quite knew where anyone else was, and when you might vanish for a magical mysterious hour of your own . . . 'Let's run away to the boathouse, Theo . . .'

It was on the crest of this memory that Theo saw, quite definitely, a flickering light inside the boathouse.

*

He unlocked the French windows and stepped outside. Cold night air, dank from the nearby river, breathed into his face and he stood on the step, listening and trying to see. Was the light still there? Yes. But who was creating it? How mad would it be to investigate on his own? Should he try calling the local police? But a vagrant light in an old boathouse was hardly cause to call out the cavalry. In any case, by the time they got here the light would probably have disappeared. He frowned and went back into the dining room to pick up the poker. Twice in two days, he thought wryly. He tried to remember where a torch might be kept and could not. He would have to trust to luck that he could see the way.

Once outside he locked the French windows behind him and pocketed the key. Then he went warily down the twisting path that he had once known as well as he knew his own reflection. Here was the little rockery where the lavender bush had been, and here were the four mossy steps to the lower level. Once down the steps, a big old apple tree screened the boathouse, and Theo could no longer see the light. Supposing he reached the boathouse to find someone waiting for him? Charmery's murderer? Or Charmery herself? 'Let's run away to the boathouse,' she had said that afternoon, giving him the shining smile that had always melted his bones. She's dead, said Theo silently. She's been dead these four months and the dead don't return.

But supposing they did? Supposing they came back to a house they had loved and set its heart beating again . . .?

There was no longer a light, and Theo paused, his heart pounding. I'll have to go inside, he thought, and taking a deep breath, walked up to it and peered into the dank interior.

It was very dark inside. The far end of the small structure was open for the boats to come and go and a faint misty radiance came in from the river itself. Waterlight rippled on the walls and on the staging where a small rowing boat used to be tied up. The memories rose up like a solid wall but Theo pushed them away and scanned the shadows.

There was nothing here. He could see traces of the police investigations – some polythene sheeting rolled up and presumably forgotten, and tattered remnants of tape that had probably once said crime scene and been wound round the entire structure. But there was nothing else. If I saw anything it was simply a shaft of moonlight, he thought with relief, and turned to go back up to the house. The dining room light shone like a beacon, and Theo unlocked the French windows and stepped thankfully inside. The warmth of the room closed round him, and he locked the windows again and drew the curtains against the night. Safe.

He was crossing the room to the hall, thinking he would make some supper, when he saw that the portrait of Charmery was no longer in its place. He looked round, wondering if it had fallen off its hook.

It had not fallen off its hook. It was on the table, near his laptop, set upright against the desk lamp. This was surely not possible, because he had absolutely no memory of putting it there. Had Innes done so? No, they had not even taken it off the wall when he was here. Walking a bit unsteadily Theo went over to the table. The desk lamp was still on; it shed a golden glow over Charmery's enigmatic stare. But something had changed about the sketch. Was it just the light? Was the frame damaged? But even as the questions formed, Theo saw what was different and his mind tumbled in disbelief.

In front of the sketch, half propped against it as if it had been placed there very carefully, was a dried flower. Its colour was faded and cobwebby, and although Theo knew very little about flowers, he recognized this one. Several times in those long-ago summers he had cut one and laid it on Charmery's pillow for her to find when she went to bed.

It was a Charmian rose.

Theo had no idea how long he stood staring at the fragile, sinister outline of the flower against Charmery's portrait. He had managed to convince himself that the chiming clock in the bedroom was due to some quirk of the weather or the house itself, but there could only be two explanations for what he was seeing now. One was that someone really was managing to get into the house and that someone had waited outside and crept in while he was investigating the boathouse light. But this was so elaborate and pointless, Theo could not bring himself to believe it.

But outlandish as it was, the other explanation was so bizarre Theo did not intend considering it, even for a second. It was that Charmery herself had returned.

CHAPTER SIX

Theo had been almost twenty-one, at the end of his third year at Cambridge, and Charmery was seventeen, still at school, but already making plans for what she would do when she left.

'But it doesn't sound as if she'll need to do anything, if she doesn't want to,' said Theo to his mother who drove him to Melbray at the end of June. Theo was spending the whole of the summer there; Petra would stay for one night, then go off again.

'Won't she want to try for university? Or at least get a job?' said Petra, concentrating on the road.

'She says not. She says her father will give her an allowance and she'll probably get herself a flat somewhere trendy like Chelsea or Holland Park. I suppose,' said Theo thoughtfully, 'the allowance will be quite generous. Uncle Desmond and Aunt Helen are very well off, aren't they?'

'I hope so,' said Petra rather wryly. 'Helen certainly spends enough to give that impression – remember the party they gave for the millennium?'

'Nancy had to be decanted into a taxi at two a.m.,' said Theo, grinning at the memory.

'The legend is that Desmond made a lot of money a few years ago when he was attached to the Treasury.'

'The unpronounceable Middle-European state,' said Theo, smiling, because the elder Kendals still occasionally planted a gentle jibe about Desmond's months in some exotic country, just emerged from communism and needing help with its new monetary policy. Great-aunt Emily Kendal, who was Theo's godmother and who liked to regard herself as the matriarch of the family, was fond of saying it was Desmond's sole claim to fame. 'He never lets anyone forget about it,' she said.

'Wherever it was that Desmond went, I think he did get some huge fee for the work,' said Petra. 'But I wouldn't like to say whether there's any of the money left.' She frowned, then said, 'I wonder if Charmery will turn into a kind of It-girl. A bit of modelling, a bit of publicity work. Travel and smart parties and getting her name in minor gossip columns.'

For once Petra sounded bitter, which was unlike her. Theo said, 'What an aimless existence. I should think she'd want to work properly. It's far better – far more satisfying – to be paid honest coinage for working—'

'Oh God, next you'll be quoting Karl Marx at me.'

'What's wrong with Marx?' demanded Theo.

Petra glanced at him, and said, warmly, 'D'you know, you're a constant delight to me.'

'Lot of slop,' said Theo, which was a family saying, generally used if someone appeared in danger of getting emotional or over-demonstrative. The Kendals, en masse, were not great on being emotional or demonstrative.

It had been an oppressively hot summer but there was an unsettled feeling that had nothing to do with the weather. Looking back, Theo thought it had been the summer of endings: Charmery, seventeen, was approaching the end of her school life, and Theo was facing his final Cambridge year that September. Even Lesley, who was fourteen, had left her school for a new one that had a better art department.

Despite the thunderstorms, the clans, as Desmond said, had gathered in force that year. Desmond himself came and went at intervals, pleading pressure of business, sometimes bringing sheaves of paperwork with him, and shutting himself away in the small room off the hall which Helen had designated as the study, but which was not much more than a general dumping ground for things people could not be bothered with.

Guff was at Fenn as he was most summers, although this year he was calling it the summer solstice because he had recently become interested in ancient religions. He had met a young lady who was instructing him in the history of the druids, he said. There was still an Order of Druids in existence it appeared, and he was hoping to accompany them to their midsummer's vigil at Stonehenge, although some kind of endowment was apparently required before he would actually be allowed to join the Order itself.

'She drove him here and spent the night,' said Helen, after the high priestess of druidism had left next morning.

'Just don't tell me which bed she actually ended up in,' said Nancy.

'I gave her the spare bed in Lesley's room,' said Helen, to which Nancy said that was as maybe, but there had been a suspicious amount of creaking of landing floorboards around midnight.

'Oh, Guff's encounters are never physical.'

'I should think not at his age,' said Nancy tartly.

Nancy herself was at Fenn House that summer because Helen had invited Great-aunt Emily, and Nancy was going to help with her. She was very good with elderly people, said Nancy, and did not hear Aunt Emily telling Charmery and Theo if she had known that old bat Nancy was coming she would have gone to Frinton-on-Sea instead.

But even though it had been a peculiar summer, what with Guff's druidism and Nancy's bossiness and Great-aunt Emily's bluntness, and what with Lesley's two small brothers turning the lawn into a football pitch, there were no quarrels. The Kendals did not go in for quarrels any more than they went in for emotions. They sniped a bit and grumbled a bit, but in the main they were civilized and polite to one another.

'I love them all madly,' Charmery said to Theo one Sunday afternoon towards the end of that summer. 'Of course I do. But don't you sometimes just want to run away from them, as far as possible?'

Theo looked at her. She was wearing her big 1920s-style straw hat, and she had tucked a vivid pink Charmian rose into the band which ought to have clashed with her bronze hair but somehow did not. The hat shaded her eyes, deepening their colour almost to jade, casting light shadows over her high cheekbones. She had on a thin silk skirt and a white cotton top – simple but probably expensive – and her bare arms and legs were tanned. He wondered if he would ever stop feeling this overwhelming surge of love and desire every time he saw her. But when she said this about running away from the family, he said, very lightly, 'I often want to run away from them. Shall we do it together, right away?'

There was no knowing how she would answer which was why he had kept his tone flippant, but she looked at him thoughtfully for a moment, then said, 'Yes, let's. Where shall we go?'

'To the river?' Theo's heart had performed a double somersault. 'The boathouse?'

The boathouse was a bit of a joke because the river frontage was supposed to be the house's main attraction. Desmond always said ruefully that it had added thousands to the purchase price and when he was declared bankrupt they could all blame the River Chet. In practice, the boathouse was hardly ever used although there was a rather battered rowing boat moored in its leaky gloom. Charmery kept suggesting to her father that he buy a motor launch, and Helen got leaflets about boat furniture and cabin fridges so they could drink chilled wine on deck, but Nancy and Great-aunt Emily said it was a waste of time. 'In high summer the river smells like a sewage farm,' said Aunt Emily. 'I don't care if Desmond buys the *Queen Mary*, I'm staying on dry land, thank you.'

Guff had taken the rowing boat on the river a couple of years ago. He had been interested in photography that summer and wanted to capture dappled river banks and weeping willow trailing into the water. There was a very nice young person in his local photographic shop who had been advising him on what cameras he should buy. Lesley had gone with Guff to help carry the light meters and flash attachments which he had bought from the young person's shop, but unfortunately they had capsized the boat, the cameras had sunk irretrievably, and Guff had to be fished out and given rum toddies to ward off a cold.

The river did not smell like a sewage farm today. As Charmery and Theo went along the rather uneven garden path towards the boathouse, and down the mossy steps there was only the scent of roses and of the lavender from the little herb garden lying on the warm afternoon like a drug.

'All the perfumes of Arabia,' said Theo, who had been studying the Elizabethans that term. 'So perfumed that the winds were love-sick.'

'If you're going to start waxing poetical I warn you I shall counter it with "'Twas on the good ship Venus".'

'Dear me, what do they teach children at schools these days, I wonder?'

'You needn't play the po-faced older cousin, because you taught me that one,' said Charmery, and grinned. Somehow their hands had linked, and the feel of her fingers against Theo's palm was the strongest aphrodisiac in the world.

The boathouse was dim and secret. There was the faint lapping sound of water and soft green waterlight rippled on the walls.

'It's an enchanted cave,' said Charmery, pausing in the doorway with delight.

'It's very old,' said Theo. 'That's one of the things that always intrigues me about it. It was here long before Fenn House was built. My mamma once told me there's a local legend that people used to see will o' the wisps dancing across this part of the river like human fireflies. They'd beckon to you, but if you followed them they led you to a watery grave.'

'We should have brought a bottle of cider or something,' said Charmery. 'We could have cooled the bottle in the river like they do on films. Except the river's too muddy, isn't it? We'd probably catch typhoid or dysentery. Let's sit down – preferably not on the floor, those planks look disgusting.'

But Theo spread his cotton sweater on the planks and Charmery sat down, then pretended to shiver at the cool miasma from the river so that it was the most natural thing in the world for Theo to put his arm round her for warmth. She pulled off the straw sunhat and a swathe of her hair tumbled loose, brushing against his face. The sheer intimacy of this was like the igniting of a touch-paper, and Theo's long pent-up desire exploded like a thousand sky rockets. Before he knew it, he had pulled her to him and was kissing her with such desperate urgency that she half flinched.

'I'm sorry,' said Theo, releasing her at once. 'I didn't mean to do that. I didn't hurt you, did I?'

'No, but I wouldn't care if you did.' The soft radiance of the boathouse reflected in her eyes. 'Kiss me again, Theo. Do it so hard I faint.'

This time, when she freed her lips, she said, 'Why did you never do this before?'

'Did you want me to?'

'God, yes. For about a year now.'

'A whole year wasted,' said Theo, and then somehow they were lying on the planks, and the dank wood of the boathouse floor no longer mattered. Her body was pressing against him and his mind was spinning with the ecstasy. But I can't, he thought. I daren't. She's only seventeen, she's my cousin . . . 'Oh God, Charmery, we must stop.'

'No! Don't stop.'

She pushed aside the thin skirt she was wearing and he realized with a fresh surge of desire that she was naked beneath it. When his hand slid between her thighs she shivered with delight, and he felt her hand reach for him.

'So this is how you feel and this is how you behave when you're being passionate,' she said suddenly. 'Isn't this weird? We know each other so well, but we don't know any of this about each other. You're a different person all of a sudden. You're not the cousin I've known since I was small.'

'You're different as well,' said Theo, but this was not true, because this was a Charmery he knew very well indeed from all the fantasies and dreams over the years. But five minutes later – five minutes of breathless and increasingly urgent passion – he sat up and said tersely, 'Charmery, we really must stop. Apart from anything else, someone might come in.'

'No one ever comes down here. Anyhow, I don't care if the whole family stands in the boat and watches us. Put your hand back . . . Oh God, Theo, that's such bliss . . .'

'This is something I've dreamed about for so long – but I don't want to do anything you'll regret afterwards.'

'I won't regret anything. Not with you. Will you regret anything?'

'God, no! I've wanted to make love to you since you were about fourteen,' said Theo.

'Perv.'

'Lolita.'

They smiled at one another.

'Our thoughts fit, don't they?' she said. 'We understand each other without needing explanations.'

'Yes.' Theo stared down at her, wanting to print her face on his memory, wanting to fix the moment so that he could keep it for ever.

Her hand slid inside his jeans, at first tentatively as if she was not sure about what she was doing. Theo gasped, and Charmery took her hand away at once. 'I'm sorry – isn't that all right?'

'It's so incredibly all right that you'd better stop or I might lose control altogether.'

'Please lose control,' she said at once, her eyes glowing. 'I'd love that.'

'But you might hate me afterwards.'

'Shouldn't that be my line? But I'll never hate you. And don't you feel this is the right time for us?'

'The inevitable step forward?'

'Yes. Only – have you got something we can use?'

'Not right this minute.'

'I thought all university students went round with a permanent erection and a pocket stuffed with condoms,' she said, and Theo blinked with surprise at how worldly and grown-up she suddenly sounded.

'Not all the time we don't.' He hesitated, and she leaned forward and began to kiss him, and Theo, tumbling helplessly into the whirling, desperate ecstasy all over again, thought: It will be all right. I can't break the mood to go back up to the house and ferret around for a condom – I'm not even sure if I've got any. Just this once, it will be all right. I think I'll be able to stop in time.

She tasted like sunlight and summer, and her fingers were like velvet and her skin felt like silk ... Several layers down he was thinking he would have to exercise iron control and be so gentle, because she would never have done this before.

But she had.

The way she was twining her legs round him, pulling him in deeper and moving with the smoothness of practice, were the unmistakable products of experience. He shouldn't have been surprised: Charmery was beautiful and unusual and any man seeing her would instantly want to have her.

He was in no position to criticize; he had not been as wildly promiscuous as some of his friends and fellow students, but he had not lived the life of a monk either. He had been seventeen himself when he lost his virginity at the end of his final school term, and he had had several girlfriends at Cambridge. All of them had been intelligent and attractive and companionable, and with two of them things might easily have developed into something lasting and good. The fact that they had not was quite simply because they were not Charmery.

Afterwards he propped himself up on his elbow and looked down at her. Her hair was tumbling over the timbers of the landing stage and she was smiling at him.

'So,' she said, 'finally and at last, we've done it.'

'Finally and at last and for ever,' said Theo, managing to beat down the stabs of jealousy that someone else had been first with her.

'You stopped in time, didn't you?' she said, suddenly. 'I mean – you withdrew in time?'

'It was a bit of a close thing,' said Theo, aware it had been more than close. 'What happens now? When my finals are over and I've got a job, we could—'

'No,' she said at once. 'No, *don't* let's do all that undying devotion, love for ever stuff.' She pulled her skirt back in place, and put the sunhat back on to hide the disarray of her hair. 'Not yet anyway. Let's just go back to the house and be ordinary again.'

It was absurd to feel as if she had dealt him a blow, just as it had been absurd to assume she had not had boyfriends. Theo could not recall her ever mentioning any, but that didn't mean anything; she could be very secretive at times. But he had always visualized the time after making love to her as deeply intimate and sweet – as a time when they might even glance at a shared future.

61

But she had said, 'Not yet', so Theo managed to match her tone. 'OK,' he said lightly. 'But are you all right?'

'What an unoriginal question. Still, at least you didn't say "How was it for you." Of course I'm all right.' She brushed the dust from her skirt. 'What I am,' she said, 'is absolutely starving.'

Words and tone came like a blow. Had this just been an adventure for her? Something intriguing and new to while away the afternoon because the family were exasperating her or she was bored? After all his years of hoping and planning and dreaming ...? Only moments earlier, she had said, 'Our thoughts fit,' but it seemed they had not fitted enough for her to sense how he felt about her – how he had ached for today. But he clung to that 'Not yet', and said, 'I'm quite hungry as well. Let's go and raid the larder.'

'People don't raid larders these days. You sound like something out of a 1940s children's adventure story.'

'Enid Blyton? *Famous Five go Shagging*?' said Theo.

'You're so vulgar I don't know how you stand yourself.'

They walked back to the house, but this time the width of the garden path was between them.

She left Fenn House four days later.

'Final school year ahead,' she said, standing among the piled-up luggage in the hall, and kissing him with a light cousinly kiss that anyone could have witnessed. 'A levels and all kinds of tedium. But we'll be together when it's my half term, of course.'

'Do you want to be?' Theo could not believe she was going to leave without any further acknowledgement of what had happened.

'Of course I do.'

'Come to Cambridge for a weekend before that,' said Theo, a bit desperately.

'Yes, if I can. But I can't talk now. Pa's bringing the car up to the door in about half a minute, and he'll get impatient if I'm not there.'

'But promise to try?'

'Of course I promise.' She glanced round to make sure no one was in earshot, then said softly, 'It's all right, Theo. Really, it is. I do love you. One day we'll talk about it properly.'

'Soon?'

'Yes.' Her hand came out to curl round his, holding it tightly for a moment. 'Promise you won't say anything to my parents, though – not even a hint. Not yet,' she said again.

'All right.'

'Good.' She glanced towards the half-open door, and Theo heard the car. 'It's only seven weeks to half term anyway,' she said, and with that, and with the elusive promise contained in 'Not yet', he had to be content.

He left Melbray three days later because he could not bear Fenn House without her.

'Revision for next term,' he said to Charmery's mother and Aunt Emily.

'Work hard, but remember to play hard, as well,' said Aunt Emily, who was planning to buy a new outfit for his graduation. Guff had discarded the Druid female and had now met a sweet young thing who ran a little boutique in the Brompton Road and was going to advise Aunt Emily on what to wear for the occasion. When Theo said there might not even be a graduation ceremony for him because at the moment there was more chance of ignominious failure than a degree of any kind, Aunt Emily said, 'Nonsense'. She and Guff were going to sit in the front row where they could applaud Theo enthusiastically.

Back at Cambridge he wrote to Charmery several times – he did not dare email because she would be using the school computer which was not likely to be very private. He tried phoning, but her phone was nearly always on voicemail, and on the rare occasion he did get her, she always seemed in a hurry. There was a class she should be at, she said, or a sixth-form meeting. She was sorry if he kept getting voicemail, but there was a rule about not having phones switched on between 8.30 a.m. and 6 p.m.

'Really tedious, but I've only got another couple of terms of it,' she said, and Theo tried not to think that this new gushing way of speaking struck an unpleasantly false note. 'It's lovely to hear you, but I'll have to dash because it's the debating society in ten minutes and I'm one of tonight's speakers.'

'But I'll see you at Fenn in October?'

'Yes, of *course*.'

I've lost her, thought Theo bleakly, and it's my own fault. I should never have let that afternoon in the boathouse happen. But she was as eager as I was. She was loving and warm and we were so close.

He tried to compose sonnets to her – paeons of praise to her beauty, and burning words of love and longing. Unfortunately, his first attempt was unpleasantly lewd, the second sounded like a reproving head teacher and the third had the dubious rhythm and scansion of a limerick. All three endeavours were crossly consigned to the bin in screwed-up balls, which was highly suitable since Theo's own life at the moment seemed to be screwed-up and ballsed-up and might as well be thrown into the bin or down the loo and flushed into the Cam.

He reminded himself she was still very young. Perhaps in another year? Or two years. Oh God, two years is a lifetime, thought Theo. I'll feel like some medieval knight serving seven years for his lady. It had better not be bloody seven years, though, or I'll forget what to do in bed. I'll bet when Lancelot stopped riding around on quests and finally got it together with Guinevere he wasn't exactly a tiger in the sack.

On the crest of this last thought, he returned to composition, and at white-hot speed wrote a satirical sketch for the Footlights in which Lancelot had to embark on a new crusade, not in search of the Holy Grail this time, but of the Round Table equivalent of Viagra, blaming his sorry state on his long enforced celibacy. The sketch was performed with gusto, and caused considerable mirth among the students. Theo, fêted and congratulated after the show, told himself he could one day recover from Charmery and there might even be a life to be lived that did not contain her. He did not believe it, though. He did not think anyone who had loved her would ever recover from her.

CHAPTER SEVEN

———◆———

Theo counted the days until that October holiday at Fenn House. The Kendals liked Melbray in autumn, and Helen and Desmond nearly always went to Fenn for two or three weeks. As Helen said, Charmery's half term usually coincided with the half terms of Lesley and the twins, and Theo could generally come down for a long weekend as well. There were walks through crunchy autumn leaves and one or two local events which they enjoyed, and there was Desmond's mulled wine which was nearly a legend by itself.

Guff was not there that year; he had gone to Scotland, having become enamoured of fishing – the sweet young thing from the boutique had obtained waxed jackets and waders for him, he said, although he had been shocked at the cost. Nancy was there, though, because of helping with the local Halloween Festival. You could not really trust the residents to get the decorations right, she said, they were apt to tip the thing over into outright paganism if not watched.

'It *is* outright paganism,' said Great-aunt Emily who had arrived in a hired car, pleased to be part of the festivities, but not best pleased at finding Nancy in self-appointed command of the kitchen. 'It's an old Celtic festival – I know that because I once had an admirer who was Irish and he told me about the Samhain bonfires. I believe there used to be all kinds of wild goings-on.'

'Well, we aren't going to have wild goings-on here,' said Nancy. 'I daresay we might run to a bonfire, though. You wouldn't mind a bonfire, would you, Helen?'

'Well . . .'

'Desmond can make his mulled wine and Lesley and I can go into Melbray to order suitable food. Sausages and spare ribs, I think, don't you? The twins can come with us, it'll stop them tearing about the house like ruffians.'

'Listen,' said Theo, managing to draw Charmery out into the hall, 'if we're to get any time at all to ourselves it'll be now while they're unpacking pumpkins and calculating spare ribs. You only wrote to me once, and your phone was hardly ever switched on when I called. I've missed you like grim death for the last seven weeks, in fact it's felt more like seven years. I've been through seven separate kinds of agony.'

'I don't think there *are* seven separate kinds of agony,' she said. She was standing in the deep bay window, staring out at the autumn gardens. The soft light cast a golden radiance over her skin.

'Charmery, come down to the boathouse with me now. I don't mean for . . . I just want you to myself for half an hour.'

She turned to look at him thoughtfully. 'All right.' The remembered intimacy was in her voice again and she was the Charmery of Theo's childhood – the cousin he had known since she was born and who was impossibly beautiful and unbearably exciting. 'But I hope you want a bit more than just being alone,' she said in a low caressing voice. 'In fact after seven weeks I hope you want a lot more.' She reached for his hand and Theo felt as if he had received a 1,000-volt electrical charge.

They went stealthily across the hall, trying not to make a sound.

'Grab a couple of coats from the hall as we go,' said Theo.

'It's almost like being children again,' said Charmery, doing as he asked.

'Tiptoeing away from the grown-ups, trying not to giggle.'

'I never giggled.'

'Yes, you did. I loved it when you giggled. Only don't do it now. And mind the squeaky hinge on the garden door.'

'What if somebody sees us?'

'If it's Nancy she'll get the shock of her life to see me in this condition.'

'Do her good,' said Charmery, stifling one of the giggles.

The boathouse was cool and dim and smelt of autumn. Theo spread out the coats on the planks, then pulled Charmery against him, kissing her and cupping her face between his hands.

'Will we hear if anyone comes down the path?' she said, when he finally released her.

'I wouldn't hear if the Four Horsemen of the Apocalypse rode through the shrubbery.' A sudden stab of conscience made him say, 'Charm, listen, I honestly didn't mean to steamroller you into anything. We can just be on our own down here and talk.'

'I didn't trek all the way down here just to talk,' she said, unbuttoning her coat.

'Yes, but I don't want this to seem like a . . .'

'Quick casual shag?'

'Well, yes. Although there's nothing casual about it as far as I'm concerned. You must know how much I love you. You do know, don't you?'

'Yes, but stop talking about it and demonstrate,' she said, pulling his mouth down to hers, and Theo was lost to everything in the world save the soaring bliss of being with her again.

'Don't make the boards creak so much,' she said, after a moment. 'Supposing they give way and we go down into the Chet?'

'I don't care. We're going to celebrate a pagan festival later, and the pagans didn't care about creaking planks,' said Theo. 'I'll creak boards and I'll ford the Chet with all the ferrymen of the world and sail into the sunset with you. I'll chant pagan spells so that you love me for ever, and leap through bonfires, and—'

'You sound drunk,' said Charmery, laughing.

'I am. I'm drunk on you. I'd quote poetry to you if I could remember any. Wait a minute ...' He foraged in his jacket for the condoms and pushed her back on the folded coats. Her body, when he entered it, felt like silk and she gasped and arched her back, pulling him deeper. Ecstasy seared Theo so violently that his mind seemed to splinter into hundreds of fragments, and the dim boathouse shivered and blurred all round him. For a moment he was afraid he might be about to pass out or have a heart attack, and it would surely be the ultimate irony to die now.

He did not die, of course, and he did not pass out. He tumbled into a helpless explosive climax. He felt Charmery shiver and heard her cry of delight at almost the same time. He wanted to grab this moment and save it for ever.

They were still tangled together, Charmery's hair tumbling over Theo's bare chest, when there was the crunch of footsteps outside, and a voice said, 'Theo, are you in here? Because they want some help pacing out a site for the bonfire.' The voice stopped, but Theo, jolted out of the warm half-sleep of pleasure, had already recognized it as belonging to Helen Kendal. Her footsteps came along the path, and a shadow fell across the timbers of the landing stage. For a moment there was only the dark outline of her figure against the golden autumn afternoon. Then she stepped into the boathouse itself and Theo saw the horrified shock on her face as she took in the scene that confronted her.

He managed to pull his jacket across his thighs and sit up and say, with as much dignity as possible, 'Helen – I'm really sorry you had to find us like this, but—' He broke off. Helen Kendal was white and there was a pinched bluish look round her lips. 'I know it's a shock,' said Theo, wanting to banish the dreadful look, aware that Charmery was sitting up beside him and pulling on her

69

jeans. 'But you've probably suspected how I feel about Charmery,' he said. 'I've always loved her.'

'Oh, dear God,' said Helen and for a moment Theo thought she was about to faint. Then she stood up a bit straighter, as if squaring her shoulders to receive a great weight, and although Theo felt absurd and at a disadvantage sitting in the draughty boat-house like this, he said, 'This isn't so very terrible, is it? I know Charmery and I are cousins, but our fathers weren't brothers, they were cousins, so we're only second cousins. And I want to marry her in a year or two – it's what I've always wanted.'

Helen was not quite crying, but she was not far off and she was clearly distraught.

'Theo – you can't marry her.'

'I don't mean right now.'

'You can't marry her – ever,' she said, as if Theo had not spoken. 'Not ever.' There was a moment when she seemed to struggle with some huge inner conflict, then she said, 'You're brother and sister.'

The golden afternoon outside spun into a confused blur, and the world narrowed to the dim confines of the boathouse. For several moments Theo could not speak and he could scarcely even breathe. This is a nightmare, he thought. It must be. This is the really bad moment just before you wake up. At last, he managed to say, 'I don't believe you.'

'It's true,' said Helen, and now she was crying properly. 'I wish it weren't. Charmery, my dearest girl, I'm so sorry.'

Charmery was huddled over, hugging her knees, her hair falling forward to hide her face. When Helen made a clumsy movement to kneel next to her and put her arms round her, Charmery brushed her away with an angry gesture. Theo was unable to tell if Charmery was crying, so he turned back to Helen, and with difficulty, said, 'Could you explain? Is Desmond my real father? Is that what you mean?' But he was already aware of disbelief, because it was impossible to think of his mother and Desmond together, and it was equally impossible to think of his mother betraying Helen by sleeping with Helen's husband.

For a while he thought Helen was not going to reply. She was still half kneeling on the landing stage, her arms wrapped about her as if for warmth, but she finally managed to go on.

'Desmond isn't your father, Theo. It's the other way round. Your father was Charmery's father. John Kendal and I had an affair just before he died. I have no excuses,' said Helen, help-lessly.

'Haven't you?' said Theo, through the choking fury against his father. 'Did Desmond know? Did my mother know?' He thought there was a split second before she replied, but then she said, 'No. Neither of them knew.'

From behind the curtain of hair, Charmery said, 'Are you sure about that?'

'Yes,' said Helen. She made another of the tentative gestures towards Charmery, then recoiled and looked back at Theo. 'Desmond was very upset at John's death – they had been as close as if they were brothers, in fact they practically grew up together. I think that's why he accepted the overseas contract – that Eastern European state you all laugh about. He left in January – mid-1980s it was – and I went out there to be with him in May. You were born out there, Charmery – we stayed until you were old enough to travel back to England.' She stopped, and Theo saw she was fighting tears again. 'I told lies and I deceived people,' said Helen. 'People I cared about very deeply. But out of it all, I got you, Charmery. I could never regret that. Even now, even this afternoon, I don't regret it.'

'Well, thank you,' said Charmery, and Theo could not tell if she meant it or if she was merely embarrassed. The thought flickered in his mind that he would have expected Charmery to challenge her mother – almost to attack her, but she did not.

'Theo, in other circumstances I wouldn't go up in smoke about this,' said Helen, looking back at him. 'It was my generation who

71

thought it invented the permissive society, anyway. But given the real relationship marriage would be illegal, and what's happened today – what's clearly already happened between you – is certainly unnatural.'

Theo wanted to say it had felt like the most natural thing in the world. Instead, he said, 'If we made sure never to have children— I'd have that operation – a vasectomy.'

'No!' said Helen. 'Theo, my poor dear boy, there's no way round it. It can't happen, not under any circumstances. I couldn't let it happen. I'd have to tell people the truth.'

She was crying all over again, and Theo said, 'All right. I understand. I suppose you're right.' At his side, Charmery was still huddled over silently, as if hugging the misery of it all tight inside her. Theo ached to put his arms round her, but knew, with sick despair, that he could not. Not ever again.

'For the moment we'd better focus on the immediate,' said Helen, the tears drying on her cheeks. 'On getting through the rest of this holiday, including, oh dear God, Nancy's bonfire. It'll be a nightmare, but it'll have to be done. Can you do it?'

Theo did not say he would have to focus on getting through the rest of his life. He managed to say, 'Yes, I can do that.'

'Thank you,' she said, and without looking at Charmery, went out of the boathouse and back to the house.

Only then did Charmery push back her hair and sit up straight to look at him.

'I'm sorry,' she said. 'That isn't what I intended to happen.'

Theo had hoped the world would stop spinning when Helen went away, but Charmery's words and her tone were sending it spinning in a different direction. She's apologizing, he thought, and before he realized it, he said, 'You knew.'

'I knew Desmond wasn't my father,' she said.

'How did you know?' Theo made an angry gesture. 'It doesn't really matter,' he said, 'but tell me anyway.'

'If you must have the sordid details,' she said impatiently, 'I found some old letters last year – mother was having a bedroom re-fitted and there was a massive clear-out going on. There was a big envelope at the top of an old wardrobe stuffed with ancient medical cards and hospital appointments and things, so I looked to see if there was anything interesting.'

'And?'

'And there was a letter addressed to Desmond Kendal, dated way back – 1981 or 1982. It was confirmation of some tests.'

'What kind of tests?'

'Fertility tests,' she said. 'Only he wasn't – wasn't fertile, I mean. It was absolutely clear on that. Zero score. Sad, isn't it? Some childhood illness, it said. But it was absolutely definite and clear. He could never father children, not ever. So I knew he wasn't my father.' She reached for his hand. 'But honestly, Theo, I didn't know the truth.'

'Didn't you ask Helen?'

'No, I couldn't. At first I wondered if she'd had – what do you call it? – in vitro fertilization, but I don't think that was very common or successful in the 1980s. So then I thought she might cry among all the paint-pots and stepladders and give me a lot of guffle about star-crossed love and doomed romances – like *Brief Encounter* or something equally nauseating. Massively embarrassing to hear one's mother bang on about some torrid old love affair. I didn't want to hear it. Lot of slop,' said Charmery, on a sudden sob.

'But *did* you guess the truth? Charm, tell me honestly.'

She bent her head again. 'I did think it *might* be your father,' she said. 'He sort of fitted the profile – he seems to have been very much part of the scene, and according to all the stories he was very charming.'

'So I believe,' said Theo in a hard voice.

'I didn't know for certain, though. Does it matter so terribly much? We could be really secret about it . . .' She suddenly leaned over to kiss him, and Theo's lips opened involuntarily and his

73

body responded with the familiar hard longing. When she stopped kissing him, her eyes were wide and shining.

'It'd be a really exciting secret to be lovers like this, wouldn't it?' she said.

'It's not exciting at all,' said Theo. 'It's sick.' But he remained where he was, and after a moment she slid her hand down between his legs. I'll push her hand away in a minute, he thought. In just a minute . . . His emotions were in turmoil, but the familiar longing was already spreading through him like a fire. She doesn't understand, he thought, but in the same heartbeat remembered how she had made him promise not to tell anyone about their love-making in the summer. 'Not to my parents,' she had said, and the memory of those words sent a spike of anger through Theo. Had she known the real truth all the time? Had she manipulated him, purely for the excitement of it. *It'd be a really exciting secret to be lovers like this . . .*

He managed to say, 'Charmery, we can't turn our feelings off like flipping a switch, but we've got to try.'

'Why? No one needs to know. As long as we keep it from my mother and Desmond.'

'That's not the point.' Theo clung to the flicker of angry suspicion that Charmery could have known the truth and it gave him the strength to push her hand away. 'We can't do this, Charmery. Helen's right. Not now. Not ever again.'

A look he had never seen before came into her eyes. 'What a hypocrite you are,' she said. 'So bloody moral and righteous when all the time, you're bursting your skin to fuck me.' She stood up. 'Well, fuck you, brother dear, because you won't get the chance to do it again.'

Without looking at him, she half ran out of the boathouse. Theo sat for a long time, his mind a churning mass of raw agony. But within the agony the spikes of anger were still jabbing into him. He thought if anything were to drag him through this sick despair, it would be that anger. What if she really did know? She could have done. After she found the medical report on Desmond's infertility, she'd have been tuned in for any clues about who her father really was. Maybe she came across a letter Helen had kept, or Helen had said something unguarded. Charmery was sharp enough, intuitive enough, to piece together any small fragments. But if Theo once believed this, he might start to hate her instead of loving her.

He realized he was shivering as violently as if he had a high fever, and he managed to go back to the house and up to his bedroom. He pulled on a sweater and sat on the bed, wrapping his arms round his body in an attempt to bring some warmth back. Then he washed and got ready for Nancy's bonfire. As he did so, he wondered how he could ever forget the sweet softness of Charmery's lips and the helpless hard arousal between his legs when she kissed him. Even if he really did hate her now, he would go on wanting her for the rest of his life.

He returned to Cambridge and his final year, but when it came to the finals he did not get the prophesied double first. 'A very near miss, apparently,' said his tutor ruefully. 'I suspect you've burned the candle at both ends these last few months.'

'I have but it gave a lovely light,' said Theo.

'Don't quote to the converted,' said his tutor sharply. Then, relenting, he said, 'I think it was more a matter of the mental energy going in other directions, wasn't it? All those sketches for the Footlights for instance.'

But Theo knew he had lost the double first because of Charmery. There were endless nights when he lay awake aching for her, and when he thought he heard her voice inside the rain pattering on the windows. On those nights he almost wished himself living in the Middle Ages so he could order an alchemist to conjure her up there and then, and he came very close to reaching for the phone, just to hear her voice. But if once he talked to her he would want to see her, and he was afraid of discovering he did not care that she was his sister.

Despite what Helen had said, he wondered whether his mother had known or suspected the truth. She had never, for as long as he could remember, stayed at Fenn House for longer than was absolutely necessary. Was it because she knew Charmery was her husband's love-child and could not bear to see her more than she had to? But if so, surely she would have hated Helen, and she never had. So it looked as if she had not known. Theo considered asking Petra, but knew he could not. If she really didn't know it would tear her apart.

But although he won the many fights not to phone Charmery, news of her filtered back to him in gossipy trickles. She left school the following year, and as Petra had prophesied, did not go on to university or seem interested in doing so. The family grapevine reported that she travelled quite a lot – there were two or three months in America, and six months in France, and then another six months in Switzerland. Theo guessed Helen had deliberately arranged this to keep Charmery out of his reach. The rest of the family viewed these travels with disfavour, even Aunt Emily, saying anybody would think Charmery was a debutante or an eighteenth-century fop taking the Grand Tour. Nancy thought it all very extravagant and just hoped Desmond had enough money to fund all this gallivanting. Better if Charmery had trained for a proper job, said Nancy; Helen and Desmond should have insisted on it while the girl was still at school.

'I don't know what century Nancy lives in or how she copes with her sixth formers,' observed Aunt Emily. 'Parents haven't been able to insist their children do anything for at least twenty years, even I know that.'

Unexpectedly, it was Theo's mother who said, 'But nobody's ever been able to insist that Charmery does anything she doesn't want to do.'

CHAPTER EIGHT

After Theo left Cambridge he avoided the family as much and as politely as possible. His absence was noticed and commented on, of course, and apparently became the subject of considerable conjecture. Opinions ranged from the possibility that he had become entangled with some disreputable adventuress who could not be introduced to anyone (Aunt Emily's belief), to speculation that he had taken to drink or drugs or both (Nancy), and the suggestion by a mild-mannered aunt on Helen's side of the family that he might be contemplating a religious retreat from the world. According to Theo's mother, who attended a fortieth birthday party for Lesley's mother, this last idea caused much ribaldry among the bluffer uncles who said what about the vow of chastity, ho ho, and added that hell would freeze and pigs would fly before Theo would enter a monastery. Guff thought the absences might be due to Theo having been enlisted by the government to work in a secret capacity, and pointed out that Burgess and Maclean had been Cambridge men.

'They were also double agents,' said Nancy, tartly.

'Yes, but Theo wouldn't be a double agent.'

'So there you are,' said Petra, recounting all this to Theo.

'You're either in the hands of a gold-digger, you're an alcoholic or a drug fiend, you're about to become a monk or you're James Bond.'

'I've just had a bit too much of family,' said Theo, hating himself for deceiving her.

'A little of them goes a long way,' agreed his mother, apparently accepting this with perfect equanimity.

'But I expect I'll wander back into the Kendal bosom at some point.'

'I expect you will,' she said, as if it was not important. 'One usually does.'

In time life became slightly more endurable. His Footlights' sketches had caused a few ripples in the world that existed beyond Cambridge's rarefied atmosphere, and some review work came in, along with the acceptance of a couple of articles for one of the heftier Sunday papers. In the wake of this was a modest commission for a series of four short radio plays.

'And very good they were,' said Guff, who had written to the BBC to praise the plays and had received a very nice reply from a young production assistant whom he intended to take out to lunch.

The radio plays led to scripting work for a couple of TV documentaries, which was gratifying and enjoyable. None of it provided a huge amount of money, but for the moment there was enough on which to live and it was possible to view the financial future with a degree of optimism. With some trepidation, Theo embarked on a full-length novel, and after a few false starts and some rejections, his first novel was published when he was twenty-six. When he received the call saying it had been accepted, he found himself longing to tell Charmery, and to see her eyes glowing with admiration and delight for him. He tried not to mind when she did not so much as send him a note or even an email of congratulation.

There were congratulations from other quarters though, because the book received considerable acclaim. 'Dark,' said the critics. 'Dark and dense, and although not entirely comfortable to read, very compelling indeed.' When it won a small, but prestigious award, they all said they had foreseen it, and began to talk about the Man Booker Prize as a future possibility.

On the strength of this Theo scraped together a deposit for a tiny sliver of a house on the northern outskirts of London, and tried not to think how he would be shackled to the building society for the next twenty-five years.

But his new life was not so bad; there were agreeable contacts in the world of publishing and radio and newspapers, and there were a few girlfriends along the way, although he never viewed any of these relationships as serious. Once again this was because none of them were Charmery. He wondered if he would ever stop thinking about her and wanting her.

And then, five years after that never-forgotten autumn afternoon at Fenn House, midway through an ordinary working morning in the little north London house, he answered a knock at the door and she was standing on the step.

Theo's emotions spun in wild confusion, but when she said, 'I can come back later if this isn't a good time. Of if you're just going out?'

'It's fine,' said Theo.

She came into the comfortable untidy room which was strewn with his books, and sat down as easily as if they were back at Fenn or in her parents' London house at Hampstead.

'This isn't quite as I visualized it,' she said, looking about her. 'But it's nice.'

'Did you visualize it?' Theo could not take his eyes off her. He could not say any of the conventional things about whether she would like a drink, or what she was doing here. Half of him wanted to pull her against him and kiss her until they were both dizzy, but the other half kept replaying that autumn afternoon. 'It'd be a really exciting secret to be lovers . . .,' she had said.

'Oh yes, I often visualized it,' she said. 'Masses of times.' Her eyes went to the shelf with Theo's book on it, and to the desk where the proofs of his second book were spread out. 'You're almost famous, aren't you? *The Times* and the *Independent* are saying what a brilliant writer you are. I've read your book. It's very good – I didn't realize how good a writer you'd be. All those years ago, I mean.'

'Thank you.'

'I'm here because there's some bad news,' she said, 'about my mother and Desmond. I wanted to be the one to tell you.'

'What's happened?'

'Well, it's all frightfully traumatic,' she said. 'They were on the M25 – driving too fast as usual, you know what Desmond was like, and there was a pile-up.'

'A crash? God, what happened?'

'Oh, they're both dead,' she said. 'Right out of it, completely gone.' She shrugged and blinked several times, and if there had been a sudden glisten of tears, they vanished. 'Terribly sad, isn't it?'

'Oh, Charm, I'm so sorry . . .'

'Yes, well,' she said, in a brittle uncaring voice.

Theo waited, but when she did not say anything more, said, 'I really am dreadfully sorry. Does that mean you'll be in this country more now?'

'Actually I'm often in this country,' she said. 'I always go to Fenn in the spring – didn't you know that?'

'Yes.'

'But where I go now rather depends on you.' She had been curled up in the armchair, like a luxurious Persian cat; now she came to perch on the arm of Theo's chair. Her mouth was on his before he realized it and his lips opened involuntarily. She tasted sweet and warm and five years dissolved into nothing as

Theo's body responded with the familiar hard longing. When she stopped kissing him, her eyes were wide and shining. 'So,' she said, 'it *is* still the same for you, as well. I wasn't absolutely sure if it would be.'

The beloved and familiar curve of her cheek and the scent of her hair were like tinder igniting a fire that had never quite died, and Theo wanted to make love to her more than he had ever wanted anything in his life. But he fought down his emotions, and said, 'Charmery, what's going on? I'm truly sorry about Helen and Desmond, and I'll do everything I can to help you through it. Practically and emotionally, and—'

'Emotionally,' she said, in a soft silken voice. 'Ah yes. That's the thing, isn't it, Theo?'

'I don't understand you,' said Theo, but in a corner of his mind, he did understand.

Charmery said, 'Don't be dense, darling. The two people who knew the truth about us are both dead. No one in the world knows. We can be together.'

They looked at one another.

'We can't. Charmery, I'm sorry. I still love you just as much – I think I always will – but no.'

She recoiled as if he had struck her. 'I thought it would be all right,' she said, and for a moment it was not the flippant tone she had used earlier; it was the uncertain voice of the real Charmery.

'No,' said Theo again.

Her eyes darkened briefly, but then she sat up straighter. It was as if she had reached once again for the enamelled surface and the slightly bored flippancy.

'Oh well, worth a shot. Quite a day for me – I'm not used to encountering rejection. But then you always hit a nerve with me that no one else has ever found since. I'd better go, hadn't I?'

'You don't have to.'

'I think I do. Goodbye, Theo, darling. Maybe one day . . .' She stopped and shook her head. 'Or maybe not,' she said, and went out, quickly and gracefully. There was nothing to show she had ever been in the house, except for a slight dent in a cushion and the faint drift of her scent. That, and the feeling that a knife had been plunged into an old wound that had just started to heal.

Theo's mother asked Theo to accompany her to the double funeral. 'I know you haven't had much to do with the family for a long time, but I'd like to have you there if you could bear it,' she said.

'Of course I could bear it.'

'Helen was very kind to me when I came into this family,' she said. 'The Kendals didn't really approve of me in those days.'

'Why not?'

'Oh, because they thought I was different. Or they wanted your father to marry somebody with a lot of money. I had no money at all, of course. But Helen was a good friend to me,' said Petra. 'I feel as if a large piece of my life has suddenly vanished.'

There would probably never be a better moment to open the subject of the man who had been Charmery's father as well as Theo's. Theo framed several approaches in his mind, and found he could not say any of the words.

He sat at the back of the church during the funeral, and managed to slip out through a side door before he could get caught up in the wake that Lesley's parents had arranged. He spoke briefly to Great-aunt Emily, congratulated Lesley on having been accepted at the Slade, which had just happened, and exchanged a brief word with Lesley's brothers. But the only glimpse he had of Charmery was a remote, elegant figure at the front of the church, wearing expensive-looking black.

'Nancy seems to think Desmond was cooking the books,' said his mother when she telephoned him that evening to report on the wake. 'I said it didn't matter now if he'd cooked them until they boiled over onto the stove.'

'Trust Nancy to home in on the finances,' said Theo. 'I'll bet if Desmond did any cooking it was to keep pace with Helen and Charmery's lifestyle. Aunt Helen might be easy-going but Charmery must be very high maintenance.'

'You might be right about struggling to pay for the lifestyle,' said Petra thoughtfully.

After the death of Helen and Desmond, the half-serious prophecy Petra had once made about Charmery seemed to come true. She apparently lived a darting, butterfly life, going from one party, one smart weekend to the next, occasionally modelling clothes or cosmetics for the smaller fashion magazines, once or twice getting her name or her photo in gossip columns. She had a small flat in Pimlico – Lesley, now in her second year at the Slade, had stayed with her once or twice and when asked, said Charmery's life seemed hectic – but she apparently spent every spring and often part of the summer at Fenn House. This worried Guff, because Fenn was so solitary, but Nancy said Charmery was not likely to be solitary at Fenn or anywhere else, and the pity was that she did not invite some of her family to stay at Fenn, and continue the tradition her parents had started.

'But I daresay we're too dull for her smart friends,' said Nancy, tartly.

There were vague reports of love affairs between Charmery and a series of more or less eligible, semi-famous men. The younger members of the family regarded this with envy and Lesley's brothers were popularly supposed to have conceived a romantic passion for this glamorous cousin whom they only distantly remembered from the Fenn House holidays. But the older ones pursed their lips, said they had never heard of any of the men and it was to be hoped Charmery was not going to bring shame and disgrace on the Kendal name. Or even, said Nancy, to meet some appalling fate – and they might all laugh and look incredulous but you heard of these high-flying girls getting tangled up with gangsters and the like, thinking crime was glamorous, and ending on a mortuary slab, their names headlines in the newspapers. In light of what eventually happened to Charmery, it was later agreed to be unfortunate Nancy had made that remark about headlines in newspapers and mortuary slabs.

But in the end, Charmery was not a butterfly but a mayfly. Four years after her parents' deaths, Charmery herself was dead and Theo came back at last to the remote Norfolk house which held so many memories. The house that had its own air of secrecy, and that against all logic, he was starting to believe might be haunted.

Haunted. Since returning to Fenn House the word had kept coming to the forefront of Theo's mind. Haunted, he thought. Something's haunting me.

It occurred to him that the portrait of Charmery might be responsible for his jumpiness, but he could not bring himself to remove it. His emotions about her were a complex tangle, but he was unable to shut the sketch away in a dark cupboard. But whenever he looked at it, he thought the artist had over-emphasized the slightly slanting eyes, and missed the manipulative charm.

If anything was really haunting Theo, it was Matthew.

Matthew never really felt entirely safe, even when all the doors were locked and his father was at home. After the men had asked him to spy on his father he felt even less safe than before.

His father never talked about the men and Matthew did not talk about them either; he was afraid of finding out that what they said was true and his father really was a traitor. He did not think anyone would have seen the jeep driving up to their house because it was in a lane that did not lead anywhere much. Wilma was not very likely to tell people about it, because she had known Matthew's mother as a child and would do anything for Matthew and his father.

Two days after the men's visit, Wilma came stumping into the kitchen to say that his friend had vanished. She had heard it from the milkman.

'Friend?' said Matthew, who was getting ready for school. 'Who?'

'That Mara from Three Lanes Cottage,' said Wilma, banging pots around on the stove.

The words of the man exploded in Matthew's head. 'You'd want to help your friends,' he had said. 'You'd want to make sure they were safe . . .'

Matthew felt sick, but he managed to say, 'I 'spect it's just people making things up. I 'spect she'll be at school like always.'

He prayed that Mara would be waiting for him in the usual place, but she was not and her brother was not there either. Matthew walked to school by himself, thinking all the time that Mara would be there ahead of him, or there would be some news at school about her. But there was not. Even when her small brother came to school by himself the next day, white-faced and silent, Matthew could not find the words to ask him about Mara. He noticed, though, that the others kept away from the boy, as if they were afraid of catching something from him. Matthew was ashamed to realize he was doing the same thing.

On Friday afternoon, when he came out of school at four o'clock, one of the men was waiting for him at the entrance to the lane leading to his house. It was the man he had thought of as the leader, and he walked a little way along the lane with Matthew. He had brought a little book for Matthew about a school where people could go to learn how to draw and paint. Matthew turned the pages over while they walked along. The book was made from thick satiny paper, and the pictures showed huge light-filled studios and people a bit older than Matthew doing nothing but drawing and painting all day.

'We saw your drawings when we were in your bedroom,' said the man, 'and we thought how very good they were. I'd say you like drawing and painting better than anything.'

85

'Yes, I do.' There seemed no reason not to admit to this, anyway they apparently knew already.

'Well then, this is what we thought,' said the man, 'if you help us, Matthew, we could arrange for you to attend a proper art school in a few years. Perhaps even the very one in this leaflet – or one like it. It couldn't be for five or six years, and you'd have to work hard at school in that time. But we could arrange it for you. But in return you would have to help us.'

'Find out where my father goes and tell you?' said Matthew, looking at the man.

'Yes. There might be notes about the times of trains or something of that kind. An address where he stays. And we'd also like to see any articles he writes – any copies of articles. A bargain, that's what it will be. Well?'

Matthew did not answer immediately, but his whole body ached with longing. An art school – a place that taught you how to draw and paint properly, where you would do nothing else all day. The chance to go away from this bleak dull village which his father sometimes said was the end of nowhere, and perhaps live in a city – a big exciting city with people and shops. It's one of those worlds you want to escape to, he said to himself, and it would be the best world of them all because you'd be drawing and painting the whole time.

'But you want me to spy on my father,' he said. 'I can't do that. I told you I couldn't.'

'It wouldn't be spying,' said the man at once. 'It would be helping to prove his innocence.' He looked thoughtfully at Matthew. 'Let's suppose he goes out this weekend,' he said, 'just into the town to buy things. That's possible, isn't it?' He waited, and when Matthew did not answer went on, 'You could go into his study while he's out, and look for copies of the articles. Notes about his journeys.'

'He always locks the study when he goes out,' said Matthew.

'But you could find the key, surely. And wouldn't it be better to know once and for all? Then we could forget the whole thing. You can understand that, can't you?' The man paused, then said very deliberately, 'I think, Matthew, that your friend Mara would be very disappointed if you didn't help us.'

The sick feeling came rushing back and Matthew stared at the man and thought: So they really have got her! 'Where is Mara? What's happening to her? Please tell me.'

'One of us will be in the lane you call Three Lanes Corner each day at half past four,' said the man, ignoring the question. 'We'll wait there for a quarter of an hour so you can bring us anything you find. Do you understand that? Can you tell the time?'

'Yes, of course.' The dreadful thing was that half of Matthew wanted very much to do this, to make everything safe, to have Mara back home and prove to the men that his father was not a traitor. To go to that marvellous school where people drew and painted all day, and learned how to do it properly. But he did not trust the men, and so he said, 'I can't do it. I'm very sorry indeed.'

CHAPTER NINE

———❖———

'Your friend Mara would be very disappointed if you didn't help us.' The words kept repeating themselves in Matthew's head and the more he thought about it, the more he wanted to do what the men had asked: to search the study and find something that would prove his father's innocence. If he could do that everyone would be safe and Mara would come home.

He waited until his father went into the nearby town – he had suggested Matthew go with him, but Matthew, hating himself, said he had horrid homework. By three o'clock the house was quiet, but at least it was its own ordinary quiet, not the frozen frightened stillness that meant the men were around. Wilma was snoozing in the kitchen at this hour, and his father was not likely to be home until at least five.

Trying not to shake with fear, Matthew walked across the hall, not tiptoeing or creeping which would look suspicious if Wilma woke up and came out, but walking naturally and ordinarily. The study was locked as it usually was, but a key was kept inside the big ginger jar on the hall table. Matthew took the lid off, and reached inside for the key. So far so good. Hardly daring to breathe he slid the key into the lock, turned it, and went inside, shutting the door after him.

The familiar scents of old leather from the bindings of the books on the shelves closed round him. The desk stood near the window so Matthew's father could look at the garden when he was working. On one side of the desk was a photograph of Matthew's mother in a silver frame. Matthew could not remember her, but he liked the photo. He liked the dark hair, which was slightly untidy, a bit like smoke, and he liked the way she looked as if she was about to laugh at whoever was taking the photo. Her name had been Elisabeth, and looking at the photograph, the enormity of what he was doing almost overpowered Matthew, but he remembered about proving his father's innocence and about saving Mara.

The desk's surface was covered with sheaves of typed manuscript and notebooks filled with notes for plots and ideas and characters, all in his father's squiggly writing. The men had talked about articles and diaries, although Matthew did not think his father kept a diary, except for the kitchen calendar, on which they wrote down dates that had to be remembered. He began to search, opening desk drawers, trying not to catch the eyes of the photograph.

His father kept typed copies of the books he wrote: smudgy carbon sheets which he stored inside large envelopes or cardboard folders, burning them when the book was published, but Matthew did not know if he kept copies of his newspaper articles. He did not know if there would be lists of train times or addresses, although presumably his father would stay somewhere when he went away. Matthew had never thought much about that. He knew there were places called hotels where people could book a room with a bed. It was said to cost a great deal of money, though.

The clock on the mantel ticked away a whole thirty minutes while he searched, but although he looked in all the drawers and cupboards, and crawled behind the desk, there did not seem to be any articles or any details about the journeys. There were some letters, but they were mostly to his father's bank arranging for money to be put into a savings account or asking for a quarterly statement. Matthew was not very sure about the value of money; he wondered if the amounts were large and if his father was well off. Not many people were well off these days, everyone said that. It was something to do with communism.

There was one small cupboard by the side of the window, half built into the wall, that he had not tried. Matthew eyed it doubtfully, but it was important to look everywhere, so he climbed carefully onto a chair and reached up. The cupboard was locked. Matthew looked worriedly at the clock because it could not be long before his father got home. Where would the cupboard key be?

He found it taped to the back of his mother's photograph, under a square of thick brown paper. It was only lightly stuck down – it would easily re-stick. With trembling fingers he unlocked the door and it swung open with a little creaking sigh that seemed to say, *secrets . . .*

There was not much inside: a cheque book and a small box of cash and in one corner was a large envelope, and when Matthew opened it he found several sheets covered in his father's writing. His heart racing, he drew them out still standing on the chair, with his mother's eyes on him.

His father's writing was not very clear, but he managed to make out most of it. At the top of the page, in block capitals, it said, PRISONS WITHOUT NAMES: PRISONERS WITHOUT IDENTITIES. This did not make very much sense, but Matthew began to read.

Despite all the protestations to the contrary it is a fact that innocent people are still being torn from their homes and carried off to places that are no better than medieval gaols, but that are as cut off from the world as an inland Devil's Island. Most of these people are guilty of nothing more than following their own religions and their own beliefs – in some cases it is merely the accident of birth that damns them. Their lives were ordinary, unthreatening, unremarkable – everyman's life and everywoman's. But for these people, one night came the growl of wheels across the streets, the midnight knock on the door, and they vanished as abruptly and completely as if by sorcery. Their identities and histories vanished too, but there is no enchantment about that. It's a bureaucratic vanishment, a systematic process of erasing their identities from the world.

The regime inside those prison houses is brutal; many of the inmates are subjected to torture of a cruel and subtle kind: beatings, forced labour for impossibly long hours, their sustenance so meagre it is extraordinary they can remain alive. Not all do remain alive, of course, but those that do become wraiths, living ghosts in a world that will soon have no memory of them.

Or will it? 'There is no such thing as ultimate forgetting: traces once impressed upon the memory are indestructible.' Those are the words of an Englishman – his dreams were sometimes the flickering hag-ridden dreams of opium, but that does not matter so very much because the sentiment is true and sound. The iron grip that is closing so relentlessly round this country will not be able to erase those forgotten ones entirely.

Under a more humane regime, it might be possible to obtain the release of these lost ones and arrange for their return to the world, but there is a massive obstacle to that: a man who already holds too much power and who is poised to sweep his way to even more power. He seems unstoppable. But if these prisoners are not to become lost for ever – if other innocent citizens are to be safe from midnight

91

knocks on their doors by members of Ceauşescu's infamous Politburo – then a way to stop him *must* be found. Even if it means his death.

The present

Theo sat back, staring at the computer screen, his mind whirling. Nicolae Ceauşescu. Everything was falling into place like the pieces of a child's kaleidoscope. The actual driving force behind the writing of his book was still a mystery but Matthew's setting had finally become real. The place Theo was writing about was a dark, dramatic country, a ravaged beautiful land, resonating with violent history that stretched back a thousand years and as close as 1989.

Romania. Sometimes written Roumania or Rumania. Its very name was akin to the word romance. Bordered by the old principalities of Wallachia and Transylvania, the vaguely sinister Carpathian mountains as its spine and dozens of wild legends and rhapsodic fairytales within its soul. A country that for a large part of the twentieth century had virtually been a police state, ruled by a draconian authority. Whose people had endured crippling poverty, deprivation, cruelty, repression and the overweening ambition of two people who ruled with the iron hand of dictators: Nicolae and Elena Ceauşescu.

Theo had been eleven in 1989, the year of the Romanian revolution. He supposed that for most children there was probably a single event that caused them to register for the first time the existence of the world's stage: a presidential assassination, the declaration of a war, sudden menacing hostilities between major powers, an earthquake or famine. For Theo this childhood event had been the execution of Nicolae Ceauşescu and his wife on Christmas Day. The accounts and video footage of the courtroom and of how the Ceauşescus had been tied up before being led out to be shot, had made a deep impression on him. 'Did they have to treat them like that?' he asked his mother, after the television news report. 'Shot in that courtyard? They're old – the man said seventy-five.'

'Oh yes, they had to kill them,' Petra said, her eyes on the screen. 'They were cruel and harsh, those two, and they destroyed a great many lives.' She stared at the television for a few moments, and then, in a voice Theo had never heard her use before, she said, 'Switch it off, Theo, I can't bear seeing this. Or put on something livelier.'

He had done so, realizing the reports of the bleak gaols and the political prisoners locked inside them had upset her. This was unusual; Petra normally allowed life to flow past her. Nancy said Petra was light-minded, but Theo knew it was just that his mother did not allow her emotions to appear on the surface. But that day she had done so and his memory of it was vivid.

It was almost six p.m. and he suddenly realized he was ravenously hungry. He remembered disinterring some chicken from the freezer that morning, but when he tried to remember if he had had lunch he could not. It occurred to him he had been subsisting on soup and the occasional sandwich since he arrived at Fenn House a week ago, and this might be contributing to his current peculiar mental condition, if not actually causing it.

The chicken had thawed and he put it into a casserole dish along with stock made from a cube and a couple of diced potatoes. There were mushrooms in the fridge which he had bought on the way here. They would be a week old but they looked all right so Theo added them to the dish, then put the whole thing in the oven. He went back to re-read the day's work, polishing where it was necessary, until he reached the close of the chapter where Matthew had found the article referring to Ceauşescu.

By this time he had decided that if the book ever got finished, anyone reading it would probably say, 'Oh dear, poor Theo Kendal, this is the thing he wrote when he was a bit dotty. Sad, isn't it? He was such a promising writer until then.'

This was all so depressing that Theo poured himself a glass of wine which he drank while eating some of the chicken casserole which had been bubbling invitingly in the oven. He left the dish on the kitchen table to cool, pleased to think the rest of it would re-heat for tomorrow's supper. Then he returned to his story, thankful that at least he finally knew where he was writing about. What he did not know was why he was plugging into this particular section of recent history.

Romania, early 1970s

As Matthew finished reading the article his father had written, sick horror swept over him. There were several words on the page he did not know and there were a few he thought he might not have read right because of the squiggly writing. But even allowing for a few mistakes, the images his father's words conjured up were terrible ones: poor helpless prisoners shut away in dark gaols, in cold stone cells with barred windows, no one knowing they were there – only small traces of them remaining in people's memories. The forgotten ones.

And I know about them, he thought suddenly, and the untidy familiar study blurred. I know about those stone cells – I know there are women there as well as men, and I know some of them are quite young. They're all miserable and hungry, but some of them are angry and the angry ones force the others to keep alive and keep trying to escape. How do I know that?

He managed to push these pictures away and, locking the cupboard, he returned the key to its hiding place. It's all right, he said to his mother's photograph as he climbed down from the chair. I know what I've got to do. I know no one must see this paper because it tells about things that aren't supposed to happen – things the cold-eyed men want to keep secret. But somehow my father's found out the secrets and written about them, so they want to stop him.

He took matches from his father's drawer – his father occasionally smoked a pipe which Wilma said stank the house out, but which Matthew quite liked. He was not supposed to use matches, but he would only need one and he would return the box afterwards.

He had the feeling that eyes watched him as he went along the garden path, the dreadful piece of paper folded in his pocket. The sheet of paper caught fire at once and Matthew scattered the crispy black shreds over the garden. He returned the matches to the study, careful to put them in the exact same place he had found them.

He had saved his father, but there was still Mara. Matthew tried to think she would soon come home and everything would be all right, but the days went by and she did not. In the end, he knew he would have to tell his father everything. This made him feel instantly better, because his father would know what to do.

His father listened carefully, not saying anything until Matthew had finished, but seeming to listen not just with his ears but with his eyes and his mind as well. He always did this; it was one of the really good things about him.

Matthew explained how the men had wanted to know where his father went two or three times a year, and how they had wanted papers or diaries or writings that might tell them his father was a traitor. He stumbled a bit over this word because it was a shameful thing to be saying, but his father made an impatient gesture as if to say, Never mind about that, and Matthew went on. He had thought he would say how he had found the writing his father had done about the prison houses and the people whose names were lost, but he could not. He told him everything else though, and when he came to the end he felt weak and a bit trembly but better, like being sick which was horrid while it was happening but which made you feel better afterwards.

'And so,' he said, 'it's my fault she's been taken away, and we must find her and bring her home.' He waited confidently for his father to say they would do so at once, even that he knew people who would help. He'll make everything all right, thought Matthew confidently.

But his father did not make everything all right. His face took on the white strained look he always had when the men came to the house and when he came back from his mystery absences.

'Matthew, if I could help Mara, I would. But I can't. And you must promise me very solemnly that you won't try to find out what's happened to her. Not ever.'

'I can't promise that,' said Matthew. 'We must rescue her. You can do it, can't you? You can do anything.'

'I can't do this. If I so much as try, something far worse will happen.'

'What? What will happen? Nothing could be worse than this,' cried Matthew desperately. 'Nothing . . .'

'Oh Matthew, yes it could,' said his father, his eyes like dark pits. 'It really could.'

For the first time ever, Matthew saw that his father was frightened.

Mara was trying not to show how very frightened she was.

She had always known deep down that one day the men would come and she thought her grandmother had known it as well, but she always imagined it happening in the middle of the night. The midnight knock, people called it, telling how you were jerked out of sleep, too befuddled to put up any kind of resistance or think how to outwit the men.

But when they finally came to Three Lanes Cottage it was the middle of the evening. Mara and her brother had been playing a game by the fire. She liked this hour before bedtime with him; she liked watching his small absorbed face and seeing how his eyes lit up when he scored a point in the game.

The knock on the door made Mara jump, spilling the counters on the board. She looked across at her grandmother and saw her face had a dreadful pinched look. Then she saw the dimmed headlights of the jeep shining through the curtains and heard the thick growl of its engine. Her heart began to beat fast as if she had been running very hard and she remembered they had planned she would snatch up her brother and run to hide him in the shed outside. But there was only the one door leading outside and the men were already there, and there was no time to hide.

Or was there? Her grandmother was pointing to the latched door that led to the stairs and Mara nodded. She grabbed her brother's hand – he did not entirely understand what was happening but he sensed the fear – and half carried, half pulled him up the narrow stairs to the two tiny bedrooms. In the one Mara shared with her grandmother was a flap opening into the loft, and by standing on the bed on the tips of her toes, she could just reach it. She pushed it back, and lifted her brother up, scrambling after him, then closing the flap, laying a finger on her lips to indicate they must be quiet.

They crouched in the dark, cramped space under the roof and waited. The men were inside the cottage. Their voices came up through the floor, rapping out orders, telling Mara's grandmother to stay where she was and not interfere. Doors were opened and closed loudly. Mara's heart was pounding so furiously she was afraid they might hear it all the way downstairs.

She put her arms round her brother to make him feel safe. He was shivering with fear and smelt of soap and clean hair. He was the most precious thing in her whole life. If she lost him tonight, these clean-hair, clean-skin scents would be part of the memories she would have of him. She was very frightened indeed, but there was a good chance the men would not see the little hatch in the bedroom ceiling.

But they did see it because they knew what to look for; they knew all about hiding places – cupboards and lofts into which people crammed themselves to avoid being taken away. They pushed the hatch open, crashing it back so that dust clouds rose up and the old timbers groaned. A man's head came up into the loft and Mara pressed back into the dark corner, hoping he would not see them. But even in the dim light she saw him smile. He reached out, and his hands closed round her wrists, and although she struggled, he held her firmly. As he pulled her down through the open flap she risked a quick look back and saw her brother still crammed in the corner, thrusting knuckled fists into his eyes which was what he always did to stop himself crying. Mara wanted to call out not to be afraid and to say she would be back very soon, but it was just possible the man had not seen the small huddled figure so she did not.

As they carried her out to the waiting jeep, she managed to look across at her grandmother who was standing by the fireplace, one hand clutching the brick mantel, the other pressed over her heart. Would she be all right? There was no time even to call out that she would come back very soon, because they were already through the door and outside. A thin cold rain was falling. In the jeep's headlights it looked like little shards of broken glass pelting down from the skies; there was a hot oily smell from the growling engine. Mara struggled again, this time managing to kick the man who was carrying her. He swore and said she was a vixen and they knew how to deal with creatures like that inside the Black House.

It was not until he said this that Mara stopped telling herself she would be returning to the cottage soon, and knew there was no point in struggling any longer.

CHAPTER TEN

———————◆◆◆———————

Romania, early 1970s

The lane winding up to the Black House was narrow and lonely. A spiteful little wind blew through the trees, like somebody sobbing somewhere in the darkness. The trees partly screened the house, but the lane twisted and turned sharply so that little bits of it kept coming into view and then vanishing. Each time this happened the house was a bit nearer, until the jeep went round the last curve of the track and they came out into a clearing and there it was, rearing up in front of them.

It was built out of harsh black stone, and all the walls seemed to be leaning in the wrong direction so it looked twisted. It was surrounded by blackness – a thick oozing darkness like black goblin juice bleeding into the sky, shutting out all the light for ever. Old trees grew right up to it, and some of the upper branches leaned down to the windows like bony fingers trying to get inside. There were bars at some of the windows, and shutters closed over others as if it might be empty, but when the men pulled Mara from the jeep, she saw a thin curl of smoke coming from one of the chimneys.

At the centre of the building was a thick iron-studded door, and when one man pulled on a bell rope it made a dry rusty scraping inside the house like bones rattling together. There was the sound of footsteps, somebody fumbled with a bolt or a lock, and a woman wearing a grey dress opened the door. Her face was pale as if she did not go into the fresh air very often, and she was thin and sharp-featured. She took Mara into the bad-smelling dimness of the house, closing the door with a heavy clanging sound and turning the key in the lock. Mara gave a sobbing gasp and tried to pull her hand free, but the woman held her too tightly. In a sharp angry voice that made Mara think of tiny hard pebbles, she said, 'None of that, now.'

'Please – why am I here?' said Mara, desperately. She saw the woman look down at her in surprise as if she was not used to being questioned, and this brought some of the courage back. 'I won't try to run away, but tell me why I've been brought here.' Greatly daring, she said, 'Who are you?'

At first she thought the woman was not going to answer, but then she said, 'My name is Zoia – no need for any other name. I look after everything inside the Black House. As to why you're here – see now, you're eight, aren't you?'

'Nearly nine.' Mara thought this sounded a lot older than eight.

'Then that's not too young for you to understand what goes on in the world. You're what they call a pawn.'

Pawns were something in a game that clever people played for hours and hours at a time, taking it very seriously. Mara did not really understand what the woman meant, but she was not going to let her know that, so she said, 'Why am I a pawn?'

'There are important people who need to know certain things,' said Zoia. 'Things your very particular friend knows.' She grinned nastily as she said this, as if the word friend meant something different to her.

'Friend?' But Mara had already guessed who Zoia meant.

'Your friend Matthew. Those important people want to find out the secrets from him. The Party doesn't allow secrets, so they tried bargaining with him – you know what a bargain is, do you?'

'Of course I do.'

'The bargain was that if Matthew told them all the secrets, you would be allowed to go back to your home. Do you understand that?'

'Yes. Matthew will tell them whatever they want,' said Mara, confidently. 'As soon as he knows it's to rescue me, he'll tell them. Only I'm not sure if he knows any secrets,' she said, suddenly doubtful.

'It's not Matthew who has the secrets, you silly little girl, it's his father,' said Zoia. 'It's Andrei. He's the one they need to know about.'

'Why?' But even as Mara spoke she was remembering the whispers about Matthew's father, and she remembered all the things her grandmother had said.

'Andrei Valk is what we call "an enemy of the people",' said Zoia. 'That's a very wicked thing to be. You're not too young to start learning that, either.' She tightened her grip on Mara's hand and took her along a corridor and up a long flight of stairs. 'You're to be kept here,' she said. 'If your friend talks, you'll go home. If not, you'll stay.'

They went up another flight of stairs. The walls were dingy, and there were wall lamps every few metres. Mara thought they were lamps that burned oil: her grandmother told how there had been oil lamps in the house where she had lived as a girl, but they were a terrible nuisance and, if you did not clean them properly, they began to smell. The oil lamps in the Black House smelled as if they had not been cleaned for a hundred years: it was a fatty, greasy smell like rancid butter. A few of them were lit and burning with a thick smeary yellow light, and several dripped with hot bad-smelling oil which ran down the walls. In the narrow passage they looked like yellow lidless eyes peering down to watch everything that happened, with tears oozing out.

'In here,' said Zoia and, opening a door at the end of the corridor, she thrust Mara inside.

Beyond the door was a big room – bigger than any room Mara had ever seen. There was grimy plasterwork near the ceiling with cobwebs hanging from the corners, and a smeary bluish light came in from two narrow windows set high up near the ceiling. Six or seven iron beds stood along the wall but no one was sleeping in any of them – Mara could not decide if this was a good thing or not. At the far end was a huge elaborate fireplace with a squat black stove where the fire would normally be, and a wide grille at the front like a grinning mouth, big enough for a person to be fed into.

'Into bed.'

'But it isn't my bedtime.' Mara had no idea where she had found the courage to say this, but the small show of defiance made her feel brave for a moment.

'Times don't matter in here,' said Zoia. 'You'll be less trouble if you're in bed. You'll be fed when it's tomorrow morning. The lavatory's along the passage, so no dirty wet bed, mind. There's a punishment for wet beds in this place. There're punishments in this place for a lot of things.' She did not say this as if she enjoyed telling about punishments or as if she was threatening Mara. She simply said it, then went out closing the door behind her.

Until now Mara had managed not to cry, but alone in this terrible room tears sprang uncontrollably to her eyes and she huddled against the pillow, sobbing miserably. But then she remembered about being brave and getting back to her brother, so she wiped her eyes on her sleeve, took off her shoes, and got under the covers. The bed was uncomfortable with scratchy stale-smelling sheets, but the sooner she went to sleep, the sooner morning would come and they would let her go home. Matthew had probably told them the secrets already; Mara thought this ought to make her feel better.

But she did not feel better at all. She felt frightened and lost. The wind breathed gustily in the room's massive stone chimney, and there were little rustlings and tappings as if something was trying to get in. The faraway ceiling had fungus growing on it, like the mushrooms Mara and her brother sometimes gathered in the autumn and toasted on the fire for supper, and her bed was under a really big bit of mushroomy growth. If she went to sleep it might break off and fall on her face and smother her.

I can't bear this, she thought suddenly. I can't lie here like this all night – I *won't* lie here like this. With the thought, anger came surging up, and she looked about her, trying to see if there was any way of getting out without anyone knowing. The door of this room was not locked; could she tiptoe through the darkness and find a door leading outside? Sister Teresa at school said if you were frightened you should take several deep breaths and ask God to help you, so Mara took several deep breaths and asked God to help her get out of the Black House. If she could get back to Three Lanes Cottage she would be safe. Even if the men came looking for her again, her grandmother would help her hide and this time it would be a proper hiding place where she would not be found. Or she would run away for miles and miles and no one would know where she had gone.

She had not undressed because she had not had anything to undress into, so she pushed back the blankets, slid her feet into her shoes, and tiptoed across the room to the door. If anyone caught her she would say she was going to the lavatory. Zoia had said it was along the passage so it would be a reasonable thing to be doing.

The door made a scraping sound, and Mara waited, but nothing stirred so she slipped out into the dark passage, closing the door behind her. All she had to do was find her way to the ground floor, and look for an unlocked door or even a window. Once she was outside she would run down the hillside as fast as her legs could carry her. But the Black House was so big and so full of puzzling corridors and shadowy echoing halls that Mara began to panic. As she went warily through the shadows, glancing back over her shoulder every few minutes, the oil lamps stared down at her, and the Black House sighed and creaked to itself. She crept down the stairs, trying not to listen to the whispery echoes, and was just thinking the main staircase with the panelled walls should be ahead when she became aware of a sound that made her skin prickle with terror. Footsteps. Someone was walking through the dark corridors of the Black House. Zoia?

Mara did not wait to hear if the footsteps were coming towards her; she fled into the darkness, not caring where she went, only intent on finding somewhere to hide. She was out of breath and her heart was pounding so hard she thought it might burst out of her chest. She could no longer hear the footsteps, but there was another sound now, which was not the wind moaning in the chimneys or the windows rattling. Mara's skin prickled and she forgot about escaping and hiding from the footsteps, because this was a thin crying. It made her think of her brother, because it was how he used to cry when he was very small and afraid of the dark. Was it children she was hearing? Very young children, frightened or in pain?

She was in a narrow, stone-floored passage, and the crying seemed to be coming from behind a door a little way ahead of her. It'll be locked, thought Mara, staring at the door. Even if it isn't, it won't lead outside, and I've got to find a door that leads outside. I mustn't think about anything else. She was starting to feel unreal, almost as if she might be asleep and inside a nightmare that had a fairystory mixed up in it.

She had not meant to open the door, but another sound came that changed her mind. The footsteps were coming back and now they were coming straight towards her. In panic, Mara reached for the handle of the door.

She tumbled instantly into a nightmare far worse than anything she had ever dreamed in her whole life. The thin sad crying had prepared her for the sight of children, but it had not prepared her for what was beyond the door.

A windowless chamber, very like the one she had been taken to earlier, but with a grey light filtering in from somewhere, showing up damp-looking walls. There was straw on the floor and several of the oil lamps hung from the walls. The room was divided into sections by iron grilles – frameworks made up of bars that did not reach all the way up to the ceiling, but created four or five enclosures, each one open-fronted but each one forming an unmistakable shape. Cages, thought Mara in disbelief. They're *cages* like you'd have for animals.

But these cages did not contain animals, they contained children. Each cage held two small figures and there was just enough room for them to sit up and lie down. Most of them were little more than babies, and she had a sudden vivid image of her brother at this age, and how he had crawled at top-speed across the floor of the cottage, chuckling as he went, delighted with his own ability. Mara and her grandmother had laughed with him, snatching things out of his way so he could not knock them over or cannon into furniture. But these children could not do that; they could not toddle or crawl, because there was no room. All they could do was sit or lie in the tiny space inside the bars. This was dreadful, it was *dreadful*.

Several were crying with thin wailing sounds, but they stopped when they saw her and turned their heads, curious at this small interruption. Bright intelligence shone from most of their faces and several of them held out their hands. Mara wanted to run to them and take their little hands in hers and comfort them, but she did not dare.

The pity of it all slammed into her throat like a fist, and tears stung her eyes because these mites were so tiny, so helpless, and most of them were so pretty under the uncombed hair and shapeless grey garments. A scalding anger burned up, and she clenched her fists and made a silent vow to the children. I can't help you

105

now, said Mara to them, not this very minute, I can't. But if I get away from here I'll tell people about you. I'll tell what I've seen and you'll be rescued – I *promise* you'll be rescued, even if it takes years and years.

She stepped back from the terrible room and closed the door. She was still trembling from seeing the room with the children, and had almost forgotten about escaping and about the footsteps. But to her horror, Zoia was standing in the narrow passageway. In a voice like a nail scratching across tin, she said, 'It's a pity you tried to run away, Mara. We don't let people run away from here. It's an even greater pity you snooped into that room because we don't like people knowing the Black House's secrets. Especially when we aren't told secrets in return.'

Mara managed to say, 'Matthew will tell you the secrets, I know he will.' She tried to speak bravely but her voice came out muffled and hiccupy.

'I hope he does. But until then, you'll have to learn a lesson,' said Zoia. 'A lesson that will show you what can happen to snooping children who see things they shouldn't, and who won't share their secrets.'

CHAPTER ELEVEN

———————◆◇◆———————

Zoia had heard people say the Black House was filled with ghosts, but she always denounced such remarks as superstitious nonsense. People who claimed the Black House was haunted were simply letting themselves be influenced by its slightly sinister appearance. Zoia would allow the sinisterness, but ghosts were tales for the credulous. She liked living in this shadowy old mansion with its tucked-away corners and twisty stairways and empty halls. It was one of the many things for which she was grateful to Annaleise.

Annaleise ... Even touching the name in her mind brought a deep satisfaction. It was Annaleise who had brought Zoia to the Black House, and Zoia would have coped with far worse than living in this decaying grandeur to please her. She coped with the children who came here and was firm with them because she knew it was what Annaleise wanted. Occasionally some of them had to be punished, and Zoia did so efficiently and with detachment. She had been punished herself as a child – her father had a heavy hand with his leather belt and the belt had a thick buckle that cut her skin when it hit her bare bottom. No sense in beating a child through its clothes, he used to say, lifting his daughters' skirts and taking down their cotton undergarments, his thick labourer's hands lingering over the smooth young skin of their thighs.

Zoia, who was beaten more often than her sisters, had wept at the pain and the humiliation of those beatings, and crept into a corner afterwards to hide, but looking back she could not see that any of it had done her any lasting harm. Punishing the children at the Black House would not do them any lasting harm either.

It was unfortunate that the inquisitive child, Mara, had found the babies' room. A punishment would have to be administered to her – something that would enable Zoia to show Annaleise how sensible, loyal and firm she, Zoia, was. She did not allow herself to think, even for a second, that this was the only means she had of impressing Annaleise nowadays, because such thoughts might have made her maudlin, and Annaleise would have no patience with that. She had no patience with sentiment or with any emotion. It had taken Zoia a long time to understand that and even longer to accept it.

Particularly since Annaleise had not always been so un-emotional.

It had been more than fifteen years ago when they met. Zoia had been seventeen, a student, shy and awkward in the bewildering university world, determined to conceal her background from everyone. She was ashamed of her family who worked on the land for a pittance and who all thought Zoia had ideas above her station. Her father had always said it was enough if you could read a little, write your name and add up your accounts. The idea of education was a fanciful thing for the rich, for the rulers of the country, not for the likes of them, he said. Her mother, reduced to a whispering subservience from years of fear, said it was best Zoia did what her father wanted. There was plenty for her to do: she could help with her brothers and sisters and bake and cook and do women's work. It was good enough for most girls, she said, pleadingly.

But it was not good enough for Zoia. One of her teachers at the tiny local school, seeing the bright intelligence of this pupil, gave her extra lessons in secret. Later, she helped Zoia get a university place, providing a tiny sum of money which would cover the journey and help her through the first weeks. Zoia took it eagerly, and one morning simply walked out of the crowded cottage without telling anyone where she was going, boarding a bus – several buses – to the exciting new world she was entering.

For the first year of her university studies she worked very hard indeed. She was too timid to make friends or become part of any of the student activities, although there were plenty of parties and clubs she might have attended or joined. There were political activities as well – it was the late 1950s, and although the communist regime was as firmly entrenched as ever, people were daring to speak out against it and protest groups had sprung up, often small groups working in cautious secrecy, many of them within the universities. There were a number of these anti-communist groups at Zoia's own university but she steered clear of them as much as possible, because, clearly, they trod a dangerous path. Some of these students were caught and branded enemies of the state, all were expelled and some were even arrested. Stories filtered back of forced labour camps and prisons where conditions were so appalling and the warders so brutal, prisoners sometimes committed suicide. These things were seldom spoken of in public, because the Securitate was everywhere, listening, spying, reporting to their masters.

Zoia remained on the fringes of it all, afraid of becoming too close to anyone in case they found out about her background: the illiterate mother, brothers and sisters, the father who beat his children and whose hands sometimes strayed between the thighs of his daughters. Once or twice she thought about letting her family know where she was, but she was too afraid that one of her brothers or sisters might come to find her. Best let the past be forgotten.

She watched, without envy, the senior students, glittering and assured demi-gods whose smallest word was received with respect and admiration. How did people only a few years older than Zoia herself come to be like that? Was it because they were cleverer than the rest? Because they were more attractive? Or because they came from families who had money and position? Occasionally she heard whispers that some of them supplemented their incomes by acting as informants – ferreting out people's secrets and selling them to the Securitate. Hearing that made her even more careful and watchful about what she said and who she talked to. And then one night, hurrying to her small lodgings on the edge of the town, she ran into, not a demi-god, but a demi-goddess. Literally ran into her, so that the armful of books Zoia was carrying slipped from her arms and tumbled into the gutter.

'I'm so sorry,' said the demi-goddess. Her voice was strangely unresonant, at odds with her graceful movements, the slender ankles and heavy black hair like a raven's wing. Zoia, kneeling on the pavement to scoop up the precious books that she had scraped together the money to buy and that were already mud-splattered, stared up at her.

'Let me make amends by buying you a glass of wine,' said the harsh-voiced, exquisite-featured creature. 'There's a wine bar just along here – I often go there. I expect you know it.'

Zoia did not say she had never dared venture into any of the bars or restaurants the other students frequented. She did not have time to wonder if she would be expected to buy wine on her own account, the goddess had already taken her arm and was propelling her along the street. They were suddenly inside the hot smoky bar and somehow a table in one corner was free, and they were facing each other over a carafe of wine.

'A bit rough,' said the goddess, grimacing slightly, 'but drink-able. Let me fill your glass.'

Perhaps if Zoia had been used to wine there might have been a different outcome. Perhaps if she had not been so nervous, she might not have fallen so easily or so completely under the spell of the beautiful harsh-voiced one.

'I'm Annaleise,' said the goddess as if, thought Zoia, she might not know the name of one of the most glittering people in the whole university. As she lifted her glass again the wine cast a reflection in her eyes giving them a red glow. Devil's eyes, thought Zoia, mesmerized. No, not devil's, angel's! She's clever and admired and everyone knows who she is and I'll have to pretend more than I've ever pretended in my life.

'You're an odd little thing, aren't you?' said the angel with the glowing red eyes. 'I've noticed you watching me quite often. Why do you do that?'

Zoia managed to stammer something about being interested in student groups.

'Political groups? Not those squalid little anti-communist people, surely?'

'Oh no,' said Zoia, who had not thought much about political beliefs, but flinched from being thought squalid.

'Then you're for the State,' said Annaleise, at once, 'and I'm always on the look-out for recruits.' She leaned closer. 'Why don't you join us?' she asked, and for a moment the harshness was smoothed out of her voice.

Zoia thought about saying she was too shy, but before she could speak, Annaleise said, 'Let me pour you some more wine and we'll talk about it.'

The taste of the wine was enjoyable, but far more enjoyable – far headier – was the knowledge that this goddess-creature was talking to Zoia as if they were equals. She talked with intensity about things Zoia had never dreamed existed: about how the world was going to change; how they were the people, the generation, the Party, who would change it; how there would be massive upheavals to bring about that change, but also how upheavals were sometimes necessary for the common good.

Zoia listened, entranced. But when Annaleise said she must

come to tomorrow's Party meeting, she drew back. In such an unknown situation she might betray herself; people might see through her. So she said she could not go – she had to study.

'Oh, study can wait. And I want you there,' said Annaleise, and this time the rasping voice slid down into something almost like a caress. 'Do come, Zoia,' said Annalise, and when she said her name, Zoia felt as if Annaleise had reached out to stroke her face.

Almost as if Annaleise had heard her say this, she reached out a hand across the table, and took Zoia's own hand in hers. Her skin was like velvet or a cat's fur, the nails polished and smooth. Zoia could hardly bear the comparison with her own rough-skinned hand. Annaleise did not seem even to notice. She turned Zoia's hand over between hers, and brushed the centre of the palm lightly with her fingertips. At once an extraordinary sensation shot through Zoia's body – a deep secret tingling, so that she gasped and her eyes flew to Annaleise's face. Annaleise was smiling, her eyes narrowed. 'All right?' she said, and Zoia heard herself whisper, 'Yes,' without knowing what was all right or what she had agreed to.

What she had apparently agreed to was seduction of a kind she had not previously realized existed. But as they walked along the streets together, Annaleise's arm came round Zoia's thin waist. When they passed into the shadow of an old church, she bent and kissed Zoia on the lips, forcing her mouth open so that Zoia tasted the wine on Annaleise's breath. She drew back, startled, but Annaleise only laughed and pulled Zoia very close against her so Zoia could feel the press of thighs and the swell of breasts through her clothes. Marvellous. Shameful. One ought not to feel like this, not about another female.

Later, in Annaleise's rooms near the university which were silkenly and expensively furnished and which overlooked a quad-rangle, she was lain on a bed and her clothes gently but firmly removed. Once she protested and tried to push away the questing hands, but Annaleise only laughed. 'What a nervous little virgin,' she said. 'Don't struggle against me. If you really don't like it I'll stop, but let me just do this – and now this … Oh, you're not struggling now, are you?'

By 'this', Annaleise meant the butterfly fingertip touches on Zoia's body – on her breasts which had become tip-tilted with passion, and then, shamefully and marvellously, between her thighs. Zoia was distantly aware of the chiming of the clock from the old church, but the outside world had ceased to exist for her; there was only this dimly lit room and the smooth porcelain skin of this goddess, and the mounting excitement that Annaleise was creating.

Then Annaleise drew back and stood up, reaching for her own clothes, and the excitement was cut off suddenly and painfully, like being prevented from drawing a deep breath or strangling a sneeze. Zoia half raised herself on one elbow and looked mutely at her goddess.

'An introduction,' said Annaleise, pulling on a silk robe the colour of the wine they had drunk earlier. 'A prelude. You're a very promising pupil, Zoia.' She turned away, opening the bedroom door. After a moment, Zoia got up from the bed and fumbled for her clothes.

Walking home, her body remembered with a throbbing urgency, the feel of Annaliese's hands. Lying in her own bed in the shabby lodging house, she went through the lonely ritual of self-satisfaction. It was not until she was finally falling into a troubled sleep that she remembered Annaleise had used the word prelude. Her heart lifted. Prelude meant just the start. It meant there was more ahead.

Zoia smiled in the darkness. She would go to the meeting as Annaleise had suggested, and they would be together again.

She did go to the meeting, and to many more after it. She met a number of people, mostly other students, but also lecturers. Some of the speakers who addressed the meetings believed in communism and believed in putting down people who rebelled against it. She lost some of her fear of saying the wrong thing, but she never volunteered any information about herself, other than to say, if asked, that she was reading history, and yes, it was an interesting course, thank you. She did not exactly make friends but she made acquaintances.

She had not previously known or thought much about politics or economics or world affairs. Her father had said it was not for the likes of them to know about these things and her mother would not have dared question his attitude. There was no money for newspapers, even if anyone could have read them. When Zoia was seven, her father caught her reading a children's storybook the kindly teacher had lent her, and beat her for wasting her time when she should have been helping to cook the supper. Afterwards, huddled miserably on her corner of the bed she shared with her sisters, she heard her brothers whispering that there was always a bulge in Father's trousers when he hit the girls.

The teacher who had helped Zoia get to university had possessed a small wireless to which the enthralled Zoia had listened once or twice, but when she left the village there was no money for such luxuries. She spent all her vacations doing whatever work she could get to provide money for term time, but even so there was barely enough money for food and lodgings.

But Annaleise and her friends had books and newspapers and radios, and Zoia was made free of them all. She tried to form her own opinions but always returned to the belief that Annaleise's views were the right ones. Annaleise said Romania's government had the well-being of the people at heart. The nationalization of large businesses and banks was sound and logical, she said, and collective farming – the sweeping away of individual ownership and the creation of one massive agricultural cooperative – was logical, as well. It meant the pooling of labour and income for the greater good of all. Those farmers who did not want to give up their land were simply clinging to the selfish old ways of capitalism, insisted

Annaleise, her eyes glowing with fervour. Admittedly the government had used force to make them yield up their land, and yes, it was true that large numbers of the farmers had ended up being arrested or deported.

'Made homeless?' asked Zoia doubtfully.

'Oh, they all have friends and families where they can go to live. You must understand, Zoia, this is the natural progression of Stalin's original five-year plan of the 1920s – it's revolution from above. It's not a goal that can be lost because ignorant and recalcitrant farmers are jealous of their few paltry acres.'

Because these were Annaleise's beliefs, Zoia knew they were right and they became her beliefs as well. She repeated Annaleise's phrases with as much reverence as if they were charms or incantations.

Annaleise. She was like a glittering thread running through Zoia's new life and Zoia sometimes felt she was living inside a dream. She had never met anyone like Annaleise and had never expected to experience even the smallest part of the emotions Annaleise aroused in her – mentally as well as physically. She had not even known such emotions existed. They certainly bore no relation to the grunting poundings which used to come from the tiny upper floor of the farm cottage, mostly on nights when her father had been helping to get the harvest in and the workers had been given ale afterwards.

Zoia and her brothers and sisters were grateful to escape his attention on those nights. Sometimes Father became angry and called Mother ugly names and blamed her if he was not able to do what he wanted to her. Cock-shriveller, he called her, belching his beery breath into the small cottage. It was embarrassing to have to hear all this, but it was worse on the nights when Father had not taken too much beer, and the poundings on the rickety bed were fast and fierce. Mother would gasp and say please stop, they could not afford another child, the birth would kill her and there was not enough food for them all as it was.

Father never stopped, though. He shouted that she was a bitch to expect him to do so, and it was against the law of the country to withdraw. A man should spend his seed in his wife, that was the law and the teaching of their religion, and anyway it was every man's right. Then there would be an urgency to the sounds, followed by a groaning cry and moments later would come the creak of the bedsprings as he moved off Mother. And in just under the year there would be another baby in the overcrowded cottage.

But none of this needed to be remembered now, years afterwards. It was all in the past, and all that mattered to Zoia these days was the goddess she had discovered: Annaleise.

After that first startling and bewildering night when Annaleise had poured wine into Zoia's glass – the night that had been so agonizingly incomplete – there had, as she had prayed, been other times. Evenings spent in the perfumed bedroom of Annaleise's beautiful apartment, afternoons spent on the riverbank, with dappled sunlight falling over their naked limbs, and the guilty, but wildly exciting knowledge that someone might come along and catch them. Occasionally and blissfully there were whole nights spent together. To wake up and see Annaleise's tumble of silken hair on the pillow next to her, then to feel Annaleise's knowing, skilful hands moving over her body, gave Zoia such a deep and complete joy she would not have cared if she died in that moment.

When Annaleise, three years older than Zoia, graduated and made plans to move on from the university town, Zoia was distraught. She pleaded with her to stay – or at least to take her with her wherever she went. She did not care where it was.

'Don't be ridiculous,' said Annaleise. 'You can't run out halfway through university. Think of the waste.'

'I don't care about the university. Let me come with you. Please let me.'

A smile curved Annaleise's lips and for the first time Zoia saw it not as a beautiful and loving smile, but as self-satisfied. 'You've become quite a little slave, haven't you?' she said thoughtfully. 'I wonder how much you would do for me, Zoia. I mean – really how much?'

'Anything,' said Zoia at once. 'Truly, I would do anything.'

'Yes,' said Annaleise. 'I believe you would.' Then, speaking very slowly as if selecting her words carefully, she said, 'There might be work you could do. It might sometimes appear to be quite menial, at least on the surface. Washing, serving food, cleaning. But really you would be working for the Party. For the government.'

'Then I wouldn't mind menial work.' Zoia would have scrubbed floors or cleaned out sewers if it meant staying near Annaleise. Hesitantly, because Annaleise did not like to be questioned too closely, she said, 'What would the real work consist of?'

'Gathering information,' said Annaleise. 'Doing so in secrecy, of course.'

'What kind of information?'

'About people mostly. About what they do and what they think. About their families and movements. It's probable the Securitate would give you names of people to watch specifically – people already under suspicion. The Securitate are keen, you know, to get more control over people – to know more of what goes on in their lives. It's vital to know who the agitators are.'

'Know thine enemy,' said Zoia, half to herself.

'Exactly. As an instance,' went on Annaleise, 'just purely as an example, that young student who has rooms near the old quadrangle – her name is Elisab—'

'I know who you mean.' Zoia cut in before Annaleise could finish saying the name because she was afraid there might be the caress in Annaleise's voice that once had been exclusively reserved for Zoia herself. She had seen Annaleise watching the elfin-faced Elisabeth for some weeks, and a bitter jealousy had scalded her soul because Elisabeth was so very lovely, so graceful and amusing, all the things Zoia was not. To cover her emotions, she said, 'She's reading political history.' But because she was truthful by nature, she added grudgingly, 'They say she's extremely clever.'

117

'A brilliant student by all accounts.'

And you like the brilliant ones, thought Zoia miserably. The brilliant, beautiful ones.

'My masters believe she's dangerous,' said Annaleise, and Zoia looked at her because she had not been expecting this. 'They think she's a conspirator – an enemy of the Party. Therefore an enemy of the people. We suspect – very strongly – that she's working to uncover secrets.'

'Are there secrets?' asked Zoia, and then, seeing Annaleise's sudden severe frown, added hastily, 'Within the Party, I mean?'

'All people in power have secrets, Zoia. All kinds of things have to be kept quiet and private. It isn't good for the masses to be told everything.'

The masses ... she peddles the maxim that everyone is equal, thought Zoia, but underneath she's as arrogant as any old-style aristocrat. That's what I love so much, I think. Aloud, she said, 'So the work I would really be doing would be finding out about people like Elisabeth?'

'Elisabeth would be a good starting point.'

Zoia did not speak, and Annaleise said, 'Zoia, when a country is undergoing change – when it's being re-shaped – it's sometimes necessary to do rather underhand things. Perhaps to read private papers or listen to private conversations. To tell lies. There is,' she said, in what Zoia thought was a careful voice, 'a particular profession that comes into its own at such times. There are people who regard it as rather despicable, but it is necessary.' She stopped and in the silence that fell between them, Zoia could hear the popping of the worn gas fire on the hearth of her small room. She could feel her heart beating.

'You want me to become a spy,' said Zoia at last. 'An informant for the Party. That's what you mean, isn't it?'

'Yes,' said Annaleise, 'that's exactly what I mean.'

CHAPTER TWELVE

The present

Theo hit the Save key and leaned back, turning his head from side to side to ease his aching neck and shoulder muscles.

He noticed he seemed to have a surname now: Zoia had referred to Matthew's father as Andrei Valk. Valk did not sound very Romanian, but that was the name it seemed to be.

It was half past three and he needed a break from Zoia and Annaleise, and their machinations. He glanced at the uncurtained window wondering whether to take himself for a walk. Shadows were already creeping across the garden and it would be completely dark in another hour. He switched off the laptop and went out.

He enjoyed his walk and he enjoyed the sharp winter scents that prickled his nose and made his eyes sting with cold. He went past the convent gates, glancing along the drive. What would the nuns be doing at this time of day? For a wild moment he considered ringing the bell and asking if Sister Catherine was free. Probably she would be busy with patients and, in any case, he had no real reason to see her. He went briskly on, through the grey, sepia lanes. The troubling ghosts of Annaleise and Zoia receded a little as he walked, although Matthew's ghost did not. Theo thought Matthew walked with him, and he smiled at this idea.

The cousins had walked along these lanes hundreds of times. In the autumn they went blackberrying, and in the summer there were raspberries and strawberries – there was a fruit farm on the other side of the village that grew the most delicious raspberries. Mostly it was Theo with Charmery and Lesley, but other members of the family came and went. Lesley's brothers were often there; when they were younger they ran back and forth along the lanes like unruly puppies. Once, when Charmery's and Lesley's parents had gone off somewhere for the day, the five of them had tried to make raspberry wine but something had gone wrong with the process and a container had exploded, splattering the kitchen wall. Lesley had been horrified and had wanted to rush out to buy paint so they could cover the marks up before anyone saw it, but Charmery only laughed and said no one would care and she was not getting covered in paint for anyone.

A thin icy rain was starting to fall, and Theo retraced his steps, turning up the collar of his coat and hunching his shoulders against the rain. As he went past the convent gates again, he smiled at the prospect of Wednesday's talk and of seeing Sister Catherine again.

Fenn House, when he got back to it, felt chilly, and he turned up the heating. The water was hot, though, and he thought he would have a bath to warm up. Last night's chicken casserole could be re-heated at the same time.

It was one of life's minor luxuries to lie in a hot bath, and the water out here was so soft it felt like silk. Theo let his mind drift. He wondered vaguely at what point he would phone his agent to explain that instead of a book with a flawed hero suffering from post-battle trauma, she would be getting children living in Ceauşescu's bleak Romania, and a predatory female whose appetites ran rapaciously to her own sex.

When he went back downstairs the casserole was ready, and he ate it watching the television news, smiling rather wryly at the staid ways he was falling into since coming to Fenn. Supper on a tray in front of the television – it was hardly the high life. But he knew the solitude and the extreme quietness of Melbray was responsible; it had a soporific effect and it was one of the reasons he had come to Fenn anyway.

The drone of the newsreader's voice on the television was soporific as well; by the time the weather forecast started Theo was almost falling asleep. Once he sat up sharply, thinking he had heard a sound outside, but he seemed to be mistaken and lay back in the chair. The weather forecast finished and he got up to take the plate back to the kitchen, but a sick dizziness engulfed him and he had to grab the back of the chair to stop himself falling. Eventually, he managed to reach the kitchen, but he felt so giddy he simply put the plate and used casserole dish in the sink and staggered back to the sitting room, half falling into the chair.

This was ridiculous. Perhaps he was coming down with flu. In the space of half an hour? he thought, disbelievingly. He felt as if he was being pulled down into a spinning black tunnel and although he fought it, the room wavered and blurred. Once he thought he heard Charmery's clock chime the hour, but then he remembered he had muffled its chime.

Little by little, threads of light started to trickle across the darkness, and Theo came slowly and fuzzily back to a semblance of consciousness. The room was still blurred as if it was under water and he felt as if his brain was wrapped in thick flannel, but his sense of hearing had returned – he could hear the television which he had left on. But there seemed to be other sounds, that were not from the television. He frowned, trying to make sense of what he was hearing. Then he did make sense of the sounds, and horror flooded over him.

Someone was in the house. Footsteps, soft and stealthy, crossed the hall, and through the mist he saw the sitting room door slowly open. Theo, still fighting to climb out of the spinning tunnel, tried to call out, but the thick flannel wrapping round his brain seemed to have wrapped his tongue as well. It's the prowler, he thought in panic. He's got in. Oh God, what do I do if he attacks me?

A dark-clad figure came through the door, paused for a moment as if looking round, then crossed the room and came to stand by the chair. Theo could not make out who it was, but he had a sense of the figure bending closer, as if inspecting him. He managed to move his head slightly and look up, because if only he could see clearly, and if only he could speak ... With the small movement the figure seemed to flinch and step back. This time Theo managed to lift his hand, and the figure moved out of his vision altogether. There was the sound of a door opening and closing. He's gone, thought Theo. Did he even exist? He stayed where he was, thankful to realize the blurriness was starting to dissolve – he could see the mantelpiece clock now. Incredibly, it was just after nine o'clock. Could he really have been out of it for a whole two hours? How? But he was starting to feel slightly better, and he managed to sit up and look about him. There was no one in the room, and everything was exactly as it should be. Did I dream that figure? he wondered.

He got shakily out of the chair and switched off the television. Silence descended, but it was not a very comfortable silence. Even though Theo was still not sure if the figure had been real, he knew he would have to search the house. He was furious to find his legs were still unsteady, but by dint of holding onto furniture, he managed to get to the downstairs cloakroom and sluice cold water on his face. This revived him sufficiently to make a wary search of the house. None of the rooms revealed anything sinister, but when he went into the dining room he was aware of something different and he frowned, trying to pin it down. Was a light on – or off – that had not been earlier? Was something in a different place?

Then he knew what it was. The laptop. He had switched it off before going out for his walk earlier and closed down the lid, but now it was open and running. Theo could see the slight glow of the screen saver – it was this light within the unlit room that had attracted his attention. The screen saver was called 'Starfield', a kind of travelling through space pattern: thousands of pinpoint stars whirling on a velvet-black background. He had always found it rather restful, but not now; he found it terrifying.

He made his way to the table and sat down, staring at the screen with its journey through the cosmos graphics. Could he be mistaken about having closed it down? He had been more or less unconscious for two hours, and the laptop, even if it had been on, should automatically have gone into its complete sleep mode; it was programmed to do that if it was not touched for an hour. But it was still in the half-power state, which meant someone had touched it in the last forty minutes or so. While he was unconscious? The memory of that hazily seen figure returned, and he felt a shiver of fear. Without touching the laptop, he got up to close the curtains against the darkness beyond the windows and switched on the lights to dissolve the watching shadows. Then he returned to the table. If he brought the computer out of its slumbering state what would he see on the screen? He hesitated, then reached for the keyboard.

The instant he touched a key the starfield fled and an ordinary Word document appeared. The menu bar showed it to be three pages long, and it was in the font and typesize Theo normally used. He read the first words and felt them stab into his eyes.

'Four months ago, I killed Charmery Kendal.'

Cold horror engulfed Theo and he sat motionless, staring at the words. He had absolutely no knowledge of how – or when – they had got there, but he realized with panic that there was quite a lot of text on the screen. His mind shied away from reading it. He went out to the kitchen to make a cup of tea, trying to convince himself that when he went back the words would have vanished. I dreamed them, he thought. I was still in a half daze. Maybe there was something wrong with the chicken. But he had eaten the chicken last night and been perfectly all right. Unless a rogue mushroom had got in? Amanita muscaria, fly agaric. He seized on this flimsy explanation eagerly. I've had a dose of LSD without realizing it. I'll bet that's quite possible.

But when he sat down at the table again, the document was still there.

'Four months ago, I killed Charmery Kendal.'

Theo had no idea how it had got there. Could it have been on the computer's hard drive all along, and some quirk of its workings – even some peculiar blip in Fenn's power supply – had flipped it out of its rightful place and opened it onto the screen. It was a wild idea, but he checked the list of files anyway. There was no record of it anywhere. He checked the stored emails next, in case it had been emailed to him some time, and was not surprised when this even wilder idea drew a blank.

It's just floating on the screen, he thought, appalled. It's been typed straight onto a blank page and it hasn't been saved – it's just been left here for me to see. He remembered again the shadowy figure, and a sinister image of himself semi-conscious in the sitting room while the faceless intruder sat at the computer typing, rose up. He considered deleting the whole thing without reading it but he knew he could not, and with the feeling of plunging neck-deep into black icy water – water which might hide all kinds of macabre things below the surface – he began to read.

I came to Fenn House in the middle of a long drowsy day – the kind of day when the air is scented with lilac for miles around and the only sound is the hum of bees, and the whole world seems to be slumbering. The kind of day when no one quite knows where anyone is. Certainly no one knew where I was that day, and I'm as sure as I can be that no eyes saw me arrive at the house. Throughout all the investigations into Charmery's death, no one has ever mentioned seeing me there; nor have I really been questioned, other than perfunctorily. A lot of people were questioned in that way, though: eliminating them from inquiries, the police called it. Creating a timetable. I was certainly never slotted into a timetable – I didn't expect to be.

Charmery was in the garden when I arrived, sprawling half naked on the lawn just below the French windows. The tiny bikini she wore would no doubt have some extravagant designer label and would have cost a ridiculous sum of money, and the little soft shoes that revealed her painted toenails would be expensive leather.

The stone statues with their pitted faces and lichen-crusted limbs looked down at her, and I remember thinking only stone figures would be unmoved by seeing her like this. I had never been able to look at her without feeling a surge of such wild longing it sometimes made me dizzy. It happened that day, as I went down the mossy steps, and it annoyed me because I did not want any distractions. So, to counteract it, I reminded myself that there used to be ugly names for women who lay around practically naked, waiting for people to call on them. It helped a bit to think like that.

There was a flush of colour on her cheeks because she had been drinking wine – the bottle was at her side, in a plastic sleeve to keep it cool. She looked – and this is no exaggeration – impossibly beautiful. In any other female the flush would have been an unbecoming alcohol floridity, but in Charmery, with her rioting hair and smooth skin, it gave her a slumberous incandescence and the painters of the Pre-Raphaelite era would have fought each other for the privilege of painting her like this. I would have fought them for her as well, if I thought it would do any good.

I have no idea whether she was pleased to see me, because she pasted on the false, bright smile that fooled most people nowadays but that could never fool me. She offered me a drink, of course, suggesting chilled lemonade as an alternative to the wine. It was such a hot day to be flogging round,

125

she said in her languid, slightly too-breathy, voice, pouring the lemonade, and apologizing for doing it so awkwardly. This stupid sprained wrist, she said, waving her left hand. *So* tedious and the bandage horridly uncomfortable in this weather. She talked about a tumble down the garden steps which had caused the sprain, making a story of it, saying how ridiculous she must have looked lying all anyhow on the ground, but clearly believing she had looked beautiful and helpless.

When I suggested walking down to the river she was agreeable. She was not drunk, but she was very relaxed and amenable – a state of mind and body in which she loved the world and everyone in it.

It took some time to embark on the walk, because the vain creature needed to don a sunhat and sunglasses to keep the glare from her eyes. She pulled a thin silk wrap over the bikini.

'I daresay you think I'm impossibly frivolous,' she said, with a sideways glance.

'Not at all.' Here was the boathouse. I waited for her to make some comment, but she only said, 'Goodness, this place is looking a bit battered, isn't it? I haven't been down here for ages. I suppose it ought to have a coat of paint some time. And the timbers need something doing to them, don't they? Creosoting or something – *I* don't know.'

'I'm afraid they might have gone a bit beyond creosoting,' I said, studying the low outline of the boathouse critically.

'Might they? Oh well, I don't know about these things.'

A pause. I let it stretch out, not wanting to spoil this part of the plan by being too eager, but thinking I would give it a count of ten and then, if she didn't say it, I would have to say it for her.

But she did say it. She said, 'While we're down here perhaps I ought to take a look inside, just to check. I'd hate it to collapse and float out into the Chet one night all by itself.'

'It would be a shame, wouldn't it?' My voice was vague, disinterested. I was neither of those things, of course, but I gave an Oscar-winning performance that day.

Surprisingly, there was a moment when she hesitated and this disconcerted me. I could not tell if it was because some half memory from her past waited for her in there, or if she was merely worried about the unsafe timbers. But she went inside and I followed her. The boathouse was dim and secretive and filled with waterlight, and if ever there was a perfect place for a murder ... The blood was pounding in my veins, and a little voice was hammering inside my mind, saying, 'Don't fumble it. Stick to the plan.'

I did not fumble it and I stuck rigidly to the plan. That's the secret of a good murder: a carefully calculated plan, and the ability to keep to it all along. I pointed out a sagging section of rotten plank on the landing stage – goodness knows there were enough of them. I had thought there might be. She leaned over, pushing the ostentatious sunglasses up into her hair, in order to see better.

The plan worked as smoothly as if it had been rehearsed a dozen times. The boathook was in its place – I didn't even have to look round for it. It was heavy but not unmanageable, and she barely registered the small unhurried movement when I picked it up. Then I raised it above my head and brought it hard down on her. The steel end hit her between the shoulder blades and the force of the blow sent her toppling off the landing stage into the water. She yelled and clawed at the edges of the planks, screaming for help, but she was already half submerged. Her hair was draggled with weeds and her flawless complexion was stained with river mud.

'Help me! For Christ's sake, get me out! Don't just stand there – I'm fucking drowning in this shit-hole—'

It would have been a good refinement to let the foul-mouthed bitch climb halfway out and then shove her back in, but I didn't risk it. I lifted the boathook again, this time pushing her completely under. The water isn't very deep at that point because the bank slopes, but it's deep enough to drown in if you're held down.

Charmery Kendal was held down very firmly indeed. Once the boathook slipped and knocked a large piece of the staging away, tearing into her shoulder. Blood, thick and viscous flooded out, staining the silk wrap and when she yelled in pain, I felt – I may as well admit it – a surge of triumph, shockingly close to sexual arousal.

She flailed and thrashed wildly, grabbing at the boathook, and there was a bad moment when her hand actually closed round it making it necessary to exert more force. But her lungs were filling up with water – disgusting green river water that would clog her whole cheating body – and her hands fell away. She stopped fighting. I didn't move, though, not yet: I wasn't risking her rearing up from the water again. But she didn't rear up. She lay under the surface, her hair streaming out round her head, her eyes open and staring. The water rippled across her face so it looked as if it smiled and moved. By then I knew she was dead, so I gave her a good hard shove so her body would float out into the main part of the river. I didn't much mind where it ended up; my idea was to delay it being found. The longer that was, the less easy to pinpoint the precise time of death.

Remembering all this warmed me for a long time afterwards. It was something to savour, to re-live during all the nights when sleep would not come and the nightmares crawled from their corners. The image of that selfish, vain, butterfly creature, drowned and smeared with river mud, brought vast satisfaction.

It was somehow like her to become wedged in the struts

of the landing stage and disrupt the final part of the plan. But the secret of a good plan is that it should be fluid, capable of being adapted. So I adapted and deceived, and I lied. I lied to myself quite a lot, as well. People do that. Especially murderers. I'm a murderer. It looks shocking written down like that, but it's what I am.

The press with their customary habit of coining phrases, dubbed the boathouse the murder place and talked about the Fenn House Drowning, and I daresay that's how it will go down in Melbray's history. They're probably already saying the boathouse is haunted, telling one another that murdered people always come back.

I always thought that belief was nonsense, but it's not. Charmery has come back – she's come back to me, and that's what I can't live with. That's why I'm writing this – typing it, if we're going to be accurate, and since I'll shortly be dead myself I suppose I had better be accurate.

I can live with my conscience – with the knowledge of what I did that afternoon – perfectly well. I have no particular contrition about it. What I can't live with is Charmery herself. She's haunting me, and that's a statement I never thought I'd make. But it's quite true. At first she was no more than a darting shadow or a scarcely heard footfall, but these last four nights I have seen her. She's no longer the beautiful creature stepped down from the Pre-Raphaelite painting. She's the thing they dragged out of the river four months ago – a pale, bloated corpse, the eyes eaten by the fish. *That's* what lies down with me in my bed every night and comes in to sit with me every evening. That's what I can't bear.

It's been progressive, this haunting. At first she was just a shadow, then she gradually became clearer. The clock in her room began to tick again – it doesn't sound much, but it was disturbingly eerie. Before much longer I think my nerves will crack completely and I shall be judged completely mad and carried off to some bleak asylum. For me that would be a living death.

Last night, for the first time, Charmery spoke to me. In a clear and recognizable voice. She said, 'Theo, why did you murder me?'

'Theo, why did you murder me?' The words keep echoing in my head. 'Theo, why did you murder me?' That's what she said, whispering with hateful spite through her nibbled-away lips. Then, this morning when she came to me; she wasn't alone. There was a child with her. And *that's* the thing I can't bear – the sight of the child, with its huge, knowing eyes watching me.

So I am going to kill myself. There's even a sort of symmetry to it – to die here in the place where it all began. I shall finish typing this, then I shall do it.

Hopefully it will be clean and quick. It will be very simple – no untraceable drugs or exotic potions. I shall blunt my senses by swallowing a triple dose of the diazepam prescribed for me in London. They were meant to help me sleep after Charmery's death, and I've got enough left although I'll make sure not to take too much so that I'm incapable of carrying out the next step. That next step will be to slash both my wrists with the sharpest of the kitchen knives. It will take some resolve but it won't be all that difficult. It's very easy to kill, I know that already.

I wonder if she will be here when I do it? I wonder if the child will be here, too?

But whoever is or is not here when I die, this document is my confession that I murdered my cousin, Charmery.

Theo remained, absolutely motionless, in front of the screen. If the opening words had burned into his eyes, the whole dreadful, damning text of the rest of the document had skewered deep into his brain. Where has this come from? This is a confession, and I didn't write it, I know I didn't. His eyes skimmed the screen again, and words and phrases danced jibingly before his eyes, like demons with pitchforks.

'Some half memory from her past waited for her . . .' The words dredged up the image of two people making explosive love in the middle of a long-ago afternoon, but more vivid was the statement about her hair being draggled with weeds and her flawless complexion stained with river mud, because this was the image Theo had had since she died. People thought drowning a beautiful way to die – the water would just take you, they said poetically – but there was nothing poetic or beautiful about drowning in the foetid waters of the Chet, or being half blinded by the rank slimy weeds . . . For a moment Theo thought the sick dizziness was returning and he sat very still, willing it to go away. After a few moments it passed and he was able to look back at the screen.

'A triple dose of the diazepam prescribed for me in London . . .' Who else knew about those sedatives, suggested by Theo's doctor four months earlier? He could not remember ever mentioning them to anyone.

The dreadful possibility that he might have written this himself trickled across his mind. Was that remotely conceivable? Maybe he was going mad – maybe that was the explanation to all the strange happenings in Fenn House, or maybe he had been harbouring some deeply buried guilt about sleeping with his half-sister. He could have committed the murder exactly as it was described – he could have come to Fenn without anyone knowing, and killed her in the boathouse. But why would he have done that? He had tried to hate Charmery and at times he thought he had succeeded, but he had never really stopped loving her.

And what about that mention of a child? He scrolled back up to re-read it. 'This morning . . . she wasn't alone. There was a child with her.' *A child*.

If Theo had been suffering from fifty kinds of madness, he could never have written that – there had never been any hint that Charmery had ever had a child. But could she have become pregnant and gone into a discreet clinic for an abortion? The implication that it had been Theo's was unmistakable, though. For a moment an image was vividly before him of the child he and Charmery might have had: tip-tilted eyes filled with light like Charmery's, and hair like beaten bronze in sunlight. Beautiful, thought Theo. Any child of Charmery's would have been beautiful and filled with her particular charm. But another part of his mind snapped across this and he thought, but nature plays cruel tricks when it comes to inbreeding. More likely it would have been misshapen in some pitiful way, or missing a chromosome and prey to God knows what awful mental condition.

But who would have known enough about Charmery's and Theo's past to type that? No one except Helen, and Helen was dead.

His hand hovered over the Delete key but he knew he would not delete this. No matter how damning it might be, he would save it in an obscure corner of the hard-disc drive. He could not simply wipe it out. Not yet. Because of the child, he said to himself, because of the little lost thing, the might-have-been. He created a miscellaneous file, saved the document into it, then with an abrupt gesture shut down the computer. After this he hunted out the briefcase he had brought with him, which contained the documents relating to Charmery's death. As sole beneficiary he had been regarded as her next of kin and had been sent various papers, some of which had to be signed, others which the solicitor appeared to think he should have for the record. He had not read them all in detail; he had simply glanced through the ones for signature, and returned them to the solicitor, hoping he had understood the complexities and his own obligations.

He shuffled the loose documents out of the folder and began to sort through them. There were letters from the solicitor and from Charmery's bank; there was the official registration of her death;

police and forensic reports. There was the post mortem report, in grisly detail. Theo had not been able to read this, but he forced himself to a scholarly detachment, and began to scan the printed pages.

The report stated that the deceased was a young woman in the mid-twenties, apparently in good health at the time of death. She had been sexually active. Fair enough, thought Theo. I haven't exactly lived the life of a monk myself. The primary cause of death was given as 'suffocation due to immersion of the mouth and nostrils in liquid'. It was concluded that the deceased was alive at the time of submersion – there were unpleasant details verifying this, describing froth and blood-tinged foam in the airways and also the presence of silt and weed and large quantities of water in the lungs and stomach. Theo managed to skim over most of this. However, said the report severely, the mechanism of death by drowning was neither simple nor uniform: there were a number of variables. Drowning as a method of murder was uncommon and required either physical disparity between the victim and the assailant, or a victim who was incapacitated by drink or drugs, or had been taken by surprise. The evidence pointed to this latter circumstance, stated the pathologist, and it could be concluded with reasonable confidence that the deceased had been forcibly held down in river water until asphyxiation occurred.

'She flailed and thrashed wildly, grabbing at the boathook, and there was a bad moment when her hand actually closed round it making it necessary to exert more force . . .'

Theo pushed the words away and went on reading. There was reference to an old appendectomy scar. Reading that, Theo was jerked back to Charmery's twelfth birthday, when she had complained of tummy-ache and everyone had thought she was simply suffering from too much trifle, until she doubled up with pain halfway through the party and was sick on Helen's new carpet. She had enjoyed herself afterwards though, languishing on a hospital bed surrounded by flowers and fruit, then convalescing at Fenn.

But it was the last sentence that leapt from the page and etched itself into his mind like acid. 'Within the last five to ten years deceased had given birth to a child.'

Given birth to a child. *Given birth.*

It can't be true, thought Theo, his mind spinning in disbelief. It's a mistake. I would have known about it – an abortion could have been done in secrecy, but an actual birth surely couldn't? And what happened to the child?

He put the report to one side, and went determinedly through the rest of the papers, wondering what he would do if he found a birth certificate for a child born nine months after that enchanted, tragic summer. But there was nothing to be found.

CHAPTER THIRTEEN

As Catherine helped prepare the day room for Mr Kendal's talk to St Luke's patients, she realized she was nervous. She examined this feeling and discovered it was because she wanted Theo Kendal to give a good account of himself. She could not bear it if he was hesitant or mumbly, or – even worse – if his talk was boring. She could not imagine him being boring under any circumstances, but people were constantly a surprise.

He arrived on time, which pleased her, ringing the big old-fashioned doorbell, and smiling when she opened it, saying he had not expected to see her.

'There's a rota for door-answering,' said Catherine, as he stepped inside. 'But I lay in wait because I thought you might like to see a familiar face. Convents can be a bit disconcerting if you aren't used to them.'

'It's certainly not terrain I've ever explored in any detail,' he said with the mixture of slight amusement and gravity Catherine remembered.

He was wearing an olive-green corduroy jacket over a cotton shirt with a knitted tie. Catherine thought this was what people nowadays called smart casual, but whatever it was called, it was exactly right for the occasion. He had paid the nuns and patients the compliment of not turning up in scruffy jeans and trainers, but had not gone over the top. His hair looked as if it needed cutting, but probably this was how he wore it anyway. It was soft and dark; it would feel like spun cotton if you touched it.

She and one of the other nuns had set out chairs in the big day room, leaving wide aisles for wheelchairs. Catherine had polished the desk that stood in the bay window. It was a nice old mahogany piece with an inset leather blotter, and she had set out on it a notebook and pen, and a carafe of water with a tumbler. The promised flipchart was at one side – they had brought it in from the library; Sister Miriam had agreed to the loan for a couple of hours – with two felt-tipped pens for writing. Mr Kendal said this was really excellent, absolutely ideal, and he hoped his talk would be as good as the arrangements.

'I'm sure it will,' said Catherine. 'I think there'll be about twenty people,' she added a bit doubtfully. 'I expect you're used to far larger audiences.'

'I promise you I'm not,' he said. 'On rainy nights in small towns, I'm lucky if twenty turn up. Not all writers are celebrities.' The smile showed again, lighting up his eyes.

'Dr Innes is coming,' said Catherine, 'and several of the other sisters. Oh, and Reverend Mother hopes you'll have a cup of tea in her study afterwards.'

'Yes, certainly.' He prowled round the desk a couple of times, like a cat inspecting new territory, tried the flipchart and nodded, then spread out his notes. Catherine watched him for a moment, then went out to help wheel in the patients. Most of them had wanted to come, pleased at the diversion in their ordered day.

In fact it looked like being a full house. The Bursar came, very alert, carrying a notebook and pen, and Dr Innes followed her. Catherine was pleased he had managed to spare the time because he was always so busy. Sister Miriam came in quietly, and took an unobtrusive seat near the back. Catherine wondered if Sister

Miriam had read any of Mr Kendal's books and if so what she had made of them. Sister Agnes bustled in at the last moment, slightly out of breath, apologizing for her tardy arrival, explaining she had had to finish supervising the washing-up and was sorry if she had brought with her any aroma of cooking. You could not, she said to the room in general, cook chicken casserole for thirty people without it permeating your garments.

Mr Kendal gave her his marvellous smile, and glanced at Catherine. She had the strong impression he was sharing a kindly joke with her, and she suddenly wanted to smile back. This would not be a very good idea, though, so she looked down at her feet. When she looked up again, he was glancing through his notes, and she thought she must have imagined that moment of mental intimacy.

If he was nervous at talking to a roomful of strangers, he did not show it. He seemed perfectly relaxed, and when he began Catherine relaxed as well, because although he was not an outstanding orator, his voice was nice and it carried comfortably to the whole room, and what he said was interesting. Catherine listened, her eyes fixed on him, as he explained how he had started writing sketches at university for Footlights. He talked about the journey a writer took during the creation of a book, and the closeness he developed with his characters, and also a little about research methods, recounting a couple of incidents which had happened during the gathering of material for one of his books. This was done wittily and caused considerable laughter. It's all right, thought Catherine, they like him. They're enjoying what he's telling them.

Towards the end, using the flipchart, Mr Kendal illustrated what he called the unrolling of a plot, making columns for the different plotlines for the various characters. It had not occurred to Catherine that books could be divided up like this, but Mr Kendal explained it very clearly. Then he asked the audience to call out suggestions for characters and backgrounds so they could develop a basic story. There were, he said, only five or six basic plots in the world, just as there were only five or six basic tunes in music.

This went a bit awkwardly at first, because most people in the room were diffident about being the first to speak. But then one of the men made a suggestion about a man injured in a road smash, and somebody else said perhaps the man was a target for a hit-man.

'Perhaps he was. Yes, that's very promising. All right, what had he done to make him somebody's target?' asked Mr Kendal, and after this the ideas rolled in thick and fast. The Bursar and Sister Agnes both contributed several suggestions, and although Catherine would have liked to take part, she thought she had better not.

'Terrific,' said Mr Kendal, scribbling delightedly on the flip-chart. His eyes were alight with enthusiasm and energy. 'You see what happens?' he said. 'One idea leads to another – and then another.' He stepped back, to survey the results of their handi-work. 'D'you know, I think we've given ourselves the basis for at least three books there.'

'Three?' said the Bursar.

'At least three, unless we could find a Dostoevsky or Charles Dickens to bring them together into one. But you see the basic principle?' And he went smoothly into a more general discussion, inviting questions from the audience, and dealing with them, Catherine thought, very well and very courteously.

Theo had been rather touched to find how carefully the sisters had prepared for him, and he was pleased Sister Catherine was there. As she took him across the big polished hall and up the stairs to Reverend Mother's study, he noticed again how smooth and clear her complexion was. It made him think of lightly polished ivory.

'Thank you for all the trouble you've gone to,' he said.

'It was no trouble. The study's along here.'

'Is this floor the nuns' living quarters?'

'Yes. Common room, TV room, a couple of small extra studies for private visits. The bedrooms are on the top floor – they're converted from the attics in the main. The chapel's along that corridor.'

'Do you have a – what would the term be? A house priest?'

'We share him with four other villages,' said Catherine. 'It means daily Mass is a moveable feast but it's surprising how easily you get used to that.'

'Is this the lion's den?' said Theo, as they stopped in front of a door.

'Much worse. Reverend Mother's study. But she won't eat you, especially since the Bursar will already have told her you didn't preach the doctrine of the Antichrist or advocate smoking cannabis in your talk.'

While Theo was thinking how to reply to this, she knocked on the door, then opened it and left him to it.

The room was half study, half office, with a large, extremely tidy desk, glass-fronted bookcases mostly containing religious works, and framed prints – again of religious subjects – on the walls. There were several modern filing cabinets and, unexpectedly, a computer and printer with scanner.

Theo found himself liking Reverend Mother, who was fairly elderly but had bright intelligent eyes, and he also liked the Bursar who came in a few moments later and was sturdy and forthright. They both thanked him for sparing time from his busy schedule to talk to their patients. The Bursar said she had enjoyed his talk and found it very instructive. She added that she had read his last book and found it perceptive and well constructed. 'You have a remarkable insight into people's emotions, Mr Kendal.'

'Thank you,' said Theo, not daring to ask which of his characters' emotions the Bursar had in mind.

'The Bursar writes a little on her own account,' said Reverend Mother.

'Dabbling,' said the Bursar gruffly.

'She wrote and edited our centenary booklet last year,' went on Reverend Mother serenely, 'and made a very good job of it.'

'Is it still available? I'd like to have one,' said Theo.

They looked pleased, and the Bursar promised to look one out. There was a box of them somewhere around.

'And,' pursued Reverend Mother, 'she has long planned to write a history of this area. Its folklore and legends and so on.'

'Only for local circulation, you understand.'

'I like folklore and legends,' said Theo. 'They spin a tapestry more or less by themselves, but they're the fabric of a country's heritage. Any country.'

'One day I'll get round to it,' said the Bursar. 'Although not if it means learning how to operate that machine.' She indicated the computer in the corner. 'None of us are very well-versed in the ways of modern technology. I typewrote the centenary material and just handed it over to the printers, smudgy erasures and all, I'm afraid. Sister Catherine attended a one-week course about computers last year, though.'

'So that we could send and receive emails,' explained Reverend Mother. 'People expect it nowadays.'

'And we don't want anyone thinking we're living in the Middle Ages, still using quill pens and parchment,' added the Bursar.

'Of course not,' said Theo, secretly entertained. 'But you must get round to your history. People like reading about the place where they live. Don't forget the centenary book for me as well, will you? And I'll expect an invitation to the launch party of your local history book when it's published.' He was pleased when they both smiled appreciatively at this.

It was as the Bursar ushered him back to the ground floor and across the hall that he saw, in a rather shadowy corner, a pair of framed sketches: one of St Luke's, the other a view of the Chet's tributary from one of the banks. They were quite small, each one roughly fifteen inches by ten, executed in what looked like charcoal and neatly framed in narrow surrounds. The convent was shown against one of the lowering skies so typical of this area, and behind it the fields looked bleak and unfriendly. But both sketches had a quality that was distinctive and Theo's attention was caught.

'Are you interested in art, Mr Kendal?' asked the Bursar, as he paused.

'Only in a general way.' He paused, then said, 'There's a sketch at Fenn House that I think might be done by the same hand as these.' Charmery's portrait, he thought, but he only said, 'I wonder if it's someone local.'

'I've no idea. I don't even know how long we've had these,' said the Bursar. 'This hall had to be completely cleared last month – we found woodworm in the panelling and everything got moved or tidied away or swapped round. I don't think anything is back in its original place yet. Never let anyone tell you the Church is a rich institution, Mr Kendal, because after paying that bill we're verging on bankruptcy, and— Yes, what is it?' She turned as a very young nun came into the hall.

'Sorry to interrupt, Bursar, but they're on the phone from Norwich about the fractured pelvis. He wasn't due here until Friday, but the ambulance service can only manage the journey tomorrow. Sister Catherine's with a patient and I can't find anyone else.'

'Wretched people. Are they holding on? I'll speak to them. Mr Kendal, would you . . .'

'I can find my way out,' said Theo at once. 'Take your phone call.'

'Would you mind that? The outer hall's just through there and the door won't be locked at this hour. You'll come to see us again?'

'I'd like to,' he said, meaning it. 'Thank you.'

He waited until she had gone, then looked at the pictures once more, seeing the similarities to Charmery's picture even more strongly. There were the same light pencil patterns – almost like the random scribbles of a child – indicating shadows. And there were corners of darkness that contained different and more intricate patterns, suggesting there might be something slightly sinister hiding within them. There was a faint suggestion of drowned faces just beneath the surface of the river and of sightless eyes staring upwards into the gunmetal sky. Charmery, dead under the boathouse, thought Theo, her body in the cloudy green water for three days before it was found. What had she thought in those last frantic moments before she died? Had she thought about the child – had she wanted to survive because the child was somewhere in the world? If so, where was it now?

It was very quiet in the hall. Theo glanced about him, and then reached up carefully and lifted the sketch of St Luke's from its hook, turning it over. The back was covered with the same brown paper as Charmery's portrait, and taped in place in the same way. But the back of Charmery's portrait had been completely blank and anonymous. This was not. Across the lower corner was a slanting signature. 'Matthew Valk'.

Theo stood in the dim hall for a very long time, staring down at the signature, aware of a feeling that something had reached out to clasp his hand.

When he finally forced himself to replace the sketch he felt as if he had severed a very fragile link, although he was not sure what the link was. He made sure the picture was hanging exactly as it had been, then crossed to the main doors. As he did so, somewhere behind him an inner door closed very softly. Theo looked back, but everywhere was wreathed in shadows and nothing moved. Or did it? Probably he had simply heard one of the nuns going about her lawful business. He was getting neurotic about being followed and watched, but after last night's scare and the bizarre confession on the computer, he thought this hardly surprising. He opened the main doors and went out into the dark afternoon.

It had started to rain again, but he scarcely noticed. His mind was filled with Matthew. Matthew existed – or had existed in the recent past. More than that, he had been in Melbray. He had not only sketched Charmery, he had sketched St Luke's and that view from the bank. How recently had he done that?

Theo went down the narrow road leading back to Fenn House, his feet making squelching sounds on the rain-sodden road. He and Lesley had always liked squelching through the rain; they had worn wellingtons and vied with one another to see who could make the most spectacular splashes. Charmery had had wellingtons as well, but they were patterned ones, bought specially from one of the big London stores. Lesley had drawn Charmery in the wellingtons, making a semi-cartoon of it. Charmery had at first been furious, saying Lesley had made her look ugly, but later she had laughed at the cartoon, and said she would keep it and when Lesley was a famous artist, she would sell it for a lot of money.

And years afterwards, she had sat in front of an artist called Matthew and looked at him with that warm and vulnerable intimacy.

CHAPTER FOURTEEN

———◆◆———

Catherine had had to fight with herself not to stand at a window and watch Mr Kendal walk away down the drive. Even so, as she went about her normal tasks, tending to the various patients for whom she was responsible, she watched him in her mind: he would walk with his shoulders slightly hunched against the cold, and the soft dark hair would be misted with the thin rain. When he got back to Fenn House he might towel it dry in front of the fire, in the room where he worked that smelt of memories. Later in the evening, he might cook himself some supper and eat it by the fire on a tray. He had seemed to be on his own when Catherine called, but he could have been joined by a female companion since. Catherine still did not know if he was married or in a relationship. But if someone was with him tonight, after they had eaten and per-haps shared a bottle of wine, he might talk to her about his work. And at some point during the evening they would find themselves lying on the thick soft hearthrug together. What would Theo Kendal be like in that situation? What was any man like in that situation?

I don't mean any of that! thought Catherine, appalled. None of those are serious thoughts! I chose this way of life ten years ago and it was the right choice and I knew exactly what I was doing. (At eighteen? said her mind, sneakily. Are you sure about that?) And, thought Catherine firmly, I'm entirely content and my faith is strong enough to deal with these insidious images.

She made her way determinedly to the sluice room, where there was always something to do on any given day. No one could clean out a sluice room and harbour impure thoughts at the same time, not even about Theo Kendal. But even amid bleach and disinfectant her mind stayed with Fenn House. It was raining quite hard now – she could hear it pattering against the windows – and it would be wonderful to be in the slightly shabby living room at Fenn, with the curtains drawn against the night and that bottle of wine and the hearthrug. Catherine frowned and dug her fingernails into her palms in the hope that the small jab of pain would dispel these thoughts. It was just as likely that Mr Kendal would be impatient and wanting to get on with his work which had been interrupted by this afternoon's talk. He would shrug off any solicitude and tell her not to make a fuss.

Exactly as his cousin, Charmery Kendal, had told Catherine, nine years earlier.

'Don't make a fuss,' Charmery had said on that early March afternoon when Catherine had called at Fenn House to see if any of the family would support a charity afternoon St Luke's was holding in its grounds.

'I have no idea which of the Kendals will be there,' Reverend Mother had told Catherine. 'They come and go, particularly during summer – sometimes in autumn as well and the odd Christmas. But I saw lights on last evening, so somebody's definitely in the house at the moment.' As Catherine hesitated, Reverend Mother said, bracingly, 'They're very nice people, and you don't have to be shy, Sister,' and added a little homily about shyness not being permissible when one was doing God's work. Humility, on the other hand, was a different pair of shoes, said Reverend Mother, and something they should all strive to achieve although not when they were having a charity afternoon with stalls and tombola and the nice old-fashioned pursuit of bowling for a pig.

'Oh, and on that subject,' she said, 'Sister Agnes wants it making clear to everyone that the pigs are in the form of chops and joints and sausages for the freezer. Don't forget to explain that, will you?'

Catherine had promised not to forget, but as she walked up to Fenn House, she was wondering if she would be able to explain about the pigs if she were confronted with the severe-looking lady who was sometimes seen in the village, usually admonishing shopkeepers for sending the wrong groceries to Fenn. But perhaps it would be the nice bumbly gentleman who was often here, or the plump domestic-looking lady Catherine thought was Helen Kendal. She had a rather vain, rather supercilious-looking daughter who was around Catherine's age. Catherine had encountered her once or twice in the lanes; she had given Catherine an offhand nod and very coolly looked her up and down as if to say, How *can* you go about looking such a frump? Catherine had had to remind herself very firmly about the marvellous thing she had in her life which was God and all His people, and how that was immeasurably better and would last far longer than looking like a Burne-Jones painting.

When she reached Fenn House, no one seemed to be around. Catherine rang the bell and then plied the knocker, but there was no response. It was rather an endearing house. It had bits stuck on here and there and unexpected jutting roofs that did not seem to quite line up with the rest, like a child's exuberant drawing. The back of it was visible from St Luke's. Catherine had sometimes looked across to it and wondered about the people who owned it and came here at intervals. How would the view of the convent look from here – Alice peering out of the looking glass, so to speak? She thought no one would mind if she walked round the side of the house to look across at the convent. There was a wrought-iron gate on one side; she unlatched it, and went along the path. She would take a brief, polite look, then she would go back. Perhaps Reverend Mother could write a note about the charity afternoon which could be delivered later.

There was St Luke's, visible through the trees, looking a bit severe and institution-like, except for the gardens which several of the nuns enjoyed tending, and which blazed with different colours throughout most of the year.

Fenn House had mossy paths leading away from the house, and a huge lawn where Catherine had seen some of the younger members of the family playing rounders and cricket. The supercilious girl was often there, and a dark young man was generally with her. They looked a bit alike; he might be her older brother. It would be nice to be part of a large family like that and have brothers and sisters and cousins, and spend holidays in a house like this. Catherine's own childhood had been a rather solitary one.

At the far end of the grounds the land sloped steeply down to the river and there was a boathouse, low and a bit gloomy-looking even on this bright afternoon. Catherine had not known about the boathouse which was not in the convent's sightline, and she studied it for a moment, imagining the family embarking on river picnics, with wicker hampers of food, the ladies in white linen frocks, feathery willows trailing into the water as they went along. It would not be like that at all, of course: the river smelt disgusting when it was high, the trailing willows would get into your hair, and people had not worn white linen to go boating since the 1930s. She was retracing her steps towards the iron gate when she heard a faint cry from the direction of the boathouse. It sounded like someone calling for help, but it might have been a bird screeching or the shout of someone from the lane. She waited to see if it came again, and it did a second then a third time, and it was unmistakably the word 'Help'. Had someone fallen and sprained an ankle, or even fallen into the river? She took a deep breath and went quickly down the path towards the boathouse. The cry came again, this time filled with a kind of angry pain, and Catherine called out, 'It's all right, I'm coming. Where are you?'

'Boathouse. Please help.'

A female voice, unrecognizable, but blurred with pain or fear. Please don't let it be the Burne-Jones girl, thought Catherine.

But it was. She was lying on the planks of the boathouse, hunched over, her face twisted with pain. Her extravagant hair was stringy with sweat and hung over her face as if she could not manage to push it back. Despite the cool March afternoon, she had on a thin cotton skirt which was pushed up almost to her waist and there was blood on her thighs, smearing the rug under her.

For a shameful moment Catherine wanted to run away and find someone who would take charge of this situation, but she managed to go forward and kneel down and take Miss Kendal's hand.

'You're hurt. Tell me how I can help.'

'I'm not hurt, I'm having a bloody baby!' she said, and as she doubled over again, gasping with pain, Catherine saw the bulge of the child under the thin cotton. After a moment, the girl said, 'I thought I'd be able to do this on my own – I'd got everything worked out, but it's coming sooner than it should and I didn't know it would be like this, it's sheer sodding agony.'

'But you can't have a baby on your own,' said Catherine, horrified, scarcely noticing the language. 'And you're – you're bleeding and I don't know if that's right— I'll go up to the house and call an ambulance—'

'No! If you call anyone I'll throw myself into the river,' she said, and her eyes were so wild Catherine was afraid she meant it. She glanced uneasily towards the lapping green waters. 'I've kept it secret all this time,' she said, clutching at Catherine's hand, 'I'm not letting anyone find out now. You're from St Luke's, aren't you – that's a hospital, right?'

'I'm only in training, Miss Kendal.'

'Charmery. I'm lying here bleeding everywhere with my skirt round my waist. It's not a time to be formal.'

'All right. I'm Catherine.' The pain seemed to have receded. Did that mean they were between contractions? People timed contractions which was all very well if you knew what to do after you had finished timing them. 'Charmery, isn't there anyone at the house? Your mother?'

'I'm at Fenn on my own. No one knows I'm here.'

This was terrible. Despite Charmery's threat, help would have to be summoned. Charmery hunched over with another spasm of pain and tears ran down her face, but even like this she was beautiful.

'I was going to get rid of it,' she said, when the pain eased again. 'But when it came to it . . .'

'When it came to it, you couldn't.'

'Not that, no. The clinic wouldn't do a termination. They said it was too far advanced.' A half grin lit her face. 'I thought it happened in October – you can't rely on condoms one hundred percent after all – sorry, I probably shouldn't say that to a nun. But anyway, apparently it had happened two months before that – the end of August – which made more sense when I thought about it.'

'But weren't there any signs?' said Catherine, not trying to unravel this slightly bewildering information.

'Nothing to speak of. I never had regular periods anyway,' she said, and Catherine realized they had gone beyond being polite or reticent. 'And— Oh, God!'

This time the pain sent ripples across her stomach as if the child was fighting its way out, and she screamed and twisted her body round on the hard wooden floor. Catherine stood up, and said, 'I'm calling for help.'

'No, I told you—'

'If you keep screaming like that half the village will hear. And if it – uh – was conceived at the end of August, that means it's only six months old. Charmery, you must let me get help. What if the child dies?'

149

'I don't care if it does,' said Charmery, but the words came out on an angry sob and Catherine saw how frightened she really was.

With the idea of seeing if there was any other way of persuading her, she said, 'What about the father?'

'He doesn't know about it,' said Charmery. 'And since you didn't ask, I'll tell you who it was. My . . . cousin, Theo.'

Theo. The dark-haired young man who was almost always at her side. Of course, thought Catherine. She said, 'I'll go back to the house to call Dr Innes.'

'Who?'

'He came to Melbray a couple of months ago. I think you could trust him to keep it all secret.' She waited for a reaction, but Charmery was deep in the pain again. Catherine took a deep breath and half ran back up the path to the house, praying a door would be open, praying she would find the phone.

There were French windows overlooking a terrace; one was partly open and she went in. The room was quite dark and beyond the windows the sky was like a violet bruise. A storm brewing, thought Catherine in dismay, but she found the phone in the hall, a local directory lying beside it. She dialled Dr Innes' number, her heart pounding in case a polite receptionist answered.

But the doctor answered on the third ring, and Catherine managed to explain who she was and how there was someone at Fenn House who desperately needed help.

'Did you phone an ambulance yet?' he said.

'She doesn't want anyone to know. She threatened to throw herself in the river if I got an ambulance. Dr Innes, she's having a child, but I think it's quite premature – only about six months – and I think something's gone wrong.'

'Stay with her. I'll come at once.'

Catherine replaced the receiver, then picked it up again and this time dialled St Luke's. She asked for a message to be given to Reverend Mother or the Bursar, saying she had encountered Dr

150

Innes in the village and her help was needed with an emergency patient.

The hour that followed was like a nightmare. The storm rolled in from the North Sea in earnest; huge heavy rainspots fell and thunder growled menacingly as Dr Innes knelt down and made a brief, impersonal examination.

'We'll need to carry you back to the house,' he said at last, standing up. 'Sister, will you help me?'

'Yes, of course.'

'Wait – I'm going to be sick,' said Charmery suddenly, and hunching over vomited onto the wooden floor, sobbing and shuddering with pain and disgust.

'Not unusual,' said Dr Innes in a calm voice. 'But now—'

'No! Oh God, it's coming out! I can feel it . . .'

'Get towels from the house and, if you can manage it, warm water, as well,' said Dr Innes to Catherine. 'We can't move her now. The head's crowning.'

As Catherine sped back up to the house lightning crackled over to the east. She ignored it, and going inside found a linen cupboard with neat stacks of clean towels, which she snatched up and threw into a plastic carrier, along with a half-full bottle of Dettol that was near the sink. After this she filled a big plastic bucket with hot water from the tap. It was heavy but she managed to get back down to the boathouse without spilling much.

The rain was beating against the wooden sides of the boathouse and splashing into the river. Earlier, the water had been splintered with the sun's reflection and dappled sunlight had filtered through the willows, now the trees dripped water and the river's surface was lightless, like black glass.

Charmery was half sitting against the wooden wall of the boathouse, her knees drawn up and her thighs spread wide. The child had just been born: it lay between her legs in a bloodied mass, not moving, tiny and impossibly fragile. It was a boy. The son of that

151

dark-haired cousin Theo. But it's not moving, thought Catherine. There's something wrong. Thunder crashed overhead again and she shivered.

Dr Innes was oblivious to the storm. He wrapped the child in one of the bath towels, wiping the eyes and the mouth with damp tissues. Please God, let it be all right, thought Catherine. Let it cry and open its eyes.

She watched Dr Innes put his lips to the tiny mouth to breathe life into the lungs, but no flutter of movement disturbed the small chest and the eyes stayed closed.

'It's dead, isn't it?' said Charmery, after what seemed to be an extremely long time. Her voice was weak and languid. She doesn't care, thought Catherine. Or does she care too much? She hasn't looked at the baby once.

'Yes. It's a boy. I've done everything I can, but – I'm so very sorry.'

'Was it because I didn't have proper check-ups and things? Or because he was born too early? Is it my fault?'

Dr Innes did not immediately answer, then he said, very gently, 'Not necessarily. The autopsy will tell us more.'

'Autopsy?'

'There must be one, of course. This is a stillbirth, not a miscarriage. A six- or possibly seven-month child.'

'Six months. The end of August last year,' said Charmery. 'I won't let you do an autopsy.'

'Charmery, it needs to be established whether he died in the uterus, or if he died during labour.' Dr Innes frowned. 'Is it because your parents will find out you were pregnant?' he said. 'They might be shocked at first, but they'd support you, wouldn't they? It's hardly the nineteenth century.'

'You don't understand,' said Charmery. 'They mustn't know – not ever.'

Dr Innes handed the child to Catherine, and for a moment she held the tiny, still shape against her. Its little body was still warm –

it might suddenly move or start crying for food or comfort or love. This is the son of that dark-haired young man, she thought, looking down at the sprinkling of soft dark hair. One night, or maybe one afternoon, or maybe several nights and afternoons, he was in a bed with Charmery and because of it this little thing has come into the world. After a moment Catherine put the baby down carefully on the wooden floor near Charmery, hoping she would pick him up, just once, just to say goodbye.

Dr Innes was half kneeling on the wooden floor. His eyes were shadowed, but he said, quite calmly, 'Charmery, as soon as you feel up to it we'll take you back up to the house. We'll talk about the autopsy there. For the moment, there's still the afterbirth to come – we need to deal with that.'

'It's all so squalid,' said Charmery angrily. 'I didn't think it would be like this.' She still did not look at the tiny shape in the bath towel. 'I know you're both thinking I'm a cold-hearted bitch,' she said. 'But I'm not. It's just that I didn't want this child and also it might have been—' She broke off. 'It wouldn't have been a good idea,' she said, and Catherine saw tears in her eyes.

Dr Innes turned away to close his medical bag, and Catherine got to her feet to help him. In that moment Charmery reached forward and scooped up the small sad bundle. Before Catherine realized what she intended, she leaned over and dropped it, quite gently, into the lapping green waters of the river.

Catherine and Dr Innes both turned, startled, as the towel-wrapped shape was carried away. Innes lunged forward to the edge of the landing stage and knelt down, his arms reaching out.

'It's too far out,' he said. 'I can't reach it, and—'

'And in any case, it's dead,' said Charmery in a flat voice.

Catherine stared at the dark river through a curtain of rain. In another couple of minutes the baby would be out in the river's main flow. The towel was already sodden and falling away from the little body. It did not matter, except that it exposed what was inside, making it seem doubly vulnerable. She looked at Charmery who was sitting upright, her face pale in the stormlight, her eyes unreadable. Tears poured down her face, and through the drumming rain, Catherine heard her say, very softly, 'I'm sorry, Theo . . . I loved you so much.'

Catherine looked back at the river. In the glowering light of the storm, from out of the unravelling towel, a little starfish hand came upwards as if its owner was trying to hold on to the world it was about to leave. Catherine cried out at once, and darted to the edge of the landing stage, then felt Dr Innes grab her arm and pull her back.

'Sister, it's dead,' he said. 'I promise you, there's no question about it.'

'But it moved!' cried Catherine, kneeling on the edge of the timbers, trying to stretch her hand out to the small shape. It was too late, of course; the child was already being swept away. Soon the water would close over the small pale body.

'It was the river's undertow,' he said, still holding onto her. 'Catherine, please believe me, that's all it was.'

Catherine was still staring at the dark river. How would it feel to drown in the cold black water, with the angry storm all round you? The baby was becoming a pale blur in the rainy darkness, already swept out into the main undertow of the river. Catherine suddenly said, 'Charmery, you can't let him go like this. Not into that darkness without even a name.'

'But . . .'

'He never had a life,' said Catherine, beyond caring what Charmery thought of her. 'Give him that, at least. Let me say the words of baptism.'

'That's for Catholics. I'm not a Catholic.'

'Does it matter?' cried Catherine, angrily.

'All right,' she said. 'If it makes you feel better.'

'Yes, it does. And it might make you feel better when you get on the other side of all this. What d'you want to call him?'

'I don't care.' But her eyes were on the dark swirling river.

'It's St David's Day,' said Catherine suddenly. 'Can we call him David?'

'I suppose so.' And then, with sudden entreaty, 'Yes – please call him that.'

Catherine turned back to the river. 'I baptize thee, David, in the name of the Father, and of the Son, and of the Holy Ghost.'

As she pronounced the brief words, the small shape vanished completely, and Catherine stared at the rain-misted river. David, she thought. His body would probably never be found. He would lie on the river bed of the Chet for ever and no one else would even know he had existed. I'll know, though, thought Catherine. I won't forget about you, David.

Somehow they got Charmery back to the house and onto a sofa in the long, low-ceilinged sitting room. Catherine brought a bowl of warm water and soap for her to wash. 'And could I make tea or soup or something?' she said.

'A good idea,' said Dr Innes. 'You do that while I deal with Charmery.'

Catherine explored the kitchen, discovering that Charmery had stocked the fridge and larder very thoroughly indeed. The fridge was stacked with cheese and eggs and vacuum packs of ham, and when Catherine opened the big chest freezer it was filled to the brim with prepared meals and bags of oven chips and pizzas. The shelves of the deep, old-fashioned larder held rows of tinned fruit, meat and soup. It looked as if Charmery had intended to hide out here until after the birth.

Catherine opened two large cans of mushroom soup, and removed a packet of bread rolls from the freezer. She was just putting the rolls under the grill to thaw when Michael Innes came into the kitchen.

'She's fine,' he said. 'The afterbirth's out, and although I'm not a gynaecologist, I don't think there are any complications.' He watched Catherine for a moment, then said, 'The birth of that child should be properly registered and also the death.' He paused, then choosing his words carefully, he said, 'But there are times when a doctor has to take things onto his own conscience.'

'And ignore the law?'

'Yes. No crime has been committed. The child was dead when it went into the river.'

'You promise that?' Catherine was still seeing that last uncertain movement.

'Yes, I promise. So,' he said, 'I don't want to report any of this. Only you'll have to agree. And you'll have to be comfortable about it.'

Catherine stirred the soup, not speaking, trying to sort out her thoughts.

'When she put the child in the river,' said Michael Innes, 'I think she was trying to – to erase the whole thing. She'll probably realize later that it won't ever be erased, but for the moment . . . Catherine,' he said, with a pleading note in his voice, 'please agree to this. She's extremely young.'

Catherine wanted to say that Charmery was only a little younger than she was herself, and no matter how young that might be, she had still managed to have a lover and give birth to a child.

'It's all a front, that flippancy,' said Innes, as she still did not speak. 'Under it she's distraught at losing the child. It meant a lot to her – I think her cousin Theo meant a lot to her.'

'I know he did.' Catherine looked at him. 'All right,' she said. 'If you believe it's the right thing to keep it all secret, I'll trust your judgement.'

A wry smile touched his face. 'Conventual obedience, Sister Catherine? I would have thought you struggled with that a bit.'

'I do struggle with it,' said Catherine. 'But I think this is more doctor/nurse obedience. You have more knowledge – more experience – than I do.'

They looked at one another. 'Your conscience would be clear?' he said.

'Yes, I think so. Will Charmery be all right? I mean – physically?'

'There's nothing I can't deal with over the next week or two. I'd rather she came into the local infirmary to get everything double-checked. I'll try to persuade her, but I think she'll refuse.' He paused, then said, 'Thank you, Catherine,' and went quietly out.

When Catherine carried the soup into the sitting room Charmery was saying, 'No. I absolutely won't go to hospital. If you try to make me I'll think of something to stop you. I mean it. Anyway, you can't force me.'

'No, I can't. But the law—'

'Sod the law,' said Charmery, 'the child never existed.' Catherine heard the vulnerable note in her voice and knew Dr Innes had been right about the flippancy being armour.

'If you won't go to hospital, will you stay quietly here for the next week or so?' said Dr Innes. 'Rest on your bed or on this sofa, and let me call at the house each day to make sure you're all right? Perhaps even let Sister Catherine look in as well?' He glanced at Catherine who immediately said, 'Of course I'll do that.'

'Well, OK, then,' said Charmery. 'Is that soup? Thank God. I'm utterly famished. Nobody tells you that giving birth is such a hungry business.'

As they drank the soup, Michael Innes said, 'What I don't understand is why you were here on your own in the first place. Surely your family—'

'None of them knew,' said Charmery. 'Certainly none of them know I'm here. Just before Christmas I forged a letter from my ma to the school saying I was going to America with my family at the start of January and I'd be away for a month. The school was fine with it – they think travel's educational, and it was my last half year there anyway and I wasn't bothering much about A levels. I told my parents I was going on a long school trip – St Petersburg and all those tzar places. They believed me; they believe anything I tell them.'

157

Catherine thought people had probably believed anything this girl told them ever since she was born; she thought it had probably resulted in Charmery being spoilt.

'It was only in December that I started to look a bit, well, chubbier,' Charmery said. 'But I wore really tight girdles and it was winter so I could wear loose sweaters most of the time. Oh, and I pretended to have a torn ligament in my knee, so I could duck out of games and swimming.'

'But the school couldn't have believed you'd be in America all this time,' said Catherine, 'not since January until now.'

'No, but I wrote halfway through January saying I'd picked up a virus while I was there and I'd be away until the end of the summer term. I got a friend in Boston to send it for me so it would get there by airmail. I told her I was having a wild fling with a new boyfriend. Actually, of course, I was here at Fenn all the time.'

'Since January?'

'Yes. I travelled by train – I couldn't use my car because I wasn't supposed to be here at all, you see. I got a train to Norwich and bought masses of food there – packs and packs of frozen stuff and about a zillion tins, and long-life milk and stuff.'

'I saw it,' said Catherine. 'If nothing else, you won't starve out here.'

'I got a taxi here and the taxi-driver helped me to carry everything in – it was a Norwich taxi firm so he had no idea who I was. And I've been here ever since. It's been pretty boring, actually. I've never been on my own for so long – I've done nothing but read and sketch and watch TV and DVDs, can you imagine the tedium?'

'But the birth,' began Catherine.

'I was going back to Norwich in time for that. I was going to order a taxi and book into one of the big anonymous hotels – a Travellodge or something – then dial an ambulance when it all started. It would have been an emergency admission, and I was going to give a false name. Only it happened before it was meant to.'

'What were you doing in the boathouse anyway?' said Innes.

'I like it there,' said Charmery, off-handedly, but Catherine heard a defensive note behind the words.

Dr Innes seemed to hear it as well. He said, 'Fair enough. But listen, what about the child? Once you'd got yourself to a hospital and given birth, what would you have done about it afterwards?'

'You hear of people walking out of hospitals leaving babies behind,' said Charmery. 'That's what I'd have done.'

'Would you?'

'Yes. Yes!' she said angrily.

'It's a mad plan,' said Dr Innes, 'but it might just have worked.'

'I'd have made it work,' said Charmery. 'I didn't want it to happen like it did this afternoon and I know you think I'm utterly soulless. But I dealt with it in the best way I could, and as it is, only the three of us know what happened. Will you both promise me never to tell anyone? No one else must ever know the child existed.'

'Yes, I promise,' said Dr Innes after a moment.

'Catherine?'

'Yes,' said Catherine. 'Yes, I promise, as well.'

CHAPTER FIFTEEN

The present

Theo awoke on the morning after his talk at St Luke's feeling mentally and physically restored. He refused to be spooked by his discovery that Matthew was real, that he was a man who had sat on the Chet's banks and in the grounds of the convent, and drawn what was in front of him. He would find explanations for everything that had been happening, even that grisly document on the computer.

The sun streamed into Fenn House as he ate breakfast, after which he made a pot of coffee and headed for the dining room and the computer. He had saved the confession onto the hard drive, and he was considering the possibility that someone had got into the house and coolly sat at the dining table and typed it while he was virtually unconscious. This was a pretty wild theory, but it was just about credible, although Theo had not yet worked out who the mystery typist might be. But it would not have taken very long to actually type it. Presumably it had been pre-written. Could it have been prepared on another computer, saved onto a disk or a memory stick, and uploaded onto Theo's laptop? That would be the work of a few minutes and it would not need a particularly deep knowledge of computers. But that meant the document would have to have been saved, not only on the laptop – which it had not been – but also on the original computer – which would have meant leaving evidence. Whoever had typed it would surely not have risked that. It could have been hand-written and then typed but that meant he had been drugged beforehand. Was that really likely? Something in the casserole after all? Theo shivered at the thought that someone could have been watching him so closely, and remembered that the someone had also known about the sedatives prescribed in the summer.

And what about the child? he asked himself. The post mortem report had been clear that Charmery had given birth. Had this faceless watcher found out about that, as well? How? Theo was as sure as he could be that the family had not known – they could never have kept something like that to themselves. Could a journalist, hell-bent on scraping copy out of Charmery's murder, have gained access to the report?

After he had finished his breakfast he hunted out a phone directory to find the number of a local locksmith. There was only one firm, but they were helpful and efficient and could send someone that afternoon to fit new, heavy-duty security locks. When Theo gave the address, there was a sudden pause at the other end. 'You know the place, I expect?' said Theo.

The voice said, rather apologetically, that yes, they did know it, bit of a landmark really, Fenn House. No, there was no problem about the work, unless Mr Kendal wanted anything out of the ordinary. They did not keep a very large stock.

Theo did not care if they fitted steel grilles and dug a moat round the place if it would keep out prowlers who typed bizarre documents on the computer while he was zonked from a spiked casserole, but he said he simply wanted the house made as secure as possible with whatever was to hand.

'Fair enough. We'll be there at three,' said the voice and rang off.

Theo went into the dining room, his mind already leaping ahead to Matthew.

But it was not Matthew who was waiting for him, it was Zoia. As Theo began to type, he found himself curious to know if Zoia would be able to cope with Annaleise's demands about spying.

Romania, early 1960s

At first, Zoia thought she would not be able to cope with Annaleise's demands about spying. Stripped of the fancy words and honeyed tones, it boiled down to Annaleise wanting Zoia to pry and snoop and tell her all she discovered. Annaleise explained it in detail, saying there were rebels and dissidents everywhere.

'But how will I recognize them?' Zoia asked. 'How will I know which ones to watch?'

'You'll recognize them. I'll give you some pointers, but they're usually easy to spot. They're arrogant; they walk round as if they own the world. They're dangerous and must be stopped, taught a lesson, removed from circulation if necessary. I hope you understand, Zoia.'

She reached out a hand to caress Zoia's breast as she said this, and Zoia, her body leaping with the familiar desire, gazed longingly at Annaleise and said she understood it very clearly. What happened to these people? she said.

'They aren't all guilty, of course,' said Annaleise. 'Most of them are, though. My masters in the Communist Party are very clever and very watchful and it's not often they get it wrong. The innocent are let go, of course.'

'And the guilty?'

Zoia thought Annaleise hesitated, then she shrugged and said it was necessary to think of the common good. The guilty ones were taken to suitable places to be kept out of the way for a while. That was really all Zoia needed to know.

'Prison?' said Zoia.

'That's a harsh word. But whatever's done is for the common good. Such people are a danger. The sensible, logical thing is to put all the rotten eggs in one basket.'

'Yes, I see that,' said Zoia thoughtfully.

'There is one egg who is very rotten indeed,' said Annaleise. 'Someone I would like very much to bring to justice. It's up to the Party to make the decision, of course, but I'm preparing evidence, a little here and a little there. I shall persuade my masters to investigate her in the end, though, because she's a very dangerous lady indeed. Very much of a threat to us.'

'Who is she?'

'You knew her at the university,' said Annaleise and her lips thinned with hatred. 'But she has since married. Her name now is Elisabeth Valk.'

The present

The shrilling of the doorbell shattered Theo's absorption, dragging him out of Zoia's dark and unhappy world. The bell was followed by a cheerful tattoo on the door knocker, and Theo opened the door to the locksmith. He let the man in and explained the requirements, after which the locksmith proceeded to clatter breezily round the house, whistling to the strains of a minuscule radio which he switched on as soon as he started work. 'You don't mind, do you, squire? I like a bit of liveliness while I work.'

'Not at all,' said Theo, closing the dining room door firmly, and trying to recapture Zoia and that intriguing reference to Elisabeth Valk.

'No one really knows what happened to Elisabeth,' Mara's grandmother had said. 'And no one knows where she is either, not now, not for sure.'

Elisabeth Valk, who had laughed out of the photo on Andrei's desk – the photo Matthew had liked – and whom even the ungenerous Zoia had said grudgingly was beautiful and clever. Theo began to write a description of Elisabeth who was starting to look as if she could be a major player in the story, but was interrupted again by the locksmith who had finished his work and wanted to explain the workings of the locks.

'I'm sorry it's taken so long, squire, but these old places are real shockers to work on. Oh, I had to plane that kitchen door a bit to get the new lock on properly. I've swept up the wood dust, but you might want to run a vacuum over it as well. Here you are – three keys for each door, and that's your five-lever for the front, so you're safe as houses. Had a bit of trouble with snoopers, I expect.'

'Just a bit.'

'That's murder for you,' said the man philosophically. 'No offence and all that if you were related to the lady, but people like a murder. No accounting for tastes, I say.'

Theo said there was no accounting at all, paid the modest account, added a substantial tip to cover the planing of the door, and returned to Elisabeth and Zoia.

Romania, early 1960s

If Elisabeth Valk had not been so vividly alive, she might never have come to the attention of Annaleise, and subsequently to Zoia's. But at university, Elisabeth had been a leader, an innovator, at the centre of everything. She had not been called Valk then – Zoia had never known her maiden name and it had not really mattered, because if anyone ever said 'Elisabeth' people had always known who was meant, and had smiled. Zoia had never smiled though. She envied Elisabeth who was beautiful and clever and possessed of the indefinable gift called charm, and because of that she had disliked her without knowing her. She had thought, in a vague way, that it would be deeply satisfactory to teach such a vain, privileged little madam a lesson. Was she now going to get the chance to do that?

Zoia's departure from the university did not cause much comment; if anyone noticed they assumed she had gone because she had no money to continue, or because of some man. These things happened and the awkward angular female had never really been a part of student life. After leaving she worked mostly in cafes and bars; a couple of months in one town, a few weeks in another, going wherever Annaleise thought would be most useful. She had expected to dislike snooping and prying, but when it came to it she found it deeply exciting and for the first time she understood properly the saying about knowledge being power. She had knowledge of the people with whom she worked or who came into the cafes and the bars; she found out their secrets and that gave her power over them.

She went about her work diligently because it was for Annaleise. She eavesdropped and became a sympathetic listener to people's troubles. She found that people who went into bars to get drunk were apt to disclose their most private thoughts to the waitress or barmaid. After a little while she hit on the idea of inventing a large mythical family, nothing like her real family, consisting of relations who had similar troubles to her customers. It created a bond; people opened up far more when they heard that the sympathetic girl serving their wine or food had a cousin or sister or aunt who was in the exact same situation. Several of them even invited Zoia to their houses or apartments, saying how wonderful it was to talk to someone who really understood. On more than one of these visits Zoia contrived to read their letters or bank statements.

She loved it when she could take a really useful piece of information to Annaleise. Perhaps someone might be receiving rents for land or property they ought not to own – there were sections of the community who were prohibited from owning land nowadays but some people found ways of dodging the law. Sometimes there were people who wrote what was called sedition – inciting others to rebel by means of articles or pamphlets. Often these were students who came into the bars and talked indiscreetly after a few glasses of wine.

When Annaleise was pleased with some particular nugget of information she would take Zoia to an expensive restaurant and smile at her across the table, and afterwards take her back to wherever she or Zoia might be living, and cause the longed-for explosions in Zoia's body and mind. Zoia lived for these meetings and, after a time, if the supply of information about people's plans and secrets was sparse, she made things up. This one was writing a pamphlet, that one was forging land ownership papers. It was extraordinarily easy to find out what Annaleise's masters wanted to know and fashion information accordingly. In the beginning it worried her slightly in case these made-up tales resulted in official interrogation or even a spell in prison, but after a time she ceased to care. The guilty would be punished and the innocent would be able to prove their innocence. All that mattered was pleasing Annaleise and, in any case, who ever said life was fair? It had certainly not been fair to Zoia.

A few times she approached other women, curious to know if they could give her the same explosive pleasure as Annaleise. She was careful about who she approached. Sometimes she got it wrong and the woman would recoil from her, but mostly her instinct was right. The trouble was that once in a bed – or more likely a quiet back street or a deserted park – all other women were disappointments as far as Zoia was concerned. They knew the mechanics, some of them were very expert indeed with fingers and tongues, and one or two possessed devices shaped for female pleasure – it was Zoia's first experience of these. Some demanded money afterwards, which she generally refused to pay. Usually she got away with this, although on a couple of occasions the women attacked her and one sent a shifty-looking man to beat her up. Zoia recovered from the beating which was not much more than bruises and cigarette burns to her arms, and was more wary about who she approached afterwards. In any case, none of them created the wild throbbing of the blood she sought.

Once, curious for further knowledge, she picked up a man in a late-night cafe and went into a nearby park with him. She did not much like it; his penis forcing itself inside her was hard and thick, and it took her back to the nights in the cottage when her father unbuckled his belt to thrash her and her sisters, one hand wielding the belt, the other hand moving with rhythmic urgency between his legs. Still, she thought she might as well know this side of the sex act, so she endured the man's banging thrusts to the finish and tried not to flinch. Back in her own lodgings, she washed for a long time in lukewarm water from the chipped enamel basin on her washstand. The man's climax, when it finally happened, had been messier than she had expected and she could not bear the smell or the feel of him on her skin. But the exercise had not been entirely without its value, because now she knew what men were like. He had assumed she was a prostitute and given her money.

She had been living like this for almost a year when Annaleise came to the small apartment where Zoia was living, her face flushed with uncharacteristic colour, her eyes blazing.

'The Party have agreed to officially investigate Elisabeth Valk,' she said.

Elisabeth had married at the end of her final year at the university: her husband was a lecturer from another college. His name was Andrei Valk, and he was several years older than Elisabeth, and said to be intelligent and fairly well-off.

'As much as anyone is well-off these days,' Annaleise said curtly.

Elisabeth and Andrei Valk had left the university town after their marriage. Annaleise had not yet found where they had gone, but it was said to be not very far.

'It will be easy to find the exact address,' said Annaleise. 'Andrei took up writing as a profession, so we might be able to trace him through his books. But a couple like that would stand out in any community.'

She had read one of Andrei's books and said she thought it pretentious.

'He dedicated his first book "To my beloved Elisabeth, who possesses all the graces". Can you believe that? Nauseating, isn't it?'

Zoia agreed. She remembered how the lecturers had looked at Elisabeth with proud fondness while Zoia herself had barely earned a second glance from them and she was pleased to think Madam Vanity was about to be taught a lesson. 'I have a great deal of information about her,' said Annalcise. 'But so far nothing quite damning enough for the Party to take action.'

Zoia thought how marvellous it would be if she could get the final damning evidence Annaleise wanted.

And exactly two months later, she did get it.

It happened completely out of the blue, and was due to one of the customers in the bar where she had been working for the past three months. He was a youngish man who came in every Saturday night to wait for his girlfriend and sometimes they had a meal in the tiny dining room. Zoia had cultivated a cautious friendship with them, not because there was any indication that they might be grist for Annaleise's mill, but because she had learned by now that almost everyone could be made use of in some way.

On this particular night something emerged from the casual talk that could be used very definitely indeed.

'I was listening to the wireless before I came out,' said the young man, accepting the glass of beer he always drank before his girl arrived, clearly relaxed after his week's work and looking forward to the evening ahead. 'Remarkable, isn't it, the things people manage to get broadcast nowadays.'

Zoia, polishing glasses, said she supposed it was.

'Brave of them, when you consider it,' he said. 'The way they speak out against—' He glanced furtively over his shoulder to see who was in earshot, and drew nearer to Zoia and the bar.

'Against whom?'

He gave a small shrug and drank some more of his beer.

Zoia's mind had sprung to attention by this time. Trying another approach, she said, 'What do you mean, brave? What was the programme?'

'One of those protest radio stations,' he said. 'There've been a few of them over the years but this was the first one I'd ever heard. A mistake, of course,' he said hastily, looking round to see if anyone had heard this statement. 'I was trying to find a play I wanted to hear and I tuned in by accident. The October Group, it calls itself. Of course, I switched off almost as soon as I realized what it was.' He said this fairly loudly.

'But what was it exactly?' asked Zoia, her heart starting to pound, the palms of her hands suddenly clammy with sweat. Was this going to be a really big lead? A protest radio station, she thought. That's something Annaleise's people would want to know about.

'What it was,' said the young man, taking a deep draught of his beer, 'was sedition, nothing less. Clear as a curse. They were publicizing a meeting – a rally to freedom they called it – and asking questions most of us wouldn't even dare to think, if you take my meaning.'

'Such as?'

'Best not say,' he said, with a wink. Then, half turning, he smiled, 'Here's my lady,' he said, and Zoia saw the girlfriend come through the door. He got up from the bar stool, then looked back at Zoia. 'I'll tell you this, though,' he said. 'Before I switched off, I noticed the woman who was talking had one of the most attractive voices I've ever heard.'

'Really?'

'People don't give the voice enough weight as an attraction, do they?' he said. 'But sedition or not, this one's voice was an absolute sizzler. Her name was Elisabeth Valk.'

*

169

The next night in Annaleise's apartment, Zoia and Annaleise spent almost an hour turning the dial on the wireless to find the wavelength of the October Group. Annaleise knew about them, of course. 'They call themselves that because of the Russian Revolution of 1917,' she said. 'But it's also an acknowledgement of the start of the Hungarian Revolution in October 1956. They think we don't know they exist, but of course we do, although I'd have to admit we don't know much about them. But,' she said thoughtfully, 'Elisabeth Valk is one of their number, is she?'

'It looks like it,' said Zoia. She was pleased it was Sunday and her day off so she could be involved, but Annaleise was inclined to be sceptical about whether this would lead anywhere. They did not know how far they could trust Zoia's customer, she said. He might just be making mischief. As the wireless's dial screeched its way along the various channels, her scepticism increased.

'It's the same time of the evening,' offered Zoia. 'He'd been listening before he came in, so it would have been about this time.'

'Yes, but they might only have made that one broadcast. Or they might not bother on a Sunday. They might even have been discovered in the last twenty-four hours and closed down.'

Then, quite suddenly, between a blast of music and a discussion about farming, it was there.

'The October Group calling,' said the voice. 'The October Group calling . . . Elisabeth Valk here, wishing a very good evening to all my friends . . .'

Elisabeth Valk. Zoia stared at the wireless. One of the most attractive voices I've ever heard, the man had said, an absolute sizzler. Infuriatingly and unfairly, it was a remarkable voice, like violet midnight or warm honey or newly spun silk. If you lay in bed with the owner of this voice you would feel as if your skin was being caressed by sound.

Elisabeth was talking about the meeting which Zoia's customer had mentioned. She called it a rally, and said details as to time and place would be given soon on this wavelength. In the meantime, here were some things for their overlords to ponder. Why had labour camps been created and why was there vicious physical and psychological torture of prison inmates – many of whom had committed no crime? asked the beautiful voice. There were other references, more homely. Why was the food in the shops of the poorest quality but the most expensive of prices? Why was it necessary for bread to be bought with ration cards in an agricultural country? But most damning of all were the warnings she gave. A change of government was coming and there would be appalling restrictions of human rights, there would be censorship, and what was called relocation – people would be forced from their homes. Beware of it all, said Elisabeth. Fight against it, for it would ruin the country and other countries as well. When she bade her listeners goodnight and urged them to listen again at the same time tomorrow evening, Zoia saw that Annaleise's eyes were blazing with triumph. She turned her head and smiled.

'We have her,' she said softly. 'Proof positive and clear. If my people can track down where that broadcast is coming from – and that should be possible – then we have Elisabeth Valk tied up tighter than a caterpillar's cocoon.'

She reached out and pulled Zoia hard against her. 'It's arousing, isn't it?' she said. 'And so you and I are going to bed now, and I'm going to have you so many times, by dawn you'll be crying for mercy.'

'I would never cry for mercy with you.'

Annaleise smiled.

'I wonder if you'll still be saying that by the time dawn comes,' she said, and began to tear off Zoia's clothes.

Nothing happened for several days and Zoia began to think Annaleise's people had failed to find the source of the broadcast. Or perhaps it had been found by others and closed down. She wished she had a wireless of her own so she could tune in to the

171

October Group herself, but wirelesses were expensive and there was a waiting list of at least a year.

But a week later, Annaleise came into the bar where Zoia worked. This was something she had never done before, and Zoia's heart leapt with a mixture of delight and apprehension.

Without preamble, Annaleise said, 'Can you be ready to make a journey early tomorrow morning? Around seven o'clock?'

Zoia did not finish at the bar until one a.m. and it took forty-five minutes to get back to her apartment, so she would only get four or five hours sleep, but she would have gone without any sleep at all for Annaleise. She said, 'Yes.'

It was a bitter, unforgiving morning as the large car jerked its way across the frozen countryside and a sharp frost rimed the hedges and the roofs. A man Zoia had never met was driving, with a woman, also unfamiliar, seated next to him. She was around forty, bony-featured and striking without being actually good-looking. Her eyes, as she turned to look at Zoia, were piercing.

Annaleise said, 'Elena, this is Zoia Calciu. I told you about her.'

'You did,' said the woman. 'We're all very pleased with your work for the Party.'

'This is Madame Elena Ceauşescu,' said Annaleise. 'She's a very hardworking and respected member of our cause. Her husband is a senior member of the Politburo.'

Zoia had not expected to meet anyone so highly connected. Her sense of inferiority returned at the reference to the Politburo, but she tried not to appear intimidated and managed to ask where they were going.

'Across the border into Yugoslavia,' said Annaleise. 'To Krivaca, then to a small village on its edge. It's about seventy miles from here – we should do it in two hours.'

Before she could say any more, Elena said, 'We're going to find Elisabeth Valk. Annaleise particularly asked that you be there

172

when we catch her – you were the one who provided the information, Zoia.'

'What will happen to her?' asked Zoia, aware of sudden pleasure that Annaleise had made this request.

A thin smile lifted Elena's lips. 'She will be dealt with,' she said. 'The Party has a very particular way of dealing with enemies of the state.'

CHAPTER SIXTEEN

———◆◆◆———

The present

Well! thought Theo, sitting back and staring at the screen, no one can say I'm not importing real people into this book! Elena Ceauşescu, no less. Married to one of the greediest, most corrupt dictators of modern times – Nicolae Ceauşescu, convicted of genocide and shot with his wife on Christmas Day, 1989.

He did not know a great deal about Elena Ceauşescu, and he certainly did not think he had known enough to introduce her into the plot, but there she was. He got up to scan the bookshelves in a corner of the room, where a motley collection had assembled itself over the years. There were ragged paperbacks the cousins had brought to read during the holidays and forgotten to take home, cookery books belonging to Helen, ordnance survey maps and tourist books about the area which no one had ever consulted. But there were a few standard reference books as well, all foxed and faded-looking and among them was an elderly *Oxford Concise Encyclopedia*. Theo reached for it, bringing out a shower of dust and dispossessing several indignant spiders of their homes.

The encyclopedia turned out to have been published in 1933, and described Adolf Hitler as being Germany's new Chancellor.

Theo swore and returned it to its place in disgust, and was just thinking he would have to drive to the nearest library when he saw, at one end, a couple of books dealing with Eastern European history. Memory stirred and he remembered a summer when Guff had brought to Fenn House a young Ukrainian student, in England to improve her languages. She had, as far as the family was concerned, been one of Guff's less worrying escapades, partly because she had not seemed interested in money but also because on the second night of her stay she had taken over the kitchen and cooked borscht followed by a truly inspirational beef stroganoff. She had also, in the wake of several bottles of Bulls Blood that evening, taught the younger Kendals several satisfyingly explosive swear words in Russian. Theo had no idea what had eventually happened to her, but it looked as if Guff, rather endearingly, had tried to acquaint himself with Eastern European history, either during or as a result of, the association.

He sat down on the floor and began to riffle the pages of both books. The first was of no help, but the second had a whole section on Romania. Theo began to read, working his way through various aspects of the country: its folklore, which included rusalkas and mild-mannered vampires; its many invasions by Goths, Bulgars and Turks and assorted marauding armies, and the complexities of its royal dynasties and rulers which he found confusing, largely because most of them had names ending in 'escu'.

There was a brief section on Elena Ceauşescu near the end. Theo read it carefully.

Elena Ceauşescu (c.1916–89), was the wife of the infamous and power-hungry Nicolae Ceauşescu, dictator and president of Romania between 1967 and 1989. Elena, also sometimes written as Ilena, rose to power when Nicolae became Secretary General of the Romanian Communist Party in 1965 and then President of the State Council in 1967. Although she styled herself at one stage as Mother of the Nation, Elena was not, in fact, particularly maternal, and was to become one of the most hated people in Romania during her husband's 25-year reign.

She was involved in, and finally found responsible for, many of the human rights abuses in Romania between the 1960s and 1980s.

That seemed to sum up Elena fairly well and to provide all the information Theo needed, but he read to the end of the section.

She brought in many of her own reforms, one of which was the outlawing of birth control and abortion, creating a flood of unwanted babies, many of whom were housed in what can only be described as substandard, state-operated orphanages. There has been speculation since about her motives for this particular policy, but at the time of writing, the reasons have still not been satisfactorily explained.

Orphanages. Theo went back to the laptop and recovered the earlier chapter where the small Mara, trying to escape from the Black House, had accidentally stumbled on the room with babies in cages. It had horrified her, just as the newsreels of the Romanian orphanages would later horrify the Western world. It had horrified Theo when he was typing it.

After the coup that deposed Elena and Nicolae Ceaușescu in 1989, they both fled the country but were caught, arrested, tried and executed on Christmas Day in 1989.

He was about to close the book when he saw the footnote, in a typeface so minuscule he had to take it across to the table to read under the desk lamp.

There are unsupported and undocumented claims that Elena Ceauşescu, shortly before her rise to power, relied very much on a female friend who was extremely active within the Communist Party. Little is known about this woman, except that she apparently assisted Elena in tracking down a number of so-called political agitators and enemies of the state. The woman died in violent and mysterious circumstances. Elena attended the funeral and paid public tribute to the work of Annaleise Simonescu.

Annaleise Simonescu. *Annaleise.* Theo stared at the printed name and tried to remember whether he had ever read this book, but was sure he had not – he thought he would have remembered. He turned to the front, curious to see if Guff, the sentimental old spaniel, had written in it, or even if the Ukrainian girl had done.

There was no message either to or from Guff. There was just the title page, various acknowledgements to people who had helped with research, and the date of publication: 2003. That settled the question of whether he could have read it and forgotten. He had not been to Fenn House since that half term when Helen had caught him and Charmery together. It had been the autumn of 2001, two years before this book was even published, which meant he could not possibly have read it. And yet he had chosen the unusual name of Annaleise, and had described how she and Elena Ceauşescu had worked together to hunt down Elisabeth Valk.

He put the book back, frowning and wondering where he went from here. Back into the plot, he said to himself at once. Just dive back in and don't worry about where any of it's coming from. Don't worry, either, about how a young boy, mixed up in Ceauşescu's bleak Romania, could have drawn scenes in Melbray, as well as that remarkable portrait of Charmery. Theo looked across at the sketch. Matthew had lived in the grim Romania of Ceauşescu's rule, somewhere between 1960 and 1989 and

Charmery had not been born until the mid-1980s, and had died at the age of twenty-six earlier this year. Theo supposed it was possible they had met, but it did not seem very likely.

But even if they had met, it was still curious the way that Romania and its troubled history was tumbling so insistently and so consistently into Theo's mind.

Romania, early 1960s

As the car with Elena, Annaleise and Zoia drove across the countryside, the cold monochrome morning gave way to a watery sunlight.

This was the longest journey Zoia had ever made – she had been born in the little village on the east side of Resita, and had only ever travelled to the university town some thirty miles distant. That had seemed a huge undertaking, filled with terrifying prospects and unknown horizons, but it had been a journey she had wanted to make because it represented escape. This jolting drive across unfamiliar countryside, with dark forests and brooding mountain ranges, represented the opposite of escape: it represented imprisonment for Elisabeth Valk. Zoia stared out of the window and thought how Elisabeth must have made this journey many times. Had she been planning the things she would say on the wireless as she travelled, or had she been wondering if her husband was all right at home without her? Did they have any children?

It was a lonely road to travel – presumably Elisabeth had made the journey by car. Not many people had cars and very few could actually drive, but Elisabeth was the kind of privileged creature who might actually own a car.

They stopped in a small market town just beyond Pescari for coffee and food. 'A delayed breakfast,' Elena called it. Both Elena and Annaleise were disdainful about the primitive lavatories behind the cafe, and Zoia wondered what they would have thought of the privy in the garden of her childhood home.

As they went on again a distant church clock struck ten – Zoia counted the chimes – and Elena said, 'There's the Yugoslav border,' and indicated a checkpoint a few miles ahead. Zoia knew a moment of panic because she had no papers of any kind with her – nobody had told her to bring anything – but Elena simply showed the soldier some kind of document, and he sketched a respectful half salute and they were through. At Zoia's side, Annaleise murmured something about the power of the Party, and Zoia nodded.

The mountain smudge had moved round to the west and the sun streamed down making it uncomfortably hot in the car. But presently they drove through a cluster of narrow streets, not unlike the streets of the university town, and this seemed to be their destination. The driver stopped to consult a map with Elena, stabbing a finger questioningly at it. Elena studied the map then nodded, and the car moved off again. Ten minutes later they drew up in front of a tall narrow house, four stories high, with a chipped and peeling facade and long windows, most of which were shuttered. Annaleise touched Zoia's arm and indicated the thin metal structure on one of the roofs.

'Wireless transmitter,' she said. 'This is it, all right.'

'Are we sure she's there?' asked Elena.

'Yes. Our people on the ground here were very clear. She's here for these two days – working out the filthy treason she intends to broadcast, I suppose. She goes home, then comes back for the evening broadcast twice a week.'

'Will anyone else be in the house?' asked Zoia, eyeing it doubtfully.

'Our people said not. There's only ever one – at most two others – with her, and that's for the actual broadcast. Even if they're here now, Vasile is armed.'

Zoia had not been prepared for that. She asked if they were all going in.

'No. Elena and I will go in with Vasile. If we need you, we'll call.'

So Zoia waited in the car, the strong winter sunlight shining down on the quiet street, making the wireless transmitter glint like the betrayer of secrets it was. Nothing much stirred. Once a black-scarfed woman went hurrying along, her head bowed, a basket over one arm, and once a couple of youths on bicycles clattered along. They looked curiously at Zoia, but continued on their way. The church clock chimed the half hour, then the hour and Zoia wondered if she should go into the house in case they needed help. But as she reached over to open the door Elena appeared. She looked up and down the street, then looked back into the house and nodded. Zoia sat up straighter, anticipating a struggle, because Elisabeth would surely not give in without a fight.

But she did not fight. She came out between Vasile and Annaleise, both of them holding her arms, and they pushed her into the back of the car, wedging her between Zoia and Annaleise. Vasile got back into the driver's seat and the car moved off.

For a while Elisabeth did not speak, then she said, 'I suppose you're going to lock me up somewhere. Well, you can imprison me, but you won't imprison the cause I'm fighting for. There are others who will keep fighting.'

'Your husband, d'you mean?'

'My husband knows nothing of this,' she said at once, and Zoia heard the sudden fear in her voice, and guessed she was lying to protect him.

'And your small son?' said Annaleise, and Zoia half turned her head, hearing a menacing note in Annaleise's voice.

'How do you know I have a son?'

'We make it our business to know.'

'You'll never imprison my son,' said Elisabeth, glaring at Annaleise like a small feral cat. 'Andrei will kill you all first.'

'Are you sure?' said Annaleise softly, and this time Elisabeth flinched visibly.

'Where are you taking me?'

'Pitesti Gaol. We're driving there now.'

Zoia felt as if something had struck her across the eyes. Pitesti Gaol, she thought. Oh God, is that really where we're going? An old, deeply buried memory stirred uneasily.

Elisabeth was staring at Annaleise, and for the first time there was fear in her eyes. 'Pitesti,' she said. 'Pitesti means "to hide" because the town is hidden between hills. And it's as well it does hide, because it's said to be the worst place in the world – the place where people become lost for ever. It's where gaolers brainwash the prisoners until they have no memories of their real lives.'

'It's called re-education,' said Elena at once, glaring. 'Brainwashing was outlawed years ago.'

'Whatever you call it, you know as well as I do that it's a very particular kind of mental torture,' said Elisabeth. 'I *know* what goes on inside Pitesti.' Huddled next to her, Zoia thought, Oh no you don't. Not everything.

'But one day the prison walls will be torn down,' said Elisabeth, her voice full of anger and contempt. 'And then the world will see all your cruel secrets.'

Elena said, 'Pitesti's a useful place. It's where troublesome cats like you are put. Once inside, you'll be forgotten by the world.'

'You're so naive, aren't you?' said Elisabeth. 'Don't you know there is no such thing as ultimate forgetting – that traces, once impressed on the memory, are indestructible.'

'Don't flatter yourself,' said Elena tersely. Elisabeth shrugged and turned up the deep collar of her coat as if to shut them all out. In the strong sunlight her profile was fragile and her skin like ivory. Zoia could not help staring at her, because she had forgotten how small and fragile Elisabeth was, and how extremely lovely. She glanced at Elena and knew a moment of doubt. Was this really right? Shouldn't people be allowed to speak out against what they believed to be injustices? Zoia knew, of course, that nothing really unjust was going on – Annaleise would not ally herself with anything wrong or unfair – but it was not so long since people had fought wars for the right to speak their minds. Wasn't that all Elisabeth had been doing? And what about her husband and her little boy who would be left without a mother? The boy could not be much more than a baby.

Then Annaleise, who had been looking out of the car's window, turned her head and sent Zoia a smile. It was their own private smile, and Zoia relaxed because, of course, this *was* all right. The Valk creature was dangerous and rallies and protests against the government and the Party could not be allowed. Elisabeth's husband would have to get on without his wife. He would look after the child like other men had to look after children.

The car sped down the lonely road with the thick forests and smudgy mountains beyond. Bright winter sunshine still flooded the road, bathing the trees in emerald brightness. Zoia's head began to ache from the glare and from the knowledge that they were approaching Pitesti with its dreadful history. She closed her eyes against the dazzle, but the headache increased and she started to feel sick from the jolting of the car. As they rounded a sharp curve, nausea rolled over her in such insistent waves that she sat upright and cried out in panic that they must stop and let her get out.

Stumbling to the roadside, she bent over, retching miserably, sobbing with humiliation because it was dreadful, degrading, to be sick like a drunken beggar with Elena and Annaleise watching. But after a few minutes the spasms ceased and she mopped her face as well as she could with her sleeve and climbed back into the car, saying she was sorry, so sorry, but the journey had been such a long one.

She sank into an uncomfortable half slumber, only dimly aware that they had reached Pitesti itself, although she roused sufficiently to notice that it was clean and attractive and there were churches and pleasingly laid-out parks. Elena's voice said, 'We are here,' and Zoia opened her eyes and saw the rearing bulk of the gaol in front of them.

182

Something black and bitter closed around her. Pitesti Gaol. The prison of the lost ones. Rearing walls and rows of small mean windows, and a massive double door at the front – an ogre's front door, thought Zoia with dim memories of childhood fairytales. It was wreathed in a shimmering heat haze. If you were shut away behind those stone walls you would bake in this weather. You would not survive very long in this place. Sickness lurched in her stomach again, but this time she managed to fight it down.

She stayed in the car while the others got out, but she wound down the window to get some fresh air and see and hear what happened.

And now, at last, Elisabeth fought. She kicked and struggled, and clawed at Annaleise's face. When Elena and Vasile grabbed her arms, she sank to her knees and tried to curl into a defensive ball, the dark hair falling over her face. The three of them grabbed her and hauled her to a standing position, and between them carried her towards the huge doors. She was screaming by this time, still fighting them, but Vasile had her shoulders and Elena and Annaleise her legs. Even so, she tried to kick out at them. Then, across the heat and the listening silence of the gaol, she shouted, 'So this is your revenge because I wouldn't have you in my bed, is it, Madame Simonescu? This is what you do to people who reject you!'

I didn't hear right, thought Zoia, staring at Elisabeth, but the cold sickness was washing over her again, and she knew she *had* heard right. It was a spiteful lie, of course, Annaleise would tell her that afterwards. But she found she was clutching the windowsill of the car so tightly she had drawn blood from the palms of her hands.

Annaleise and Elena both ignored Elisabeth's angry accusations. Annaleise released her hold on Elisabeth for long enough to reach for what Zoia thought was a bell pull. She heard a faint jangling deep inside the prison, and then a small inset door opened. Elisabeth was dragged inside and the door clanged shut.

CHAPTER SEVENTEEN

Romania, early 1960s (continued)

The sounds of Elisabeth Valk's screams and the clanging of Pitesti Gaol's doors stayed with Zoia for a very long time. Sometimes she woke gasping and covered in sweat, hearing again the desperate screaming. Did she still scream from within whatever cell they had put her? Did she plead to be set free so she could be with her husband and child? But she shouldn't have plotted against the Party, argued Zoia. She should have remembered her responsibility to her son and not taken those massive risks.

Annaleise did not refer to Elisabeth's accusations. At first this worried Zoia, but then she realized that, of course, Annaleise would consider it beneath her to justify anything. Annaleise was clearly delighted with Zoia for having helped track Elisabeth down and Zoia could cope with any number of nightmares about screaming revolutionaries in order to please Annaleise. She could even cope with that image of Pitesti itself, crouching between the hills.

The evening after they took Elisabeth to Pitesti, Annaleise gave Zoia an expensive and luxurious dinner at a restaurant. Zoia had done immensely well for the Party, she said, pouring the wine.

Once Zoia would have said it was the purest luck that had led her to Elisabeth's illegal broadcasts – a chance remark by a customer in the bar – but she had learned to slant the truth in her favour, so she smiled in a deprecatory way, and asked what would happen to Elisabeth.

'She'll be kept in Pitesti most likely,' said Annaleise. 'She'll soon be forgotten.'

After the lavish dinner, they went back to Annaleise's apartment, and lying in the big soft bed, warm and replete from the lavish dinner and the love-making, Zoia wondered if this was one of the times when Annaleise would let her stay the whole night. She loved to lie watching Annaleise sleeping, and when it grew light she liked to slip out of bed and make breakfast. Once she had picked a flower out of the window box and laid it on the tray, but Annaleise had said, Good God, were the flowers wilting and falling onto the plates, so Zoia had not done it again.

The apartment had been newly fitted out since Zoia's last visit, and the rooms were all in shades of gunmetal grey, ebony black and soft sensual ivory. Zoia thought it very smart and sumptuous, and tried not to compare it with her own rather meagrely furnished set of rooms or to wonder how Annaleise could afford such beautiful things. Weren't there waiting lists for quite ordinary things these days? Zoia herself had been waiting six months for a kitchen stove for which she had diligently saved almost three months' wages from her wine-bar job.

As they lay on the bed she listened with attention to Annaleise talking about Elena, saying now her husband was First Secretary of the Romanian Communist Party he and Elena were people of considerable importance. Nicolae Ceauşescu had, in fact, recently met President Tito in Bucharest. The first of a series of what would be yearly meetings, said Annaleise, with unmistakable reverence. Zoia said it was gratifying that she had been able to help Elena.

'I work with Elena a good deal,' said Annaleise at once, 'so I get to know quite a lot about what's going on within the Party. We're very close, she and I.'

Zoia felt a spear of jealousy go through her at this, but managed not to show it.

'She's very pleased that we were able to close down that radio station. In fact, Zoia, she wants me to put forward an idea for your future.'

'What is it?' said Zoia, prepared to be suspicious.

'The Party have recently acquired a very large old house.' Annaleise's voice was deliberately offhand, and Zoia thought, Ah yes, we all know what 'acquired' means when the Party is involved. 'It's known locally as the Black House,' said Annaleise. 'I don't know what it's original name was – I don't think anyone does. It's one of those places whose name seems to have been lost or forgotten.'

As Elisabeth Valk's name is to be lost and forgotten. Zoia asked where this place, this Black House, was.

'Only about fifteen miles from here,' said Annaleise. 'Quite close to Resita. You remember Resita? We drove through it on the way to the Yugoslav border.'

Zoia did not say she knew Resita quite well because she had lived near it as a child. She said she remembered.

'Elena drove me out to see the place earlier today,' said Annaleise, with pride. 'It's in a very remote village, and the house is quite grim-looking from the outside, but once you get inside it's better than you expect. Perfectly habitable. The plan is for it to be a centre for what's called deep interrogation – detailed questioning of people suspected of working against the Party.'

'And they'd be held in this Black House while they were being questioned?' asked Zoia.

'Yes. It's quite large enough; there are about thirty bedrooms and some could be partitioned. People could be kept there very securely until it was known if they needed to be sent to one of the gaols. It would be a kind of halfway house.'

186

'Where would I come in?'

'You'd be virtually in charge of the entire running of it,' said Annaleise, and Zoia turned her head to look at Annaleise in surprise.

'You'd have to be properly trained and briefed beforehand, of course, in fact you'd have regular training sessions. And you'd have to be approved by senior members of the Party, but if Elena wants you – and she does – that will be little more than a formality.'

'Would I have to live in this Black House?'

'Yes, you'd need to be there all the time. Once the project was properly launched you'd be expected to oversee any suspects held there – some of them might be kept for several weeks. You'd have to coordinate the gathering of information from all parts of the country and arrange for it to be passed to Party Headquarters. There'd be the transporting of suspects and prisoners, as well. It would all have to be very secret and it would be a very responsible job, but I told Elena you could be trusted completely.' She glanced at Zoia. 'It's a small place,' she said, 'bit of a backwater, in fact.'

I know that, thought Zoia. I grew up in one of those villages.

'The Party want a backwater, though,' Annaleise went on. 'Elena told me so herself. They need a place where no one will suspect what's really going on. But for all its remoteness, it's to be an important centre for some of the Securitate's work.'

'I would be working directly for the Securitate?' This sounded quite promising. It sounded as if it might even be some kind of reward for the months of unremitting dreariness in the bars and cafes.

'You would. At times for the Politburo also.'

'I see,' said Zoia, thoughtfully.

Annaleise had been lying on her back, her hair spread over the pillow, but she turned onto her side and reached out a hand. Her nails were long and enamelled with scarlet; they began to trace little scratchy paths of pure pleasure over Zoia's breasts. But they had made love twice already, so Zoia tried to appear uninterested

187

in case she appeared to be too easy a conquest. It was no use, though. The light scratching of Annaleise's nails was dredging up a throbbing response and Annaleise would know it. She knew exactly how to reduce Zoia to a helpless slave.

'The Securitate has a very wide net,' she was saying, her fingernails beginning to scratch a little deeper into Zoia's skin. 'They employ spies at all levels, in all walks of life. We both know how it works, and we know the methods of persuasion sometimes needed to get at the truth. You might have to get involved in the questioning yourself. You might need to be a little bit hard on some people. Could you do that? It's all for the good of the country, remember.' As she said this her hand ceased its movements for a moment.

'I think I could,' said Zoia, her mind going back over the years to the labourer's cottage and the things done to her there. 'People have been cruel to me in the past.'

'Then you could hand out a bit of what you had to endure. Have what the Americans call payback.'

'Payback,' said Zoia, trying out the word, and felt a sudden surge of power. My turn to dish out the punishment. 'Yes,' she said after a moment. 'I could do whatever was necessary.'

'Good. Oh, very good.' Annaleise's voice was suddenly soft and thick with sexuality, and her hand slid lower, the questing fingers were no longer teasing but demanding. She sat up in the bed, and leaned across Zoia's prone body. Her hair, which had become unpinned, brushing against Zoia's thighs and as Zoia felt Annaleise's warm moist breath between her legs, she gasped, then gave herself up to the familiar tumult of sensations, and everything else vanished from her mind.

Much later, when she had washed and put on her clothes and joined Annaleise in the living room, Annaleise returned to the question of the Black House.

'We need to get a few more details clear before you go home,' she said, and she was no longer the sensuous partner of the bedroom, but the sharp ambitious woman who intended to work

188

her way up to a position of real power and influence. 'There's plenty of time to discuss it – your bus doesn't go for another hour, does it?'

That meant Zoia would have to queue up to catch the last bus to her own rooms, and she could hear an icy rain pelting against the windows which meant the bus would be crowded and she might not be allowed on.

'The house has to be provided with a cover,' said Annaleise. 'Those are Party orders. People in the immediate area must think it's been opened up for some innocent use. They mustn't be allowed to suspect what's really going on inside. That shouldn't be a problem, though. We'll think of something credible.'

She got up to open a bottle of wine. She seemed to Zoia to be drinking more these days. 'In your place,' said Annaleise, handing Zoia a glass, 'I'd be inclined to build up a bit of a local legend about the Black House as soon as possible. This is a country full of legends, folklore and myths: use whatever you can. Make the place feared and shunned. It's a small village; they're probably credulous and superstitious, and it shouldn't be difficult to foster a few dark stories.'

'Will there be anyone in the village itself worth watching?' said Zoia and Annaleise smiled.

'What a clever, intuitive creature you are. Do you know of the existence of the circle in life's pattern, Zoia? Fortune's wheel that turns the fate of men? Did your studies at the university cover any of the philosophers? Boethius?'

'Well, a bit,' said Zoia uncertainly, loath to display ignorance.

'There's the turning of a wheel in the pattern of this,' said Annaleise. 'Because there's a man living quite near the Black House who will be very worth watching indeed.' She sipped the wine for a moment. 'His name is Andrei Valk,' she said, and, as Zoia looked up in surprise, she smiled. 'Yes, Elisabeth's husband. If we could get evidence that he's playing the same kind of game as his wife, we would be very pleased indeed.'

It was then that Zoia knew Elisabeth had not lied when she flung that angry accusation at Annaleise. Annaleise was indeed wreaking revenge on Elisabeth Valk for having rejected her, and that revenge was not going to stop at Elisabeth's imprisonment. It was going to include her husband and perhaps even her entire family.

Zoia was impressed by the Black House – by its age and size – but she was not in awe of it or its former owners, whoever they had been. When she considered this, she thought it was because it was so neglected: its fabric was crumbling, paintwork and woodwork were dull and worm-eaten, and most of the upper-floor rooms were mouldy with damp. It was impossible to be in awe of people who could allow such decay to creep over a building.

Over the fireplace in the main hall was the outline of a coat of arms: Zoia tried to make out the motto, but the stone was too worn away. To whom had the crest belonged? What margravines or boyars or voivodes might once have walked these rooms and fought and loved and quarrelled and conspired here? What rich hunting parties might have stayed in the house when it was young, riding through the forest to be greeted by the doffed caps and tugged forelocks of villagers? That's where I'd have been, thought Zoia. Down in the village with the serfs, and not so very far away, either. She was not very knowledgeable about geographical distances, mostly because she had hardly travelled anywhere, but she thought her own village was about ten kilometres away. No one knew that, though. Not even Annaleise knew where Zoia came from, and this gave her confidence. The Black House did not belong to her and never would, but she could come and go as she liked, giving orders, surveying the surrounding countryside from the windows of the upper floors. She could feel herself on equal terms with the house's ghosts.

But what about her own ghosts?

One day she walked through the overgrown grounds, trying to

work out exactly where the Black House's boundaries lay. A track led down to the high-road between the trees: it was just wide enough for a car and there were already deep ruts made by the Securitate's jeeps. The ancient forest that once had covered this hillside, had almost vanished and the remaining trees were dry and twisty-looking, their roots and trunks buried in the thick undergrowth. But there were splashes of colour everywhere: gentians and star flowers and Zoia was enjoying these. She had almost reached the foot of the hill when she caught sight of something deep in the trees, something that was not part of the forest or the undergrowth, but something that, even from this distance, dredged up the very darkest of her ghosts.

Her heart began to bump with fear, and she was plummeted back into the past.

It had been an afternoon when her father came home more drunk than usual, and began berating Zoia's mother for not having food ready for him. She scurried about the tiny scullery, setting pots to boil and cutting bread, her hair falling over her face in her panic-stricken haste. But when Zoia and her sisters went to help and Zoia said they should throw the food in Father's face, she said they must forgive him because he had a thwarted life and no money. Zoia and her sisters did not know what thwarted meant, but they knew what it meant when Father came into the room they shared, the girls on one side of a thin curtain, the boys on the other, and they knew what it meant when he seized whichever of the girls was nearest. The three boys said one night they would stand up to him and defend their sisters from his beatings and from the way he slid his fingers inside their clothes. It was a sin, they said, and as the girls got older the stroking would lead to other things. Zoia, who was eight, did not really understand this, but her eldest sister, who was eleven, seemed to. Over the years they had made a lot of plans to stand up to their father, but they never did. Zoia did not think any of them dared.

But her father had heard Zoia's remark about throwing the food in his face, so today she was the one to be grabbed and subjected to the swishing leather belt. She submitted without struggling, because when his violence was at its height it was no use fighting back; he was as strong as three men put together. But she had discovered that while it was not possible to shut out the pain and fear entirely, it was possible to make it a bit easier by reciting in her head the pieces of poetry she learned at school. She tried to do it tonight, but for the first time the poetry failed her, and something snapped inside her driving out the fear and engulfing her with cold hatred for her father.

After he had finished beating her, she crept into a corner of the cottage, wrapping her arms round her as she always did, and waited for him to go up the rickety stairs to the space under the roof to sleep off the drink, which he always did. Would he do it today? How drunk was he?

It seemed he was very drunk indeed. Zoia heard him climb onto the bed, and within a very few minutes he had fallen into repulsive snoring sleep. She waited a while longer, her heart thudding, scarcely aware of the pain of her bruised back and legs. Her brothers and sisters were somewhere outside – they all had tasks to do on Saturday when it was not a school day – and her mother was cleaning pots in the scullery. Zoia took a deep breath and went up the stairs, moving a bit awkwardly because of the beating, and praying the worn treads would not creak and give her away.

The tiny sliver of room smelt hot and sour from the belched and farted beer. Her father lay on the bed, half on his side, still fully dressed, his eyes closed, his face the colour of bad cheese, a dribble of saliva running from his mouth. Zoia hated him so much it burnt up her whole body. Did she hate him enough to do what she had planned? How would she do it? She smiled, because she knew exactly how. The thick leather belt with the hard shiny buckle was hanging on the end of the bed, as it always was, and when Zoia picked it up the leather felt strong but soft. It would wrap round a neck very easily indeed.

He was in such a deep drunken sleep he was not even aware of Zoia kneeling on the edge of the bed and looping the belt round his neck. For a moment it lay there like a thick flat snake, then Zoia slotted one end through the buckle of the other end and pulled hard. At once his eyes flew open and he stared straight at her, then gasped, gusting stale beer-breath sickeningly into her face. He would not gust his horrid beer-belch into any of them ever again. Zoia kept her mouth firmly shut so as not to breathe in more of the smell than necessary, and pulled again on the leather. This time it tightened all the way to his neck, and the buckle bit into his skin so that beads of blood sprang out. He grunted and flailed with his hands, threshing and writhing like a hooked fish, but, as Zoia had hoped, he was too fuddled from the beer to put up a real fight. If he fought properly she would let go and run away, pretending she had not done anything.

But he did not fight. He plucked feebly at whatever was constricting his throat, too far gone even to realize that by knocking Zoia away – which he could easily have done – he could free himself. Zoia was beyond fear by this time. She kept hold of the belt, and although she thought there was a step on the stairs behind her she dare not let go for long enough to look round.

Her father's face was flooded with scarlet and his eyes bulged – they were flecked with blood and his tongue was protruding from his mouth. Zoia lost all sense of time. There was nothing in the world any longer but the feel of the leather and the harsh choking sounds of the man on the bed as he slowly strangled. The scarlet deepened to crimson, and livid purple blotches showed on his cheeks. He's *dying*, said an exultant voice inside her head. He's dying and once he's dead everything will be better.

From a long long way off, she could hear a voice telling her to come away, to let go of the belt. Then someone prised her hands free and she saw they were bloodied and bruised and that some of the nails were broken and bent back from where she had forced the belt tight. But the thing on the bed had stopped struggling. Its eyes were fixed and staring, the coloured parts rolled up leaving only round white globes.

Someone was crying very hard. Zoia looked round to see who this might be and realized it was her mother. It struck her as extremely silly that her mother should cry, because there was no longer anything to cry about. There would never be anything to cry about again. It seemed a long time before the crying finally stopped, and Zoia's mother wiped her eyes and face, and took Zoia's hand. Best they should go downstairs now, she said. Her face was creased and still tear-stained, and her voice shook, but she asked if Zoia knew what had just happened.

'Of course I know,' said Zoia. 'I've killed him. I did it for us all. For you and for the others.' She saw, then, that her brothers and sisters were huddled together at the top of the stairs, their eyes huge and frightened. 'I know it was wrong,' she said. 'You aren't supposed to kill people, so I 'spect I'll have to be punished. I'll confess next Saturday though, and if I explain why I did it, it'll probably be all right.'

'You mustn't confess,' said her mother at once. 'Zoia, you must promise never to tell anyone what you've just done.'

'Oh yes, I have to tell the truth.' The nuns at school said you should always tell the truth; if not, God would be very cross and Jesus would weep. 'I'll be given a penance,' she said.

Mother seemed not to be listening; she reached for a thick woollen scarf, said they were going on a small trip, just a very little walk.

'Why? Have I got to confess it now? Is next Saturday too late?' Killing somebody would be a mortal sin, and mortal sins were very bad indeed. Perhaps you had to confess them right away.

Her mother said, 'Yes, Zoia, it's because you're going to

194

confess.' She looked down at her. 'You have to keep silent,' she said. 'And if you won't promise to keep silent, then you'll have to be silenced.'

CHAPTER EIGHTEEN

Silenced. The word and the way her mother said it, frightened Zoia. People in stories were sometimes silenced. If it was a fairy-story the silencing might be done by throwing them into a dungeon or imprisoning them in a windowless castle where they would be forgotten for ever. She knew those stories were not real, of course, but she knew other stories about people being silenced – stories that the grown-ups whispered and that were very real indeed. In the grown-up world 'silencing' could mean far worse than dungeons. It could mean your tongue might be cut out of your mouth so you could never speak again. It could even mean you might be killed.

Zoia knew Mother would not do anything like that, but still . . . She glanced up at her and began to feel far more frightened than when she crept up the creaky cottage stairs to strangle her father.

They did not walk through their village and onto the road as she had expected. Instead, they walked out of what people called the back of it, onto the fields, with the forest in the distance, and the mountains beyond. It was nice here in summer, with sun-light pouring down over the mountains and glinting on the trees, but there was no sunlight this afternoon. Everywhere was grey and cold, the trees had swirls of pale mist clinging to them and the mist lay thickly on the fields, so it was like walking through damp grey wool. Zoia shivered as the mist curled around her ankles and wished she had brought a coat, but her mother had not given her time.

They walked fast and every few paces her mother looked over her shoulder as if afraid they were being followed. With her scragged-back hair and frightened eyes she looked like a bolting hare. When they were across the field and at the edge of the forest, she stopped and pointed and said, 'I'm sorry, Zoia, but you'll have to go in there. It's the best hiding place there is.'

Zoia looked about her, puzzled, not seeing anything except the fields behind them and the trees in front. Then her mother pointed again, and this time she did see and it was absolutely the worst thing she had ever seen in her life.

On the edge of the forest was a small building, low and ugly, made of pale old stones, crumbly and pitted and covered with moss and lichen. It was not very high – a tall grown-up, standing on tiptoe, might just touch the lower edge of the roof with their fingertips, and the roof itself was domed like the hairless skull of an old, old man. At the centre was a wooden door, and on each side of this door, just under the roof, were two windows exactly in line with each other, oval-shaped and framed by lichen-encrusted bricks. There was a terrible thick blackness about these narrow windows; they were like sightless eyes with the lichen for the eyelashes. They were dead, empty eyes, and yet if you looked at them for too long they might blink. It looked exactly like a stone face to Zoia, as she stood there staring at it. A massive stone face jutting up out of the ground, watching everyone with its blank staring eyes.

'It's the old well-house,' said Zoia's mother. 'It used to serve several of the villages until everyone was given water in pipes and taps in the houses. But we used to hide here as children – it was our secret hiding place. No one ever found us and no one will find you. You'll be quite safe.'

But Zoia did not think she would be safe at all. She was dreadfully afraid that this stone face had once belonged to a real person – a monster or even a giant – and that the empty eyes might suddenly blink into life.

When her mother pulled her forward Zoia resisted, but her mother was surprisingly strong and Zoia found herself being half carried towards the building. She thought she would make sure not to look up, but at the last minute she could not help it and in that moment, something flew out of the trees, disturbing the branches so that shadows shivered across the stone face.

She hoped the door would be locked and they would have to go back home and forget about hiding, but it was not. There was a black hook latch across it, and when her mother lifted this the door swung open with a groaning creak, like an extremely old man trying to move after a long time or like something dead trying to come back to life. A dreadful sour dankness breathed outwards; it was a smell that made you think of dishcloths that needed boiling in soda crystals or old drains that had been clogged for years. As her mother half pushed her inside, this bad-drains smell closed over Zoia and she began to shiver uncontrollably. The well-house was not much bigger than the main room of their cottage, and although it was dark some light came in through the open door and the two eye-windows.

In the centre, taking up at least half the floor, was what looked like a square black iron box, a few inches deep. Squitch-grass grew round its edges and a handle was set into it on one side. Dozens of scuttly black-beetles, disturbed by the light from the open door, ran about, and Zoia turned to look pleadingly at her mother, because she could not possibly stay in here. Her mother could not mean to leave her here.

But it seemed she did. She pointed to the shallow iron box, and said, 'That's the lid over the shaft of the well. There used to be a winch mechanism and the villagers would come along the lane to fill their buckets with water, then carry them back to their houses. I don't remember that, but my mother told me how people used to meet at the well each morning to get their water. I don't know if the well is dry or not, but the cover's always in place so no one can fall in. The cover will be too heavy for you to move, but even so you mustn't go near it.'

Zoia gulped and said, 'How long will I be here?'

'Not long.'

'I won't be here in the dark, will I?'

'No.' Her mother suddenly bent down and gathered Zoia to her in a hug. This was so unusual that Zoia was not sure what to do. Her mother never hugged any of them; she was always too busy and too fearful of Zoia's father. She put her arms round her mother's neck and hugged her back. It made her feel a lot better, but after a moment her mother stepped back, and said in a trembly voice, 'One of your brothers will come for you later today.'

'Not you?' The memory of that sudden hug was still warm round Zoia's heart.

'I may not be able to. But you won't be here long, I promise.' She paused, then said, 'Goodbye, Zoia. Always be a good girl,' and then she was gone, and there was the sound of the door creaking back into place and the hook latch being fastened across the outside.

Zoia sank miserably on the floor, trying not to cry, remembering her mother's promise that she would not be here when it was dark. Light came in through the windows and fell across the floor in the same oval shapes so it was as if a second pair of eyes were watching her in here. She tried not to look at the floor-eyes and sat with her back against the door so the eyes could not see her.

She had learned to tell the time at school, and she thought it might now be about three o'clock. How long away was the dark? Six o'clock? Then she would only be here for about three hours, she could pass the time by saying the poetry she had learnt.

Between poems she rattled the door as hard as she could, but the latch stayed firmly in place and the door did not move.

The hours went on and on, the light coming through the eye-windows began to fade, and there was no sound of anyone coming to let her out. Zoia waited and waited. She tried not to look at the well cover or think about the deep shaft under it. Most of all she tried not to think about the stone head coming back to life.

The bad-drains smell was making her feel very sick. This was worrying, because it would be terrible to be sick here where she could not see anything. She tried to open the door again so she could at least be sick outside on the grass but it still did not yield, so she swallowed as hard as she could to keep the vomit down. In the end she could not hold it in any longer and she ran blindly into a corner and was sick as tidily as she could manage. It made her feel cold and shivery, and it added to the bad smells already in here. She walked to the corner farthest from the pool of sick and sat down.

The threads of light had almost completely vanished when, finally, she heard the wedge on the door being removed. Zoia hoped it would be her mother, but it was one of her brothers, the second eldest. She shot out of the terrible, sick-smelling darkness as fast as she could, and drew in deep gulps of the cold evening air. She wanted to be back in her home – she was thirsty and hungry – but she also wanted to be a long way away from the stone face.

Her brother would not look at her as they walked back across the field, and so Zoia, in a voice that was dry and cracked from crying and from being sick, asked what was happening. Remembering what she had done earlier in the day and how her mother had cried before making her hide in the well-house, she said, 'Is Mother all right?'

But her brother did not reply. He hunched his shoulders, and walked faster so she had to run to keep up with him.

*

She never saw her mother again and no one mentioned her. Zoia did not dare ask anyone what had happened to her. Life in the cottage went on. The meals were cooked mostly by her eldest sister, who was fourteen and whom Mother had always said was a good little housewife and would make any man a fine wife. The others helped.

Zoia's father's body had been taken away. Zoia thought there would be a funeral, but no one told her when it was, and none of her brothers and sisters attended any kind of service. Once or twice the neighbours murmured something about 'Pity', and pursed their lips if Zoia's family walked through the village.

It was not until she was fifteen and her eldest sister was leaving the cottage to marry one of the farm workers in the next village, that she told Zoia what had happened. Their mother had strangled their father, she said, her face serious and sad. Zoia was old enough to know the truth now – she was passing it on to her. After the years of beatings and drunkenness, their mother had finally turned on their father and strangled him with his own belt. Then she had run to the village priest to confess and ask him to tell the Poliţia Comunitară what she had done.

The priest had done so and their mother had been taken away to prison because she was a murderess. It was not 'Pity' Zoia had heard the neighbours whispering all those years ago; it was Pitesti. Her mother had been taken to Pitesti Gaol on the very same afternoon Zoia was hiding inside the well-house.

She had not been at the gaol for very long. A month later she had been taken out to the yard behind one of the cell blocks, stood against a wall and shot. It was what happened to murderesses, and serve them right. Zoia's sister said their mother had not died at the first round of firing because the soldiers forming the firing squad had all been drinking the night before – most of them had still been half drunk, and their aim had been wide. She had died at the second round of firing, though.

*

Zoia never dreamed about her mother being shot or her father choking out his life, but the thought of Pitesti itself remained like a hard lump of bitter misery inside her. On that nightmare car journey with Elisabeth Valk, the sudden realization of where they were bound, had brought the misery chokingly into her throat, sending her tumbling out of the car to be sick on the roadside. But if she did not dream about her parents, she dreamed about the well-house. Even when she went to university she had nightmares about being dragged towards the sinister stone head, sobbing and struggling, waking drenched in sweat with tears pouring down her face.

And now, in the grounds of the Black House, she was facing another well-house – not the one she had hidden in all those years ago, of course – this one was older and more encrusted with lichen and moss because of standing in the deep shadow of the old forest all its life. But other than this it was almost a mirror image of the one in Zoia's childhood village. The stone face. The place of punishment. The place for being silenced. She stood looking at it for a very long time, and it was only when she suddenly realized the sun had gone in and night was creeping across the hillside, that she turned away and went back up the track to the house.

It was not very remarkable that there should be two such well-houses, of course; probably the same builder had built them. There might be a whole series of similar well-houses in this part of the country – a succession of stone faces, places of punishment.

After a while Zoia began to understand the work she was expected to carry out for Annaleise and Elena Ceauşescu and for the Party. Results, Annaleise said at the very beginning, the Party wanted results. Zoia must deliver them.

She did deliver them. She gradually built up a network of people who listened and watched – her own months in the cafes and bars meant she could train others – and after a while she gained sufficient knowledge and confidence to send the minor officials of the

Securitate running this way and that. There was someone who must be investigated in Carasova or Moldova Noua, she said, handing out addresses and names. Or there were people in Dognecea suspected of dodging the land laws and it must be looked into. When the suspects were brought to the Black House in the big jeeps, Zoia saw to it that they were held in solitary confinement in one of the many rooms until the Party's interrogators came sweeping through the night in one of their sleek cars.

The Securitate were pleased with her. After a little while they suggested she take a more active part in the interrogations themselves.

'A reward for all your good work,' Annaleise said, smiling, and Zoia thought anything that made Annaleise smile like that must be worth doing.

The interrogations usually took place in the big stone-floored room beneath the house, deep in the hillside. It had been fitted out as a wine cellar, but she thought it might once have had a more sinister use. Those long-dead overlords who had lived here would not have flinched at throwing their enemies into these cold cells.

Zoia sat with the two Securitate men behind the long table that had been set up at one end of the cellar. They had pens and notepaper and carafes of water. Until today it had been one of Zoia's task to make sure these things were set out; now she was one of the people writing on the paper and sipping the water.

The first interrogation was of a weasel-faced man caught printing seditious leaflets. The leaflets were set on the table, and Gheorghe Pauker, the more senior of the Securitate men, read one, pursing his thick lips.

'You challenge the Party's practice of collective farming, do you?' he said, looking at the weasel-faced man.

'Yes. It's cruel and barbaric.'

'It's a system based on common ownership of resources and on pooling of labour and income,' said Pauker coldly.

'What about the other cooperative principles of freedom of

choice and democratic rule?' said the man defiantly. 'Only one quarter of the peasant farmers gave up their land voluntarily. The rest were beaten and deported.'

'The *kibbutzim* in Israel are collective farms, and they work very well,' said Pauker.

'That was voluntary collectivism,' said the man. '*Kolkhoz* in Stalin's Russia was a different story.'

'You aren't here to argue,' said Pauker angrily. 'You're here to answer for sedition.'

'I am here to argue. The people I work with believe collectivism – cooperative farming – is only the start. The next step will be turning people from their homes and creating apartment buildings for tenants. Every person to be given one cell in an egg box. And,' he said, his eyes alight with anger, 'you can throw me into as many prisons as you like, I'll still say what I think.'

'But,' said Pauker, 'you won't say it where anyone who matters can hear you.' He went to the door and called to the guard outside, and the weasel-faced man was led away, his hands still bound. Zoia realized the man's name had never been mentioned.

'Where will they take him?' she asked Pauker.

'Pitesti,' he said, off-handedly. 'He's guilty of subversion, no question about it. But his ideas will be lost.'

'And the man? Will he be lost, as well?'

'Oh yes,' he said, sounding uninterested, and then, with more animation, 'Are we having lunch here? You served some very good wine on my last visit.'

A small stock of wine was kept for visiting Party officials, and Zoia had learnt what was good and what was not. She said, 'Lunch will be ready for you shortly, and I've asked for wine to be served.'

'Good. I always find these interrogations hungry work,' said Pauker. 'The prisoners always stink to high heaven.'

All the prisoners stank to some degree because they were usually kept in one of the cell-like rooms of the Black House without water or washing facilities, and the weasel-faced man had been there for nearly two weeks. Zoia did not say any of this, though.

Some prisoners were defiant and articulate, like the weasel-faced man, but others were frightened and squirmed away from the truth, trying to twist what they had done to make it seem acceptable. It was never acceptable, of course, and they never squirmed away from the truth altogether. Zoia rarely got it wrong and almost everyone who was brought to the Black House left it for incarceration inside Pitesti Gaol. They might be there for years, joining the ranks of the forgotten ones. Zoia's mother had not been there for years, she had not even been there for months, but the end result was the same. They were all silenced and eventually forgotten.

Occasionally Zoia felt uneasy at the factory-like despatching of these people to Pitesti Gaol, but it was important not to think too deeply about what happened to them there. You could almost argue they were luckier than her mother had been, because they still had their lives. Annaleise said their punishment was deserved.

'In some countries and in some centuries they would have been executed,' she said. 'Shot.'

Zoia thought, But people are sometimes shot for things they have not done. They sometimes take the blame to protect others. A mother protecting a child, for instance ... And even the ones who are shot don't die instantly if the firing squad has been drinking.

She had been at the Black House for almost a year when Annaleise arrived one night, and without preamble said, 'We have decided on a disguise for the house.'

'Yes?' They had been waiting for this, because there was now quite a lot of coming and going, and there was an increasing danger that the people down in the village might grow inquisitive. Zoia said, 'What is the disguise?'

Annaleise said, 'How would you feel about looking after unwanted children?'

*

It did not happen all at once, of course. Orphanages did not spring up overnight, and it was some time before the orphanage within the Black House – the 'disguise' as Annaleise termed it – was established. But it did not take so very long and Zoia knew it came about because of one of the new Party laws.

'One of Elena's laws,' Annaleise said with pride. 'Her husband wanted to increase the birth rate, and she thought up this regime. Abortions are illegal, of course, but contraception itself is now prohibited. And – a very clever addition, this one – childless couples are required to pay higher taxes.'

'Isn't all that a bit harsh?' asked Zoia after a moment.

'Oh no,' said Annaleise. 'Elena is always very fair. Very just. As she told me herself, she has even biblical authority for the law. Genesis. God slew Onan when he withdrew and spilled his seed on the ground. That's clear enough, isn't it?'

'Well, yes.' The nuns at school had skimmed rather rapidly over this part of the Bible, although there had been furtive giggling among some of the older girls about it.

'Anyway, women who are over the age of forty-five, or have at least five children already, are exempt.' Annaleise paused, then said, 'But there is an unfortunate result of this law, Zoia. Much as I admire Elena, just between ourselves, I will admit that there's an unfortunate outcome.'

'Unwanted children,' said Zoia, understanding at once. 'And a lot of people won't have enough money to feed them.' Memory spun an image for a moment: herself and her brothers and sisters hungrily eating the thin, unsatisfactory stew which had been made with the cheapest cut of meat obtainable, and filling up on plain bread afterwards.

'Exactly,' affirmed Annaleise. 'Children whom parents can neither feed nor clothe.'

'And a whole crop of orphanages springing up because of it.'

'Yes. The State will fund such places, of course, although it can't be on any very lavish scale.'

Zoia said she still thought it rather a harsh law.

'I don't think so. Contraception might be forbidden, there's still good old-fashioned abstinence. They're not actually forced to have children at all, these—'

'Peasants?' It came out more angrily than Zoia had meant, but she had felt a stab of bitterness at Annaleise's words. She looked at her, and thought: when did you ever practise abstinence! When did you ever suffer hunger? Not just a few pangs because a meal was delayed, but permanent aching hunger for weeks on end? But she had already gone further than was wise, so she smiled and said she was sure Elena and the Party knew what they were doing. Elena was so intelligent, said Zoia.

It did the trick; Annaleise smiled the wolf-smile that meant she would share Zoia's bed tonight.

And so the children came to the Black House in twos and threes, in forlorn trickles, sometimes brought furtively by guilty-looking mothers or grandmothers, less often, by defiant fathers. Occasionally minor members of the Politburo brought them, although this did not happen very often.

Zoia dealt efficiently with these children, seeing they were fed at regular intervals, making the best use she could of the sparse money doled out. Sometimes the smallest children cried for quite long periods. It was irritating and exhausting and it took Zoia back to the unhappy years of her own childhood, but she could just about cope with it.

But Annaleise could not. 'That constant wailing drives me distracted,' she said, angrily. 'I can put up with a good deal, but not grizzling babies for hours on end. For pity's sake shut the brats away somewhere.'

'But they're too little. They might fall and hurt themselves and lie injured without anyone knowing.'

'Then we'll get one of the workmen to fashion something to keep them enclosed,' said Annaleise. 'Other places do it – they have a kind of half cage with compartments. I've seen them. It's up to you, Zoia, but I'm not coming here again if that row's going on.' She stood in the draughty hall and looked about her disparagingly. 'This place is falling apart. If I'm to come here again, you'll have to get it in better condition. I'm not staying in a house where rainwater spatters into the rooms and gutters leak.' She made for the door and Zoia said, desperately, 'But there's no money for repairs.'

'Don't be naive. Hive some off the allowance and spruce the place up a bit. Let me know when it's done and I'll see about coming back for a night here or there.'

Zoia did as Annaleise wanted. She was not very happy about the cages for the smallest children, but it meant Annaleise came back which was all that mattered. And looked at sensibly, there was no point in giving young children elaborate meals which might make them sick: plain fare was much better. It had been what she and her brothers and sisters had been given, and it had not harmed them. There was no point, either, in dressing the children in fancy clothes which no one would see and which they would soil within twenty-four hours. Clothes were difficult to get anyway, and the cost was prohibitive if you did get them.

The years went along and the Black House's sinister reputation became safely established in the area. Not a place to approach after dark, and not really a place to approach in the daylight, either. The people who knew it was an orphanage were the ones who had placed children there, and they did not talk about it. They considered it shameful and sad. Somewhere best ignored and best forgotten.

Zoia's stock within the Party rose quite high. Elena Ceaușescu was known to be pleased with her work, and if Elena was pleased, Annaleise was pleased. When Annaleise was pleased, she visited Zoia frequently – she still turned Zoia's bones to water simply by touching her hand. She prepared little suppers for Annaleise herself, going down to the cold-floored sculleries and cooking appetizing meals, and she made sure that on those nights a big log fire burned in the hearth, and fresh sheets were on the old-fashioned tester bed. Life was not ideal, but life was never ideal. Zoia was as content as she could hope to be.

And then the spying snooping child, Mara, was brought to the Black House.

CHAPTER NINETEEN

Romania, early 1970s

When Zoia caught her outside the room with the caged children, Mara was very frightened indeed. She was afraid Zoia meant to shut her in the room itself – perhaps in one of the cages like Hansel and Gretel. She had always thought Hansel and Gretel was just a story, but now she was not so sure. Supposing it was true? Suppose all the stories her grandmother had told were true and there really were wolves and witches and giants?

But Zoia did not put her in the room with the crying babies. She took Mara back to the long room with the empty beds and the mushroom growths on the ceiling and this time the door was locked. For a while Mara sat on the windowsill and stared outside, trying to see Matthew's house across the tops of the trees, wondering what to do if he did not tell the secrets and she had to stay here for ever. Eventually she fell into a frightened sleep on one of the beds, waking at intervals to sit up and peer through the darkness in case the black stove was lurching towards her or the mushroomy things had fallen onto the bed. Somewhere before dawn it occurred to her that she might be inside a nightmare and none of this was really happening. This was such a comforting idea she promised herself she would soon wake up in her own bed at home, with grandmother downstairs and her little brother asleep in the next room. For a moment she could see Mikhail's small curled-up outline under the sheets in his small bed, and she seized on the image and went to sleep with it in her mind.

She woke to find she was still in the dreadful room but it was morning now because daylight showed at the windows which made Mara feel a bit better. Perhaps locking-up for the night had been the punishment. Probably Matthew would already have told them all the secrets, and she would soon be allowed to go home.

Presently a woman she had not seen before came in with a mug of milk and a bowl of some porridge stuff. The milk was a bit watery and the porridge was lumpy and tasted faintly of cabbage, but Mara was hungry so she ate and drank it all. Afterwards the woman took her to the lavatory which was a terrible place with rusty pipes and a huge wooden box encasing the lavatory itself and damp floorboards all round it. When Mara ran water from the tap it came out rusty, but she managed to wash her face and hands.

The woman was waiting for her when she went out; she took Mara's hand and led her down the stairs. Waiting in the big dim hall, was Zoia. She gave the woman a nod of dismissal and took Mara outside. Bright sunshine flooded the courtyard and the hillside; it was dazzling after the dim rooms and Mara put up her free hand to shield her eyes. A man came out of one of the outbuildings to join them. He was wearing a dark uniform – Mara thought he might be one of the people who drove the jeep – and he had little squinty eyes. They led her down the slope and, just as Mara was starting to think she might be going home after all, they turned off the path and went into the trees.

It was cooler here and everywhere was very still, almost as if they had stepped into a different world or even a different time. Mara remembered her grandmother's tales again, but if this was a fairytale it was not the kind where a friendly woodcutter or a passing prince in disguise would come along to rescue her.

211

'We're here,' said Zoia. 'This is our place of punishment.' She pointed, and Mara saw with horror that in front of them was a lump of stone thrusting up out of the ground like a giant's face. There were narrow slitty windows for eyes, and over the door were lumpy pitted stones for a nose.

'It's an old well-house,' said Zoia. There was a note of fear in her voice.

Mara was staring at the stone structure in panic. She did not believe it was a well-house at all. She was dreadfully afraid it was the hacked-off head of a giant, like in one of her grandmother's stories. She wanted to run as far away from it as she could, but Zoia had a tight hold of her, and the man was opening the door. It stuck for a moment, then gave way, swinging inwards to show a dreadful gaping blackness like a toothless mouth. When Zoia and the man began to pull her forward, Mara struggled, then screamed for help. Her voice echoed through the forest, sending birds flying wildly up from the trees, but no one came running to see what was happening. She screamed again, but this time Zoia smacked her across the cheek to silence her. Mara gasped and began to cry. Tears ran down her face and into her mouth because Zoia and the man were holding her hands and she could not wipe them away.

They had got her to the door when Zoia suddenly half turned to look back towards the track. Mara looked as well, and saw movement within the dappled sunlight of the forest. Her heart gave a thump of hope. Someone heard my screams after all. The guard stood up straighter, and Zoia's face lit up and in a soft voice, she said, 'It's Miss Simonescu.' And then, with a kind of reverence, 'It's Annaleise.'

Annaleise. The last shreds of hope dropped away from Mara and she knew there was no longer any point in trying to escape because she would be caught and carried back. Annaleise was no longer a dark wraith, a fearful whisper in the playground, a prowling ghost waiting to pounce on children, she was a real person. She wore a long dark coat with the hem trailing on the ground and the deep collar was turned up to frame her face. Her skin was pale and smooth as if she had been carved out of ivory, and she had black hair looped up into a kind of coil on top of her head. Little tendrils had escaped from this coil; they curled over her neck like crawly spiders' legs.

'Miss Simonescu likes to oversee punishments whenever possible,' said Zoia, and Annaleise said, 'Sadly, punishments are sometimes necessary, especially for children who see things they shouldn't.' Her voice made Mara think of cold lumps of granite in the depths of winter.

'The cages,' whispered Mara, staring at her. 'The babies in cages, that's what you mean, isn't it? But I wouldn't talk about them, not to anyone. I really wouldn't.'

'But we have to make sure of that,' said Annaleise – Mara could not think of her as Miss Simonescu; in the stories she was always just Annaleise. 'We have to show you what happens to silly little girls who might tell their friends and families about secrets they shouldn't have seen.' She took a step nearer and Mara cowered back. 'Secrets,' she said softly. 'I hear your friend Matthew hasn't shared his secrets with us, Mara.' Her eyes, which Mara had expected to be dark, were pale, like pebbles.

'Matthew doesn't know any secrets. It's no good keeping me here. He can't tell you anything.'

'Not even when he knows you're shut away in the place of punishment?' said Annaleise, and Mara sent a scared glance at the dreadful well-house.

'How long will I be here?' she said.

'Until we know all we need to know about Andrei Valk,' said Annaleise.

'We don't mind what we have to do to find out,' said Zoia.

Mara saw that although they wanted to make sure she did not tell people about the cages, Matthew's father was of far greater interest.

Before she could screw up her courage to run away and hide in

213

the trees, Zoia and the guard had picked her up and carried her through the open door. Great swathes of pale cobwebs hung down over the opening as if they were strings of saliva inside the mouth. Zoia pushed them impatiently aside, but they still brushed against Mara's hair and her face. The bad-smelling darkness closed about her. It was smothering and confusing, and before she could gather her senses, she had been set down on the brick floor and Zoia and the guard were outside, closing the door. It scraped into place and the light was shut off altogether. She could just hear Annaleise and Zoia going away through the forest. She could hear their voices getting fainter and fainter.

She was inside the stone face, and panic swept over her. It wasn't a real stone face, of course, Mara knew that, deep down. Or was it? Supposing these weren't stones and bricks but bones and skin. Supposing those trickles of moisture weren't rain, but blood or the stuff that came out of people's eyes when they had colds. She reminded herself she was not locked in; there was no lock on the door. That meant all she had to do was find the door and she could be out in the forest, then she could run down the track and be home.

It was not absolutely pitch dark because of the eyeholes, but for the first few moments it nearly was. Mara's eyes adjusted slowly to the dimness, and she could eventually see the bricks of the walls and the floor. The floor ... At the centre was a black yawning hole. That's the well itself, she thought, staring at it. It was like a massive lipless mouth and round it was a tiny wall, only as high as Mara's ankles. She stared at it in horror. It would be a long deep tunnel, going down and down, and all kinds of things would live there. Worms and spiders and blind crawling things that did not like the light. If you fell down it you would never climb back up. The thing to do was not look at the well at all but to stay close to the wall, find the door and get out. Mara said this to herself several times.

The door was not easy to see, but it was situated between the

214

eyes, so she stood up and began to feel her way cautiously along the wall until the eyes were on each side of her. Here was the door: she could feel the break in the stones. She moved her hands all the way up and down, expecting to find a handle or a latch. But there was nothing. The door was old and its hinges had shrieked like a screaming animal when Zoia opened it, but it was a thick heavy door, and once shut it fitted absolutely flat and smooth into the stone walls.

Panic rose in her all over again, but she fought it down and tried to prise the door open with her fingernails. It would not budge. All that happened was that Mara tore several of her fingernails, which was just about the most painful thing in the world. She sank to the floor again, huddled against the door in the terrible darkness, putting her raw fingertips into her mouth to suck them clean of the blood. After a little while she tried again, trying to forget the spiky pain in her fingers. But it did not move, so she went to stand on tiptoe under one of the eyeholes, shouting to be let out. She shouted until her throat hurt, but she did not think anyone could hear. The eyehole was too high up for her to reach, and her voice bounced back on the brick walls, sounding muffled in the enclosed space.

She sat down again. The floor was hard and cold and there was a gritty feeling to it, but there was nowhere else to sit, and she could not stand up for hours and hours. Once she put her hand down by her side and felt a crackly little heap of something light and sad. A bird skeleton, thought Mara, snatching her hand back and shuddering.

The truth had better be faced – Sister Teresa said it was always better to face things head on, so you knew the whole truth. The whole truth here was that Mara was not going to get out until Zoia and Annaleise came back to let her out. They were leaving her inside the stone face until Matthew told them what they wanted to know about his father.

But Matthew did not know anything. Mara remembered this in

a terrible rush of fear. He did *not* know. 'There are secrets about your father,' she had once said to him on one of their walks to school, curious to see what he would say, but it had not worked. He had stopped and stared at her, and said, 'What secrets? What do you mean?'

Remembering this, she felt as if a huge clenched fist had come smacking out of the darkness and punched her in the throat.

When they asked Matthew about the secrets, even if he wanted to tell, he could not. He knew nothing.

Then how long would they leave her here?

The present

Theo had been typing at top speed, but when Mara realized she was imprisoned in the macabre old well-house indefinitely, he could not go on. He always identified closely with his characters, but this was far more than that. It was as if he was living through the whole thing with them. He could smell the sour darkness inside the well-house and if he half closed his eyes he could see the shadowy outline of the well cover. He could feel Mara's terror as if it was his own.

Had this woman, Zoia, actually existed? Annaleise had certainly existed – she was mentioned in Guff's book as being a close associate of Elena Ceauşescu, and according to the book had met an untimely death. Matthew had existed as well – he might still exist – and at some time in his life he had been to Melbray. If he really had done that sketch of Charmery – if he had been the one to make her look like that – then there must have been a strong link between them. Perhaps a love affair. If Matthew was still alive, he would only be in his late forties now – fifty at the most.

He took the sketch down from the wall and examined it yet again, deciding he needed to be sure that the hand who had created it had been the same hand that had drawn the convent pictures. He thought for a moment, then replaced the portrait, found his mobile and called the number of Lesley's studio flat in Earl's Court. It was a quarter to seven, a time when she might reasonably be expected to be at home. After she left the Slade, she had gone to work for a small auction house specializing in fine art, mostly helping with the restoring of paintings. According to Guff, who liked to send bulletins round the family, and who was Lesley's godfather, she was enjoying herself very much.

The phone rang for a long time and Theo was about to hang up when Lesley answered, sounding breathless.

'You sound as if you've just run upstairs,' said Theo.

'I have just run upstairs. In fact I've just run almost the entire length of the street because it's pelting down with rain – and then I heard the phone ringing two flights down, so I ran all the way up because there's no lift here.'

'Shall I call back in ten minutes?'

'No, I'm fine,' said Lesley. 'I'm just ferreting for a towel to dry my hair . . . Wait a minute . . .'

Theo waited, smiling at the endearing image of Lesley's short feathery hair with rain clinging to it. When she emerged from the towelling, he said, 'I'm at Fenn House for a couple of months. I don't know if you knew that?'

'Everyone knows it,' said Lesley. 'Guff was quite worried that you'd lapse into melancholy out there. He thought you might start communing with ghosts or something and he was planning on coming to see you.'

'By himself?' Guff was a gregarious soul who liked company when he travelled, and his journeys were always planned well in advance and with an attention to detail that would not have shamed a Victorian explorer bound for remote Tibetan peaks or the deserts of Araby.

'Nancy said she would drive him. It's all right though,' she said quickly as Theo drew in breath to swear, 'I headed them off. I said you had gone to Fenn to work and you wouldn't take kindly to interruptions. You did go there to work, didn't you?'

'More or less,' said Theo, knowing that by communing with ghosts, Guff meant Charmery. 'Lesley, on the subject of interruptions, are you by any remote chance free for a couple of days fairly soon? Say this weekend? I want you to help me with something.'

'What is it?'

Theo hesitated, then said, 'There's a sketch here of Charmery and I'd like your opinion on it.'

'I don't think I'm qualified to give opinions yet,' said Lesley doubtfully. 'And I don't remember ever seeing any sketch of Charmery at Fenn.'

'Nor do I. But there's one here now, and I'd like to find out a bit more about it. Just quietly and off the record.'

'Off the family's record, d'you mean?'

'Well, yes.'

'I'd have to jiggle a couple of things – the twins were coming up for the morning, but I can jiggle the twins,' she said.

'Would they mind being jiggled?'

'No, I can see them next weekend just as easily. I could probably take Monday as a day's holiday.'

'Could you? That direct train from Liverpool Street is probably still running,' he said.

'High noon on Saturday,' she said, and Theo heard the smile in her voice and knew she was remembering how Charmery had named it the High Noon Saturday train, and how she and Lesley – later Lesley's brothers – had made a small ritual about always travelling on it.

'I'll meet you in Norwich,' said Theo.

After he rang off he returned to the computer. It was starting to look as if he might have to read up on Romania's grim prison system from those years, and he contemplated this prospect with mixed feelings because it would be the darkest kind of research. It had better be done, though. He could try the library in Norwich when he drove out there to meet Lesley on Saturday, but although he could probably get the basics on Ceaușescu and the revolution, he wanted first-hand accounts of places, lists of names and dates, archived newspapers, communist-slanted articles as well as objective ones. The internet would provide some useful leads, of course, but there was nothing quite like handling and reading the real thing. Still, the worldwide web would be a good start. It was quarter past seven – was that too late to phone BT? He only needed to know how soon they could reinstate the landline to Fenn House so he could link up to the internet. Surely they had 24-hour call centres.

The call was not very satisfactory. The phone line to that address could certainly be reinstalled, said the BT operator. But since the connection had lapsed more than three months ago there would be a small delay.

'How small?' said Theo, suspiciously.

'About ten days. Perhaps two weeks.'

'Damn,' said Theo. 'Can't you make it any sooner?'

'I'm afraid not.'

'Well, all right. Will you set it up, please?'

He rang off, then on a sudden thought, hunted out the local phone directory and called St Luke's. The Bursar answered, sounding exactly as Theo remembered her, practical and down to earth. She expressed herself pleased to hear from him – they were still discussing his visit and the excellent talk he had given, she said. They hoped he would visit them again while he was in Melbray.

No plotter ever had a better opening. 'As a matter of fact, I would like to do that very much, but there'd be an ulterior motive, Bursar.'

'Quid pro quo,' she said. 'What can we do for you, Mr Kendal?'

Theo said, 'Do you suppose I could have a brief session on your computer? Say an hour or so?'

'I don't see why not. Has your own broken?'

He remembered her saying none of them were very well versed in modern technology, and smiled at the choice of words. 'No,' he said. 'But I need a connection to the internet for some research, and I can't get one set up here for a couple of weeks.'

'I'd need to clear it with Reverend Mother,' she said, 'but I'm sure it will be all right. Sister Catherine's the one who really knows about the computer so you'd probably need to have her around when you come in.'

Catherine, thought Theo, and found he was smiling at the memory of that cool irony and those direct eyes, and the hint that there might be a rebel held in check beneath the surface. He said, 'Well, if she could spare the time . . .'

'We've got a visit from several nuns from our sister house in Poland over the weekend so she'll be a bit caught up with that. What about Monday?'

'Monday would be fine,' said Theo. Then, as if suddenly remembering, he said, 'Oh, wait, I'll have a cousin staying here until Monday evening.' Lesley had phoned back to say she would come to Melbray early on Saturday morning and would not need to return until Tuesday if Theo could put up with her until then.

'Bring him with you,' said the Bursar.

'It's a her,' said Theo.

'All the better. Would you like to come along about twelve, and we'll give you both lunch before your computer session.'

'I'd love to. I'm sure my cousin would as well.'

'Don't get too enthusiastic, Mr Kendal, Monday is shepherd's pie day,' said the Bursar caustically.

CHAPTER TWENTY

———◆———

Saturday morning brought a post delivery, which was a sufficiently rare event at Fenn House to be modestly exciting.

There was a card from Theo's mother who had just got back from Paris, and wrote that it had been hot and indolent and she hoped he was enjoying Melbray and not working too hard. There was also a pamphlet inviting him to have solar heating fitted to his house, a leaflet reminding him that Jesus Saves, and a note from his agent wanting to know if he was still enduring the rigours of East Anglia, reporting some pleasantly high sales figures from a Dutch edition of his last book, and ending with a question as to how the ex-paratrooper's exploits were coming along.

Lesley's High Noon train was delayed and by the time they had collected provisions in Norwich, and Theo had negotiated the traffic, it was five o'clock before they reached Fenn House. Lesley paused in the hall, staring about her, and Theo tried to gauge her reactions.

'D'you know,' she said, 'I was a bit frightened of coming to Fenn again. I suppose I was expecting to sort of sense Charmery's presence. But I'm not sensing anything. I'm just remembering how much Charmery loved this house.'

'We all loved it,' said Theo. 'After Helen and Desmond died, Charmery used to come here on her own for long stretches.'

'I know. I always hoped she'd ask me to stay but she never did.'

'I don't think she asked any of the family,' said Theo. 'I think she liked to be on her own sometimes.'

'If she *was* on her own,' said Lesley, with a brief grin. 'You know Charm.'

'Yes.'

'She did like being on her own here, though,' Lesley said thoughtfully. 'The family never understood that – they never really understood her, did they? You were the only one who did. Everyone used to wonder why you fell out.'

'We didn't fall out. It was just a cousin thing,' said Theo lightly.

'Was it? My mother once said it was because of Charmery that you stopped smiling.' She was not looking at him and Theo was glad. 'It's so good to be here again,' said Lesley. 'I'm going to walk into the village tomorrow, I think, just to re-visit a few old haunts. But . . .' She looked back at him.

'But it's sad, as well, isn't it?' said Theo, gently. 'Coming back to Fenn like this, without her.'

'I miss her so much,' said Lesley, and then, as if shaking off the memories, said, 'Sorry, I didn't mean to go all Gothic and gloomy on you. I'll go up and unpack. Am I in my old room? Oh good. I'll only be ten minutes.'

One of the nice things about Lesley was that she never expected people to fuss or run round after her. Charmery, arriving at Fenn, would say haughtily, 'Could someone take my case up to my room? And I'll have a bath before supper.' She would come down to supper just as it was being put on the table, freshly bathed and shampooed, while everyone else had been peeling potatoes or looking for the corkscrew or dashing into the village for milk because the fridge had stopped working.

Lesley simply picked up her case and carried it upstairs before Theo could forestall her. He heard her opening doors and running the taps in the bathroom, then she came down again. She had on what looked like an Elizabethan tabard over purple tights and pixie boots. Theo thought she looked like a Tudor pageboy and wondered whether she would wear this outfit for the convent visit, and if so what the nuns would make of her over the shepherd's pie.

'Come and see the sketch before we eat,' he said. 'It's in here.'

'Why are you so interested in it?' said Lesley, following him into the dining room. 'You sounded really mysterious on the phone.'

'Because whoever did it must have known Charmery quite recently,' said Theo, noncommittally. 'And I don't think it's an angle the police followed up.'

'Isn't it signed?'

'No. And I'd like to know a bit more about the artist,' said Theo. He switched on the light and stood back, seeing her eyes widen as she saw the portrait. After a moment, he said, 'It's extraordinary, isn't it?'

'Yes, it is. Not just the sketch, but – Theo, it's almost as if a whole new persona took her over when that was done,' said Lesley.

'I know.'

'It's good,' she said.

'I thought it was. There are a couple of similar ones at St Luke's Convent and I think it's the same artist, but I'm not sure.'

'Someone local,' said Lesley. 'Yes, that might make a link to Charmery, mightn't it?'

'I'm hoping you can tell if they're by the same artist,' said Theo. 'We're invited to the convent for lunch on Monday, mostly so I can steal an on-line hour with their internet connection.'

'And so I can prowl round the sketches. That's fine, as long as I get the six o'clock train back.'

'I'll give you a spare key to the house anyway,' said Theo, hunting out the extra keys the locksmith had cut and handing one to her.

'Thanks. Can I have a closer look at the picture?'

Theo took it off its hook and Lesley studied it carefully, then turned it over to examine the back. Her expression was serious and absorbed and for the first time Theo saw her not as the small cousin who liked drawing pictures, but as someone who had studied art at the Slade, no less, and who might not be an expert in the accepted sense, but had considerable knowledge and also talent.

'Have you seen it before?' he said.

'No, but I haven't been to Fenn for years. Could I remove this backing paper? Only a corner of it. I'll be very careful and I should be able to put it back intact.'

'You can dismantle the whole thing if it'll do any good.'

'I don't really think there'll be a hidden signature,' said Lesley. 'But there might be a clue as to when it was done. A framer's stamp or something.'

'It must have been done in the last couple of years,' said Theo. 'It can't be any older than that. Charmery looks at least twenty-five.'

'Yes, she does.' Lesley sounded puzzled, but she fetched a very thin palette knife from her case and with extreme care began to lift the backing. At first Theo thought it would not come away or that it would tear, but eventually it came free and she laid it carefully to one side. Then she loosened the frame so the sketch itself could be removed.

'This is odder and odder,' she said, staring down at it.

'Why?'

'Because this is old,' said Lesley. 'Everything about it is old – the paper, the ink, even the glue holding the backing paper – you saw when I removed it how hard and dried out it was. Whoever he was, this artist, he used a medium-soft pencil, then a very thin sepia ink for outlining. No fixative. Most people use some kind of fixative now, but it's not a given.' She ran a fingertip experimentally over the paper's surface. 'Theo, this can't possibly have been done in the last two years. It's at least twenty years old – probably more.'

Theo stared at her. 'Are you sure? I thought it was just cob-webby. Everything in the house was cobwebby and faded when I got here.'

'I'm not absolutely sure, but I'm reasonably so. Restoration – the dating of old paintings – were subjects of their own at the Slade so I know the theory. And I've been working at the gallery for the last four months and we do quite a bit of restoration work. That doesn't make me an expert though, so don't take what I've said as gospel.'

'But this can't be twenty years old,' said Theo. 'That would mean—' He stopped.

'Say it.'

'That would mean it can't be Charmery,' he said, slowly. 'Twenty years ago she would only have been seven or about six.'

They looked at one another.

'But if it isn't Charmery,' said Lesley, 'then who is it? Because it's *very* similar.'

'Could it be Helen?' said Theo. 'If Charmery found an early sketch of her mother after Helen died, she might have decided to have it on show. No, of course it isn't Helen. The bone struc-ture is completely different. Could it be a modern sketch on old paper?'

'I don't think so. There are tests that can be done on the actual ink but there wouldn't have been any reason to use old paper. It's not as if we're in the Middle Ages where starving artists couldn't get materials and had to recycle. I think the ink's old anyway. If I make a very tiny scratch here – it's only in the corner, it won't show – it flakes. The new inks don't do that – at least, not for a good few years they don't.' She sat back, still looking at the framed face. 'Would you like me to take this back to London and see what my boss thinks of it? He's very knowledgeable, and I'd take great care of it.'

'Yes,' said Theo. 'Yes – would you do that? I'll pay whatever fee's involved.'

'No, you won't. I'll parcel it up now – I expect there's brown paper somewhere.'

'And then we'll have an early meal,' said Theo.

'Good. It's hungry work, trying to solve mysteries.'

They wrapped the sketch up, then grilled the steaks Theo had bought in Norwich, companionably drinking a glass of wine as they did so. They ate at one end of the dining table, but several times Lesley glanced through the uncurtained window to the dark gardens, and Theo saw the faint glint of tears in her eyes. He had been thinking he might tell Lesley about some of the curious things that had been happening – it would have been a relief to talk about it – but seeing the sadness in her expression as she stared at the smudgy blur of the boathouse, he knew he could not.

Instead, he got up to close the curtains, and said, 'More wine?'

'Yes, please. You only gave me about a quarter of a glass while we were cooking the meal.'

'And you already look like a naughty twelve-year-old who's been at the plonk.'

Catherine did not want to be present at Monday's lunch with Mr Kendal and his cousin.

It was only an informal arrangement, the Bursar had made that clear.

'He's coming to use the computer,' she said on Sunday evening, after the Polish nuns had left. 'Sister Catherine can show him where to switch it on. But I thought it would be courteous to invite him to lunch, we'd all enjoy meeting him again, I daresay. He's bringing a cousin with him – she's at Fenn House for the weekend.'

Sister Agnes, informed there would be two extra for the meal, said her shepherd's pie was more than equal to the occasion but she would whip up an apple pie by way of pudding. Most men liked apple pie. Reverend Mother thought Sister Miriam could show him their library: they had a couple of signed first editions of

George Borrow and the children's author Anna Sewell, both of whom had lived in Norfolk.

Catherine was appalled to realize she was considering staging a minor illness in order to miss the whole thing and that she was even subconsciously planning the details of a fictitious stomach bug. She was so disgusted with herself she went along to empty the ortho-bins by way of penance. It was hard work because the bins were large metal containers, and it was disagreeable because the discarded plaster casts were usually grubby and sweaty, but it should help to drive out all thoughts of Theo.

But it did not. The idea of seeing him again – of showing him the computer's intricacies in the enforced intimacy of Reverend Mother's study – made her stomach bounce with such pleasurable apprehension, that at one point she thought she might really have a stomach bug, which would serve her right. She wondered about the cousin he was bringing. 'Cousin' might be a polite euphemism, of course, and if you wanted to be facetious you might remind yourself that nine – nearly ten – years ago Theo Kendal had been very partial to cousins, to the extent that he had made his cousin Charmery pregnant. He would never know that on that long-ago afternoon, Catherine had held his son in her arms and felt the warmth of the small body and looked down at the vulnerable little head with the soft dark hair. And then watched the tiny body swept away by the muddy flow of the Chet . . .

She still offered prayers for the little lost David on the anniversary of his birth and death: each year she thought how old he would have been, and how he would be celebrating his birthday, going to school when he was five, learning to read and write, exploring the world around him. At other times she thought about him lying in the green depths of the river. Or had his body been washed up somewhere miles away, and found by people who had never heard of the Kendals or Melbray?

She wondered if any of the other nuns experienced this kind of struggle over a man. It was impossible to imagine Reverend

Mother or Sister Miriam or the Bursar lying in bed and staring up into the darkness, with wild thoughts of romance rioting through their minds. No, let's be honest, thought Catherine unhappily, what I'm imagining is a whole lot stronger than romance. It isn't moonlight-and-roses stuff, it's double beds and unclothed bodies. And Theo Kendal would not have given Catherine a second thought. He probably had scores of women in two separate continents panting for his attention, to say nothing of assorted cousins queuing up.

But when he came into the dining room on Monday, his eyes went round the room as if looking for someone and stopped when they saw her. A smile of unmistakable intimacy lit his face, and he gave her a nod of greeting that seemed to set her apart from the others. Catherine's heart leapt with delight and she was glad she had fought down the idea of faking illness, but at the same time came the thought that she did not want this, she did not want to feel like this.

The cousin was introduced as Lesley Kendal. She was a few years younger than Catherine, perhaps twenty-three, and she had short hair, the colour of autumn leaves, and wide-apart eyes. She was wearing a long green velvet coat, with, beneath it, an ankle-length black skirt and sweater with a rope of amber beads wound round her neck. Every time she looked at Theo her eyes seemed to take colour from the amber. Catherine could not decide if she regarded him as a much-loved surrogate elder brother or a lover. Theo's hair was slightly damp although Catherine did not think it was raining. Perhaps they had been making wild love all morning and reluctantly broken off because they were committed to eat shepherd's pie with a crowd of nuns, and he had taken a shower before coming out.

She listened quietly to Reverend Mother enquiring how Mr Kendal's work was progressing. He did not say much, other than that it had taken an unexpected turn and sometimes an author had to sit back and give the characters their heads and see where they took the story. Sister Miriam for once joined in with the discussion, offering some opinions about modern novelists which Mr Kendal seemed to find interesting.

The Bursar wanted to know what work Lesley Kendal did, and on hearing she had recently left the Slade, said they had a few paintings at St Luke's. Nothing valuable, she didn't think, but Miss Kendal might like to look at them while her cousin pursued his research on the computer?

'I'd like that very much,' said Lesley. 'All paintings are interesting and this part of the country has a terrific heritage. Alfred Munnings and Cotman. And Turner, of course. So I'd love to see your paintings.'

Catherine saw Theo glance at Lesley with a brief smile as if he was proud of her for making such a very good answer. Was it an avuncular smile – an older cousin, indulgently pleased with a younger one? Or was it the smile of a lover, proud of his lady's knowledge and warmth?

After lunch Catherine was expected to take Theo to Reverend Mother's study where the computer lived. She booted it up and explained which internet provider they used, and which email programme. He didn't really need her help, of course, but Catherine sat next to him for a few minutes, watching his hands operate the keyboard. After a moment, she said, 'If you're all right now, I'll leave you to get on with your research. Feel free to print anything you want. The printer's on that table.'

'Thanks, I might do that. My writing's practically illegible.'

'Is there anything else you need?' Let him say there is, she thought. Let me have a bit longer sitting with him like this.

But he said, 'No, nothing. Thanks for this.' The smile showed, briefly.

I was wrong about that moment of intimacy earlier, thought Catherine, but as she got up to go, Theo said, 'It's been nice seeing you again, Catherine – sorry, I probably shouldn't call you that.'

'It's my name. These days most of us keep our own names.'

229

'Well, then, Catherine, will you call at Fenn some time for another cup of coffee?'

Catherine stared at him and felt the telltale colour flood her face. I'll have to refuse, she thought. I daren't accept. Probably he doesn't mean it. Even if he does . . . I really *will* have to refuse.

'If it wouldn't interrupt your work, I'd like to call.'

'Good. Any morning is fine. I'm not being polite, you know.'

'Aren't you?'

'I'm never polite,' he said, and this time the smile was a mischievous grin.

Catherine, her heart racing, the treacherous blood singing through her veins, managed to get outside the door.

Theo had no idea why he had issued that invitation to Sister Catherine, or why he had used her name in that way. But he had the impression that she was a good listener, and he had suddenly felt a strong wish to pour out everything that was happening at Fenn House.

He brought his mind back to the task in hand, consulted his notes, and began typing in search requests. Nicolae and Elena Ceauşescu came under this heading as well, although there would be no shortage of information about those two. As he worked, St Luke's and its inhabitants ceased to exist for him. He travelled to a country with a violent and vivid history, and to an era when an iron dictator had held its people in poverty and fear.

There was a wealth of material about the years of Ceauşescu's reign – which had begun in 1965 and ended on Christmas Day 1989 – and also of the years leading up to his election as leader. Matthew and Mara's years, thought Theo. There were also several first-hand accounts written by prisoners who had been incarcerated in Pitesti Gaol or in the equally grim-sounding Jilava Gaol, and he read these carefully. They were written with varying degrees of literacy by people from widely different walks of life. Some of the automatic translations read a bit oddly, but the emotion and the suffering came through so strongly that Theo felt his throat constrict with the pity and horror of it. One account, apparently an extract from a book published by a survivor of Jilava, told of the physical and mental torture inside the prison.

They called it by many names but, boiled down to the bones, it was brainwashing. They employed torture to remove our real natures and beliefs and loyalties. One of the names they used for it was 're-education', but in fact they were systematically turning us into robots and making informers of us. We had to work for exhausting periods doing humiliating tasks – I often had to clean the floors with a rag clenched between my teeth. Our food pans were seldom washed, and sometimes we were forced to eat from them with our hands bound – that doesn't sound much, but to kneel down and lick food off a dish like an animal is degrading.

I protested, and was punished. They shut me into a tiny coffin-shaped room with a bright light permanently on, making it impossible to sleep. After three days, I managed to reach the light bulb and unscrew it – I was exhausted and dizzy; I thought I would give anything for a couple of hours' sleep. But they came in before I could replace the bulb, and I was punished even more. They tied my hands behind my back, and pushed me to a sitting position on the floor, leaning against the cold stone wall. Then they jerked my lips wide open and pushed the glass light bulb straight into my mouth, with the narrow brass end jutting out and the wide bulbous part scraping against my teeth. I couldn't move. If I tried to dislodge the bulb it would have splintered in my mouth and glass pieces would have gone down my throat.

They left me for an hour – I knew it was that because I counted the seconds and added them into minutes. The darkness was an added torture because earlier I had craved darkness in order to sleep. I could not sleep now. After only a few minutes my jaw ached intolerably with the strain of keeping my mouth open and still, and saliva ran from the corners of my lips. The pain was so fierce I wanted to cry with the misery of it.

When finally they came back and removed the bulb, I broke down, sobbing. I was so grateful for the ending of the pain, I confessed to whatever they wanted to hear. Years afterwards, trying to rebuild my life, I learned that the light-bulb treatment was an old Nazi trick.

It was the most detailed account Theo found from inside any of the gaols, although there were several others, brief and scrappy in the main, but all telling of physical and mental torture: sparse food, cramped and dirty cells, medical attention which consisted of the dispensing of an aspirin or strychnine shots.

As he read, an image formed in his mind of the woman in Andrei's photograph. Had she existed in real life, that dark-haired rebel, who had been Matthew's mother? He tried reminding himself that Elisabeth had been forged out of his own imagination, but it did not help. Matthew and Annaleise had been forged from his imagination as well, but they were also real people. He was starting to have the feeling that Elisabeth Valk was real as well, and that if he stretched out his hand he would feel her take it. He began to read a set of documents grouped under the heading of 'Student Movements in Communist Romania'. The translations were heavy and confusing and by the time he reached the fourth one he was thinking it was a blind alley. He would check this last account, however.

The final document was not a blind alley at all. Rearranged into an English structure of sentences, it read:

In the mid-1950s, events in Poland, which led to the elimination of that country's Stalinist leadership, provoked unrest among university students in Eastern bloc countries.

A clandestine group created links between all the faculties, with a view to organizing protests, and on 28 October 1956 a radio station calling itself 'Romania of the Future: The Voice of Resistance' began broadcasting. Not all the locations of this group were found, but one was certainly in Yugoslavia. The station, considered a nationalist one, presented the students' demands and incited people to rebel.

A radio station, thought Theo, recalling his story. 'The October Group calling,' she had said. 'Elisabeth Valk here, wishing a very good evening to all my friends ...' That beautiful voice challenging and defying, and calling people to a rally. But she's imaginary, he thought angrily. I gave her a beautiful voice and dark hair and eyes – she's my creation, she's not real! None of them are real, they can't be. He read on.

The October Group, which was behind so many protests and also much of the illegal broadcasting, was to last far longer than the Securitate could ever have visualized.

Oh God, thought Theo, staring at the screen. The October Group. He plunged back in.

Even in the mid-1960s, the October Group was still broadcasting from the country then known as Yugoslavia. Some of the ringleaders were caught, and one of the stations in a small village outside Krivaca, just across Romania's south-west border, was summarily closed down.

Theo's mind had spun into whirling confusion. Krivaca, he thought. That's where I sent Zoia, Annaleise and Elena Ceauşescu that morning. That bleak frozen grey morning, when they drove across the border and found the thin tall house and dragged

Elisabeth out and took her to Pitesti Gaol. He had never heard of Krivaca – he had simply looked it up in an atlas. He might easily have picked any of a dozen places near the border.

A precise list of the people involved in organizing protests is difficult to reconstruct. The primary sources are transcripts of the trials that followed the crushing of the various student movements and groups such as the October Group. But a list is appended here for the researcher or enquirer.

The names were set out alphabetically, but her name seemed to leap from the page and deal a blow straight into his eyes.

Elisabeth Valk. Incarcerated in Pitesti Gaol, November 1965, for crimes against the State. No record of a trial exists.

CHAPTER TWENTY-ONE

Theo sat back and stared at the glowing screen of the monitor. So Elisabeth was real. She had lived – might still be living – and she had been a rebel, responsible for broadcasting against the communist rulers under whose sway she lived. She had risked losing her husband and small son but she had taken the gamble and it had failed. She had been caught and taken to Pitesti Gaol and, in the enlightened twentieth century, the supposed era of justice and fairness, she had not even been given a trial to establish what she had done.

Moving like an automaton he made notes of dates and times, and even found a map reference for Krivaca that might be useful and jotted this down as well, wondering for a wild moment if he would end up travelling to Romania. He was just thinking it was more or less on the normal holiday route now, when there was an apologetic tap at the door and the Bursar put her head round.

'Sorry to interrupt, but Sister Miriam and I are taking your cousin along to the old wing to look at some of the paintings stored there.'

Theo was so deep in Elisabeth's world that for a moment he

found it difficult to focus on what the Bursar was saying. With a massive mental effort, he came back to the present, and said, 'That's fine. She'll enjoy it.'

'There's quite a lot of stuff, most of it fairly old, but we used some for a display for our centenary celebrations last year illustrating the history of this house and so on. Quite an excitement for us all. Oh, and Miss Kendal says don't forget her train's at six. She'll meet you downstairs in half an hour. If you're not there, she'll just go back to Fenn House. She says you gave her a spare key.'

'I did. But I won't be much longer – I've been at least an hour over the time I envisaged, anyway.'

'You're welcome here for as long as you want. Come again if you need to do any more research. In fact, come back to see us anyway,' she said.

Theo returned to his research about Elisabeth, but it was almost as if the small interruption had broken a spell, or sealed up a portal into the past. There was nothing else about her, although he found some useful background details: descriptions of Ceauşescu's iron rule, and of the State orphanages that had sprung up to deal with the flood of unwanted children – again, the television images rose up before Theo's eyes.

A report in the *Guardian*'s online archives, dated 2006, stated unequivocally that children had been used by Ceauşescu's Intelligence Service. They had to report to their Securitate handlers on their friends' and families' opinions on the Communist Party, on whether they listened to Western radio stations, or even if they made jokes about Ceauşescu. In some cases, the children had been blackmailed over trivial childish sins – things they had done wrong at school, tiny offences they had nervously committed. Some had been threatened that their parents or brothers and sisters would suffer if they did not do what was wanted. Theo remembered how he had described the children in Matthew's school being set a weekend composition to describe where they lived and the people around them. Had that been a sly ploy to get information about the ordinary men and women in the outlying districts, or had it come from Theo's own mind?

He sat back massaging his aching neck muscles, then seeing the half hour was up, turned off the computer and shuffled his notes into some sort of order, along with a handful of pages he had printed out. Lesley was not in the main hall, and Theo was just thinking he would have to find someone to direct him to the old wing, when she came down the stairs with the Bursar.

'Sorry, Theo, were you waiting?' said Lesley. 'I had to go back for my coat. Bursar, thanks so much – I've loved seeing the paintings. Sister Miriam's very knowledgeable, isn't she?'

'Yes, very. It's easy to underestimate her because she's generally so quiet,' said the Bursar. 'Mr Kendal, I picked up one of the centenary booklets we had printed last year – there's a box of them in those rooms. I thought you might like to look through it some time.'

'Thank you,' said Theo, taking the small glossy booklet. 'Is Reverend Mother around?'

'She'll be about to take evening reports in the common room,' said the Bursar. 'I'm on my way there now.'

'Oh, I see. Well, would you thank her for me? And Sister Catherine as well?' He was annoyed to hear a tiny hesitation in his voice before he said Catherine's name.

'Of course I will, but it's been our pleasure,' said the Bursar.

'They're nice, aren't they?' said Lesley as she and Theo walked back along the lanes to Fenn House. It was almost dark outside, and a vapour had risen up from the river and was lying over the ground. 'We should have got to know them years ago,' she said, putting her hands in her coat pockets.

'Yes,' said Theo. He looked down at her. 'Well? You saw the sketches?'

'The ones in the hall. Yes, I did. I had quite a good look at them, in fact, and I think you're right – they're the same artist as ours,' she said. 'Only those two are signed, aren't they? The artist was called Matthew Valk.'

It gave Theo the most extraordinary feeling to hear someone use Matthew's name. He listened as Lesley explained about use of light and shade, and described some particular technique Matthew had apparently used, but he could make only brief responses.

'How did your research go?' asked Lesley, as they turned into Fenn's drive.

'It was surprising,' said Theo. 'I'll tell you about it properly when I've untangled it. There are some peculiar things going on here, Lesley.'

'What sort of peculiar?'

'Mysterious peculiar.'

'Such as sketches done out of their time?'

'That's one of them. Oh Lord, it's nearly half past four – we'd better drive straight to Norwich for your train.'

'I'll just dive in and get my bag,' said Lesley, as Theo unlocked the door.

'And the sketch.'

'I'm not forgetting that,' she said. 'I'll let my boss see it in the morning and I'll phone you with the result.'

As they drove to Norwich, she said, 'Do you want me to bring the sketch back next weekend? I have the feeling you'd like it returned as soon as possible.'

'Would you like to come again next weekend?'

'Well, I would if I wouldn't be in your way. I could bring my sketchbook and wander round the lanes,' said Lesley.

'Sounds fine.'

It was almost seven by the time Theo got back to Melbray and Fenn. He parked the car, and let himself in, hanging his jacket on the old-fashioned coat stand, and taking the St Luke's booklet with him into the kitchen. It would be interesting to read about the convent's history especially if there was a reference to Fenn House anywhere. He was just filling the kettle for a cup of tea when he thought he heard a knock on the front door. He went out at once, but there was no one there. Theo stood in the doorway for a moment, looking along the drive to the lane, shivering at the cold and unfriendly darkness, then went back inside, hearing the new lock click reassuringly into place.

But as he poured his cup of tea, he heard the sound again, and this time it was definitely not the front door. He listened carefully and it came a second time. Was it a creak? The stairs? He remembered the strong new locks on all the doors, but in the same moment a voice inside his head said, 'But supposing you've locked someone in here with you?'

The sounds came again, and this time they formed a definite pattern of someone walking very slowly and very stealthily across the main landing upstairs. Theo's heart began to pound, but he went to the foot of the stairs and looked up. The shadows clustered thickly and menacingly on the stairs. He caught a glimmer of movement above him, although he could not tell if it was someone darting across the landing or just the curtain billowing out from the long window. No, it could not be that, he had closed all the windows before they went to St Luke's. Someone was inside the house.

To make sure he called out, 'Hello? Is someone there?'

There was utter silence. Theo could hear his own heart beating. He's listening, he thought. Whoever is up there is standing still and listening. Moving stealthily, not taking his eyes from the shadowy stairs, he stepped back to the coat stand inside the door, and felt in his jacket for the mobile phone. The nearest police station was about eight miles away – would they send someone out as an emergency? How long would it take? Ten minutes, fifteen? In fifteen minutes anything could happen. Above him the landing floorboards creaked again. He's at the top of the stairs, thought Theo, I'll grab the phone and get outside. It was then he realized the phone was not in his jacket – he had left it on the kitchen table that morning when he phoned to check Lesley's train time. He turned to dart back, but as he went past the stairs, the shadows seemed to rear up and something sprang at him. There was a confused impression of dark clothes, and a long coat. Theo lifted his hands in defence, but the attacker had the advantage of being above him, and before he could do anything, something hard and heavy crunched down on his head. He gave a cry, his senses reeling, and pain exploded above his left ear. As he fell against the wall, sending a small table crashing to the ground, he was dimly aware of the figure running back across the hall, unbolting the front door, and going out into the night.

'You have,' said Michael Innes, closing his medical case with a snap, 'been extremely lucky. Whatever hit you landed on the side of your skull. A little higher or a little lower and a bit more force behind the blow – and you might have suffered a haematoma. That's bleeding in the brain.'

'I know what it is,' said Theo, who was lying on the settee of the sitting room, pressing a flannel containing ice cubes against the side of his head.

'It's often fatal without prompt treatment,' said Innes, calmly. 'But you don't have any signs of it – or even of concussion as far as I can tell. Balance, speech, coordination are all normal. No nausea?'

'A bit. I'm still rather dizzy, but nothing much.'

Innes studied Theo for a moment. 'I don't think a CT scan is necessary,' he said, 'but if the nausea increases in the next twelve hours or so, phone me at once. Or if there's severe dizziness, or double vision or actual vomiting . . . If there's any doubt or if you can't get me, don't wait, call 999 for an ambulance.'

'I will.'

'The nausea should fade after a few hours. You'll have a bad headache though.'

'I have, but I'll take some paracetamol in a minute.'

'I've got something a bit stronger in my bag. Here you are. It's got mildly anti-nausea properties as well.' He waited until Theo had swallowed the pill, then said, 'It's lucky you managed to get to the phone.'

'I'm surprised I did.' Theo had half crawled to the kitchen after his assailant ran out, praying he did not black out again, praying the intruder would not return, and had managed to phone the police and then Michael Innes.

'How long will the police be?' asked Innes. 'Are they coming from Loddon?'

'They're getting a CID man to come out. I'm not sure where from. I don't think Loddon has a CID division. It didn't sound as if it would be too long, though.'

'Would you like me to stay here until they arrive?'

'In case that bastard comes back to finish me off?'

'Yes. It would probably be good if I monitor you for the next hour anyway.'

'Then please stay,' said Theo gratefully. 'Even if it's only to tell the police that in your professional opinion I'm relatively sane and not given to hallucinations about intruders.'

'There's nothing hallucinatory about that blow on your head. You'd better have some more ice for it – no, don't move, I can find the fridge.'

'I suppose,' said Theo, as Innes returned with the ice cubes, 'that I can't have a whisky?'

'Not for twenty-four hours at least. Sorry.'

'I thought not.'

The police arrived several minutes later, headed by a very young CID sergeant who introduced himself as DS Gavin Leigh, and a largish uniformed constable who was despatched to examine the doors and windows. DS Leigh listened carefully to the details of the attack, and to Theo's description of how someone had seemed to be prowling around a few days earlier. Theo omitted to mention the wound-up clock and the teleported rose, because he had no proof of either incident and it would not help his case if the

241

police or Michael Innes thought he was mad. He kept the laptop confession quiet as well, because while that was proof positive, the police might wonder if he had typed it himself.

'We need to find out how your intruder got in,' said Leigh. 'But I'm bound to say it doesn't seem like a break-in.'

'It wasn't a break-in,' said Theo. 'He was waiting in the house when I got back.'

'In that case— Yes?' He turned as the large constable came back.

'No signs of a break-in anywhere as far as I can see, Sergeant.'

'Ah. Check the gardens as well. It looks as if you were right, Mr Kendal,' said Leigh, turning back. 'He got in with a key.'

'He can't have done,' said Theo. 'I had the locks changed a couple of days ago – the morning after I thought there was someone prowling round.'

'Sensible of you. Better safe than sorry,' said Leigh, making a note of the local firm who had done the work.

'That's what I thought. I didn't report the prowler because I wasn't certain about it. I thought it might be just a local snooper, or even a stray newshound looking for a new angle on my cousin's murder.'

'There were,' observed Innes dryly, 'enough of them at the time.'

'There were indeed,' agreed Leigh. 'Well, we'll make a few enquiries among the local bad boys and I'll have a word with one or two news editors, in case a journalist's getting a bit above himself. And we'll talk to the locksmith in the morning as well, although he's kept a handyman shop in Melbray ever since anyone can remember and he inherited it from his father. Very reliable set-up. Still, we'll make sure nobody could have got an extra key cut without him knowing. That means you're the only one with a key, then?'

'Yes – no, hold on, I gave a spare key to my cousin this morning,' said Theo, suddenly remembering. 'She didn't actually need it in the end, but she didn't give it back. I'd forgotten it until now.' He looked at the clock and saw it was just after half past seven.

'Will she be home yet?' said Leigh.

'She might be just about – it depends on the Tube.'

'Would you call her, so we can check that other key is where we think it is.'

But Lesley's phone was on answerphone, and when Theo tried her mobile it went straight to voicemail. He left messages on both, merely saying he was making sure she had got back all right, and asking her to call him.

'Let us know when she does,' said the sergeant. 'You might just jot down her numbers for me, as well.' He passed the notebook to Theo, who scribbled them down. 'Thanks. Now, how about the attacker? Did you get any impression of anything about him? Any glimpse of his build, or a scent or body smell?'

'Nothing at all. It was just a dark figure – and it was on the stairs above me, so it could have been any height.'

Leigh nodded. 'We'll try for fingerprints, but any number of people have probably tramped in and out of this house over the last few months. I suppose you didn't spot anything unusual when you came out here, Doctor?'

'Nothing. I wasn't looking for anything unusual, I was concerned to get to Theo as quickly as possible.'

'Fair enough. I'll get a statement drafted and bring it out for you to sign in the morning,' said Leigh to Theo. 'We'll get your prints at the same time, just for elimination. Yours, too, Doctor.'

'They're already on file,' said Innes. 'They were taken when Charmery Kendal was killed. That was for elimination purposes as well,' he said, and Theo saw Leigh's flicker of annoyance.

But he only said, 'If you think of anything else that might help, Mr Kendal . . .'

'You'll be the first to know. Sergeant Leigh – is he likely to come back?'

'I'm supposed to say no in a reassuring voice, but I don't think we can rule it out,' said Leigh. 'You're on your own here, are you?'

'Yes.'

'I'd happily stay,' said Innes, 'but I'll need to get back home soon because I'm on call from nine to eleven.'

'Ah.'

'I'll bolt all the doors,' said Theo. 'And I should think the locksmith would come out first thing in the morning.'

'There'd be one of those twenty-four hour emergency locksmiths in Norwich,' said Leigh. 'You could try that, although by the time they got someone out to you ...'

Theo said that in his experience, twenty-four hour services were never able to come out when you needed them.

'We'll check the bolts before we go,' said Leigh. 'And I'll call the locksmith in the morning as well, just so he knows it's a priority case. I'm sorry we haven't the manpower for a permanent watch, but I'll make sure the local patrols know to stay around this area. Here's my direct number, and I'll get you the number for the patrol, so you can get straight through to them if anything happens.'

'You're taking this quite seriously,' said Theo. 'You don't think it was just an opportunist house-breaker?'

'No, and I don't think you do, either. I think it might be linked to your cousin's death.'

'Because the killer's still at large, and for all we know still in Melbray,' said Theo.

'I'm aware of that,' said Leigh. 'I was drafted in to the murder investigation team.' He studied Theo for a moment. 'We really did do absolutely everything we could to find her killer,' he said, 'but we had nothing to work on: no leads to follow, no forensic evidence to speak of, no witnesses who saw or heard anything. It was as if her murderer materialized out of nowhere, then went back into nowhere. It's easier to track down a killer – or any criminal – in the middle of a city or a big housing estate. People see things, there are shops, parked cars, sometimes CCTV cameras, you can piece together a pattern. But in a place like Melbray you've got nothing at all.'

'Yes, I understand that. But, Sergeant, why would Charmery's killer come back? It's not as if there's any damning evidence to be found anywhere. If there was, you'd have found it in the summer. Unless he's simply a madman.'

. 'Even madmen have their own logic,' said Innes, softly.

'Yes, they do, and we never fathomed the logic of Charmery Kendal's murderer.' Leigh shut his notebook and stood up. 'Don't open the door unless you're sure it's us, will you, Mr Kendal?'

'On no account whatsoever,' said Theo. He accompanied Sergeant Leigh to the door, then returned to the sitting room.

Michael Innes was standing in front of the blank wall where Charmery's sketch had been. As Theo came in, he said, 'You've moved the portrait?'

'Yes,' said Theo, not explaining. But as Innes did not move, he suddenly said, 'Michael, how much do you really know about Charmery?'

'Well . . .'

'Did she have a child?' The words were out before he could stop them.

Innes turned sharply. 'How did you know? Oh wait, it'd be in the autopsy—'

'Then it's true? Don't take refuge in patient confidentiality,' said Theo. 'You've already given yourself away. What do you know about it? When was it?'

An expression of infinite sadness crossed Michael Innes' face. He said, 'About nine years ago.'

'Nine years,' said Theo. 'Dear God. What happened? Where is it?'

Innes sat down facing him. 'It was stillborn,' he said.

Stillborn. Theo was not expecting the pain that closed around him. He half shut his eyes against it, but the image he had had the night he read the eerie confession on the laptop, was strongly with him. Tip-tilted eyes and beaten copper hair . . .

'I was with her when it happened,' said Innes. 'It was an emergency birth. Premature. She said you were the father.'

Theo managed to say, 'We had one of those brief, cousinly affairs one summer. Ten years ago.' Half to himself, he said, 'I wish she'd told me about it.'

'I don't think she wanted anyone to know.'

'Did she intend to give it up for adoption?'

'I think so.'

'Did anyone know? The family?'

'She said she managed to hide it from them – I don't remember the details at this distance. I know she came to Fenn for the actual birth. She said no one was ever here in March and she'd be perfectly safe.'

'Did anyone here know?' It did not really matter, but Theo found himself asking anyway.

Innes paused, then said, 'One person knew – someone who helped me with the birth. But there was a promise of confidentiality given.'

'All right, I won't push you. You said it was stillborn? Was it a boy or a girl? Michael – I need to know!'

'It was a boy,' said Innes. 'He was named David because it was St David's Day, the first of March.'

'David . . . Was there a funeral? A grave? I don't know what happens with stillborn babies.' Innes seemed even more reluctant to answer this, so he said, 'I meant it about needing to know everything.'

'All right. The child was born in the boathouse,' said Innes. 'It happened suddenly. We – I – only found Charmery by purest chance. The baby didn't survive – maybe simply because it was premature, but without an autopsy there was no way of knowing exactly what had happened. Charmery was distraught – because of the birth, because the child was dead – everything. We couldn't stop her— There was a storm – the river was churning – he went out of reach ... Oh God, he was out of reach before I could do anything,' he said. 'He was so small, so fragile.'

Theo stared at him, unable to speak, and after a moment, Innes said in a stronger voice, 'I think that's why Charmery kept coming back here. She never had what some people call closure.'

'So she kept coming back for him,' said Theo, softly.

'Yes. I think in some odd way of her own she felt he was still there, in that part of the river. Still just under the surface of the water, so that all she'd have to do was reach down to find him. Once she talked about a rusalka – it's an old folk tale,' he said, seeing Theo's questioning look. 'A rusalka is supposed to be the soul of a drowned infant. I think she'd read the legend somewhere and it stuck in her mind.' He smiled. 'There was a lot more to your cousin than all that flippant frivolity, wasn't there?'

'Yes.'

Innes made another of the impatient gestures. 'I had all kinds of responsibilities that I didn't shoulder that day. I should have tried to – to recover the child's body, or got the police to try. They could have dragged the river ... There should have been an autopsy, the registering of the birth and the death. And I should certainly have reported what Charmery did.'

'Why didn't you?'

'To protect her,' he said. 'You must have guessed how I felt about her. Even all those years ago she was quite simply the most beautiful thing I'd ever seen in my life. I'd have done anything she wanted. Then, years after the birth – this last summer – she and I ...'

'I guessed that,' said Theo. 'Did she feel the same about you?'

'No,' he said, very definitely. 'I was a diversion. For a few weeks that was what I was. You were the one she really loved.'

CHAPTER TWENTY-TWO

———◆◆◆———

Michael Innes left just before half-past eight, and after he had gone the old house seemed to fill up with stealthy creaks and rustlings, and with shadows that moved of their own accord. Theo sat by the fire, watching the rain beat on the uncurtained windows.

At the end of that drowned garden, somewhere below the river's surface might be the tiny body of a child who had never drawn breath in the world. My and Charmery's son, thought Theo. David, because it was St David's Day. And she came back here every year on the anniversary of his birth – letting everyone think she liked Melbray in the spring, but really coming back before spring began so she would be here on the first of March. 'She never had closure,' Michael Innes had said. 'She felt he was still there, in that part of the river.'

Had Charmery left Fenn House to Theo because she thought David was still here? Was that romantic and sad, or was it merely mawkish? Theo could not decide, and nor could he decide if it was an emotion Charmery would have had.

He made himself a sandwich and tried to watch television, but although the pills had stopped the throbbing in his head, his balance had not entirely righted itself, and the flickering screen made it worse.

It was still only a quarter to nine, but the pills were having a slightly soporific effect. Theo lay back on the sofa, staring into the flickering warmth of the gas fire. When they were children there had been an open fire here. They used to sit on the hearthrug, staring into the flames, taking it in turns to describe the pictures they saw. Lesley had been by far the best at it. She could conjure up entire fleets of ships and caves with dragons and rose-red cities half as old as time . . .

He was aware he was moving into the borderlands of slumber, and he tried to push it back but, as he did so, Matthew and Mara began to come to the forefront of his mind. He was not exactly hearing their voices, but he was starting to see something that illuminated their lives – rather as if he was reading an old, cob-webby manuscript by candlelight, and as if the flickering light showed up fragments of the pages, lighting up sentences and names at random.

Elisabeth and Andrei and Pitesti Gaol . . . Mara and the Black House . . . Zoia loving Annaleise with that sad lonely desperation . . .

Theo was hardly aware of sitting up and getting off the sofa, but he found he was no longer sleepy. He went into the dining room and switched on the lamp and the computer. He began to type, almost without noticing it. At first only disjointed phrases and sentences materialized on the screen, but then whole paragraphs started to form, and he was as deep inside Matthew and Mara's world as ever before.

Romania, early 1970s

It was very quiet inside the well-house. Mara had remained in a frightened huddle against the wall for so long, her legs were getting cramp. She stood up and tried to bicycle them, like in gym at school, but she was frightened to move too much because of the black lipless mouth that was the well. From time to time she had the impression that it was breathing out, with evil-smelling breath.

It was impossible to know how long she had been here because time seemed different. Several times she stood under the eye-holes and again shouted to be let out, but after a while her voice became cracked. She tried again to get the door open, but her fingers were too bruised and tender from where she had torn the nails, and the door was clearly not going to move anyway.

It was still not absolutely dark, but it was a lot darker than it had been. It might be just that the sun had gone in, but the trees were whispering to themselves in the way they did when it grew dark, and the forest was full of night sounds. Mara did not like these sounds, so she worked her way round the walls until she was facing the eyeholes. If anything was going to climb in through them, it would be better to know about it. The light coming through the eyeholes had taken on a thick bluish tinge; that meant it was nearly nighttime, which was worrying. Mara's grandmother told tales of wraiths and shadow-beings who could not go abroad in daylight and walked the world after dark. Trolls came alive at night as well, and if they did not go back into their lairs before dawn they were turned into stone. For the first time, Mara had the terrible thought that this building might once have been a troll who had been turned to stone and the stone made into a well-house. Until now she had been trying to be brave, but this was such an extremely bad thought, she put her head down on her knees and sobbed.

She cried for a long time which made her throat even more painful and gave her a headache. She was just trying to dry her eyes on the skirt of her cotton frock, when, somewhere beneath the sobs, a tiny, thin thought nudged its way upwards. It was so light and so frail that at first Mara was not sure what it was, but the more it worked its way through her mind, the more she began to feel it might be important. Was it something that had been part

250

of her grandmother's tales? It was not anything about trolls or wolves, that was for sure, but it was certainly something her grandmother had once told her. Something about her own village? Something about Matthew's family? Yes, that was it! She stopped crying altogether, and sat up a bit straighter, trying to imagine herself back in her grandmother's cottage. There was her grandmother rocking by the fire as she liked to do each evening and there was Mara herself, curled up in the warm little place by the side of the hearth, on the thick rag rug. She could hear the creak of the rocking chair and her grandmother's voice, and she could hear her saying some of the stories might be true . . .

The memory was suddenly there, exploding inside Mara's mind like a huge light. There had been a night when she had been falling asleep because the room was warm and it was nearly her bedtime, so she had missed some of what was said. But she had roused at the sound of Matthew's name, and she had heard – she could hear it now – her grandmother talking about Matthew's mother, saying she was not dead as everyone thought – as even Matthew himself thought. Mara had been wide awake by then; she had leaned forward, hugging her knees with her arms, listening intently.

Matthew's mother was in prison. That was what her grandmother had said. Years and years ago she had done something terrible – no one in the village knew exactly what it was and it had happened when Matthew was a baby – but she had been taken to prison because of it.

'And she's still there,' Mara's grandmother said in a whisper, almost as if she had forgotten Mara and was talking to herself. 'Still there, shut away in the stone cells. Andrei Valk hushed it up to save distressing that poor child, Matthew, and hardly anyone knows the truth.' The chair rocked downwards, and her grandmother put her mouth close to Mara's ear so that even if anyone was standing outside the window listening or looking in, her words would not be heard.

'You must never tell it, Mara, but ever since Elisabeth was taken away, Andrei Valk has tried his hardest to find her. There's an organization called the October Group who've helped him. A few years ago they found out Elisabeth was in Pitesti Gaol, and Andrei and the October Group made a plan to rescue her, but somebody talked and at the last minute she was moved, and no one knows where she is now. Andrei avoided prison by the skin of his teeth, but he's still trying to find Elisabeth, he still means to rescue her.'

'How would he do that?' It was impossible to get people out of prison, Mara knew that.

'They'll find a guard who can be bribed,' said her grandmother. 'But this must all remain the darkest secret ever, because if the Securitate find out what Andrei's doing . . .'

'Yes?'

'It's said there are worse things than prison in this land,' she whispered.

Mara did not want to know what might be worse than prison. 'How do you know all that?'

'Some people know,' said her grandmother. 'Sometimes they let things slip without realizing.'

'What people?'

'The nuns at your school,' said her grandmother, and Mara stared in surprise.

'People like Sister Teresa, d'you mean?' This was a very sad story but it was also pretty exciting, much better than wolves and giants.

'Oh yes, people like Sister Teresa. Trust nuns to know secrets. And the Church has a long history of helping people escape oppressors, always remember that, Mara.'

Mara was not sure what an oppressor was, and she was not sure if she believed Sister Teresa was part of all this. She wanted to know more, but her grandmother refused to say anything else. She told Mara she had said too much already, but as she rocked in the chair she was smiling. Mara knew this was not because

Matthew's mother was in prison, but because her grandmother loved secrets.

Secrets . . .

Huddled inside the well-house with the light fading, Mara thought how Zoia and Annaleise had wanted to know about Matthew's father. 'You'll be here until we know all we need to about Andrei Valk,' Annaleise had said. Was this the thing they wanted to know – this plan about finding Matthew's mother and bribing a guard and rescuing her? It was an enormous thing to suddenly remember, and Mara was still trying to put it into shape in her mind when there was a sound from outside. Was it Annaleise or Zoia coming back to let her out? She scrambled hopefully to her feet, and as she did so, the thick old door made a soft groaning sound and a thin line of dusklight appeared round the edges. The door was pushed further inwards, and light fell across the floor, showing the yawning cavern at the centre. Annaleise and Zoia stood in the doorway; Annaleise held a big electric torch which she shone all round the well-house, before directing its beam onto Mara. After the hours of dimness the light was dazzling and Mara had to put up a hand to shield her eyes.

'Well, Mara,' said Annaleise, 'we're sorry to say that your friend Matthew hasn't told us what we want to know.'

'Which is a pity,' said Zoia, 'because we really do want to know about Andrei Valk.'

Mara said, 'Matthew hasn't told you because he can't. He doesn't know.' She thought, I'm sorry, Elisabeth, I'm really truly sorry, because if I tell them what I know something dreadful might happen to you. But if I don't tell them, they'll leave me here. 'I've remembered hearing things about Matthew's father and his mother. I can tell you what you want to know.'

She saw they did not immediately believe her. They looked at one another, then Zoia said, 'Why is it you're only telling us now?'

'We don't like children who lie to get away from a punishment,' said Annaleise.

'It's not a lie. I remembered it while I was here,' said Mara. 'Just a few minutes ago. It's true, I promise.'

'Lies can be checked,' said Annaleise.

'Tell us and we'll see,' said Zoia.

'It's not lies,' said Mara. 'Years and years ago Matthew's mother – her name's Elisabeth – was put in Pitesti Gaol.' For a dreadful moment she thought this might all be just a story after all and they would say she was lying, but they did not.

'We know about that,' said Annaleise, glancing at Zoia.

'Matthew's father tried to rescue her,' said Mara. 'Only he was found out and Elisabeth was moved. So he's looking for her now, and when he finds her, he has a plan to rescue her. The October Group are helping him.' Neither Annaleise nor Zoia spoke, so Mara said, 'They're going to find a guard at the prison who can be – um – bribed. That's the plan.'

Annaleise said slowly, 'If Matthew doesn't know all this – if hardly anyone knows it, how is it that you know?'

For a moment Mara could not think what to say. If she said her grandmother had told her, they might take her grandmother away and her brother would be on his own. Would they put him inside the Black House, in one of the cages? The thought of Mikhail helpless in that dreadful place was not to be borne. She would sacrifice anyone else to save him. She had already sacrificed Matthew's parents anyway. So she looked Annaleise straight in the eye, and said, 'The nuns at school know about it.' It was not quite a lie because her grandmother had said the nuns knew, but Mara knew it was very nearly a lie. But as long as her grandmother and Mikhail were safe that was all that mattered.

Then Annaleise said, 'Which nuns were they?'

'I don't know.' Mara had no idea where the courage came from to say this but somehow it came out. 'I heard some of them talking about it,' she said. 'But only about the plan – they weren't going to help with it.' This was better, it made it sound as if the nuns were not involved.

'If you won't tell us names, we shall have to visit the convent and question them all.'

Questioning did not sound too bad. It just meant they would ask the nuns what they knew, and the nuns would say they knew nothing. People believed nuns, so it would be all right. Anyhow, she could not go back on what she had said.

'I can't remember, truly I can't. There was a group of them talking in a classroom. I heard some of what they said, but I didn't see who it was.'

It seemed as if Zoia and Annaleise accepted this. They exchanged looks, and Zoia nodded slightly. 'Mara, you will stay here until we have made sure this is true.'

'No!' said Mara at once. 'Oh please, no! I've told you the truth, I really, honestly have.'

'Then,' said Zoia, 'you don't have anything to worry about.'

They turned and the torchlight moved away and darkness closed down once again. Angry despair flooded over Mara. She might have to be here until the morning, or even longer. I can't bear it, she thought. I hate them! With the hatred came a spurt of fierce strength and courage, almost as if it was being poured into her like hot water. It boiled up, threatening to scald her. She screamed at them, 'You shan't shut me in here, you shan't!' Her screams echoed round the walls, '*Shan't . . . shan't . . . s-s-shan't . . .*'

She bounded forward, round the edge of the gaping well mouth, her hands reaching for the door's edge before it closed on the precious threads of light. Annaleise was half through the door, but she turned back, lifting the heavy torch defensively. Mara sobbed with fury and lunged straight at her. Her clenched fists hit her in the centre of her stomach, causing Annaleise to gasp and double over. The torch fell from her hand and rolled into a corner; light skewed round and shone straight onto Annaleise's face.

Zoia now barred Mara's way. Mara flew at Zoia who dealt her a blow across the face so that Mara fell back, colliding with Annaleise who was still winded by the punch and half blinded by the glare of the torch. The force of the collision sent Annaleise toppling backwards. Zoia shouted a warning, but it was too late. Annaleise stumbled against the low surround of the well itself. She flailed wildly at the air with her arms, trying to regain her balance, but the brick parapet was old and crumbling, and it gave way. She fell screaming over the edge of the well and down into its greedy black depths. The sound echoed with dreadful shrillness inside the well's shaft. The noise she made when she hit the bottom was terrible, a squelching smashing sound, but what was far worse was that she went on screaming after she had fallen. Mara wanted to clap her hands over her ears to shut it out. She wanted to run away as fast as she could – she did not care where, just somewhere she would not have to hear the screaming.

Zoia was shouting something about getting Annaleise out, something about rescuing her. She grabbed Mara's hand and dragged her across the ground to the parapet.

'You evil wicked bitch!' shouted Zoia as Mara sobbed and struggled and tried to prise her hand free. Zoia snatched up the torch, and still holding Mara tightly, knelt at the well's edge and shone it down into the blackness.

'There!' cried Zoia. 'See there! See what you've done. She's dying! Oh God if she dies! I can't bear it!'

Mara, in an awkward painful heap on the ground, stared into the well and sick horror washed over her. It was terrible. What she saw was the worst thing she had ever seen in her life – the worst thing anyone ever could see.

The well was a dark narrow shaft, and at the very bottom of it was the small, faraway figure lying on its back. Mara could not think of it as a person; it had the shape of a person but it was no longer human. Its mouth was stretched wide, and it was screaming like a trapped hare, over and over, the sounds echoing and bouncing inside the well. Blood was coming out of the ears and there was blood in other places – over the legs and arms. Bones stuck out from the body – legs and ribs and wrists. I did that, thought the horrified Mara. I made her fall down there and I made all those bones break and stick out through her skin. And there's something else – something about the face. . .

Zoia leaned over the brick edge – she leaned so far that Mara thought she might tumble down as well, but she did not. She was shouting that she would get help, saying things Mara did not understand – things about loving Anneleise very much and how they would be together again very soon, and Annaleise was not going to die.

'Because if you die, I'll die as well,' shouted Zoia, tears streaming down her face. 'I can't live without you.'

Mara's head was spinning with panic and fear, and although she had not meant to say anything to Zoia, she heard her own voice, saying shrilly, 'There's something wrong with her eyes. What's wrong with her eyes?'

Zoia rounded on Mara with such fury that she cowered and threw up a hand in defence. 'You've fucking blinded her!' she screamed. 'You've smashed most of her bones and you've blinded her! She hit the bottom of the well so hard, the force has driven her eyes from the sockets!'

CHAPTER TWENTY-THREE

Romania, early 1970s

Mara was shivering and icy-cold with fear and shock. She no longer fought against Zoia when the woman dragged her out of the well-house. They started up the track towards the Black House, but they had only gone a few yards when two guards came through the trees towards them.

'Oh, thank God you came down here,' said Zoia. 'We need help – quickly.'

'Routine evening patrol,' said the man. 'What's wrong?'

'It's Miss Simonescu. She's fallen ... she's dreadfully injured, perhaps even dying—' She broke off, then, in a stronger voice, said, 'Fetch ladders and ropes – long ladders. We must get her out, we must get her out *now*.'

'Where is she?' said the man, preparing to go back to the house.

'In the well-house. We need ropes and ladders, *fast*. And keep hold of this child.' She thrust Mara at the second guard. 'She's to be locked up eventually, but there isn't time to do it now. Just make sure she doesn't get away.'

The hours that followed blurred in Mara's mind. She sat on the ground, which was cold and damp and added to the misery of everything, and wondered if she would ever stop being frightened or ever feel warm again. She wondered if she would see her grandmother's cottage or her brother, and then she wished the screaming from the well-house would stop. This was a dreadful wish to have about someone who was lying broken and blinded and in agony, but Mara could not help it. The force drove her eyes from their sockets, Zoia had said. Mara kept hearing these words over and over, and seeing the terrible thing lying at the bottom of the old well. Bones and blood and eyes . . .

She thought the guards felt the same about the screams. As they carried the ladders towards the well-house, she heard one of them say, 'Jesus Christ, I can't stand that row much longer. It's like a bloody animal in a snare.'

'Don't let that one hear you,' said the other, nodding to where Zoia was standing at the open door, wringing her hands, calling to Annaleise that they would get her out, just to wait a very little longer.

'Simonescu will likely be brought out a piece at a time if she fell all the way down,' said the guard. 'Any takers on how many pieces she'll be in?'

'No. Let's get on with it.'

When one of the guards came back outside a bit later to pick up a length of new rope, he passed the tree where Mara was curled up, and she plucked up courage to ask him what was happening.

'No idea. They can't get the ladders down,' he said. 'There's not enough space to manoeuvre. They need very long ladders because the well's so deep, but the well-house is too small for them to tilt the ladders and drop them into the shaft.'

'She's very badly hurt, isn't she?'

'Yes.' He picked up the coil of rope and went back.

Zoia and the guards did not exactly forget Mara, but they did not take much notice of her. At one point the ladders became stuck in the doorway, and shortly after this men came with pickaxes and massive hammers and began to break through the roof. They carried the ladders onto the roof, and lowered them into the shaft.

While they were intent on this, Mara cautiously stood up, hoping to tiptoe away into the trees without being noticed, but one of the men saw and pounced on her, dragging her back. 'None of that,' he said. 'We don't let children run away from us. You try that again and I'll tie you up and leave you for the wolves to eat.'

'There are no such things as wolves any more,' said Mara, clinging to defiance for as long as possible.

'Aren't there? You stay in this forest on your own after dark, and you'll change your mind,' said the man nastily.

The screaming stopped eventually and Mara thought they had finally been able to reach Annaleise. After a time, something swathed in blankets was carried out. Mara tried not to look at it, but could not help herself. The face was covered but one hand, smeared with dried blood, hung down. She's dead, thought Mara. They wouldn't have covered her face if she wasn't. I killed her.

Zoia came out. Her face was smeared with grime, her hands bloodied and torn, and she looked as if something inside her had shrivelled and died. She beckoned to one of the guards.

'Take a couple of the other men and bring Andrei Valk to the Black House. You know where he lives? After that go to the convent school.'

The guard had not looked surprised at the mention of Matthew's father, but he did look surprised when Zoia said this. 'The convent? At this hour of the night?'

'I don't care what hour of the night – or day – it is. Just do as you're told. Go to the convent and ask for Sister Teresa. The nuns – all of them, mind – are to be assembled for questioning in an hour's time.'

The guard nodded. Zoia walked across to where Mara was still sitting by the tree, her arms wrapped round her knees, trying to get warm. She bent down so her face was level with Mara's, and in a voice that made Mara shiver, she said, 'You're an evil little cat, and you're bound for hell. All murderers go to hell, and once they get there, they burn for eternity. That's what will happen to you.' She paused, then said, 'But I'll see you live in hell for the rest of your life on earth. I'll make sure you're shut away and never see the world again.'

Mara stared up at the thin white face and thought, She's going to put me back inside the well-house, but Zoia did not. She straightened up, and called to two of the guards. 'Take her back to the house. See to it that she's locked up.' The guards nodded, and half-carried Mara back to the cold, sour-smelling room with the black stove. This time, the door was locked.

Mara huddled miserably on the bed, crying at intervals, wondering whether Zoia would tell her grandmother and brother that she had killed Annaleise. It was still night, but she had no idea what time of night it was. She sat by the window hoping to hear the church clock chiming the hour; it would make her feel she was not so very far away from her home and she would be able to count the chimes and know the time. But either the Black House was too far away or the windows were too tightly closed, because although she sat there until she was cramped and frozen through, she did not hear the familiar friendly chimes.

Eventually there were footsteps in the passage outside, the door was unlocked, and Zoia and Sister Teresa came in. Mara had not expected this.

She wiped her eyes on a corner of the scratchy sheet and sat up because Sister Teresa always made people sit up straight; she said a sloppy posture meant a sloppy mind. She was quite strict which meant no one ever dared play around in her class and, although she looked strict now, she did not punish people unless they really deserved it. She and Zoia sat together at the narrow table under one window. Mara knew it was important to listen to what they said, but she was frightened and exhausted and found it difficult to follow.

Sister Teresa took control of the discussion at once, by asking why Mara had been shut inside the well-house in the first place.

'A harsh penance for such a small child, surely, no matter the sin?'

Zoia mumbled a bit and for a moment there were two scarlet patches on her pale cheeks. 'Mara had been wilful and unruly,' she said at length. 'The rules here are strict, but I have to do what my masters say.'

Sister Teresa did not look as if she entirely believed this, but before she could say anything, Zoia said, 'The question of the child can wait, Sister. You know we're holding two of your nuns on suspicion of plotting the escape of a prisoner?'

'I do know and it's a ridiculous idea. None of the sisters know anything about Elisabeth Valk or any other prisoner. None of us even have any idea where she is.'

'The child was clear about it, though.'

'The child was mistaken,' said Sister Teresa at once. 'Frightened and confused. She'd have said anything to get back to her home. Can I take her with me now?'

'No. She's not going home for a very long time.'

Mara was so sick with disappointment at this, she had to will herself not to cry, and did not hear what was said next. By the time she had fought the tears down, Sister Teresa and Zoia were talking about appropriate treatment for a child, and whether a doctor should be called for an examination. This was worrying in a whole new way because nobody went to doctors if they could help it. Mara had never been to one in her life. Doctors, always supposing you knew where to find one, were for rich people, her grandmother said.

Sister Teresa said they were in a situation that had probably never arisen before. In some countries there were special places for such children, she said – hostels and institutions, but out here ... She gave the bony-shouldered shrug she gave in class when people had not done their homework. It usually meant she was annoyed but puzzled at such bad behaviour.

She was annoyed and puzzled now, Mara could see that.

'I should like to hear what Mara has to say,' she said, and without waiting for an answer, went over to the bed. 'Well, Mara? What have you to say for yourself? Miss Simonescu is dead and I'm told you were responsible. You know that killing someone is a very grave sin. A mortal sin. God is good and merciful and loves all children, but He will find it difficult to love you if you've killed another human being.'

'I didn't mean to kill her,' said Mara, not knowing whether to be relieved that this was not about the lie, or frightened that God might not love her any longer. 'I was trying to get out of that place – the well-house, because it's got a face and I thought it might be a troll turned into stone.' She started crying again, but Sister Teresa waited and after a few moments, Mara was able to say, 'Truly, Sister, I was fighting them to get away. I didn't mean Ann – I didn't mean Miss Simonescu to fall into the well.' This sounded a bit ridiculous, like the nursery rhyme about the cat in the well.

But Sister Teresa gave a small nod as if this was enough, and went back to the table. 'I believe there was no malice,' she said. 'No serious intent.'

'You didn't see it,' said Zoia, her lips folded into a thin hard line like a steel ruler in a pencil-box. 'The child flew at Miss Simonescu and pushed her very hard. I saw the malice and the intent all right – it blazed in her eyes. If you won't take steps to have her shut away, I'll hand her over to the Securitate.'

'No, don't do that,' said Sister Teresa at once. 'I have a suggestion.' She looked across at Mara and then back to Zoia. 'We have a convent just outside Debreczen.'

'In Hungary?'

'Yes, but only just over the border. It's not too difficult a journey – I go there two or three times each year. But it's a very poor House in a remote area and if Mara went there, she would be expected to help with the running of the convent – cleaning and cooking. She would be given teaching as well, of course, as she must have at her age.'

'Why should I hand her over to you? The Securitate will deal with her very satisfactorily.'

Sister Teresa thought for a moment, then said, 'There are rumours in the village that this house is to be closed.'

Zoia looked up. 'How do you know that?'

'People get to hear things. We get told some of those things. Is it true?'

'It's been considered for some time,' said Zoia, 'and after tonight it's very probable. I shall leave anyway – Miss Simonescu was a very dear friend and I don't think I shall want to stay in the place where ...'

'I understand.'

'They probably won't replace me if I go. What has this to do with Mara?'

'Am I right in thinking you have some very young children here?'

'Yes,' said Zoia after a moment. 'A dozen or so. It's difficult to provide care for them – we aren't given the money or the facilities.'

'I understand.'

'There never was enough money in the first place,' said Zoia with sudden anger. 'The ruling made by Elena Ceauşescu – the ruling intended to increase the birth rate – forced an impossible situation on this country. People had babies without being able to feed or clothe them.' She stopped and looked scared. 'I shouldn't have said that—'

'It won't go beyond this room. It was in confidence between us.'

'And will the two nuns being held by the Securitate keep what they know in confidence?' said Zoia.

'I've already told you they know nothing,' said Sister Teresa.

'The Church keeps its own counsel?' said Zoia a bit sneeringly.

'It always has done,' said Sister Teresa. She frowned, then said,

264

'Miss Calciu, if the Black House is to be closed, what will happen to the children in your care? Will they be sent to another orphanage?'

'I suppose so.'

'Will that be your responsibility? Won't it be difficult to find places for them?'

'Yes. Most of the other orphanages are overcrowded.'

'You would have to – to hawk the children around the countryside like a pedlar,' said Sister Teresa, nodding. 'Very unpleasant and exhausting. But I have a proposal that might make that unnecessary. I sometimes visit another House within our Order – a convent in England.'

Zoia looked interested; Mara guessed it was the mention of England which everyone said was a marvellous place, a place where everyone was rich and you could walk into shops and buy anything you wanted.

'We have strong links with the English House,' said Sister Teresa. 'It's in a tiny place, it's not a school as we have here, but the sisters are hospitable and generous and if I were to approach them it's possible they would take in some children for a while. They might find them homes with English families – at worst places in good children's homes. Papers would have to be in order – visas and so on, however.'

'Papers could be arranged,' said Zoia at once. 'I know people who would help with that.'

'It would mean you could leave this place much sooner,' said Sister Teresa. 'You could put the sadness behind you much quicker.'

There was another silence and Mara saw that Zoia was thinking about what Sister Teresa had said. 'This place in Debreczen,' she said at last, 'is it a house of correction?'

'No, but if Mara went there she would have to keep to a strict regime. No distractions. Prayer and study and work.'

'Would there be other children?'

'There might be. The sisters sometimes take one or two in for various reasons. If parents die, for instance.'

'If I were to agree to your suggestion,' said Zoia, not sounding as if she was yet convinced, 'how long could Mara stay there?'

'A few years, certainly. Say until she reaches young adulthood – sixteen, seventeen. It's possible that by then she will have become imbued with the way of life – with the outlook of the sisters – and decide to take her vows.' Sister Teresa sent another of the quick glances towards the listening Mara. 'We wouldn't force that if there's no real vocation, but if she did join the Order it would indicate full contrition. An atonement for her sin.'

Zoia said slowly, 'I might find that acceptable.'

'And in turn, we would also be solving the problem of the Black House orphans for you.' Sister Teresa stood up, as if she considered the matter settled. She stood up. 'I'll collect Mara early tomorrow morning,' she said and went out.

Mara thought it might be a bit scary to be on her own with Sister Teresa, but it was not, although the journey was longer than Mara had imagined any journey could be. She had never been outside the village before, and had no idea how they would travel. Did Sister Teresa have a car? Mara had been in a car twice but only for very short distances. They might go on a train, of course. She had never been on a train, in fact she had never even seen a train, except for pictures in books.

They did not go in a car, but on trains and buses. Sister Teresa had made the journey before so she knew what they had to do and was able to tell Mara where they were, and how this was the border between Romania and Hungary they were crossing.

Mara was fearful about what was ahead and worried about her grandmother and brother, but it was pretty exciting to be going on this journey, seeing places she had never heard of. She looked out of the windows for most of the time, seeing how the countryside became wilder and how the mountains were different.

'They're dangerous, of course, those mountains,' said Sister Teresa. 'There are bears and wolves in them. But there's also some of the most beautiful plant life you can imagine. Potentilla and gentian and things you'll never see in the towns. You'll have lessons at Debreczen, of course, and you'll have to work hard. There were a couple of English sisters there last time I went: if they're still there, you might try to learn a little English. It's a very widely spoken language and it might one day be useful for you.'

Later, when they were at the back of the jolting bus, winding its way up a steep mountain path, she talked about what had happened at the Black House.

'I'm as sure as I can be that you didn't kill Annaleise Simonescu with deliberate intent,' she said and Mara looked at her gratefully. 'But I can't be completely sure because no one can see inside another person's mind. You were responsible for her death, but if you remember your catechism, for a sin to be mortal there has to be full knowledge, free will and grave matter. I don't think you had any of those. But that woman – Zoia – thinks you meant to kill and she wants you punished very severely.'

'Am I going to be?'

Sister Teresa hesitated. 'It won't be a life of luxury,' she said. 'The Debreczen House is a poor one. But it isn't a punishment place and they'll be kind to you. What I said about you helping with the cleaning and cooking was true, though.'

'I don't mind cleaning and cooking. Would I be allowed to go home sometimes?'

'I don't know. I wish you could simply have gone home to your grandmother and Mikhail – if I could have taken you, I would. But it was too dangerous. I made a kind of bargain with Miss Calciu, you see. I have to honour that.'

'Why couldn't I say goodbye to them?' Mara had cried all over again at discovering she was not allowed to do this. Sister Teresa had brought a hastily packed bag from the convent, with a nightdress and a clean jumper and skirt and underthings. Mara had no idea who they belonged to.

'I couldn't risk it,' said Sister Teresa. 'If either of us had gone to your grandmother's house, Zoia would have known about it. Her people would have been ordered to watch us, and she would have seen it as a trick. She might have taken you back into the Black House, and I'm not sure if I could have got you out a second time.'

'She'd have shut me inside the well-house again,' said Mara in a scared whisper. 'She hated me because of what happened. Sister, I told them a lie.' There it was, admitted to at last. 'I said I heard some of the sisters talking about Matthew's father, and how he was trying to find Matthew's mother and rescue her. But really it was my grandmother who told me about it.'

She waited for Sister Teresa to be angry, but Sister Teresa said, 'Lies are very bad things indeed, Mara, but I understand you told that lie to protect your family.'

'Yes,' said Mara in a very small voice. 'Um, Sister, did anything happen because of it?'

'To the nuns, you mean? There are always consequences from a lie, and there were consequences this time. Two of the sisters are with the Securitate at the moment. We think they will be allowed home, though.'

'I'm sorry,' said Mara again. 'I'll confess the lie. But I'm glad my grandmother and Mikhail are all right.' This seemed to go down well, so feeling a bit braver she said, 'Sister Teresa, why did Zoia hate me so very much? I didn't understand that. I know what happened to Annaleise – Miss Simonescu – was bad, but it wasn't as if she was Zoia's family or anything like that.'

Sister Teresa took a moment to reply, and when she did her voice sounded awkward, as if she was not sure if she was using the right words. She said, 'God makes people differently, Mara. Sometimes people – ladies – form very deep attachments to one another. Sometimes men do so, as well. Zoia had a deep attachment for Miss Simonescu. That's all we need to know.'

'Oh. Yes, I see. Sister – do you know about the children in the Black House?'

'I know there are children there.'

Mara saw Sister Teresa's lips tighten. 'They're in cages!' It came out in an angry explosion, and Mara bit her lip. 'I saw them by mistake,' she said. 'I think that's part of why they put me in the well-house. Sister, they were crying – they were only little babies . . .'

Sister Teresa turned her head to look down at Mara. 'I did know about them,' she said. 'That was why I made the bargain.'

Debreczen, when they finally reached it, was small and old and felt somehow secretive. The streets were shadowy because the buildings were of thick old stone – Mara pressed against the windows of the trundly little bus to see better. The convent was a few kilometres outside the town: it was much nearer to the mountains than Mara had expected, and it almost seemed to be built into them.

Once inside, it was cool and dim; there were stone corridors and small cell-like rooms. Mara was shown a dormitory where she would sleep with four other girls who were living there. They were all older than Mara and she felt a bit scared of them.

'They will be your friends,' said Sister Teresa, when she left Debreczen two days later. 'You will come to know and love them.'

But Mara knew she would never love anyone as much as she loved her grandmother and brother. She would not let herself believe she would never see them again. She could not bear that. She could not bear, either, to think she would never see Matthew again.

Even though Matthew did not know where Mara was, every time he thought about her being taken away, he had a dreadful picture of her locked in a stone cell with iron bars at the windows, beating her hands on those bars to get out.

Two days after Mara vanished a jeep came snarling down the lane. Matthew had been getting ready for bed, but he ran to the window when he heard it. His father opened the door as the men walked up to the house and Matthew's heart began to race. He tried to think it would be one of the men's ordinary visits, that they would come into the house and talk to his father, then go away again, that it would be all right.

But it was not. The men did not come inside; they grabbed his father there on the doorstep and half dragged him to the waiting jeep. He protested and struggled, but the men had him in a tight hold. The one who had talked to Matthew about art school, said, 'No use in struggling, Andrei. We've finally got the evidence we need. One of the local children heard talk and repeated it to us – no, not your precious son,' he said, in a sneery voice. 'And we've got all the pieces of the jigsaw at last.'

Matthew's father hardly seemed to hear. He was fighting the men for all he was worth. Matthew was astonished to see him like that, fighting and hitting out, his hair tumbling over his forehead, his collar loosened. They would overcome him, because there were too many of them. Matthew ran downstairs, skidding on the last few and almost falling over, then pelted across the hall to the open door. He snatched up the ash walking-stick in the coatstand to beat off the men. But when he got to the door he saw it would make no difference if he had all the weapons of an army, because the jeep was already driving off and it was too late.

His father was seated in the back, one of the men keeping firm hold of his arm. He turned round and shouted above the growl of the engine, 'Matthew – everything will be all right. I'll be back very soon. Almost certainly tomorrow. So stay here – and whatever happens, remember I love you very much . . .'

Matthew watched the jeep drive away, then went back up to his room, curled into a miserable huddle on the bed and cried into the pillow until it was soaked through.

His father did not come back the next day. Nor the next day nor the day after that. A whole lot of days went by, and Matthew ran home from school every afternoon, imagining that his father would be there and the men would somehow have been dealt with, and how Matthew himself would be able to feel safe again. But each time there was the sick stab of disappointment at finding only Wilma in the house. Each evening, he ate his supper – he did not want it but Wilma said he had to keep up his strength – and then did his homework.

He concentrated fiercely on this, because it stopped him thinking about what might be happening to his father, but when there was arithmetic homework, the memory of his father saying how he used to write stories about the troublesome figures was too much to bear. Matthew would walk about the bedroom very fast, hoping to fool the memories into going away, but they would not be fooled. He could not stop thinking about the comic story they had planned to write, with Matthew drawing the figures and his father making up the story. It would have been a good story because his father always had good ideas about these things. He had said they might try selling it to a newspaper – comic strips they called them. You could make quite a lot of money from comic strips, he had said, with the sudden narrow-eyed thoughtful look he wore when he was thinking up plots. Matthew loved that look. He could not bear to think he might never see it again.

Each night he sat in the window-seat of his bedroom, watching the lane, so he could see his father's thin figure the minute it appeared. When it got dark he placed the little lamp by the window where it would shine out into the lane, so that when his father did come he would see the light like travellers in stories.

He wanted to find out where his father had been taken, but he had no idea where to start. Those typed words in the article he had found went through and through his mind. '*They vanish as abruptly and as completely as if by sorcery,*' his father had written.

Had his father been taken to one of the nameless prisons

described in the article? Was he shut away in one of those stone cells Matthew still sometimes dreamed about?

'He'll come back,' said Wilma, wrapping her fat arms round Matthew and hugging him. Matthew found this comforting because Wilma always smelt of clean hair and soap and occasionally of baking. 'It'll be all right,' she said. 'You'll see. We'll keep a watch and he'll come home very soon.'

But although Matthew watched faithfully every night from his bedroom window, his father did not come home.

And Mara did not come home either.

CHAPTER TWENTY-FOUR

The present

The shrilling of the phone sliced violently across Theo's consciousness, splintering Mara's world, and causing the images of the well-house and the feeling of Zoia's bitter grief to vanish. He reached for the phone, hoping it would be Lesley.

But it was not Lesley, it was DS Leigh. 'Just checking you're all right.'

'I'm fine,' said Theo, forcing himself to climb out of 1970s Romania. 'No more disturbances.'

'Good. Has your cousin Lesley called?'

'No.' Theo did not say he was starting to feel slightly worried about this.

'Well, let us know when she does. I'd like to be sure that other key is where we think,' said Leigh. 'I spoke to the nuns. They haven't seen or heard anything out of the way, but they were very sorry to hear about your attack. The Bursar said you could have a room in the hospital wing if you don't want to stay at Fenn on your own tonight.'

'That's kind of her,' said Theo, 'but I'll be perfectly all right.'

'Call if you need us,' said Leigh.

Theo put the phone down, suddenly aware the room was cold. He switched off the computer, thinking he had had enough of that strange other-world for the night. It was half past ten, and he supposed at some stage he should go to bed, but he was reluctant. He knew he would keep seeing that dark crouching figure on the stair and lie awake listening for the creak of footsteps treading stealthily across the landing towards him ... Because whoever he is, he's got a key.

To counteract the deep unease this thought churned up, Theo made himself go round the house to check the bolts were still firmly in place, then made a mug of tea and returned to the warmth of the sitting room. He scanned the bookshelves, hoping to find something fairly undemanding to read, and saw the glossy booklet about St Luke's hundred years, which the Bursar had given him. Just right. He took it to the sofa, pulled the rug back over him, and opened the pages.

The Bursar's style of writing turned out to be pleasantly readable: light and informative without being dull or teachy. Theo found himself drawn into the little tale of how a pioneer group of six nuns had come to Norfolk in the opening years of the twentieth century to found an English convent for their Order, and how they had struggled on slender funds and against considerable distrust from the local people. They had been shunted from pillar to post for several years – living in old schoolrooms, virtually camping out, sharing one set of plates and cups between all six of them. After about eight years they had somehow managed to acquire their present house which had belonged to a local wool merchant, and had built it up until it was a small but busy orthopaedic clinic and convalescent home.

Old photographs were reproduced, depicting various stages in the convent's life. There were group photos of WWI soldiers who had been wounded and come to St Luke's to recuperate, and of Belgian nuns who had fled the siege of Antwerp and been given sanctuary in Melbray. There were descriptions of how the nuns

274

had later coped with WWII, helping with coastal defences, raising money for the Spitfire Fund and again taking in wounded men, mostly fighter pilots this time. The photographs were clear and well displayed and the whole book was professionally presented. The cover was particularly good: a really lovely colour shot of the convent against its grounds in spring. Theo wondered if the nuns had done their own photography and whether the printer who'd had to decipher the Bursar's typewritten text was a local man.

The last section in the book gave a brief history of the Order of St Luke itself. It was primarily a teaching and nursing order apparently, with a number of other houses around the world – Theo remembered the recent visit of nuns from Poland. The founder of the entire Order, it seemed, had been an indomitable-sounding lady from Central Europe.

Central Europe. The words jumped up off the page, and Theo sat up, all sleepiness vanished. He began to read with more attention. And there it was, halfway along:

The Founder's House still exists in south-western Romania – a troubled land – and our sisters there have encountered many hardships over the years. Two of them suffered incarceration during the dictatorship of President Ceauşescu. That was a harsh and difficult period for that country and we did all we could to help.

But times are happier now, and the sisters still work and teach there, as they have always done. (See picture of the Founder House in Romania, with the pupils of the junior school, teacher-nuns and four friends.)

Romania. And two of the Romanian sisters had been imprisoned. Theo read on.

The links with our Founder House remain strong and there have been many happy connections over the years. In particular, we were delighted when, in the 1970s, Sister Teresa brought to England twelve Romanian children who lived at St Luke's for a while before going out into the world to be educated.

Sister Teresa. Theo could hardly believe what he was seeing. So Sister Teresa, too, was real. Not only was she real, she had brought twelve children to England exactly as he had written. He turned to look at the photograph. It was a large black and white shot of a big stone building standing against a backdrop of pine trees, with distant, smudgy mountains beyond. There was no caption and no date, but the nuns stood in what was clearly a school playground, smiling self-consciously. The children were grouped in three rows, the smaller ones cross-legged at the front, the older ones standing behind.

There were three ladies and one man who must be the friends referred to in the text. All were dressed in ordinary modern clothes. The man was the youngest but his face was slightly turned away so his features were not very clear. Of the three ladies, two looked to be in their fifties; they had conservative hairstyles and rather dowdy, tweedy-looking suits. The third was much younger. She had slightly untidy dark hair, worn loose and shoulder-length, and had on a light jacket with a gauzy scarf wound round her neck. The photo was a bit grainy and did not look very recent, although it was difficult to tell its age. It might have been blown up from a smaller snapshot. But grainy or not, the details were clear enough for Theo to see the features of the young woman with the gauzy scarf.

It was Charmery.

Theo stared at the photo, his thoughts in turmoil. What on earth had Charmery been doing in a Romanian convent? When had she been there? The words of Mara's grandmother re-played in his head. 'Some people know,' she had said, whispering her stories to the listening Mara. 'Trust nuns to know secrets . . .' But what were the secrets? How did they tie up with Charmery? He leaned his head against the cushions, and tried to slot the pieces of the jigsaw into a logical pattern, because this could not be coincidence.

The room had warmed up and the gas popped softly to itself; it was a soothing sound in the quiet room. Theo closed his eyes, and after a while drifted into a shallow, uneasy sleep, in which the jigsaw pieces whirled maddeningly around, refusing to slot into place. He had the vague impression that someone was standing outside the French window looking in at him, but he was not sure if it was Charmery's murderer or whether it was Charmery herself. Because Charmery's still here, he thought, she might have died four months ago, but she's still here. 'The murdered always walk, remember?' said a soft voice inside his dream, and for a moment he saw Charmery. She was smiling at him, and standing at her side, his hand in hers, was a small boy with Theo's eyes.

Theo was trying to see the boy's face, when a sound jerked him back to full consciousness, and he sat up, his heart pounding. Someone was in the house. He slid his feet to the floor, pushing aside the cushions. The phone was on the table, just three paces away, and the note with Leigh's number was next to it. He stood up and began to edge towards it, trying not to make any noise.

The sounds he had half heard came again, and this time he identified them. It was not someone inside the house after all – it was someone outside. Someone was walking along the gravel path towards the French windows. Theo looked towards them, knowing they were firmly locked and bolted, but knowing, as well, that all it would take was a stone smashed against the glass pane, and a hand reached through to the bolt.

He picked up the phone and began to move back towards the hall, his eyes on the windows. A shape, man-sized, appeared and a hand came up to rap hard on the glass. Theo was halfway across the room, but at this he froze. He had no idea if the man could see into the dimly lit room, and he had no idea if he would be heard if he made a run for the hall and the front door.

Then Michael Innes' voice said, 'Theo? Are you there? For pity's sake, are you all right?'

For a split-second doubt stabbed at Theo's mind, but then he called out that of course, he was all right. 'Hold on, Innes, I'll let you in.'

'Thank goodness,' said Innes, coming into the room as Theo unbolted the window, then re-bolted it. He shook raindrops off his overcoat. 'I rang the doorbell but there was no reply, and I could see a light on so I came round the side to see if I could make you hear. I was afraid you'd passed out or succumbed to concussion after all.'

'I fell asleep on the sofa,' said Theo. 'Those pills were stronger than I realized. I probably didn't hear the bell through the closed door.' Then, still faintly suspicious, 'Why didn't you phone?' he said.

'I haven't got your number on my mobile. I got called out to a child with appendicitis – except it wasn't – and I was driving past the end of the lane on the way home, so I thought I'd check on you.'

'Are you off duty now?'

'What time is it? Quarter to eleven? Near enough. Enough to accept a whisky if that's what you were thinking.'

'It was.' Theo gave him the whisky, and ostentatiously poured plain soda into his own glass.

'Thanks. God, that tastes good. Has anything else happened?'

'Nothing.'

'That's all I wanted to know. I'll head home when I've drunk this – unless you want me to stay the night in case your assailant comes back. Or come back to my place. I can easily make up a bed for you.'

'I don't really think he'll come back tonight,' said Theo, 'but thanks for the offer.'

'In that case, I'd better get back, in case there're any messages.' He was just putting down his glass when the phone rang.

Theo did not jump quite so much this time, but the sound still unnerved him.

'Theo?' said Lesley's voice, when he answered. 'I know it's very late, but your voice sounded a bit panicky on the answerphone.'

'It's not that late,' said Theo, 'and I can't tell you how relieved I am to hear you. Are you all right?'

'Of course I'm all right. My mobile's out of charge and when I got home the people in the flat downstairs were having a party and they dragged me in. I threw my case into the flat, dumped the sketch on the bed, and went straight down for a couple of hours. So I've only just picked up your message. What on earth's wrong?'

'Nothing earth-shattering,' said Theo. 'It's just that I need to know about the key.'

'Key?' she said a bit blankly, and Theo guessed she was having difficulty bringing her mind back from her unexpected party to Fenn House.

'I gave you one of the new keys while you were here.'

'Oh yes, so you did. Oh Lord, I didn't give it back to you, did I?'

'No, but that doesn't matter. Have you still got it?'

'Well, if I didn't give it back, obviously I've still got it.'

'Would you make sure? No, I'm not fussing, it's important.'

'Hang on a minute,' she said. 'I put it in the zip compartment of my bag so it wouldn't fall out.' There were rustlings and scrabblings as she searched, then she came back. 'Theo – I'm sorry, it's not there.'

'Sure?'

'Positive. I must have lost it somewhere – I really am sorry.'

'I don't think you've lost it,' said Theo. 'I think it was taken out of your bag.'

'Who took it?'

'I don't know,' he said. 'Lesley, listen, everything's fine, but I'll have to ring off now and sort out a problem.'

'What sort of problem? Are you sure you're all right?'

'Yes. I'll call you in the morning and explain everything.'

'If you don't, I'll turn up on the doorstep.'

Theo put down the phone and looked across at Innes.

'Your cousin Lesley?'

'Yes.'

'She hasn't got the key, has she?'

'No.'

Innes frowned, then said, 'In that case, I don't think you should stay here tonight on your own. Whoever your attacker is, we now know he's got a key to this house.'

'Well, whatever I do, I think I'd better call Sergeant Leigh and let him know what's happened,' said Theo.

He was not sure if Leigh would still be on duty, but he answered immediately, and Theo said, 'Lesley's just phoned. The key's gone.'

'Ah. Well, I can't say I'm surprised. She's all right, is she? I mean – she wasn't attacked or her bag snatched or anything?'

'No.'

'The key *could* have been lost,' said Leigh. 'But it'd be a whopping coincidence. It didn't have the address on it, did it – no label or anything? Good. But we'll need to check everywhere she's been, certainly until she got on the train. You were at St Luke's for part of the day, weren't you?'

'Yes, but I don't think we should jump to any wild conclusions about that,' said Theo. 'Lesley walked into the village in the morning. She went into a couple of the shops, I think.'

'We'll check everything and everywhere. What I'm not liking is this news that your attacker's almost certainly got a key and you're in the house on your own.'

'The doors are all bolted,' said Theo a bit doubtfully. 'But if he really did go to the trouble of stealing a key—'

'It means he's very determined to get to you,' finished Leigh, 'and he might try again. I'll try to send someone out to Fenn, but we're dealing with a massive smash on the by-pass at the moment.'

'Michael Innes is here,' said Theo. 'He's suggested he could stay here or I could go to his house for the night.' He looked at Innes, who nodded.

'That's a very good idea,' said Leigh. 'Dr Innes isn't your attacker, if that's what you're discreetly trying to ask.'

'It was.'

'He can't be. You were able to be fairly exact about the time it happened because of getting your cousin to Norwich for her train. A few minutes before or just after seven, you said. Dr Innes had a late surgery until seven, then spent at least fifteen minutes dictating some notes to his secretary. She was with him when you phoned, we've talked to her. And your call was logged at seven nineteen – we've checked it with your phone network.'

'Oh, I see. Then,' said Theo, 'I think I'll take up his offer.'

Innes drove them to his house, which was about ten miles beyond Melbray.

'You'd better not drive yourself,' he said, as Theo went upstairs to collect night things. 'You're still recovering from the bump on the head. I can bring you back to Fenn in the morning – I've got some calls to make in the village anyway.'

Innes lived in one half of a pair of cottages, which looked as if they had been converted from old farm cottages. The sitting room was warm and comfortably untidy, and there was a second bedroom with a single bed.

'Spare duvet in the airing cupboard,' said Innes. 'The bathroom's through there – I'll put a clean towel out for you.'

Theo liked the house and the tiny study off the sitting room, where Innes kept his patients' notes and medical books. As Innes checked his answerphone, Theo prowled round, looking at the bookshelves.

'No calls that can't wait until the morning,' said Innes, coming back. 'I've put the kettle on for a last cup of tea, or coffee if you'd rather.'

'Tea's fine. I see the sisters gave you one of their centenary booklets,' said Theo, still looking along the rows of books.

'Yes, but I daren't admit to them that I still haven't got round to reading it.'

'I read it earlier,' said Theo. 'It's quite an interesting story. There's an odd thing in it though – can I open this? Thanks.' He turned to the page with the photo of Charmery, and passed it to Innes. 'Curious, isn't it?' he said. 'Did you know Charmery was ever in Romania?'

Innes studied the photograph with interest. 'No, I didn't,' he said. 'But there was a lot about her I didn't know.'

'Me too,' said Theo, dryly.

'It wouldn't be very surprising if she did find her way out there, though. Specially if she became friendly with any of the nuns at St Luke's.'

'The Romanian convent's the Founder House, of course,' said Theo.

'Yes, and one of the nuns at St Luke's has a strong link to Romania. In fact— Theo, what have I said?'

Theo's heart had begun its fast-paced rhythm. 'Which one?' he said. 'Innes, which of the nuns has a link to Romania?'

There was a moment when he waited, his heart thudding, then Michael Innes said, 'Sister Miriam.'

It was the last name Theo had been expecting to hear. 'Are you sure?'

'Yes, completely. She's originally from Romania. Her real name is Mara Ionescu, and— Are you sure you're all right?'

Theo scarcely heard him. The name had exploded inside his head and it was continuing to explode. Mara. All the time his strange, ill-starred girl had been in St Luke's. I talked to you, Mara, he thought, without knowing who you were. I even sat at table with you and ate lunch.

He dragged his mind back to Michael Innes. 'How do you know that about – about Sister Miriam? Because of medical records, or something?'

'Not medical records. Quite simple. Sister Miriam – Mara – is my sister.'

This time the mental explosion was more gentle, but once again Theo had the impression of a hand reaching from the past to clasp his. He stared at Innes, and heard himself say, 'My God, you're Mikhail.'

'Yes.'

Theo's thoughts were in a confused tumble. This is Mikhail, he thought. This is the small shadowy boy who trailed after Matthew and Mara on those walks to school, who hid in the attic when the Securitate took Mara away. It's the brother for whom Mara would have done anything if it meant keeping him from the Securitate's clutches.

From somewhere beneath the tumult, he became aware that Innes was not surprised at the recognition, but he could not spare any energy to wonder about this. Forcing himself to speak as normally as he could, he said, 'Michael, later, I'll explain what I've found, but I do know a bit of Mara's story, and some of yours too, I think. I'd like to know how Mara – and you – ended up in an English village and how she came to be at an English convent.'

'You're seeing a link, aren't you?' said Innes. 'You've discovered Charmery was in Romania and you think there's a connection between the convent and her death. Perhaps even between your own attack and the convent.'

'I wouldn't put it quite so strongly,' said Theo. 'But I think it's something that would bear looking into.' Nuns know secrets, he was thinking. *Secrets* . . .

'If you're focusing on Mara you'd be wrong,' said Michael Innes. 'She could never use violence of any kind. She couldn't be Charmery's killer. If I ever thought that for a moment, don't you think I'd have warned the police?'

'I don't know. Would you?'

'Yes,' he said, angrily. 'Yes, of course I would. But if the police were to start digging up her past life after so many years – it would cause her so much distress.'

'All right. But, listen, I'd like to know about Mara. I'll respect whatever confidence you give me, and I'll explain it all properly later. But if you can bear to talk – and if it isn't too late … Michael, this is like the child Charmery had: it's something I need to know!'

For a moment Innes seemed unable to speak, but eventually he said, 'Mara had a truly appalling time when she was a child and a teenager. And I'd have to admit it damaged her – mentally, I mean. She's managed to distance herself from what was done to her when she was very young, but it's been a hard fight for her.'

Theo said cautiously, 'The damage – was that because of the Black House?'

'So you know about that, do you? No, not so much the Black House, but what came afterwards.'

Theo, listening with every nerve-ending, thought, he knows about the Black House. He would have seen it – heard the whispers. Oh God, this really is my book coming alive.

'I don't know how much you do know,' said Innes, 'but Mara spent her most of her teenage years in a remote convent near the border between Romania and Hungary. I never knew exactly why she was sent there. I was very small when it happened. And although I never saw that convent, Mara wrote to me quite a lot while she was there. I've still got the letters. It sounded like such a bleak place – absolutely in the middle of nowhere. Later I thought those years created a solitude within her mind, as if the silence and the detachment of the life closed her off from the normal world.'

'Yes, I understand,' said Theo softly, not daring to say any more in case he broke the spell being woven.

'When she left that convent, she could have adjusted to ordinary life again, I think. I could have helped her adjust. But it was what happened to her when she came out that damaged her so deeply.'

CHAPTER TWENTY-FIVE

Romania, early 1970s

Mara had not known whether the nuns at the Debreczen convent were aware that she had killed another person. She did not know if Sister Teresa would have told them, or even if Zoia might have found a way of telling them. She could not think what she would do if they all knew what had happened to Annaleise.

But it seemed to be all right. They made her welcome in a rather gruff fashion, and folded her into the pattern of their lives. As Sister Teresa had said, it was not an easy pattern. The days were filled with work: Mara was expected to help with scrubbing the stone flags in the big scullery and in the corridors and to take her turn in the laundry which was always filled with steam and smelled of starch and lye soap, and in the refectory where there was usually a mountain of washing-up. Each day at twelve there was a small raggle-taggle queue of tramps who came up to the convent for a meal – Mara was not allowed to hand out food to them, but she was expected to help with chopping vegetables to throw into the big simmering vat of stew, and to stir the steel urn of strong tea the tramps liked.

There were lessons each day, as there had been at home, but

there were only the four other girls to share them. They did arithmetic, history and geography, all of which Mara had done at home, but they also had to learn languages. Latin, which Mara found difficult, but which the nuns said firmly was the universal language of religion, and also a smattering of French and English. Mara set herself to learn these two as well as she could because by then she was allowed to send and receive letters, although she was never sure if all her letters reached Mikhail, or if she received all the ones he sent her. But in the letters she did get, Mikhail said he was learning French and English and it gave her a feeling of closeness to him. Struggling to understand the unfamiliar structuring of sentences, she was able to think of Mikhail doing exactly the same. When he wrote that he wanted to read the great writers of the world in their own language she redoubled her efforts, spending hours in the convent's small library. Sometimes she ached with longing to see Mikhail and hear his voice. She wrote to him about her days, describing everything she did. She loved it when he wrote back saying how much he enjoyed hearing from her, and telling her about his own lessons and the village gossip, and sharing small jokes about French irregular verbs and peculiar English spellings and pronunciation of words like bough and cough and rough.

She missed the company of a big classroom and the little tests that used to be set, and the playground and the games, and she missed her own village and the cottage. But Sister Teresa visited Debreczen three times a year and always brought news. Mara's grandmother was well, Mikhail was growing up, and working hard at his studies. Such a clever boy. Mara wondered if she would ever see Mikhail or her grandmother again. She wondered, as well, if she would ever see Matthew.

Romania, early 1980s

Matthew was seventeen when he finally accepted he was not going to see Mara again, and that he was not going to see his father either. It was not a sudden acceptance. It gradually crept over him during the years of going to school and running home each afternoon in case this was the day his father came back. He counted the months and then the years – one year, then two, then four and five. He worked hard during those years, mostly because it was what his father would have wanted, and he even tried to understand arithmetic which changed its name to mathematics when he went up to the senior school. Almost every moment of his spare time was spent drawing, painting and reading books about famous painters. At odd moments he drew the cartoon figures he and his father had talked about, trying to make up stories about them as his father had planned. He did not think the stories were very good, but he liked drawing the figures.

And now he was seventeen and it was eight years since his father had been taken away and since Mara had vanished. They'll never come back, thought Matthew miserably. But I'll never stop hoping or trying to think of ways to find them.

Occasionally he wondered what would have happened if he had told the Securitate about his father's articles. He understood now that his father was regarded as a dissident, even as what was called an enemy of the state. The Securitate were still around a lot of the time, prowling the village streets, talking to people. 'And listening at doors,' said Wilma, who had grown stouter than ever with the years and still fussed over Matthew as if he were four years old, and queued for hours to get the ingredients to cook his favourite goulash when he was feeling lonely.

'They're spies and murderers, those Securitate people,' said Mara's brother, Mikhail, who was two or three years younger than Matthew, but far cleverer than anyone Matthew knew. Mikhail hated the Securitate because they had stolen Mara one night. Sister Teresa had told him and his grandmother that Mara had been taken to a place where she could be looked after and that she was safe and well, but Mikhail said Sister Teresa was only repeating what she had been told to say. Nuns and priests had

288

sometimes been brave and outspoken, he said, but mostly they bowed to authority. He thought that was what Sister Teresa was doing over Mara's disappearance. What did Matthew think?

What Matthew thought was that if Mikhail talked about the Securitate so openly and so disparagingly, he might one day find himself stolen away as well.

'I don't care,' said Mikhail defiantly. 'I read in a newspaper about Nicolae Ceauşescu. He's wicked and greedy and selfish. He sends all our food and medicine to other countries so he can pay off Romania's debts. If he cared about us he wouldn't mind about a few stupid debts, he'd care more that everyone had enough food.'

'Nobody would sell food and leave people to starve,' said Matthew disbelievingly. 'And you're not supposed to read that kind of newspaper anyway.'

'It was a good newspaper and it said Ceauşescu didn't care about people starving,' said Mikhail, obstinately. 'I believe it. Newspapers don't print things that aren't right. Anyway, if he didn't sell our food, where is it? It's not in the shops. The newspaper said the next step would be rationing, like in the war between England and Germany when people only got half an egg and hardly any meat.'

'How can you have half an egg?'

'I don't know, but that's what it said. Ceauşescu says he's keeping food out of the shops so we don't get fat. I'd like to see anyone get fat on the food in the shops. Chicken wings and claws. Things made out of soy and bonemeal. Can you remember the last time you had meat – proper real meat?'

'Wilma buys sardines,' said Matthew, who could not bear sardines. 'She says they're just as good as meat, really. And she buys BucureÅŸti salami, although she says that's no more than bonemeal, soy and pork lard.'

'And the Ceauşescus have at least a dozen fine mansions and yachts, and lavish banquets whenever they want,' said Mikhail bitterly. 'I would like to kill them. I think Elena Ceauşescu's a vampire.'

'You don't do you? Not really?'

'I do. She sucks the life out of this country like Dracula. Or like the Hungarian Countess, Elizabeth Bathory bathing in virgins' blood.'

'Mikhail, where on earth—'

'Books mostly,' he said. 'The ones in your father's library.' He smiled suddenly. 'You did say I could borrow whatever I wanted, and I always, *always* return them.'

'You can read the entire shelves,' said Matthew, who liked and trusted Mikhail more than anyone else in the world, except perhaps Wilma. Mikhail was constantly surprising him.

'Some of the books are in French,' said Mikhail. 'I'm trying to learn French, a bit at a time. Some of the finest literature in the world is written in French, it'd be good to read all those books in the original language. Proust, Voltaire and Dumas. And English. Think of reading Shakespeare and Dickens in their own language. Languages are interesting, aren't they? And useful. You never know when you might travel to another country; you'd want to know how to talk to people, wouldn't you?'

On the night before Matthew's eighteenth birthday Wilma came plodding determinedly into the study. Matthew liked being in the study because it made him feel near to his father. He liked having the photograph of his mother to look at while he sketched or read, as well. He was sketching when Wilma came in. She wanted, she said, to speak about Matthew's future.

He put down his sketchpad to hear what was clearly a prepared speech.

'You need a future,' said Wilma, 'with proper training. It's what your father wanted and it's what your mother would have wanted as well.'

'I'll have to have a job, won't I?' said Matthew. He did not know what kind of job he could get, but it was what people did when they left school. There was money in a bank somewhere for paying bills and buying food. Wilma had always said there was not a great deal of it but they would manage and Matthew was not to worry. Matthew had never entirely understood how it worked, but supposed one day he would find out.

He found out that night. It seemed that when he was very small, his father had set up some kind of trust fund with a bank.

'It was in case anything should happen to him,' said Wilma. 'Maybe even that far back he thought those people would get him one day.'

'And they did,' said Matthew.

'Yes. Well now, I don't understand all this trust stuff – I never heard tell of such a thing before – but your father was a clever man, and he wanted to make sure you would have a little money. So he worked it all out with the people at the bank, without telling you. There were pieces of paper to be signed. I had to put my name to them as well, saying I had seen your father sign while I was in the room. A legal thing, so they said.'

This was exciting because it was as if his father was stretching out a reassuring hand from the past, but it was also dreadfully sad because of his father not being here to do the reassuring.

'I never read the words on those pieces of paper,' said Wilma, 'and I daresay I shouldn't have understood one word in twenty anyway. But what I do know is that it meant when you came to be eighteen there'd be money for you to study whatever you wanted. Not a lot of money, but your father thought it would be enough.'

'To study whatever I wanted,' said Matthew, staring at her, feeling something start to open up inside his head.

'The university if that's what you want,' nodded Wilma. 'You'd have to work hard at some exams or other – I daresay you'll know about that, or the teachers at the school would.'

Matthew, his heart beating very fast, said, 'Yes, they would know.'

'It would be studying painting and drawing, I daresay?' she said. 'That's what you'll want, isn't it? Although how you'd make a living from it, I don't know any more than the man in the moon.'

'I don't know either,' said Matthew, and discovered he was having to control his voice very tightly in case he started crying. My father's gift to me, he thought. Wherever he is now, will he remember I'm eighteen tomorrow and know I'm being told about this money? Will he even be allowed to remember? For a moment the old image of stone cells and prisoners was with him so vividly he could feel the dank cold of the stones and almost smell the despair and bitterness. It was unbearable to think his father might be in one of those places. Matthew struggled to summon the memory of him seated at the desk in this room, smiling his gentle smile. But it eluded him and all he could see was his father being taken away by the Securitate, shouting back the words of encouragement as they drove off. 'I'll be back very soon ... whatever happens, remember I love you very much ...'

Matthew dug his fingernails into his palm to stop himself crying because he was eighteen tomorrow and grown-up people did not cry.

After a moment he was able to say to Wilma, 'Yes. If there's enough money, it would be studying painting and drawing I'd want to do.'

There was enough money.

'But only just,' said the man in the bank, to which Matthew, nervous and apprehensive, travelled. 'You won't be able to live a high lifestyle – in fact you might have to do evening work at times. If it's art you want to study, you'll need expensive materials – paints, brushes and canvases. But a lot of students have jobs in cafes and bars and so on, and there's no reason why you can't do the same. I daresay you'll cope.'

'I daresay I will,' said Matthew, who would have scrubbed floors all night and every night if he could be taught to draw and paint during the day.

'Your school can probably advise you as to an actual place,' said the man.

'Yes.' Matthew had already talked to his art teacher, who had been surprised and pleased and was finding out what was needed and what might be available. The Royal Drawing School in Budapest had been mentioned, which sounded dauntingly grand, but which nevertheless made Matthew's heart thump with sheer joy.

'You're hesitating,' said the bank manager. 'Is it that you don't understand about the trust fund? It's a perfectly legal and usual arrangement. It was set up shortly after you were born.'

'I understand that. It's just . . .'

'Yes?'

'Sir, my father was taken by the Securitate when I was nine.' It came out in a rush and he had no idea if it was safe to say it to this unknown man. 'I've never seen him since and I've never known what happened to him.'

But the manager said, very gently, 'I know about that, Matthew. I didn't know your father well, but I did know him for a man who spoke out against injustices – against what he saw to be injustices,' he said quickly.

'I don't even know if he's still alive,' said Matthew. 'But if he is . . .'

'If he is, he could be anywhere in one of many prisons, and he could be in any of several countries.'

'Oughtn't I to try to find him? To use this money that way?'

The manager was silent for several minutes and Matthew began to be afraid he had said something wrong. But finally he said, 'I suppose it would be possible to alter the terms of the trust – they say all laws are made to be broken – but this is a very strongly worded document. I think it would be expensive and also long-winded to break it. You'd probably use most of the money in lawyers' fees and end with nothing – no funds to search for your father, and none for your studies, which is what your father wanted. He wanted you equipped to go out into the world and make your mark on it.' He thought for a moment, then, clearly choosing his words carefully, said, 'Matthew, the kind of search you're talking about would be massively difficult and probably unsuccessful. The Securitate is a formidable engine; it's very good indeed at keeping its secrets.'

'You don't think I'd find him?'

'I think it's unlikely in the extreme. What I do think is that you'd break your heart and end up with nothing. It could even be dangerous for you. Your father was what they call high profile, Matthew. His articles were scathing attacks on Romania's government, so if it became known that Andrei Valk's son was prying into the Securitate's work ... into their prisons, into the identities of the occupants ... I'm sure you can see what I mean.'

'I hadn't thought of it like that.'

'I don't think any of his articles appeared in this country, which is probably why it took so long for the Securitate to compile enough evidence to arrest him. Although I don't know what really happened.' He made an impatient gesture. 'They frequently imprison people on what seems to us a thin thread of evidence, but your father's name was known in foreign newspapers and so they'd have had to be very careful. I'd say they took their time and made sure the proof was watertight. So even if you did find him, it might be very hard indeed to disprove the accusations or the charges. My advice is that you use this trust fund in the way your father – perhaps your mother, too – wanted.'

'I'll trust your judgement,' said Matthew, meaning it. 'Thank you very much for being so frank.' He spoke truthfully; he did not think there was anything sinister behind the advice.

The manager stood up and held out his hand. 'Good luck to you, Matthew,' he said. 'Work hard, but remember to play hard as well.'

'Thank you. I'll try to do both.'

CHAPTER TWENTY-SIX

Romania, early 1980s

There were times in Budapest, at the Royal Drawing School, when Matthew felt deeply guilty for being so happy. It seemed to him the ultimate delight to be living in this beautiful city; to have a tiny studio apartment of his own with marvellous views over the rooftops; to go with fellow students to the cafes and bars; to take the metro to visit castles and churches and study the fragments of breathtakingly beautiful Turkish and Magyar art, and see the influences of the Italian Renaissance. He learned some Italian so he could understand Italian painting and sculpture better, and from there found it not too difficult to pick up a little more English and French. But to draw and paint all day and every day with people who understood that this was the most important thing in life, and who were patient in helping Matthew to become better – that was the most wonderful thing of all.

The memory of his father did not leave him. His father's words from all those years ago – the words written by the Englishman Thomas de Quincey – were vividly in his mind.

'There is no such thing as ultimate forgetting: traces once impressed upon the memory are indestructible.'

He would not forget his father ever, and if he had known how to go about finding him, he would have done so, despite what the bank manager said. But as things stood, he had not so much as the smallest clue.

But during a summer vacation visit to Wilma, who still kept the house going, a clue did come his way. It was Mikhail Ionescu, now nearing the end of his own schooling, who provided it. Mikhail had been reading about the Securitate's methods and found Matthew a sympathetic listener.

'It's forbidden reading, of course,' he said rather defiantly. 'I know that. But who cares?'

'You'll care if they find out and haul you off to some wretched prison,' said Matthew, smiling at Mikhail's earnestness, wanting to draw him in this mood, but knowing his expression would change too swiftly to be captured.

'Like Pitesti Gaol?' said Mikhail. 'The house of the lost. Well, one of them, at any rate.'

The house of the lost. The words plucked at the deeply buried memories of Matthew's childhood.

'Pitesti's where they used to practise what was called re-education,' Mikhail was saying, 'they did it in Jilava as well.'

'What's re-education?'

'A form of brainwashing. Haven't you ever heard of it? Come down from your Magyar ivory tower, Matthew, and live in the real world.'

'What is it?'

'Its eventual aim was to alter personalities to the point of absolute obedience. They made prisoners denounce personal beliefs, renounce their deepest loyalties and loves. Or maybe persuade them they'd committed some horrific crime so that everyone hated them. If anyone was particularly devout, they'd be forced to blaspheme religious symbols.'

'That's grotesque,' said Matthew, horrified.

'I know it is,' said Mikhail. 'It's supposed to have been stopped years ago before you and I were born – in fact way back in the 1950s – but there's a belief that it still goes on here and there.'

After Mikhail had gone, Matthew found his father's old atlas and looked for Pitesti. It did not look too bad a journey, but even if he went there to search for his father, he could not think how he would get inside. You could not just present yourself at the gates and ask to see a prisoner. If you had money or influence you might be let in, but Matthew had neither. He was not sure he had the courage, either; it would take a lot of nerve to demand admittance to a State prison, and he did not think he was a very courageous person. In any case, Pitesti was one of a great many gaols.

But maybe one day he would have courage, influence and money in abundance and he could travel to all the places where his father might be. Or maybe one day the world would change – something would happen to change it – and the lost prisoners in the forgotten prisons could be set free.

Mara did not exactly count the days until she would be free, but she did mark the years. She was twelve, fourteen, fifteen ... the years wheeled by, each one the same as the one before or the one that came next. A good, quiet student, the nuns said, pleased, and when Sister Teresa made her twice or thrice yearly visit, told her how well things had worked out. Would Mara be allowed home soon? Surely, when she was seventeen and her studies finished, she could be regarded as grown-up? They had heard, with sadness, that Mara's grandmother had died the previous year and they had offered up a Mass for her soul, but the brother was still living in the family house.

Sister Teresa thought once Mara was seventeen, she might be allowed home. Mikhail was living in the cottage on his own which was not absolutely ideal, but he seemed to manage well enough, despite his youth. Neighbours kept an eye on him and helped with shopping and so on. He would soon be thinking about what to do when he left school, of course. Going out into the world.

'Yes, of course he will,' said Mara, and, taking her courage in both hands, she asked about Zoia.

'As far as I know she left the district shortly after you came here,' said Sister Teresa. 'The Black House is empty and boarded up. Doubtless a few legends will grow up round it, but I should think Zoia would still have her spies around. She'd want to assure herself that the bargain we made has been kept. If you came home, what would you do?'

Mara did not really know. She had seen nothing of the world beyond her small childhood village and this convent, so she had no comparisons to make, no idea of what might be possible or attainable. All she really wanted was to live in the cottage once more. She was deeply sad that her grandmother had died, but Mikhail would be there. If she and Mikhail could live in that beloved cottage, the two of them together again, she would have everything in the world she wanted. But she understood people had to have money in order to live, and money had to be earned by working. So she said she had wondered about teaching. Might she teach at the school where once she had been a pupil? She had worked hard at her studies, and the sisters here thought she had done well.

Sister Teresa thought this might be possible. She would ask Reverend Mother about it. Teachers needed proper qualifications, but they were difficult to acquire in Romania nowadays. Still, it might be possible for Mara to be trained in their own classrooms in the Founder House school.

Lying in the narrow bed in the dormitory, Mara was gradually aware of a new fear – a fear churned up by the suggestion that Zoia would still be watching her. Was it possible that Zoia might still exact a warped revenge? That she might take an eye for an eye or a tooth for a tooth. Mara had been the cause of Zoia losing Annaleise – and in some way Mara still did not fully understand, Zoia had loved Annaleise as if they had been husband and wife. Supposing Zoia decided to take from Mara the one thing Mara loved best in the world? Supposing she tried to take Mikhail? The

298

more Mara thought about this, the likelier it seemed, and the more she became convinced she would have to be very clever about protecting him.

Zoia would admit that ending the Black House's reign had been unexpectedly easy. Sister Teresa had been partly responsible for that of course, taking the children away and sending them to England. The arrangement had been a quid pro quo, Zoia knew that. What Sister Teresa had really been saying was, Let me take Mara Ionescu and I'll deal with the children for you. But at the time it had suited Zoia to agree to the bargain, even though it had cheated her of her revenge.

But that could wait. Planning Mara's punishment was something to cling to during the long lonely nights – the nights without Annaleise.

And so the snivelling children went off to England, and everyone working in the Black House was paid off and sent back to wherever they lived. Zoia did not enquire into that. She was not in the business of giving charity to anyone, especially when she might shortly need charity herself. The Black House was suddenly empty of people, and most of its furniture removed so that Zoia's footsteps echoed eerily when she walked through the high-ceilinged rooms. As far as she had been able to make out, the house and land had been sold to some nameless department within the Party and would probably be torn down.

The Politburo man, Gheorghe Pauker came to help her close the place down and deal with the final formalities, and on the last night Zoia cooked supper for the two of them. Afterwards they sat at the big scrubbed table in the main kitchen, with the dirty dishes stacked in the sink. Zoia had not much minded cooking because they both had to eat, but she did not see why she should wash up as well. Pauker had found the small stock of wine, and had already downed one bottle while they ate. Now he was making inroads on a second.

He told her Ceauşescu was no longer as popular as he had been, at least not in his own country.

'It's the debt,' he said slurrily. 'Romania's massively in debt. Billions of dollars to Western banks for all that industrialization in the 1970s.' He tapped the side of his nose in a knowing gesture. 'It was bound to catch up with him in the end,' he said.

'With Ceauşescu, d'you mean?'

'Yes. He's det— determined to pay it back though, an' thass honourable of him. You have to 'dmit it's honourable.'

'Yes. How will he pay it?' Zoia did not care if Ceauşescu paid off Romania's debt honourably or was thrown into a debtors' prison and left to rot, but the habit of gleaning information, however small, persisted.

'Tighten the country's belt,' said Pauker. 'Tha's his plan. Starve the people. There'll be more food rationing before we're all much older, see if there isn't. You'll all be fighting each other for a loaf of bread. Cuts in electricity supplies as well, I shouldn't wonder. Sad, I call it.' He reached for the wine again and Zoia silently pushed the bottle nearer. 'The rest of the world doesn't much like Ceauşescu *or* his wife. Not s'posed to say that.' He laid a finger on his lips, in an exaggerated gesture of silence.

'I didn't know that – about the rest of the world not liking Ceauşescu.'

''s true. Other countries don' like his policies or what's happening to the people here. Television cameras get sneaked in, you know, and things get shown to other countries. England. America.'

'What sort of things?'

'Well, places like this one. Orphan – ornof – children's homes.'

'There's no money to run these places,' said Zoia defensively. 'I did the best I could.'

'Oh, there's no money for anything any more,' he said. 'All a damn shame. Course,' he downed another glass, 'Elena pushed Nicolae into things. You know that, I 'spect. Gave orders about who could be given posts in the Party and who couldn't. 'strordin'ry woman, Elena. D'you ever meet her?'

'Once.'

'Quite 'strordin'ry. An' now she's first deputy premier. They made her that in 1980.' He tried to count years on his fingers and gave up. 'It was Nicolae's doing, of course, ev'rybody knew that. Case of nep— netop—'

'Nepotism?'

'Sssh. Shouldn't say things like that. Never know who might be listening. But I'll tell you one thing,' he said, suddenly more alert, 'she's absolutely ruthless, that woman.' He was so pleased with himself for having pronounced this without a slur, he said it again, 'Abso-fucking-lutely ruthless.'

'So everyone says.' Zoia opened another bottle of wine in case Pauker was going to be indiscreet about Elena. Indiscretions could be very useful at times. And the wine might as well be drunk as left here to gather mildew or be stolen by vandals.

'Automaton, that's what Elena is,' said Pauker. 'No heart. Call her the Mother of the Nation – pshaw, load of bollocks. Not a motherly bone in her body. Set the Securitate to spy on her own children, can you b'live that? Perfeckly true, though. Cold-hearted bitch, she is. As for all those grand qualifications she says she's got – d'you want to know something?' He drew nearer, his tone confidential.

'Tell me,' said Zoia.

'Bought half of them,' he said. 'Paid for them in sordid coinage. An' the ones she didn't buy, she invented.'

'But I've seen her speak at meetings,' said Zoia. 'She seemed very learned.' She had, in fact, only heard Elena speak in public on two occasions, both times in company with Annaleise, but she had been quite impressed by Elena's public manner.

'Smoke and mirrors,' he said, waving a hand dismissively. 'If you listen properly she always defers to a "Comrade Engineer" or some such, for the real answers. Smoke and mirrors, tha's what she is.' He nodded solemnly into his wine glass, and Zoia surreptitiously topped it up.

'This is all very interesting,' she said.

'I tell you, Elena Ceauşescu's never written a thesish – pardon, thesis – in her life. My opinion she couldn't. Mind you, neither could I, but I'm not the Mother of the Nation – bloody good joke that, don'cha think? Where's the wine gone? An' why aren't you drinkin' with me? Got to drink with me. Friendly. Here.'

Zoia gave a mental shrug and drank the wine he poured almost in one go. Here's to you, Annaleise, she said silently, as she almost always did when she took a drink.

When her companion re-filled her glass, she drank that straight down as well, and followed it with a third. He was very fuddled by this time and his eyes were unfocused, but he was not too unfocused to suddenly thrust a hand into the bodice of her dress, and prod her small breasts. Zoia felt the familiar revulsion and was instantly plunged back to the small shabby cottage and the feel of her father's rough labourer's hands on her skin. But she controlled her disgust.

'Bit of comfort tonight,' he said. 'S'all right, isn't it? Sad day closing down one of our houses. Bit of comfort.'

Zoia said flatly, 'You want to fuck me?'

'Doan' need to pretend, do we?' he said. 'Romance, all that stuff, lot of balls. See you don't lose by it, though.'

'How much?' said Zoia coldly.

'Don't mess about, do you? Much as you like. Here ...' he pulled out his wallet and tipped the contents onto the table, 'have it all. No use to me.'

'Thank you,' said Zoia, scooping up the notes, not bothering to apologize or explain that tomorrow she would be homeless and jobless. 'D'you want to go upstairs or do it here?'

There had been quite a lot of money in the wallet. She put it safely in her own bag, and then, because you never knew what might come in useful, took his Politburo card as well. There was an address just outside Reşiţa. Zoia was careful to note this down, because there might be a time in the future when she needed to make use of that encounter.

If it had not been for Gheorghe Pauker's cash she would have had nowhere to live in the weeks that followed, but she was able to take a small room in a lodging house. The days were shapeless, the nights filled with lonely agony. Several times over the dreary years she thought about suicide – a bottle of pills, a jump into the river. Easy. But then the hatred of Mara and the desire for revenge burned up again warming Zoia's cold heart, and she knew she would keep on living. Annaleise would have wanted it.

Eventually she found work in a library in a town near Mara's own village and a room in a slightly better house. It was not really what she wanted, but she needed to remain near enough to Mara's home to pick up news of what Mara was doing and to know when the creature finally came home from the Debreczen convent. She counted the years, hardly noticing when the 1970s slid into the 1980s, only really recognizing the years of Mara's life. She would be fourteen, fifteen, nearing the age when the convent would send her home. Zoia did not go as far as disguising herself during those years, because it would have been melodramatic and probably would not have worked anyway, but she did not think anyone would recognize her from her time at the Black House. Her hair had turned grey after Annaleise's death – it had gone what people called pepper and salt grey, and Zoia had it cut very short, pudding-basin style. It was remarkable how it altered her appearance. She lost weight as well – she had always been thin but now she became bony because she could not be bothered to eat much. Her skin grew dry and leathery-looking. It did not really matter how she looked – Zoia did not think it would ever matter again – but it was one more thing to lay at the door of that evil spiteful child.

Gheorghe Pauker's drunken prophecies were turning out to be true. You had to queue for food – sometimes for hours. There was bread rationing. People said it was a sick joke, because you could hardly ever find a loaf of bread anyway and as for sugar for baking or sweetening coffee, forget it. In any case, you could not get coffee any more than you could get sugar or flour. A scientific diet, Ceauşescu was apparently calling it. And what was happening to the money saved by starving everyone, they would like to know? Was it paying off Romania's debts? More likely it was going towards the grand palace he was said to be building for himself and his wife.

Standing in food queues, Zoia sensed the anger in other shoppers, but it was a strange, slightly frightening anger, as if something was gradually but inexorably coming to boiling point. Once Elena and Nicolae Ceauşescu had been seen as glittering and untouchable, but Zoia had the increasing sense that the glitter was starting to be perceived as pinchbeck.

Living in obscurity, she heard a number of things, some of which might one day be useful, others which were too trivial to bother with. Matthew Valk was studying art in Budapest. That was one of the things worth knowing and Zoia tucked the information away in her mind. She wondered where the money for it had come from. It might be worth finding out about that, as well, if she could.

And then, one day towards the end of 1982, midway through a long dull afternoon at the library, she heard the news she had been waiting to hear for so long. Mara Ionescu was finally leaving Debreczen and coming home.

CHAPTER TWENTY-SEVEN

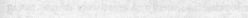

Romania, early 1980s

Zoia had never had any compunction about making use of the people she had encountered during her work for the Party. When she heard that Mara was returning home, she composed a very careful letter to Gheorghe Pauker. She was cautious, not knowing who might actually see the letter; there might be a wife – Zoia rather hoped there was – or the letter might be opened by a branch of the Securitate. Some people said the Securitate operated censorship. Zoia had no idea if this was true, but it was very likely that a Politburo official such as Pauker would be subject to surveillance.

So she reminded him of their brief acquaintance at the time of the Black House's closure. She was sure he would remember her, she wrote, they had had such a very interesting conversation about Elena Ceaușescu and she had never forgotten what he had said about their leader's wife. She smiled as she wrote this, knowing that no matter how drunk Pauker had been that night, he was unlikely to have forgotten what he'd said about Elena Ceaușescu. Zoia did not spell it out. She merely said his words that night had given her much food for thought. She was still working diligently for the Party, she said in her letter, and she had a small project in mind with which she thought Gheorghe might be able to help her. Perhaps he would contact her as soon as possible? She would enjoy renewing their friendship. It was an innocent enough letter – a note from a former colleague, a note about work for the Party. But as she addressed and sealed the envelope, she thought those comments about Elena would bring him running.

They did. He came to her lodgings two days later. He was older and coarser-looking and small red veins were prominent in his nose. Recalling the way he had downed the wine that night, Zoia was not surprised. But he remembered what had happened between them – that was apparent from the onset.

'What do you want?' he said, seating himself on the one easy chair in Zoia's room.

'Some help. As I said in my letter, there's a small project I'm minded to undertake.'

'Why should I help you?' But Zoia knew the memory of what he had said was strongly between them.

'Oh, for old times' sake,' she said, 'and because it might be safer for you.'

'Safer?'

Zoia smiled. 'Let's not pretend,' she said. 'We didn't pretend that night, did we? You wanted something then and I provided it. Now I want something and I think you can help me get it. I'd hate to tell people all those things you said about Elena Ceaușescu. What did you call her? A cheat. A liar. Everything smoke and mirrors and half her grand qualifications the result of sordid coinage. I really would hate to let people know you said all that, Gheorghe.'

'But you will if I don't do what you want.'

'Yes.'

'That's blackmail. In any case I'd deny it.'

'Of course you would. But there's the old saying about mud sticking. People would believe you, but would they believe you

306

absolutely? Mightn't they look sideways at you and remind one another you're the one who spread vicious gossip about their beloved leader's wife? Still,' said Zoia, with a shrug, 'if you want to take the risk.'

He said warily, 'Supposing I said I would help you. What exactly would you want?'

'I want a vicious little bitch inside a gaol. I want her to become one of the lost ones.'

Zoia had watched Mara for several weeks, and knew Mara and her brother had fallen into the way of taking a walk through the lanes most Sunday afternoons. Sunday was a quiet, somnolent day: people went to church in the morning, ate their Sunday dinner – or what they could scratch together for a Sunday dinner – then spent their few precious leisure hours resting or reading or visiting their friends. It was a time when a stranger walking through the streets was not likely to be noticed or commented on.

One Sunday Zoia waited until she could be sure Mara and Mikhail were clear of the village, then walked in a leisurely way down the street. There were very few people about and those who were barely glanced at her. A casual stroller, somebody visiting perhaps. Her face might have been vaguely familiar from the library in the neighbouring town, but if it was it would not matter.

The cottage was set a little way from the road; it backed onto trees and scrubland, which was very good indeed. Zoia slipped round the side and considered it. She would break in if she had to, but she hoped it would not be necessary.

Luck was with her. A small ground-floor window was slightly open near the top. Zoia peered through and saw a kitchen with a stone sink and neat rows of pans and crockery. There was a faint scent of food and she guessed Mara had made lunch for herself and Mikhail and left the window slightly ajar to blow away the cooking scents while they took their walk.

She had to stand on a large boulder from the garden so she

could reach inside and release the window latch. She glanced behind her to make sure she was not being watched, then pulled the window to its widest point and climbed over the sill. It was a narrow opening but she was wiry and active, and got inside quite easily. She stood for a moment, absorbing the atmosphere of the bitch's home, then went through to the front of the house. Everywhere was extremely neat and clean – that was the convent training, of course. The stairs to the bedrooms were behind a latched door in the sitting room. The cottage was not unlike the cottage where Zoia had spent her own childhood, although it was bigger and more comfortably furnished.

There were two bedrooms. The one at the back was clearly Mara's. There were a couple of rather drab cotton frocks hanging behind a curtain and stockings neatly rolled up on a little shelf, which also held several books, mostly with a religious slant. Nuns' training again. Zoia studied the room. There were no cupboards – where would Mara hide something secret? There was a hatch in the ceiling which must lead to the attics, but that might be a bit too inaccessible for her purpose. What about under the bed? No, too obvious. *Think*, Zoia, be subtle about this. And then she had it. What she had brought with her were just sheets of paper, and paper could be folded and slotted between books. She smiled and drew from the pocket of her jacket the things she had so carefully prepared in her own room with the door firmly locked.

There were two pamphlets describing the attempt to re-establish the National Peasant Party, which had been banned since 1947, calling for recruits. Zoia knew most of the categories of charges from her Black House years. If Mara were found to have these pamphlets in her possession, the charge known as plotting against the social order, might be levelled against her. Certainly she would be considered to be in possession of subversive literature. But the pamphlets by themselves would not be enough. What would really damn the bitch was a letter purporting to come from Mara's great childhood friend, Matthew Valk. Elisabeth's son. The symmetry of this pleased Zoia.

She had folded the letter a number of times to make it look creased and read, but standing in Mara's room now, she unfolded it and read it again.

Dearest Mara,

I was very glad to hear from you so promptly and to know all your news. When you get home we will be able to talk properly. My studies are hard work, but life in Budapest is exciting – there's so much to tell you.

I've given a lot of thought to your suggestions about my father, and if you really do know of a warden at Jilava who can be bribed, I think that would be worth trying. I like your idea of bringing my father out disguised as a guard. It would be massively risky, but I think it would work. What's life without a few risks anyway?

I don't have a great deal of money for the actual bribe, but I'll manage it somehow. I don't care if I have to live on bread and cheese for the next three months and work double shifts at the cafe to pay the rent. I don't care if I have to beg on the streets and sleep in the gutter, if it means my father can be free.

You're a dear true friend to have worked all this out, and one day I'll try to repay you.

Till soon.

All my love
Matthew

Zoia had not been able to find a sample of Matthew's hand-writing, but she knew, in a general way, the style of writing children were taught, and she knew, as well, that it was unlikely the letter would be put to any kind of test. If Matthew were ever questioned about this letter he would deny writing it, but that would be perfectly all right. In Zoia's experience, people always lied about this kind of thing. The slightly dramatic wording about not caring if he had to beg on the streets or sleep in the gutter seemed to her the kind of thing a young man studying art would say or write. She thought the whole thing would pass muster. And with Gheorghe's help . . .

She was smiling as she slid the folded letter and pamphlets between two of the books on Mara's shelf. She was still smiling as she slipped out of the cottage, carefully closing the window to its original position, then walked unnoticed down the lane to her own home.

Mara was deeply happy to be back in the familiar cottage. To curl up in the fireside corner where she had listened to her grandmother's tales, to cook and eat a meal with her beloved Mikhail, even though supplies of food were so meagre, these were the most joyful things in the world. During all the years at Debreczen she had hoped and dreamed and prayed to return, and now it had happened. If only her grandmother could be here, life would be perfect.

Mikhail still went off to school each morning, but he would shortly be leaving and decisions would have to be made about what he was going to do. There was a small amount of money which their grandmother had left. 'Hoarded under a floorboard in the bedroom, the old miser,' Mikhail said, smiling with affection-ate memory. 'She didn't want the Securitate snoopers to know about it. They can get into bank accounts and demand all kinds of payments these days, did you know that?'

Mara was not sure if this was true or if Mikhail wanted to make the Securitate sound even worse than they were. She had already noticed how very defiant he was, but after almost nine years in the quiet remote convent, the whole world seemed defiant. And loud – she had forgotten how loud the world was. Even this small village had been like an assault on her senses, so that she had wanted to hide herself in a dark corner. But she was grateful for the sturdy tin box with the money. It had to be used with extreme care, but it might be enough for Mikhail to go to university if that was what he wanted. She was going to ask Sister Teresa about that.

In the meantime, it was wonderful to be at home after so many years, to wave Mikhail off to his lessons each morning, to welcome him home each evening, and to walk with him in the lanes on Sunday afternoons when everywhere was quiet and church bells could be heard ringing. Mara wanted to trap the moments and lock them away safely somewhere so that one day, a long time in the future, she would be able to take the memories out and relive them. The convent's routines were deeply embedded in her; every night she prayed the happy times would last.

They did not. In the middle of a perfectly ordinary week, on an apparently ordinary afternoon, two Securitate men came to the cottage, knocked sharply on the door, and walked inside when Mara opened it. Her heart thumped in her chest because this was how it had all started, all those years ago, when she hid in the attic and the men found her and carried her off to the Black House.

They were not exactly discourteous, because they did not say anything, other than the initial information that they had come to search the house. Mara started to ask why, but they were already inside, opening doors, looking inside cupboards, going upstairs to the bedrooms. She tried not to panic and reminded herself that the Securitate still came summarily into people's homes like this and that, apart from the little store of money, there was nothing in the least incriminating here.

But it seemed there was. There was a shout from her bedroom, and the younger man came rattling back downstairs holding what looked like a letter and a couple of printed leaflets. He brandished them at Mara, who had never seen them before. When she said this, the men smiled knowingly, and the younger one grabbed her arm and said she was under arrest.

311

'For what?'

'Several crimes,' he said, and thrust the handful of papers in her face. 'Possession of subversive literature for starters.'

'I haven't got any—'

'And,' he said, a lick of pleasure in his voice, 'conspiracy.'

'What d'you mean? What have I conspired to do?'

'Helping free a prisoner from a state Gaol,' he said, and Mara stared at him and remembered what Sister Teresa had said all those years ago about a lie. There are always consequences of a lie, she had said. Was this one of those consequences?

'Why do you think that?' she said at last.

'We've found evidence.' Again he brandished the papers he was holding. 'Information was given to us – a very reliable source indeed it came from.'

'Who?'

'A gentleman high up in the Politburo. Never you mind about his name, that's not for you to know. But he was quite right. This is the proof. A letter from your friend – a friend who's the son of two enemies of the State.'

Matthew, thought Mara.

'It tells it all,' said the man. 'The details of the plan you were going to put into operation to steal his father away from prison. A bad crime, that, stealing State prisoners. You'll probably be a prisoner yourself because of it, and if you're a Category III prisoner that'll mean ten years at least. I doubt you'll see the world for a very long time.'

I'll make sure you're shut away and that you never see the world again, Zoia had said the night Annaleise died. Zoia was behind this, Mara knew it quite surely.

As they took her out to the waiting car – not a rattly jeep but a smart sleek car – she said, 'Where are you taking me? Am I going to be put on trial?'

'I don't know about a trial,' he said. 'But I do know where you're to be taken.'

Pitesti, thought Mara. That's where they'll take me.

But the man said, 'You're to go to the fort under the ground. The sunken prison house. Jilava Gaol.'

CHAPTER TWENTY-EIGHT

The present

Michael Innes stopped speaking, and there was a long, deep silence.

The spell's winding up, thought Theo. He's used up too much emotion in telling me all that, and he's drained. What a deeply unhappy story, though. He let the silence lengthen, then said, very quietly, 'And so Mara was taken to Jilava.'

'Yes. It's a smallish place near Bucharest – Ilfov country.' Innes seemed to take strength from suddenly realizing where he was, and from Theo's presence. 'The gaol is an old fortress, partly subterranean,' he said. 'The name Jilava derives from a Romanian word *žilav*. It means humid place. In some quarters it was known as the house of the lost.'

'They vanished as abruptly and completely as if by sorcery,' said Theo softly. 'Living ghosts in a world that will soon have no memory of them.'

'Yes.' Innes looked sharply at Theo. 'A man I once knew – a clever, brave, man – wrote that.'

Andrei, thought Theo, but he only said, 'And Mara was taken to this house of the lost? To Jilava?'

'Oh yes.'

'Were you taken there as well?'

'No, although looking back I was probably lucky not to be,' said Innes with a sudden grin. 'I was a member of an organization called the October Group.'

Theo stared at him, and thought, Well, that's something I didn't pick up.

'It was an underground movement,' said Innes. 'A lot of them were students. In the main they fought for justice for people wrongly imprisoned. We had radio stations and broadcast to try to recruit people to our cause – all illegal of course, and they were always being shut down. But for a lot of the time we managed to keep one step ahead of the Securitate. We tried to rouse international concern by sending articles to Western newspapers. Sometimes,' said Innes, 'we even managed to get prisoners out and across the borders into other countries.' He paused. 'Mara never talked about what happened to her in Jilava, but she kept diaries – a lot of the people in Jilava did. They made ink from the juice of berries growing on bushes outside their cells, although God knows where the paper came from. I think they might have stolen bits of it from the workshop. She had the diaries with her the day we got her out. She carried them in the bodice of her gown – she was afraid the guards would find them and punish her again.'

Diaries, thought Theo. Oh God, Mara's own diaries from those years ... Something darted across his mind – a faded uncertain image: fragments of brittle yellowing paper with thin pale writing, the erratic glimpse of a phrase, the fragment of a sentence. He remembered the odd impression he had had the night he was attacked – the sensation that he was reading an old manuscript by flickering lamplight.

'But even without the diaries, we all knew what went on in the prisons,' Innes was saying.

'Re-education,' said Theo. 'It was a form of brainwashing, wasn't it?'

315

'Yes. The destruction of the mind – the deliberate re-shaping of a personality. They used it in the 1940s and 1950s: Pitesti Gaol was the centre of the re-education experiments but Jilava came in a good second.'

'You said "they"?' said Theo.

'The more extreme sections of the communist overlords. Officials from the original Iron Guard. The Securitate,' said Innes, with bitterness and hatred in his voice. 'But, Theo, the horror of what happened to my sister during those months is difficult to convey.' He leaned forward as if eager to make him understand. 'It's one of those situations for which language is inadequate. Neither my language nor yours really has the words.'

Theo suddenly realized what he should have seen earlier: that Michael Innes' precise way of talking was because English was not his native tongue.

'The original aim was for prisoners to discard all past political, even religious, convictions,' said Innes. 'To reverse people's values. They forced on prisoners grotesque, wildly inaccurate versions of their own lives and their families. That's what happened to Mara. She went into Jilava as a scared seventeen-year-old on a faked charge of conspiracy. When she came out, it was as if the real Mara had been taken and another person substituted – a withdrawn suspicious woman.'

'But hadn't re-education been outlawed by then?' said Theo.

'It had,' said Innes. 'It was the early 1980s and it was more than twenty-five years since re-education had been stamped out. But it hadn't entirely vanished. Some of the old regime were still staffing the prisons and their outlook hadn't altered. If they took a dislike to a prisoner or if they were paid, they reverted to the old methods. That's what happened to Mara. She had made an enemy of a high-ranking Politburo official—'

'Annaleise Simonescu,' said Theo. 'And there was a woman called Zoia.'

'Yes. You know more than I bargained for.'

Theo saw again that Innes accepted his knowledge. Presently, he would ask Innes about that, but for the moment his whole mind was focused on Mara.

'After we got her out,' said Innes, 'I read her diaries. I wanted to understand her. I needed to know what had happened to her. Mostly they were scrappy notes, probably scribbled in secrecy or in a dark corner where she wouldn't be seen. I'll never forget the things she wrote. Later, when my English was better, I made a translation. I suppose I wanted it recorded in this country as well – writing it out in English seemed to do that.' He looked at Theo. 'I've still got the translation if you'd like to read it?'

'Oh God, yes, I would,' said Theo.

'It's rough and not very tidy, but it would help you to see that whoever killed Charmery – whoever attacked you – couldn't be Mara. Because of what was done to her, violence is absolute anathema to her.'

Theo did not reply. He watched Innes open a drawer in the desk and take out a large envelope. Innes held the envelope between his hands for a moment, as if holding on to a memory, then gave it to Theo.

'I don't think I'll ever want to read them again,' he said. 'I don't ever want to re-visit those years. I still don't really understand why you're looking backwards at all this, but if they'll help you . . .'

'Yes,' said Theo. 'Yes, they'll help me. I'll be very careful with them.'

'I'll leave them with you,' said Michael Innes. 'Go up to bed when you want.'

Theo had thought he would take the diaries up to the little bedroom, but he seemed to have gone beyond sleep. He sat back in the chair, and opened the envelope with care. Mara's diaries, he thought, as he withdrew the four or five sheets of paper. There were no dates, but he knew Mara had been in Jilava Gaol sometime in the first few years of the 1980s.

Innes' handwriting was illegible in places – Theo guessed he had

317

been deeply affected by what he was writing – and the sentences were frequently disjointed, as if Mara had written scrappy notes at snatched moments. But it was possible to piece most of it together. As he began to read, the voice of the young woman who had been Mara Ionescu came vividly into the room.

'Today I came to the sunken fortress of Jilava. A bleak grim place, cold, unforgiving and smelling of human despair . . .'

There were fragmented phrases after this – references to stone rooms with walls running with condensation, and to the unvarying routine of the days, with spells of work in the prison shop, sewing and working bewildering machinery. 'I have no idea what we are making . . .' Later, she wrote, 'I can no longer smell the despair. Is that because it's now part of me?' At the foot of the same page, describing her surroundings more fully, she wrote, 'I live in a narrow dim room, with slit windows overlooking a small brick yard. There are twelve of us. Each morning they take us to a stone-floored room with a tap – we are allowed about three minutes to wash and clean what they call the bucket – it's a kind of commode which we share. Some mornings there isn't time to clean it or even empty it. When that happens, the stench in the cell makes us all feel sick . . . .

'The other women say if I'm asked to confess to anything I should do so. It saves pain, they say. I don't understand that . . .'

Theo read on, his senses racing. There was something about being taken to a different part of the gaol – the writing was a bit skewed, but it was readable. Was this when the re-education had started?

'No matter what they do to me, I won't admit to murder,' Mara had written. 'I didn't kill Annaleise, I know I didn't. She fell.'

She fell. Theo's mind went at once to his book, to how he had described Annaleise stumbling and falling back into the gaping mouth of the old well.

'Zoia comes here sometimes. She stands in the doorway watching me with eyes as cold as a snake's. Yesterday I saw her give the

318

guards something in a big envelope – money, I think ... Is she paying them to do this to me?

'Last night, when they brought food, they tied my hands up so I had to lick the food from the plate. There were dry crustings of fat and gristle clinging to the side because they no longer bother to wash the plates. I tried to lick up a mouthful, but my stomach rebelled and I was violently sick. Being sick on the floor with your hands tied behind your back is so disgusting, so disgusting ... I can't endure this, I *can't* ... If I said what they want me to say it would end.'

Did she confess? Theo wondered. Did they keep on with this subtle, squalid torture – this re-education? That's what Zoia wanted, that's what she paid the guards for. She wanted Mara to be a self-confessed murderess so she could see her sentenced – to death, presumably. He was no longer aware of being in the warm room; he was in the sunken prison house where medieval tortures were practised in secret, and where innocent people vanished to become wraiths, living ghosts in a world that would soon have no memory of them.

'Today,' wrote Mara, after what appeared to be a gap of several days, 'they said if I confessed they would make sure my brother was safe. They reminded me how very young he is – not yet sixteen. I'm so afraid that's a threat. If I don't make the confession they want, Mikhail will be harmed.'

Mikhail, thought Theo, feeling the pity of it slam into his throat. Of course Zoia would use Mikhail to extract that final revenge, and of course Mara would give in.

'Now they say if I confess they will allow me to go home to him.'

The final turn of the screw. She could never have resisted that, thought Theo. That's the one thing she couldn't have held out against – she was only seventeen or eighteen herself.

Mara had not resisted. Straight after the entry about her brother, she had written, 'And so, finally and at last, it's over and I did what they wanted. I confessed to killing Annaleise. But I did

319

it for Mikhail's sake, for my sake, so I can see him again, so he'll be safe . . . The curious thing is that I feel cleansed for saying it, for admitting it at last. I am a murderess. It seems even more real now I've written it down.

'They were kind to me afterwards – they gave me food and blankets and tonight I'm back in the room with the other women. That's friendly. When will they let me go home, I wonder?'

'They didn't let her go home, of course,' said Mikhail, early the next morning, as he and Theo ate breakfast in the cottage's kitchen. It felt warm and safe and there was the good scent of fresh coffee, but Theo could feel the ghosts all round them. 'What they did was to keep holding out the promise of release. It never came.'

The envelope with the diaries lay on the table between them. Theo put his hand on them. 'I don't think I'll ever forget what's in those pages.'

'I never have,' said Innes. He was buttering toast and his tone was matter-of-fact, but his eyes were deep and dark. 'I never forgot how she wrote that she had done it for me – how she believed it would make sure I was safe from the Securitate.'

'How did she finally get out?' said Theo.

'I got her out. I went into Jilava with a friend and got her out in secrecy.'

'A friend?' Theo was aware of a sudden bump of anticipation, and he was not really surprised when Innes said, 'It was someone I'd known all my life – someone I knew I could trust. His name was Matthew Valk.'

Matthew. The name brushed against Theo's mind with friendly familiarity.

'It was one of those wild plans that oughtn't to have succeeded,' said Innes. 'It was like something out of adventure fiction, like those nineteenth-century heroes locked away in ancient fortresses, outwitting their captors.'

'If you've got time, I'd like to hear the final scene,' said Theo.

'Surgery isn't until ten,' said Innes, glancing at the clock. 'You've got to get back to Fenn to organize the locksmith though, remember.'

'I'll phone him in a minute,' said Theo.

Innes refilled the cups.

'We decided that two people would go into Jilava openly, as semi-official visitors. The October Group created a society called the United Communist Association as cover for us. They even printed several leaflets outlining the apparent aims of the association: a mixture of Ceauşescu's own doctrines, with a sprinkling of hard-edged Leninism. It was said to be affiliated to the Party's Humanist Prison Committee and the Politburo's Law Commission. Both were fictional, but they sounded sufficiently official, and everything was deliberately hydra-headed to make checking difficult. Once inside – well, two people would go in and two people would come out. Only they wouldn't be the same two.'

'A substitution inside the prison,' said Theo.

'Yes. I was going to remain behind – Mara would go out wearing my long coat, boots and a hat pulled down to hide her face. Once they'd gone I thought I could bluff my way out, or maybe drug the guards. I'd been taking extra chemistry and biology lessons, and I concocted a sleeping draught which I would smuggle in with me.' He smiled. 'I can't believe how naive I was,' he said. 'I still can't believe that all of us didn't end up being put up against a wall and shot. But the plan wasn't as harebrained as it sounds. The October Group found out the layout of the prison, the number of the guards, even some of their names, changes of shifts, patterns of the day, where prisoners were at certain hours. And somehow we got inside the gaol,' he said.

'And you got Mara out.'

'Yes. But what I didn't know,' said Innes, 'was that Matthew had an agenda of his own.'

CHAPTER TWENTY-NINE

Romania, early 1980s

The journey to Jilava was exhausting and maddening. The roads were hot and dusty, and the trains, when they turned up, were dirty and uncomfortable. Matthew was quite surprised to find that Jilava itself was nicer than he had expected.

'I hadn't realized it was a university town,' he said as they walked through it. 'It's sort of tucked between mountains and pine forests. I wonder what it would be like to live and study here.'

'It's five o'clock,' said Mikhail. 'We'd better not waste any time.'

They asked someone for directions to the prison and set off. Matthew had no idea what it would look like, but as they started out, his painter's mind was already peopling the road leading to it with greedy-featured goblins and long-fingered hags, and wrapping it in perpetual night. As for the prison itself, it would be a misshapen lump of brick and stone like a truncated body, or a sprawling nightmare mansion like the Black House. The images poured into his mind, but in fact the road they took was perfectly ordinary and, although the prison, when it came into view, was unmistakably an old fortress, it did not seem too formidable. But as Matthew stared at it, he saw how the stones around the small,

322

mean windows had crumbled, as if the despair and pain within had seeped out and dripped over the sills, corroding the fabric. The fortress's edges blurred with the iron sky so that it was impossible to know where the walls ended and the sky began.

'I hadn't expected it to be so ordinary,' said Mikhail. 'Are we ready?'

'No, but let's do it anyway.'

Ahead of them was a big stone courtyard. Prisoners would be brought through this courtyard, knowing the bleak future ahead of them, thought Matthew. Did they struggle, those poor creatures, or did they go defiantly, pretending not to care about what might be ahead? Had Mara done that? Had his own father? Andrei's image, never far from his thoughts, rose up vividly.

'I expected to be challenged by guards or someone by this time,' said Mikhail softly. 'I wonder if that's because everyone's so securely locked away they aren't worried by people marching up to the door and asking to come in?'

'Perhaps they aren't very efficient.'

'Matthew, no one in this regime dares to be inefficient.'

There was a massive door at the centre of the building, with a large old-fashioned bell rope that jangled discordantly when Matthew pulled it. His heart raced and sweat slid between his shoulder blades, but the guard who opened the door regarded them with indifference. Matthew, keeping to the script they and the October Group had written, was able to say firmly, 'We are from the United Communist Association. UCA.'

'Who?'

'Our visit was arranged by our headquarters.' Matthew's heart beat fast with nerves. 'Details were sent to you. We're to see the prisoner held here for the death of Annaleise Simonescu.'

The man practically sprang to attention. 'I'll need to get clearance,' he said.

'I should hope you would,' said Matthew, and they went inside.

It was like stepping into a deep dark cavern. For a moment

Matthew felt as if he was drowning in pain, despair and bitterness.

'I suppose you're expected by someone?' demanded the guard, reaching for a telephone.

'A man called Groze,' said Matthew, hoping he sounded sufficiently imperious. Groze was the name they had been given by the October Group. He was apparently responsible for transferring prisoners between gaols, which meant he was reasonably high up in the pecking order but not likely to know much about commissions or recognize that UCA was false.

The guard spoke into the phone, then said, 'Groze says he's never heard of UCA and he doesn't know anything about an appointment, but he'll give you ten minutes.'

Groze greeted them warily, and apologized for not being aware of their visit.

'We will be having something to say about that in the appropriate quarters,' said Matthew. 'What we need now is to see the prisoner Mara Ionescu.'

'Particularly why?'

'I don't know why they picked that one,' said Matthew. 'They do this from time to time – random auditing, it's called. But in view of Ionescu's history – that question mark over her involvement with Simonescu's death – the Party needs to know she's being held securely and in accordance with their rulings.'

Groze shrugged, and got up from the desk. 'I'll get someone to take you,' he said. 'I don't have much to do with the prisoners as individuals, in fact I don't know why your appointment was made with me in the first place.'

'That, too, will be looked into,' said Matthew.

Mara was brought to a small, bare room – Matthew thought it was some kind of interview room. She was ragged and thin and she looked at them with such wary suspicion, clearly not immediately recognizing them, that Matthew felt a deep spiking pain of compassion. And then Mikhail said softly, 'Hello Mara,' and recognition flared in the distrusting eyes. Matthew expected her to fly into Mikhail's arms, but she did not; she looked nervously towards the door. She thinks it's some kind of test, he thought. She thinks people might be watching us. He realized with a shock that this was likely.

Mikhail must have realized it as well and although he must have been deeply hurt at her lack of emotion, he said, 'Mara, there's a plan. Just do everything we tell you and don't question anything because we haven't got much time.'

'All right.'

It was as Mikhail started unwinding the thick scarf half-hiding his face, that Matthew said, 'No. Mara's changing clothes with me.' As Mikhail turned to stare at him, he said, 'There's no time to argue. You're both going out, and I'm staying here.' He stripped off the long coat he wore and unwound his own scarf. 'Mara, put this on – it'll be a bit too big, but that doesn't matter. Wind the scarf round so it covers as much of your face as possible. When the guard or Groze comes back, leave the talking to Mikhail.'

'Matthew, what are you doing? This isn't the plan—'

'There's a new plan,' said Matthew, thankful that Mara was doing as asked. 'It's a plan to get another prisoner out.'

Mikhail stared at him. 'Your father,' he said. 'You think he might be here. You're going to search for him.'

'Yes,' said Matthew. 'I know it's a gamble, but it's too good an opportunity to miss. If he's here I've got to get him out. So don't let's waste any more time arguing. Have you got that sleeping stuff you were going to bring?'

'Yes, but . . .' Mikhail gave an impatient shrug and handed over a small cone of paper. 'If you use it, only use half on one man – the whole dose could be fatal.'

'I wouldn't lose any sleep if I killed the lot of them,' said Matthew, pocketing it. 'Mara, I need to know where the men are kept. Can you help with that?'

For a moment he thought she did not understand, then she said,

'I don't know. There are so many rooms. But there're a couple of big workshops – people are taken there in shifts.'

'If I could find that,' said Matthew, 'I might be able to merge with the men. Do the guards keep an exact count?'

'I don't know.'

'But they'd be expecting people to try to get out, not try to get in,' said Mikhail. 'Matthew, are you sure about doing this?'

'Yes.'

'All right. I understand.'

'Good. And for the moment we stay with the original plan.' Matthew looked at them, then put his arms first round Mikhail then round Mara. 'Please be safe,' he said.

'You too.'

Matthew went to stand behind the door, and they waited for the guard to open it, calling that the ten minutes were up. When he did so, Mikhail said, 'Thank you, we're coming now.' He stepped into the doorway. 'You'll take us back to the main doors, I expect,' he said to the man. 'It's a real warren down here, isn't it?'

'I need to get the prisoner back first,' said the guard.

'She's already back,' said Mikhail, sounding surprised. 'Groze came in and took her back himself.'

'Groze never does things like that.' He sounded suspicious, and Mikhail shrugged. 'See for yourself,' he said, pushing the door of the room open.

The guard pulled the door sharply back and, seeing Matthew half-concealed behind it, gave a triumphant cry. But before he could raise the alarm, Matthew sprang at him, delivering a hefty punch to the guard's jaw that sent him staggering backwards. He went after him, prepared to give him a second blow, but the man had banged his head on the stone floor and slumped into unconsciousness.

'He's out cold,' said Mikhail, bending over to feel for a pulse, 'but breathing.'

'Give me his hat,' said Matthew, already unbuttoning the guard's jacket, and dragging it off.

'Will it fit you?' asked Mikhail.

'I don't know. I'm making this up as I go along.'

'I don't think you are.'

'I had two or three possible courses of action,' said Matthew, putting on the jacket and hat. 'Has he got any keys? Oh thank God, yes, he has.' He unhooked the heavy bunch of keys clipped to the man's belt, and looped it onto his own. 'Can we get him into that cupboard?' he said. 'The longer it is before he's found, the better.'

It was difficult because the cupboard was a small stationery store, but in the end they managed it, and closed the door firmly.

'Remember to keep the scarf over your face, Mara,' said Matthew. 'Let Mikhail do the talking, if there is any. This is the risky part.' He tilted the guard's hat so it shaded his face and led them out into the passageway. 'If we meet any guards, I'm escorting you two visitors to the door,' he said. 'We'll have to trust that there's a lot of guards and they don't all know one another.'

'And that we can find the way out,' said Mikhail grimly.

Nervous tension hold Matthew's entire body in a vice as they went along. He expected to be challenged at any minute. In his head he began to play a grim form of an old childhood game. If we get to the next turn in the passage it'll be all right. And then, when they did get to the turn, he thought, if we can reach that stairway, we won't be caught . . .

Ahead were the narrow windows of the guard room. 'This is where we'd better part. Stay safe,' he said again, and was gone, swallowed up by the dark corridors.

The present

'And so Matthew stayed behind in Jilava,' said Theo.

'Yes,' said Innes. 'And Mara and I came to England. When we

327

got out of Jilava, we simply got on a tram to Resita, where we met Sister Teresa. She brought Mara here. She thought it was sufficiently far away and that the English convent could provide the peace and safety Mara needed. The October Group helped with the paperwork side of things – I didn't ask about that, I was just grateful it was possible. But I think by then they had got a number of people out of the prisons, or just out of the country. People wanted by the Securitate for what they called crimes against the State – innocent people mostly. I think Sister Teresa and some of the nuns might have helped, although they never said. The October Group had built up a network of—'

'Forgers?'

'Well, people who could produce passports and visas that were acceptable,' said Innes. 'It was still only the early 1980s, and the computer chip for passports and so on was still in the future. I think this country was starting to wake up to what was happening in Romania, and England's always been prepared to help people escaping harsh dictators. By then I knew I wanted to study medicine and I was able to get into Queens Medical Centre at Nottingham, so I stayed. Later I got British citizenship. I don't forget my own country, but I'm actually quite proud of being a British citizen,' he said.

'You sound sufficiently deprecatory to actually be British,' said Theo.

'Good. And now,' he said, 'what about your explanations?'

Theo thought for a moment, then said, 'Can you come round to Fenn later? I should have sorted out the new locks by this evening. And . . .' He paused, frowning. 'Michael, I won't stir anything up at St Luke's – not yet anyway, and certainly not without talking to you again, but I'd like to ask one of the sisters about those twelve children who were brought here. It's in the centenary book, so it's all in the open. I can say I'm interested for a possible plot.' And that's more true than you know, he thought. 'There's the photo of Charmery, too – I can say I'm curious.'

'That sounds all right. You don't intend to talk to Mara, do you?'

'No,' said Theo. 'I was thinking of Sister Catherine. I'll say I don't want it mentioned to anyone because it's a project that might not come to anything.'

'Sounds reasonable. The children would be well before her time – early 1970s – but she might be able to find something out. And,' he said thoughtfully, 'Sister Catherine is absolutely trustworthy.'

The locksmith came out to Fenn within half an hour of Theo phoning. 'Not often we get break-ins around here,' he said. 'Still, I daresay this house is a bit of a magnet for one or two oddballs.'

If you only knew, thought Theo, but he said, yes, that seemed to be the problem, and he was grateful the locks could be changed again so quickly.

'Priority job,' said the locksmith. 'There you go, squire. Snug as the Bank of England now, not that that's saying much these days.'

He accepted the cheque Theo wrote, handed over three sets of new keys, and went off, whistling cheerfully, after which Theo called Sergeant Leigh.

'I'm just checking in to let you know I've had the locks changed and I've survived the night, and I'm hoping you've traced the missing key.'

'We're having a word with the shops this morning,' said Leigh, 'and we're going along to St Luke's later.'

'Sergeant, when you were investigating Charmery's death, did you find any record of her travelling to Romania?'

'Not as far as I remember. When would it have been?'

'No idea.'

'I can get it checked if you think there's any point,' said Leigh. 'We did look at where she'd been for the last couple of years – Paris and Italy as I recall – but there didn't seem any need to go back further.'

'It's just a mad idea I had,' said Theo. 'Probably nothing in it, but if you can check that would be great. Listen, I'm calling at St Luke's later this morning though – I want to trace something I read in their centenary book. Just a bit of research, purely for my own use. That won't confuse your enquiries, will it?'

'Shouldn't do. We probably won't get there until this afternoon,' said Leigh.

'OK. I'll make sure to be out of the way by then.'

'I'll call you later to let you know if we trace the key,' said Leigh.

Theo rang off, then remembered he had promised to phone Lesley with some explanations. It was slightly disconcerting to find her phone on voicemail, so he tried the gallery, who said she wouldn't be in today.

'She's not ill, is she? I'm her cousin – I was with her yesterday.'

'No, she's just taking a couple of days' holiday owing to her. She phoned in earlier. Can I give her a message when she gets back?'

'No, I'll probably catch up with her later today,' said Theo, and rang off, unsure whether to be puzzled or worried. But as he set about tidying up after the locksmith's session, it occurred to him that Lesley might be taking Charmery's portrait to a rival house for appraisal and did not want her present boss to know.

He checked all round the house, found no signs of disturbance, locked every door in sight, and set off to walk to St Luke's.

CHAPTER THIRTY

————◆————

Catherine was writing up some patient notes in the clinic wing when the message came that Mr Kendal had called and wondered if she could spare him half an hour. Her heart lurched with treacherous excitement, but she finished the paragraph she was writing as calmly as she could, then went along to the main hall where he was waiting.

He was standing in front of a pair of sketches of St Luke's which Catherine had always admired, but he turned at once and said, 'Hello. If I've come when you're in the middle of something, tell me at once.'

'Nothing that can't wait,' said Catherine. 'Are you all right after your attack? We were horrified to hear about it.' She did not say that when the Bursar told them, she had wanted to rush to Fenn House at once.

'Never better,' he said.

'Have they caught the man?'

'No, but they're working on it,' said Theo. 'I was reading your centenary book last night. It's very interesting, by the way, very well written.'

'Tell the Bursar that, would you? She agonized over it for

weeks. And even then she was convinced it was rubbish.'

The smile deepened, as if this was something he could relate to.

'I *will* tell her,' he said. 'The thing is, there's a reference in it that intrigued me – and I'd like to find out a bit more.'

'Well, you really want the Bursar for that. Or Sister Miriam, even—'

'No, I don't,' he said at once. 'I want you.' And then, before Catherine could think how to reply to this, he went on, 'There's a mention of some children being brought to England from Romania in the 1970s. Twelve of them, actually. I'd very much like to know more about that.'

'It was way before my time,' began Catherine.

'I know that. You're the youngest one here, aren't you? Sorry, that sounded intrusive, but you mentioned it the first time we met.'

'You remember that?' said Catherine involuntarily.

'I remember our first meeting very clearly,' he said, and looked at her so intently Catherine felt as if he could see straight into her mind. I'll look away in a minute, she thought, or he will. We can't stand here staring at each other like this. And we're in the main hall, for pity's sake! Her heart was beating wildly, and she felt as if something was squeezing the breath from her body and she did not trust herself to speak.

'It's really just a wild idea I've got,' said Theo. 'So I don't want it spread around.'

'Yes, of course,' said Catherine, thinking he probably had an idea for a new book, but wanted it kept quiet in case it didn't work out. 'I remember the Bursar getting a lot of stuff together for the centenary,' she said. 'Photographs and old records. You could look through them. I don't think anyone would mind.'

'Could I?'

'They're stored in the attic,' she said. 'I could take you up there now if you've got time. I don't know how easy it will be to find anything, though.'

'Let's go and see,' he said, and looked so pleased and eager that

332

Catherine thought the moment earlier on had just been in her imagination. He was in pursuit of a new idea, and probably still suffering the effects of the bang on the head as well.

As she led him up the two flights of stairs, and along to the narrow little stair leading to the attic, Theo said, 'Apparently, a nun called Sister Teresa brought the twelve children here in the early 1970s to escape Ceauşescu's dictatorship.'

'Yes, it's one of our bits of folklore. I should think it was all very risky and maybe even illegal.'

'I daresay the Church wouldn't necessarily have worried about that,' said Theo. 'It's harboured some odd things in its long history, hasn't it? Religious conflicts and spies.'

'It's switched sides a few times as well,' said Catherine rather caustically.

'Would Reverend Mother or the Bursar remember the children coming here?' said Theo.

'It's over thirty years ago. I don't think either of them were here then,' said Catherine. 'But it might be possible to write to the Romanian House – or email them – to ask if they've kept any records.'

'Would you do that? Or could I?'

'I'd have to ask Reverend Mother if I can give you the address. I shouldn't think she'd mind, though.'

'Thank you. Did you ever meet Sister Teresa?' he said, as they went up the second flight of stairs.

'She came over for the centenary celebration last year,' said Catherine. 'She's getting on – she must be eighty – but she's still very spry and bright. The attic's up here – the stairs are a bit narrow, so be careful.'

The attic was quiet and dim, and as Catherine found the light switch tiny cobwebs stirred in corners.

'As a storage place,' said Theo, surveying it, 'it's unnaturally tidy.'

'Is it? I haven't got much experience of attics. The centenary

333

stuff's over there, I think. Yes, look, two boxes, labelled Centenary.'

'These look like the Bursar's original notes,' he said, lifting one of the boxes out and setting it on a battered table. 'Yes, she's made a folder of odd letters and accounts. Would she mind if I read this, d'you think? Or even borrowed the folder for a day or so?' Then, seeing her hesitation, said, 'I'll ask her myself if that's easier. I can truthfully say I want to find out what happened to the children.'

Catherine looked at him. 'Is there a bit more to this than an idea for a plot?'

At first she thought he was not going to answer, but then he said, 'Yes. There's quite a lot more to it, and I hope I can tell you soon. But at the moment it's not my secret to tell.'

'Is it something to do with your cousin's death?'

'It might be. Will you trust me as far as that?'

'Yes,' she said at once. 'Will you trust me to ask the Bursar very discreetly if you can borrow her notes?'

'I'd trust you with anything, Catherine,' he said, softly, and quite suddenly the attic had become an intimate cave, and the world beyond it ceased to matter or even exist. He was standing so close to her Catherine could see the flecks of black in his grey eyes. She had the absurd thought that if he touched her she might faint.

But when he did touch her, she did not.

He put a hand up to her face, tracing the line of her cheekbone and then her lips, and it was as if his fingers set up a tiny series of electric sparks across her skin. Almost without realizing what she was doing, Catherine stepped forward, and his arms went round her.

She thought he said, 'Catherine, this is the maddest thing I've ever done,' but then he was kissing her. It was a soft, deep exploratory kiss, and she had to cling to him to stop herself falling over because the attic was whirling round, and even if this was the maddest thing ever, it was the most marvellous feeling. I'll have to stop in a minute, she thought, I can't do this, I *can't*. But just another minute . . .

When at last he released her, there was a faint flush of colour across his cheeks, and his eyes were lit to brilliance.

'I expect I should be sorry,' he said. 'I'm not, though. But I didn't mean to do that. You have the most extraordinary effect on me.'

'I don't want you to be sorry,' said Catherine, surprised to hear that her voice came out with hardly a tremor. 'Oh, Theo, I wanted you to do that ever since . . .'

'Ever since we met?'

'More or less.' Ever since I watched you with Charmery all those years ago, she was thinking, and ever since I held your dead son in my arms.

'What now?' he said. 'Do we talk about this, or do I go away politely and leave you to—'

'Untangle my emotions? Yes,' she said, frowning. 'I think I should do that. I think I need to be on my own . . .' This time her voice did tremble.

'All right. I'll come back to see you in a couple of days,' he said. 'But I'll be at Fenn if you want to talk to me before then.'

'I know.'

'Will you have to – to confess or something?'

'Yes.'

'Will that be embarrassing?'

'I should think the Church has heard worse than—'

'Than a confession of a snatched kiss in an attic? Was that what you were going to say?'

'Was that all it was? Or an experiment to see what it would feel like to kiss a nun? Sorry, I shouldn't have said that.'

'Was it what you were thinking?'

'Yes.'

'You know it wasn't that,' said Theo. 'You must know how – how strongly you attract me, and . . . Dammit, I'm even afraid to use the ordinary chat-up lines with you!' He thrust his fingers angrily through his hair. 'This is probably the most bizarre

335

conversation I've ever had – and that's saying quite a lot,' he said. 'This would normally be the point where I'd ask you out, but I suppose I can't do that. Or can I?'

'I don't know.' For a dreadful moment Catherine thought she might burst into tears, but if she did he would take her in his arms again and then she would not be able to think properly. She made a huge effort and said, 'I think we'd better go.'

As they went downstairs neither of them spoke, but when they got to the main doors, Catherine managed to recall the main purpose of Theo's visit, and said, 'I'll ask the Bursar about borrowing her notes. And I'll ask Reverend Mother if you can have the Romanian address.'

'Thank you.' In a different voice, he suddenly said, 'Catherine – will you promise me you'll be careful until – well, until I solve what's going on.'

'Is something going on?'

'I think so. I'll tell you about it properly when I can, but until then . . . Don't go anywhere on your own, and be aware that – that people aren't always what they seem.' For a moment Catherine thought he was going to reach out to touch her face again, but he did not. He merely gave her a half nod and went out into the bleak morning.

As Theo went down the drive he felt as if his emotions had been shredded. I must have been mad, he thought. Or was I actually being very sane? If he had met Catherine in the ordinary way, he would have wanted to take things further; he would have wanted to get to know her better, and he thought he might have discovered he wanted her in his life for a long time. He tried to think how he was going to deal with this but had no idea. Then he tried to imagine how Catherine would deal with it, and had even less idea. He remembered Charmery and, with a stab of wry bitterness, wondered why he seemed unable to fall for someone who was straightforwardly available.

One of the nuns was walking up the drive towards him, slightly hunched against the cold morning. At this distance Theo could not see who it was, but as she drew nearer he recognized her, and all thoughts of Catherine fled from his mind. Sister Miriam. Mara Ionescu. He experienced a wild impulse to tell her that he knew about her sad, dramatic early life. To say, I know how you listened to all those fire lit stories, and how you cowered in that appalling well-house and covered your ears as Annaleise screamed her way to her death. I know how you resisted the gaolers in Jilava and why you eventually gave in and made that confession. Did you make another confession, though, Mara? thought Theo, as the thin figure came nearer. Did you creep into Fenn House that night and use the laptop to type a confession of another murder? What's really going on behind that impassive face?

She was near enough to speak by this time, and she glanced at him in a disinterested way, as if he was no more than a chance visitor to the convent.

'Good morning, Mr Kendal.'

'Good morning,' said Theo. 'It's a sharp morning, isn't it?'

'It is. Are you recovered from your attack?'

'Yes, thank you.'

They walked on in their different directions, and Theo wondered would a killer really ask that in such an ordinary voice? Michael had said Sister Teresa believed Mara would find peace and safety at St Luke's. But had she?

From the start, Mara had found the peace and safety of St Luke's immensely reassuring. She could still remember how pleased Sister Teresa had been all those years ago when she decided to become a novice. She wrote to Mara to say it was the best outcome of all, and she was sure Mara had a real vocation. There would be many years of quiet contentment, of prayer and study and fulfilling work – in time Mara might become involved in the nursing work at St Luke's.

In the event, Mara did not take much part in the medical side of the convent. 'No vocation for that kind of work,' she said after taking her final vows, and the older nuns agreed. She was by nature a contemplative, they said, an academic. She found contact with others difficult. But everyone had something different to offer. There would be a niche for her and it would present itself in God's good time.

The niche seemed to become apparent quite naturally and gradually. Mara – now Sister Miriam – found herself looking after the convent's library, collating information about its past, liaising with the University of East Anglia when post-graduate students wanted to stay at the convent to write a thesis on the county's famous sons and daughters: the reformers Edith Cavel and Elizabeth Fry, or George Borrow. She began to write a monograph on the medieval mystic, Julian of Norwich. It was deeply satisfying to find that by now she could write smoothly and clearly in English, as if it was her native tongue. The nuns were pleased with her work, and interested in the monograph. A worthwhile study of a remarkable woman, they said, and were happy that this rather withdrawn sister was forging a quiet path of her own. They did not pry into Sister Miriam's past, but clearly there had been deep unhappiness and suffering. If she should want to talk about it at any time, they would listen and try to help. But Sister Miriam did not talk. She went unobtrusively about her work, devout and obedient, a trouble to no one.

When Mikhail finished his medical training and was a qualified doctor, Mara was immensely proud. It was wrong to be proud on one's own account – she had learned that at Debreczen, and later in the English novitiate – but it was perfectly all right on behalf of another. Mikhail was now a British citizen, known as Michael Innes. Dr Innes. There was pride in saying that, as well.

The memory of Zoia never quite left Mara. She sometimes dreamed about her. Zoia would have been filled with such anger when Mara escaped her – would she let her go so easily? Would she try to find out where Mara was and follow her? Mara seldom went beyond St Luke's confines, but on the rare occasions she did, she was careful to keep her head down and not look into the faces of passers-by.

It was Sister Teresa – dear, good Sister Teresa – who managed to put her mind at rest. The nuns liked seeing their fellow-sisters from the other houses, and they especially liked seeing Sister Teresa who came to England every few years. Sister Teresa told Mara that she could feel herself safe. 'Ceauşescu's reign is becoming a very troubled one indeed,' she said. 'They're saying his days are numbered, and Zoia Calciu will be fighting for her own survival. She won't have time to bother about one prisoner who got away from her. So be safe and content and do your work here.'

When, in December 1989, the news reports came of the revolution – of the riots and then the scrambled trial of Nicolae and Elena Ceauşescu – Mara read the newspaper articles, scanning the faces of the crowds in the photographs. Had Zoia been there? Had she seen the disgrace and downfall of that evil pair? If so, what had she felt? But the faces were blurred grey smudges.

After that the years wheeled by, quiet and untroubled, busy and fulfilling. Some of the older nuns died, and new ones came to Melbray. There was a new Reverend Mother and a couple of years later, a new Bursar. They knew little of Mara's early days, and there was safety in that, too. Life had fallen into a pattern that was orderly and safe and predictable. It should have gone on indefinitely; Mara was daring to hope it would. She began to believe nothing from the past could touch her in this English backwater. No hag-fingered memories could come bonily prodding into this safety, and expose the black mortal sin she had committed.

'Admit you're a murderess . . . confront the sin, unmask it and be penitent . . .' That was what they had said in Jilava. Well, she had done all that, and although they had not kept their promise about letting her go, in the end she had got out. She had been in England long enough to feel safe now. It was more than twenty years since Matthew and Michael came into Jilava Gaol and got her out.

And then two things happened.

The first was that her beloved Mikhail came to live and work in Melbray as the GP for Melbray itself and several of the surrounding villages. It was what Mara had hoped and prayed for. She had watched and listened for this very opportunity, writing to Mikhail at once when she heard the existing GP was to retire. Mikhail found a house a few miles away, but Mara did not mind that distance; all she cared was that he was near to her. He often came to the convent's clinic to treat the patients: he had developed a particular interest in bone damage and injuries. She did not always see him on those days, but she knew he was in the same building and that, too, was a deep delight.

He and Mara did not talk about their relationship although if anyone had asked, Mikhail would certainly have admitted it. He would have seen no reason not to. But the habit of secrecy was still with Mara, and she thought it better if no one knew. People in villages were gossipy. They had been so in Romania and they were the same in England. The new doctor has a sister at St Luke's, they might say. How interesting. Then the Romanian background might come out and this would be unusual enough for people to talk about it. And talk spread – Mara knew that from her homeland – and it gathered its own information as it went. The information might find its way to official levels, where papers would be checked, documents scrutinized. Her right and Mikhail's to be in the country might come into question – perhaps they could even be sent back to Romania. Mara felt sick at the prospect of that. So although she would not lie about Mikhail being her brother, she would not volunteer the information. This was reasonable and sensible.

But the second thing, the dreadful thing that was neither reasonable nor sensible, and that threatened to stir greedily at the silt of the past, was that Mikhail met and fell in love with Charmery Kendal.

*

Mara was never sure when the actual falling in love happened. She had no knowledge of the mechanics of love or romance and, although she supposed Mikhail had had a few adventures with ladies over the years, he had never talked about it and she had never asked. She did not want to know.

He talked about Charmery Kendal, though. How she had come back to Fenn House after several years away. He never thought he would see her again, but she had always been in some part of his mind. And now she was back.

Mara supposed Mikhail had been to bed with Charmery, which did not bother her very much: physical intimacy between two people was not something she could really relate to. It was the thought of a mental intimacy between them she could not bear. She managed to hide her feelings, but she felt as if a spade had been driven into her stomach. And one thing was gradually becoming clear: Charmery could not be allowed to take him away from her. He was Mara's, he was the one for whom she had done everything: endured Jilava, made that shameful confession.

Eventually, she managed to ask him if he and Charmery might marry. She did not really think he would say yes, because he would never want to belong to another woman in that way. She waited confidently for his reassurance. There was no reassurance. He said, 'Yes, I'll marry her, if she'll have me.'

It was as if the world had stopped turning on its axis. Everything that was dear and familiar and safe began to shiver and dissolve. Charmery Kendal would agree to marry Mikhail – Mara knew she would. No female could refuse him, that meant Mara would lose him.

Except it must not be allowed to happen.

CHAPTER THIRTY-ONE

The present

It was almost midday when Theo got back to Fenn House. His brain was whirling with images of Catherine and also of Mara who had bade him a polite good morning, so when a taxi trundled up the drive and stopped in front of the house it startled him.

From out of it clambered Lesley and Guff.

'Guff,' said Theo, even more startled. 'Is something wrong?'

'Not at all, my dear boy. Oh, it *is* good to see you,' said Guff, beaming all over his cherubic face. 'We're not putting you out, arriving like this, are we?'

'No, but—'

'We're only here overnight. Well, we can even go back this evening.'

'It's the sketch,' said Lesley, as Guff turned to pay the driver. She extricated a flat package from the taxi and Theo recognized it as Charmery's portrait. 'I talked to Guff first thing this morning, and we thought we'd better come down to discuss it all with you. It's quite complicated. I told the gallery I'd need another couple of days' holiday, and we caught the ten o'clock train.'

Guff was delighted to be at Fenn again. 'After so many years.

My word, I wouldn't like to count how many years it is since I was here, although I must say the old place is looking a bit . . .'

Theo expected Guff to fuss and fluff around for his customary half an hour, but for once he did not. He came into the dining room where Lesley had set the sketch on the table.

'I spent most of the night staring at it, trying to work out who it was,' said Lesley. 'Because if it wasn't Charmery – and I didn't see how it could be – I couldn't think who it was. Then I thought that Guff knows more about this family than anyone, so I phoned him early this morning to tell him about it.'

'I took a taxi to Lesley's flat,' said Guff. 'I don't usually go to Earl's Court, you know, so I wasn't sure of the way. My word, that area's changed.'

'Don't guffle,' said Theo affectionately, and saw Lesley grin at the use of the familiar childhood word.

'As soon as I saw the sketch I knew it wasn't Charmery,' said Guff.

'Then who is it?'

'It's your mother,' said Guff. 'It's a drawing of Petra when she was very young.'

'You're wrong,' said Theo for the twentieth time. 'You must be. It can't be my mother.' But something stirred uneasily in his mind. Charmery and I, he thought. Half brother and sister – the same father. If that's true, why would Charmery resemble my mother so closely? He reached out to trace the outlines of the face with a fingertip as if by doing so he could draw out its past.

'There's no question about it,' said Guff. 'I was around when your mother first came into this family and this is exactly how she looked. And what's more, she's wearing the pendant your father gave her to mark your birth.' He too put out a hand to the picture, touching the pencilled line of the Victorian-looking pendant which Theo had not recognized. He glanced at Guff and saw a deep sadness in the china-blue eyes.

343

'I remember her wearing it,' Guff said, 'and I remember this is how she wore her hair in those days. It's definitely Petra. This is how she looked all those years ago. I admired her so much when she first came into this family, you know,' he said. 'I remember Nancy was quite sharp with me about it: she said she hoped I wasn't going off on some silly sentimental journey. I thought that was unfair of her,' said Guff mildly. 'I'm not a sentimentalist, even if people use the word nowadays which I don't think they do. D'you know, I sometimes wonder how Nancy copes with teaching modern teenagers.'

'It doesn't look much like my mother,' said Theo.

'No, but when your father died, Theo, it altered Petra. Mentally and physically, I mean. She was absolutely devastated. She changed in some very deep way I never understood. And she was ill for a long time.' He looked down at the portrait again. 'She shut everyone out,' he said. 'She went off somewhere with you – none of us had any contact with her – then later, she and Helen went on holiday together – I was always very glad to think Helen was such a good friend to Petra,' said Guff. 'Nancy was livid about it because she would have liked to go with them.'

'Fearsome,' said Lesley and Theo both together.

'I expect it would have been. You weren't quite at school, Theo, and you stayed with Lesley's parents while Petra was away. That was before Lesley or the boys were born, of course. And you stayed with me for a while, as well. You were a solemn, silent child in those days.'

'Beautifully behaved?' said Theo, trying for a light-hearted note, inwardly grappling with what Guff was saying.

'Actually, you *were* very well behaved. I expect you only remember those years in patches, though; you were only four. When Petra finally got back – when she started to be part of the world again, she was different,' said Guff. 'Thinner and her eyes were different – as if there was no light in them any longer.' He looked at Theo, who saw a shimmer of tears in Guff's own eyes. Partially

344

understanding but not wanting to pry, he put out a tentative hand to pat Guff's. For a moment the old fingers closed tightly round Theo's, then Guff said firmly, 'Lot of slop,' and mopped his eyes with his handkerchief. Despite his own inner turmoil, Theo smiled at this time-honoured Kendal remark. He saw Lesley smile as well. She leaned over to kiss Guff's cheek.

Guff blinked several times, then said, in a determinedly prosaic voice, 'I never saw the strong likeness between Petra and Charmery, though. Not until now.'

'But,' said Theo, 'why would Charmery look like my mother?'

'Yes,' said Guff slowly, 'why indeed?'

'Theo?' said Petra into the phone. 'Is anything wrong? Are you still at Fenn?'

'Yes. Lesley's here as well, and Guff. We've had a bit of a trauma, but everyone's fine. No, I won't go into the details now,' he said, as she started to ask what had happened. 'The thing is, we've hit on a mystery and you're the only one who can explain it. But I think it's going to dredge up part of your past that might be painful.' Even over the phone he was aware of a sudden stillness. He realized he was gripping the phone so tightly his knuckles were white. He took several deep breaths. 'When I got here there was a framed sketch of a young woman. I thought it was Charmery, but it isn't. It's a twenty-year-old sketch – Lesley's more or less confirmed that – and Guff says it's you.'

'Oh God,' she said. 'Oh God, Matthew's sketch. I never knew what happened to it. I supposed it was just put away in a box somewhere.'

Theo had not realized how strongly he had wanted to hear her say she knew nothing about it. 'So it really was Matthew's work. And it really is you.' It was an extraordinary feeling to be talking to his mother about Matthew.

'Yes, it's me,' she was saying. 'But Theo I can't possibly explain over the phone. I suppose I hoped you'd never know. I can't imagine how you've found out about Matthew.' She broke off, then said, 'Listen, I'll drive down this afternoon. No, don't argue, this will have to be sorted out. What time is it? Just on one. I can set off in half an hour. I should be with you by about four.'

'But . . .' began Theo, but Petra had already rung off.

He turned to see Lesley standing in the doorway of the room.

'Matthew again,' she said. 'I couldn't help hearing that. The same Matthew who did the convent sketches?'

'Yes.'

'And probably the one of Aunt Petra?'

'Let's make some lunch,' said Theo. 'It seems years since I had breakfast. I'll tell you while we eat.'

He told Lesley and Guff the whole story while they ate soup and hastily cut sandwiches, and he was deeply grateful to them both for listening and not ridiculing anything. He described to them the galaxy of people he had believed to be his own invention, but who were turning out to be real. Annaleise and Sister Teresa. Matthew and Mara and Mikhail and their strange uneasy life in Romania. 'They've all turned out to be actual people,' he said. 'Documented. Mikhail and Mara are here. I've met them, and you've met Mara, Lesley.'

'Sister Miriam,' said Lesley, who had listened with absorption to Theo's story, her eyes huge and fascinated. 'She came with us to look at the paintings on Monday. Very quiet – rather watchful of everyone. What's Mikhail – Michael Innes like?'

'Intelligent and serious. Nice.'

'Whatever else he is,' put in Guff, 'he must be incredibly brave to do what he did. Dear me, I remember all those dreadful news reports about Romania – the orphanages, the political prisons. We never knew the half of what went on in those years. So many tragedies. You know, I do wonder how you plugged into all this, Theo.'

'So do I,' said Theo, wryly.

'I suppose you read it all somewhere and forgot about it. I mean, it's the only explanation.'

'Yes,' said Theo, unconvinced. 'Oh, and there's also this.' He reached for the convent's book, and opened it at the page with the photo taken of the Romanian convent.

'Until this morning I'd have said that was Charmery,' said Lesley, leaning over to look.

'So would I. But what if it's my mother?'

'I'd say it *is* your mother,' said Guff, peering at the page.

'But what was she doing in Romania? I never knew she'd been there, did you, Guff?'

'No, but she's always travelled about a good bit. Is there another sandwich to be had? Thank you. What about Matthew and Andrei? And Elisabeth? Is there any way of tracing them?'

'I don't know. Michael might know.'

'I hope at any rate Matthew found Andrei and got him out of Jilava,' said Lesley.

'So do I,' said Theo. 'When Michael told me about leaving Matthew in Jilava, one of the things that came strongly across was that although he tried to hide it, Matthew was very frightened.'

Romania, early 1980s

Matthew thought he had managed to hide from Mikhail and Mara how extremely frightened he was at being inside Jilava on his own. As he went deeper into the prison's labyrinth, going stealthily along the dank stone passageways, he was trying not to remember how gaunt and strange Mara had looked or the way another person – a stranger – had seemed to look at him from her eyes.

He squared his shoulders, deliberately adopting a stance of authority, and began to walk. Authority, thought Matthew, that's what I must convey if I meet anyone. Authority and a sense of familiarity – as if I know all about this place.

His plan to search for his father was simple: he would work his way systematically along the stone corridors, opening every door he came to. He could not think what he would do if he did not have keys to them all, or if the knocked-out guard was found and described his assailant. But surely if the guard had been found already, Jilava would be echoing with the sounds of warning bells, shouts and running feet.

As he went down the stone steps to the lower level, he encountered two guards. His heart leapt with panic and he expected to be recognized as a stranger and pounced on. He managed to nod casually, and experienced a huge relief when they seemed to accept him, nodding back and continuing on their way. It's all right at the moment, thought Matthew, but it could go all wrong at any minute.

He assumed he would have to unlock doors to look inside the cells. This was worrying him because there were ten or twelve keys on the keyring and it would be time-consuming and noticeable to try them one at a time. But quite a number of the doors were unlocked; they turned out to be storage rooms or offices. Twice people were working at desks, but each time Matthew glanced round the room as if looking for someone, sketched a brief salute, murmured an apology, and went out again. But his heart was hammering and sweat was sliding slickly between his shoulder blades, and he knew he was treading a very precarious tightrope.

He worked his way along, eventually reaching several intersecting passages in the bowels of the old fortress. The doors here had small spy holes at eye level. That means it'll be easy to look inside each one, then move to the next, thought Matthew, knowing it would not be easy at all, knowing that finally and at last he was faced with the nightmare of his childhood. The stone corridors with people locked away in dank stone cells. The forgotten ones, the people whom the world barely remembered. I've walked these corridors in my mind, he thought, horrified. But how did I know about them? How did I get it all so right? How did I know that human creatures were herded into such places and I would feel this knife-twisting pity at seeing them?

But here and there he saw unmistakable defiance in the faces and eyes of some prisoners, and it heartened him, even though by this time he was shaking with pity and anger. Deep down a new fear was unfolding. If Andrei was here for ten years, and Jilava might have broken him as it had so obviously broken these prisoners, he might be weak, beaten, despairing, Matthew would find that hard to bear. Even harder to bear was the knowledge he might not even recognize his father.

But he did. He looked through a spy hole and saw six men in the cell. He looked at the one who sat nearest the window and a wave of emotion so strong it almost blinded him, engulfed him.

His hands were shaking so badly he thought he would not be able to unlock the door. Then he thought the key to this particular cell was not on the keyring, and he could have wept with frustration and his own ineptness. He peered through the tiny square of window again and saw the men had heard him. They were looking up, vaguely questioning of this guard who fumbled and took so long. Matthew swore under his breath and jammed another key into the lock. It turned, the door swung open, and he saw the figure by the window stand up and walk towards him.

The present

Petra arrived at Fenn House just after four o'clock. She hugged Theo and Lesley, told Guff he was looking terrific, and went upstairs to unpack and wash. When she came down again she went straight to Matthew's sketch which Theo had put back in its original place.

'So it was here all the time,' she said, half to herself. 'I always wondered what happened to it.'

'I'd never seen it before,' said Theo, 'but it looks as if Charmery found it and decided to put it on display. I thought,' he said, carefully, 'that it actually was Charmery.'

'Charmery,' said Petra in an odd, expressionless voice. 'Yes, I see.' She appeared to give herself a small shake, and came to sit down facing Theo. 'So here's the truth,' she said, 'and probably it should have been told a long time ago.'

Theo had the impression that she squared her shoulders, as if to take on an invisible weight. 'When your father died,' said Petra, 'I was deeply saddened, but – this will sound heartless – I wasn't as grief-stricken as everyone believed.' She made a brief gesture. 'He was charming and attractive, but he was also a womanizer.' She sent Guff a quick smile. 'You knew that,' she said.

'Yes. I always hoped you didn't.'

'Of course I knew,' she said. 'But I wanted to get away from London after his death. I found this house. It was very different then, smaller, shabbier, but there was a good feeling about it. You all thought it was Helen's discovery, didn't you? But I found it long before Helen persuaded Desmond to buy it. I lived here for a little while and liked it. I felt safe. I missed John very much, but at least I didn't have to wonder whose bed he was in, or whether there would be enough money to pay next month's bills.' She leaned back, her eyes going over the warm, comfortable, rather shabby room. 'And then,' she said, 'I met someone and he turned my entire world upside-down.'

Her eyes went back to the sketch, and very softly, Theo said, 'Matthew.'

'Yes, I met Matthew,' said Petra, 'but that's not who I meant.'

'Who?'

'Matthew's father,' she said, and smiled. 'I met Andrei.'

Into the silence that followed this, Theo said, 'So Matthew did find him. He did get him out.'

'I don't know how much you know,' said Petra studying Theo thoughtfully. 'But you clearly know about Matthew and Andrei . . . Yes, Matthew got him out of Romania and they came to England.'

CHAPTER THIRTY-TWO

Romania, early 1980s

Matthew stood just inside the terrible room, and stared numbly at the gaunt man who was his father.

And then Andrei said, 'Matthew.' It came out in a whisper, but with such trust and such love, that the emotion that had held Matthew motionless vanished. He reached for Andrei's thin rough fingers and clung to them, and thought: if I live to be a hundred I will never forget how I feel at this moment. He was aware of tears stinging his eyes, and he blinked hard, because he would not – he absolutely would not – break down. Not yet. But, oh God, what had they done to him in here? He's so fragile, so frail.

In as unemotional a tone as he could manage, he said, 'Explanations later. I'm hoping to get you out, but it could be dangerous. We might be caught, and—'

'If we're caught, I'll be shot,' said Andrei. 'That's something I've faced for almost ten years. But I'm damned if I'll let you be shot as well.' Matthew heard, with delight, a flicker of the old fervour and knew that whatever else might have been done to his father, his mind was untouched. As he moved to open the door, Andrei turned back to take the hands of the other men.

'It's not goodbye,' he said. 'You know if I can come back for you, I will.'

They nodded and murmured good luck, and Matthew peered into the passageway.

'There's no one around,' he said.

'No, but there will be soon for the evening work shift,' said Andrei. 'You have keys?'

'Yes, but I don't know how many doors they unlock, and at any minute the guard I knocked out might be found.'

'I think all we can do,' he said, 'is walk out openly as if you're taking me somewhere.'

'Where? Where would I be taking you?'

'You'd better say to the solitary room. It's on one of the lower levels.'

'All right.'

'If we make it to the main doors, pretend I'm being transferred and we're waiting for transport.'

'Where would they transfer you?'

'Cluj or Aiud perhaps. I think they're still operating as prisons. Either should be safe. Did that guard have any handcuffs on him?'

'No,' said Matthew.

'Pity. If you could handcuff me it would look more authentic. What time did you come in? Don't bother to tell me the cover story, not now.'

'After five. It's nearly seven now.'

'That means the guard should have changed, so they won't recognize you from when you came in.'

'You're very sharp about details,' said Matthew.

'I've had a long time to think about such things,' said Andrei. 'The main thing to remember about an escape is to behave with panache. Bluff.'

'I'm not sure I'm very good at that.'

'You got in here, didn't you? I think you're very good.'

It seemed to Matthew that as they went along, the stone walls of

352

the old fortress closed round them, as if Jilava itself was trying to stop them escaping. With every step he expected to hear shouts and running feet, but nothing happened to disturb the brooding silence. They came in sight of the guardroom and the open courtyard.

'This is the test,' said Andrei. 'This is the dangerous part. You'd better hit me, as if I'm resisting.'

'I can't!'

'Matthew, just do it,' said Andrei sharply. 'Wait until they can see us properly. I'll give you the signal.'

They were within ten yards of the guardhouse when Andrei gave a cry, and appeared to flinch from Matthew. Matthew saw a movement within the guardhouse, and feeling slightly sick, raised his hand and dealt his father a blow, managing to land it on Andrei's shoulder, praying it would look authentic from a distance.

'Trouble?' called out the guard. Matthew saw with relief that his father had been right and it was a different man.

He said, 'Bit of a rebellious one. I've got him in hand, though.'

'It's Valk, isn't it?' said the guard. 'Trouble-maker, that one. Where's he going?'

'Cluj,' said Matthew, adding, 'Orders from higher up.'

'Oh, not far then. Where's the transport?' For the first time a questioning note sounded in the guard's voice.

'It should be here – isn't it?'

'No.' The guard had stepped nearer and was looking at Matthew more intently.

'I don't know you,' he said, suddenly sounding suspicious, and Matthew saw him reach for his pocket. He did not wait to find out what for. He sprang forward, and drove his clenched fist against the man's jaw. The guard staggered back, and Matthew dived on top of him, this time managing to knock the man's head hard against the concrete floor.

As he straightened up, Andrei said, tersely, 'Drag him into

the guardroom. Pray no one comes along, and get the uniform off him.'

'We go out as two guards?' said Matthew.

'Yes.'

As they stripped the uniform from the guard, and his father scrambled into it, Matthew saw light and energy shining in Andrei's eyes.

'Keep talking to me,' said Andrei, as they crossed the courtyard. 'We need to appear casual.'

'Yes.'

'Where do we go?' he said. 'They'll realize I've gone before much longer and they'll have the Securitate out scouring the countryside for miles.'

Matthew had already worked this out. 'Sister Teresa – you remember her? – is going to get Mara and Mikhail to England, to the sisters' convent there.'

'England?'

'I know it's a long way from here,' began Matthew.

'Yes. Yes, it's an awfully long way. There'll be so much to leave behind.' Then Andrei squared his shoulders, and said, 'But the further away the better. What about papers and passports?'

'Mikhail's getting the October Group to sort those out for himself and Mara. If they can get two people to England, I should think they can get four,' said Matthew. 'Will you risk it?'

'Yes,' said Andrei. 'I don't think there's anything to keep me in this country. Once I believed there was, but all the searching and the enquiries . . . Yes, I'll risk it.'

The energy was still in his eyes and his voice as they walked along the road, but when they came within sight of the town, he faltered and Matthew had to grab his arm to prevent him from falling.

'I'll recover soon enough,' he said. 'I'll be all right.'

He did recover, but Matthew knew he was not really all right. He knew Andrei got through the tense, exhausting, complex journey to England by sheer force of will. When they finally reached the tiny village of Melbray and St Luke's Convent, he was scarcely able to walk.

Mara and Mikhail were already there. As one of the October Group had pointed out, passports and visas could not be created overnight, and Matthew and his father had had to hide out in the Romanian convent for nearly two weeks before they could leave. That, too, took its toll on Andrei; Matthew saw him start every time he heard footsteps, and at night, in the small room they shared, he heard his father's agonized dream-ramblings.

When they arrived in Melbray, Mikhail was away attending an interview for what the English called a sixth-form college – a place where he could complete his education and go on to university. Matthew was grateful for the smattering of English he had learned in Budapest, but he could not manage the odd English place names very well.

'It's safe here,' Mara said, almost at once when she met them. 'We can't be found here.'

They were given a room overlooking lawns and lanes, and were welcomed at meals in the long refectory. No one fussed, no one asked questions; they were free to do whatever they wanted. 'We are accustomed to helping people from troubled lands,' said one of the older sisters.

England was almost exactly like the childhood worlds Matthew had created. Here were the cool green fields and silvery rivers, and the houses with flower gardens. Here were the shops with everything anyone could want to buy all arranged on the shelves. He thought Melbray beautiful, even in the midst of a frozen December. It was a strong, stark beauty, made up of blacks and whites and greys. Matthew wanted to paint everything. He had no paints with him, and did not think he had enough money to buy any. The October Group had managed to arrange for the exchange into English currency of the little he had, but it was still not much. But if he could not have paints, he could sketch the area. He would like to sketch St Luke's itself and have the results framed for the nuns who were being so kind. There were river views which would make really good subjects as well, twisty lanes, and unexpected houses made of brick, looking as they had been dropped carelessly down in their gardens. Along one of the twisty lanes, only a short distance from St Luke's, was a house called Fenn House. Matthew liked it; he liked its Englishness and its air of having been here for a long time.

'It's usually rented to people for the summer,' said one of the nuns, when Matthew asked about Fenn House in his halting English. 'So it tends to be a different set of people each year and there's no – do you know the word continuity?'

Matthew repeated it carefully, and understood the gist. He said he had admired the house and seen lights in the windows. Did people take holidays in December?

'No, but we heard there's a young widow there at the moment, recovering from her husband's death. Very sad. Her small son is with her. Her name is something rather unusual, something a bit foreign – a name we don't often get in this country, I'll remember it in a minute . . . Petra, that's it. Petra Kendal.'

Matthew liked walking to Melbray and trying out his English in the little shops. Occasionally Mara came with him, but she seemed nervous outside the confines of St Luke's. When Andrei was stronger, Matthew persuaded him to accompany him. It took a bit of doing because Andrei was still deeply hesitant about venturing far from the convent. There was also a degree of agoraphobia. Matthew had noticed this and been unsure how to handle it, but one day Andrei said, quite openly, 'Matthew, I know you're aware that I don't like going outside. It's a hangover from Jilava and I think it will eventually fade. But all those years of living in a confined space – those small cells . . .'

'I understand,' said Matthew, with the familiar twist of pain. 'Take your own pace.'

'He'll probably beat it in his own way,' said Mikhail, when Matthew reported this. 'Don't force anything. Don't fuss or crowd him.'

Matthew did not, and when Andrei occasionally spoke about Jilava and some of the brutalities he and the other prisoners had endured, he listened carefully. When once Andrei said, 'I'm not telling you all of it, Matthew, because you'll never get rid of the images.'

'I understand that. But I'll listen to whatever you want to tell me.'

He was pleased when his father finally accompanied him to the village. Andrei was nervous and hesitant on the brief walk, but when they reached the little main street with its cluster of shops, his scholar's curiosity kicked in, and he became interested. 'We'll do this again,' he said as they walked back.

The third time Matthew took him into the small inn, which the English called a pub. They drank a glass of cider each, which Andrei enjoyed, and exchanged a few halting words with some of the people in the pub who were friendly and casual.

'That reminded me a bit of home,' said Matthew as they walked back. 'D'you remember? We used to go into the little town and I always had lemonade at a teashop and we talked about the arithmetic cartoons.'

'Of course I remember. Did you ever do anything about those cartoons?'

'No. One day I might.'

They fell into the way of walking to the village two or three times a week, looking at the shops which even in this small place seemed to them to have a bewildering variety of goods, generally going into the pub for their glass of cider. Matthew tried the

357

beer which the English always seemed so enthusiastic about, and thought it tasted peculiar.

The lanes were starting to become familiar, and they shared newly acquired English expressions as they walked back, liking the quirkiness of the English speech and the casual companionship of the people in the pub. It's going to be all right, thought Matthew. He's starting to put Jilava behind him.

River mist drifted into the lanes, like wisps of thin gauze as they walked. It clung to the skeletal trees, turning the landscape monochrome, and Matthew was entranced. He had already made several rough studies of the area and had begun a detailed sketch of St Luke's. There was a small general-purpose shop in Melbray that could provide a framing service, and Matthew was hoping to present the finished sketch to the nuns on Christmas Day.

They were on their way home on one of these afternoons, nearing Fenn House, when a young woman with dark hair came walking out of the mist towards them.

Matthew thought, afterwards, that it was about as romantic an appearance as you could get. She seemed simply to materialize out of the mist and for a moment all the old legends – the tales Mara's grandmother used to tell of wood sprites and forest naiads – rushed into his mind. Then he saw she was not a wood sprite, at all, she was an ordinary human being, wearing a long woollen coat with a deep hood framing her face, and a scarf wrapped round her throat. A small boy was at her side – he had her dark hair and eyes – and Matthew remembered the sisters mentioning a young widow being at Fenn House.

The English were notoriously reserved, but the lane was narrow and the mist created its own intimacy. Matthew smiled at the woman and said, 'Good afternoon.'

She returned the smile. Her cheekbones and her eyes slanted when she smiled.

'Hello,' she said. 'Isn't it a frightful day. So cold, I'll be glad to get indoors.'

This remarking on the weather was something the English did a lot. It was extraordinary how it broke the ice.

Andrei said, 'A day for a warm fire and a hot drink.'

They were about to continue along the lane but the woman said, 'You're the two gentlemen from St Luke's, am I right?'

'We are staying there for a few weeks. The nuns are very kind,' said Matthew.

'Your English is very good,' she said, and Matthew felt absurdly pleased.

'We find it difficult, but we think we are learning,' said Andrei.

'It's a hybrid language,' she said. 'We're a mongrel lot in this country. We speak a mixture of odds and ends of a dozen different tongues.' She made to walk on again, then turned back. 'I'm at Fenn House, just along the drive there. It gets awfully lonely there for Theo and me. If you feel like calling some afternoon for that warm fire and hot drink, you'd be very welcome.'

Matthew looked at her with delight, because a drink by a fire with a wood sprite was not something to pass up. He glanced at his father questioningly, expecting him to frame a polite refusal.

Andrei was staring at the woman with an expression in his eyes Matthew had never seen before. He said, 'We should like that very much.'

It was astonishing how the light came back into Andrei's eyes during those visits to Fenn House. It was a slightly shabby place but Matthew liked it, he thought it had something of the quality of the house they had left in their own village. Then he thought it was not the house, it was the woman living in it who created the warm atmosphere. Petra Kendal had been at Fenn House for nearly a month. 'It's very quiet,' she said. 'Peaceful. I'm supposed to be in need of quiet and peace because I'm meant to be sunk in grief and misery.'

'Aren't you sunk in it?' said Andrei, and Matthew was aware

of faint surprise because his father was not usually so direct or so intimate with people. Petra did not seem to mind.

'My husband died in a car crash eight weeks ago,' she said. 'He was charming and clever and fun to be married to. But he wasn't very reliable – in a number of ways he wasn't reliable.' She looked at Andrei who nodded slightly and Matthew had the impression that some silent understanding passed between them.

'His family thought I would like to be on my own. They think it's what people do after a bereavement. And it was easier to do what they expected – they're trying to be kind – so I agreed to rent a house for a couple of months.'

'And you found this one.'

'Yes.' She looked about her. 'I quite like it, but I'd like to think that one day someone will buy it to live in. Not just to let out for holidays, but to be a real home. It needs people – children.'

There was a child with them, of course: Petra's son, Theo. He was small and rather silent and appeared perfectly accepting of the two visitors who came to see his mother. He was a self-contained child, apparently happy to amuse himself with books and pictures for hours on end. If they called in the afternoon Matthew always sought Theo out. He liked the boy's quick intelligence and the way he listened when Matthew tried to describe his own home. He was not sure how much Theo understood – often Matthew had to search for an English word to convey a meaning and often he did not know the right word – but he thought they coped pretty well. If he and his father walked along the lane after supper at St Luke's Theo would be in bed, and Petra would brew coffee and give them smoky Irish whisky, which neither of them had ever tasted.

'We learn the customs of your country,' said Andrei.

It was during those comfortable evenings that Andrei began to talk about Romania and Jilava. His English was more reliable now, and some of his former trick of making a subject interesting to a listener, was coming back. Petra listened with the absorption that was one of her attractions, curled in a deep old armchair with the curtains drawn against the night and the fire crackling in the hearth. Quite soon Matthew was going to ask if he could draw her like this, with the firelight painting fingers of colour in her hair, her eyes serious and sympathetic.

'How did you survive?' she asked once.

'People do survive,' said Andrei. 'There are some remarkable accounts – some of the prisoners kept diaries in Jilava and Pitesti. A friend of Matthew's did that.' Matthew noticed he did not specify Mara's name or say she, too, was at St Luke's.

Petra said, 'I'm glad you did, Andrei,' and somehow she had put out a hand to him at the exact same moment he had put out a hand to her. Matthew saw the expression on his father's face: love, warmth, gratitude. He looked at Petra, and knew he would not draw her in that earlier, serious mood; he would draw her like this, looking at his father with light in her eyes and longing in the curve of her lips.

There had to be a good twenty years between them – Matthew guessed Petra to be about twenty-eight; his father was nearing fifty. But seeing them together, he knew it would not have mattered if there had been thirty or fifty years. The spark, once ignited, flared up like a skyrocket, and realizing this, he stopped accompanying his father on most of the walks to Fenn House. He was working on a series of sketches, he said. Or he had promised to help Mara with some cataloguing – she was becoming interested in St Luke's small library – or he was going somewhere with Michael. He and his father were becoming used to calling Mikhail by the anglicized version of his name by this time, although he noticed that if Mara was ever with them, she stuck stubbornly to Mikhail, almost as if it made a private bond with her brother.

Occasionally, though, Matthew went with his father to Fenn House, and saw how healing it was for Andrei to be with Petra Kendal. Several times Michael joined them, and Petra cooked supper for them – huge English meals. It was still a delight to be able to see all the good food available in the shops, and to enjoy eating it after the years of deprivation. Petra introduced them to English dishes – wonderful casseroles and roast meats, and once Andrei cooked fish ciorba for them all, which had been one of Wilma's favourite dishes.

Michael talked a bit about Mara – once or twice he read out the letters she had written from Debreczen, translating as he went, Petra eagerly suggesting English words when he was stuck. Occasionally they went into Norwich to see the city, travelling in Petra's car, the small Theo wedged on the back seat, fascinatedly watching Matthew make quick light sketches of the countryside they passed through.

'Am I being very wicked?' said Andrei to Matthew one day, shortly after Christmas. 'Is this such a terrible sin I'm committing?' They were in the small bedroom they shared at the convent, ready for the evening meal.

'No, of course it isn't wicked,' said Matthew, surprised. 'She's bringing you back to life.'

'Your mother ...' began Andrei, then turned away, staring through the window at the dark gardens.

'Is dead,' said Matthew, wishing this did not sound quite so hard. 'She'd want you to find happiness, wouldn't she? After so many years ... she'd be pleased for you.'

Andrei remained where he was, not looking at Matthew. After a moment, he said, 'I don't think Elisabeth is dead. She was a member of the October Group, and was arrested for plotting against the social order – what was called a category three prisoner. That usually carried a sentence of anything up to fifteen years, under a severe regime. Matthew, I did absolutely everything I could to find her, and everything I could think of to draw attention to the plight of people like her, but I never succeeded. She's still somewhere in one of those prisons – one of the houses of the lost.'

Matthew felt as if he had been picked up and flung over the edge of a cliff. There was a rushing in his ears, like a cataract of water, and he felt as if the room was spinning round him. After a moment, he heard himself say, 'But you told me—'

'I told you what I thought was the easiest thing for you to accept,' said Andrei. He turned to face Matthew and Matthew saw that all the old ghosts – the ghosts he had been daring to hope Petra had vanquished – were back in his father's eyes.

'And you never found her?'

'No. I spent ten years trying to find her – all those years when you were growing up I tried to get inside the prisons, to find a lead. In the end – Well, in the end, I attracted too much attention, and you know what happened.' He stopped, and then said, 'She might really be dead now.'

'But she might not.'

'No. That's why one day soon I'll have to go back to find out.'

CHAPTER THIRTY-THREE

The present

'He did go back,' said Petra. 'He and Matthew both went back.'

Theo, whose mind was spinning, thought, So Matthew was here after all. He and his father spent all those winter nights in this house. Andrei had a love affair with my mother, and both of them talked to her about the agonies of those years. They poured out all the angst to her, perhaps they even had some of Mara's diaries as well as her letters, and they read them to her and she listened. And I listened as well, without realizing it. That's how I know it all.

It was remarkable he had no conscious memory of this time. But he did have a subconscious memory – he must have heard far more of what was said than anyone realized. And all these years later, because he had been in Fenn House in another monochrome winter, the memories had come to the surface. I knew Matthew, he thought. I talked to him and rode in a car with him and I watched him sketch things. Maybe I even saw him sketch those pictures in St Luke's. The knowledge of this was so immense he felt as if his mind might implode.

After a moment, Petra said, 'And, as I think Theo's already

realized from the likeness in that sketch, Charmery was a cuckoo in the nest. My own nest.'

She looked at Theo, and he pushed away the incredible knowledge concerning Matthew, and said, 'Charmery was your daughter. Yours and Andrei's.' Saying it made it real, but it did not make it any more extraordinary.

'Yes,' said Petra, 'Charmery was my daughter and his.'

His mother's words spun crazily inside Theo's head and for a dreadful few seconds he was aware of anger against her, because if she had told him the truth, then he and Charmery ... No, I'm wrong, he thought. Helen told me a distorted version of the truth all those years ago – it wasn't a father we shared, it was a mother, but Charmery and I really were half-brother and sister. We could never have been together.

'You don't need the details about the affair and I'm not giving them anyway,' Petra was saying. 'My dears, let's face it, there's nothing remotely attractive about a woman of my age confiding the details of a youthful love affair. But during that couple of months – Well, it was a shattering experience.'

'Andrei went back to Romania?' said Theo, relieved to hear his voice sounded reasonably normal.

'Yes. I tried to talk him out of it. I think Michael tried as well, but we both knew he would go. And after he left, I discovered I was pregnant.' She made a brief angry gesture. 'At first I had no idea what to do. Your father had been dead for three months, Theo, and although I wasn't especially conventional and I didn't much mind having a child by myself, the family ...' She looked at Theo and Lesley. 'The Kendals are loyal and honest, but let's face it, dears, in the main they're narrow and old-fashioned. Not you, Guff, dear, and not you, Lesley, either.'

'Nancy,' said Theo and Lesley together.

'And one or two others,' agreed Petra. 'I was distraught at losing Andrei,' she said, 'but I'd had a brief letter saying he and Matthew had reached Resita and from there had gone on to Sister Teresa's

365

convent.' She smiled. 'The nuns were always prepared to help cheat Ceauşescu and the Securitate,' she said. 'Actually, I think one of them was imprisoned for a time. But even for them, the situation with Andrei was very high-risk: he was an enemy of the State and an escaped prisoner. As far as I was concerned – well, he would have been in appalling danger wherever he was, and his health was still precarious from the years in Jilava – I couldn't hand him the responsibility, and certainly not the financial burden, of a child. I knew I'd have to make my own decisions about it.'

'You could have told me,' said Guff. 'Whatever you decided, I'd have helped you.'

'I know that, and I wished afterwards that I had told you,' she said. 'What I did was to go to the Kendal who wasn't a Kendal – the one who, like me, had married into the family.'

'Aunt Helen,' said Lesley.

'Yes. And we came up with a plan,' said Petra. 'If you think back, Guff, you remember that was the time Desmond went abroad.'

'The unpronounceable country,' said Guff, nodding. 'He left a few weeks after John died.'

'Yes. Desmond left the following January. In February I found out about the pregnancy. So Helen told everyone she was coming abroad with me for a few weeks – to help me recover from John's death. We knew we'd have to be away for longer than a few weeks,' said Petra, 'but she was going to write to the family saying she was joining Desmond. I was going to let them think I was travelling around. We left England at the end of May – the longest I dared leave it before the pregnancy began to show – and went to Switzerland. I was able to keep in tenuous contact with Andrei from there.'

'That was when I stayed with Lesley's parents, and then with Guff?' said Theo.

'Yes.'

'Did Desmond know the truth?'

'Yes, almost from the beginning. Helen had to tell him. But

366

trusted him,' said Petra. 'My idea was to stay away from the family for the rest of the pregnancy, and then fudge the dates of the child's birth – tell everyone it was born earlier than it actually was, so it would appear to be John's. It was only a couple of months,' she said. 'I was going to say the child was born in July – actually the birth was September.' She paused again, and Theo saw the sadness in her eyes. 'But shortly before the birth I became quite ill. Helen found a Swiss clinic and I was taken into it and was there right up to the birth. She paid for everything, but I was beyond knowing or caring. After the birth I was very ill indeed. I never grasped the medical technicalities, but I don't think I was expected to live.' She looked at Theo. 'I remember clinging on to the thought of you, telling myself I couldn't die because I couldn't possibly leave you on your own,' she said. 'I think that was what kept me alive. And when finally I did begin to recover—'

Lesley said, 'You decided to give the child to Helen?'

'No! Never that,' said Petra. 'I thought the child had died,' she said, with angry pain in her voice. 'That's what Helen told me. Stillborn, she said. She came and went between the *pension* and the clinic, and said she had dealt with all the formalities and I didn't need to do anything. I was still weak and pretty emotional about losing the child – as I believed – and I didn't question anything.'

Stillborn. The word twisted a deep pain into Theo's mind and, as he looked at his mother, he thought how curious that both she and Charmery should have borne the pain of a dead child. He wondered if he would ever tell Petra what had happened between himself and Charmery and about the small, lost David, and knew in the same heartbeat that he could not cause her so much pain.

'But the doctors in the clinic would have known the child had lived?' Lesley was saying.

'By then I had been moved to a sort of convalescent place,' said Petra. 'It was way up in the mountains, one of the German-speaking areas. I don't think any of them knew the truth. None of them had much English and my knowledge of German was almost nonexistent. Helen acted as interpreter – she wasn't fluent, but she had some quite good school German. It's possible she told the convalescent place that the child really had died. I never knew, though. When I had recovered a bit more, she came home, letting everyone believe she had been with Desmond all along. I followed later. But if you remember,' she said, looking across at Guff, 'I was only in England for a couple of weeks. I didn't see Helen, and the only one of the family I saw was you. I collected Theo from your house and went back to Romania with him to be with Andrei. Travelling there was difficult, but it wasn't impossible. And Mikhail still had contacts in the October Group who could oil the wheels a bit. I never asked questions about that,' she said with a sudden grin.

Theo was staring at her. 'I went with you to Romania?' he said at last.

'Yes. You weren't quite five. I told you it was a holiday before you started school. I tried to make it sound like an adventure – something from a book.'

'Where did we stay?'

'In Andrei's old house,' she said. 'Don't you remember any of it? Not even Wilma? She was a kind of housekeeper – a dear motherly soul. She had known Matthew's mother from childhood.' Petra smiled. 'Wilma had no English at all, and I only had a few phrases of Romanian picked up from Andrei and Matthew but we managed to communicate somehow. She made a great fuss of you,' she said to Theo. 'She gave you a room all to yourself at the very top of the house. She said it was Matthew's room when he was small.'

'And it had a view towards smudgy mountains, and, on the horizon, an old, crouching house with a sinister legend,' said Theo softly. Dear God, he thought, not only have I met Matthew, I've slept in his bedroom – that room I wrote about. I saw the view he saw – the Black House and the Carpathian Mountains in the far distance. 'I don't remember any of it,' he said aloud. 'How long were we there?'

'Only about a week. That's probably why you don't remember. And maybe it was fixed in your mind as being an adventure in a book. I might have overdone that. I'd meant to stay there much longer, but conditions were far worse than I realized. There was hardly any food and electricity was switched off for hours at a time. The people were so downtrodden, it broke my heart. I saw I'd made a massive mistake in taking you, and I wanted to get you back to England and safety. But before we left I went out to the convent to Andrei. You stayed with Wilma for a couple of days. The nuns were so kind to me, I remember.'

And, thought Theo, while you were there someone took a photo of you with the nuns as a little record of the English lady's visit. Then years later someone at that convent – perhaps Sister Teresa, even – sent the photo to St Luke's for their centenary book.

'So you came home properly then,' said Lesley.

'Yes. And it was to find that while I'd been gone Helen had apparently given birth to a child,' she said rather dryly.

'And that child was Charmery,' said Theo.

'Yes.'

'Did you guess she was your own baby?' said Guff.

'Not absolutely at once. At first I was suspicious because it was a whopping great coincidence, but I dismissed it. But then I put things together and challenged Helen and she admitted it. What she had done was to simply come home with the child, letting everyone think Charmery was born while she was with Desmond. She told them all she had kept the months of pregnancy a secret because the doctors feared a miscarriage, and she hadn't wanted to tempt Providence by telling anyone except Desmond. Really, of course,' said Petra, 'she had to wait to be sure she could actually get Charmery from me. The dates were a bit askew, but I think she said it had been a premature birth.'

'And Desmond went along with all that?' said Theo.

'He believed Helen took Charmery with my knowledge and my permission. Theo, what's wrong?'

Out of the tangle of complex emotions and memories, Theo said, 'But Desmond was infertile.'

Petra stared at him. 'He was, as a matter of fact. But how on earth did you know?'

'Charmery found out,' said Theo. 'She challenged her mother.'

'And Helen told her she had an affair with your father?'

'Yes.'

'And therefore the two of you were half-brother and sister?'

'Yes,' said Theo, staring at her.

'Oh, Theo,' she said. 'I'm so sorry you found out about it in that twisted way.' She studied him for a moment. 'Was it a problem for you?'

Theo returned the stare. 'No,' he said at last.

'Helen and John never had an affair, of course,' said Petra. 'That was Helen's back-up story. Desmond's infertility was the one weakness in her plan. She didn't think anyone knew about it, but it was just possible it might come out some day. If it did, she was going to say she had a brief fling with John just before he died.'

'Did you mind about that?' said Lesley.

'Yes, I did. I was furious,' said Petra. 'But when I thought about it properly, I saw it didn't really matter so much. It seemed to belong to another life.'

'When did you find out the truth?' asked Guff.

'Shortly after Charmery's first birthday. I confronted Helen with it. She broke down and begged me not to do anything or tell anyone. She sobbed for hours and clung to me and pleaded with me not to take Charmery away. She said she had wanted a child more than anything in the world, and she had been devastated – very nearly suicidal – when Desmond's infertility was confirmed.' She spread her hands. 'What could I do? I couldn't bring myself to suddenly take a small child from two people she believed were her

370

parents. Helen had registered Charmery's birth in Switzerland. She had stated she and Desmond were the parents. It would have been exhausting and cruel to Charmery as well as Helen to break it all apart. Charmery was aware of the world around her. So I agreed to let the lie stand. But it was an extraordinary sensation to know the child I'd secretly mourned was alive and growing up, and that I knew her so well,' said Petra. 'I'd bought birthday presents for her, and taken her out with Theo. But the really curious thing,' she said, 'is that after I knew, I always found it difficult to stay in this house when Charmery was here. Silly, isn't it?'

'No,' said Theo, leaning forward to take her hand.

'I didn't want Helen and Desmond to buy Fenn – there were too many memories and they weren't all good ones. But Helen had come down here with me right at the start and she fell in love with the place. She said she and Desmond would renovate it and extend it for family summers and holidays. She said I wouldn't recognize it when it was all finished. It would be like a different house. But it never was,' she said. 'For me it always meant Andrei and the start of that huge deception over Charmery.' She looked at Theo. 'I never really came to grips with my feelings for Charmery,' she said. 'I could never equate her with the baby I thought had died in the Swiss clinic.'

Theo said, 'All those times you were travelling – when I was at school – were you with Andrei?'

'Most of the time.'

'Helping him look for Elisabeth?'

Petra turned to look at him. 'So you know about Elisabeth, do you?' she said.

'Some. Not all. Not everything.'

'I expect you'll explain it to me shortly,' she said. 'But Elisabeth was the main reason for Andrei's return to Romania. The need to know what had happened to her – even if he found she had died – absolutely consumed him.'

371

'Did he find her?'

'In the end he did,' she said, 'but it was a long search. Years. By the end of 1989 Romania was a boiling cauldron. Ceauşescu was losing all touch with reality by then. He seemed to have no understanding of the violent hatred and suffering that was all around him.'

'You were there?' said Theo, incredulously. 'You were in the revolution?'

'I was there when it started,' she said. 'Andrei, Matthew and I had gone to Bucharest to try to locate some prison records. Andrei knew someone who was prepared to let him see the lists of political prisoners – I think there was a bribe involved. It was the eighteenth of December. My last day in Romania, because I was coming home to be with you for Christmas. But when it all began – when the rebels defied the curfew and ran through the streets singing the outlawed national songs, it was impossible not to be swept along by it. The whole city – probably the whole country – was sizzling with violence and anger and defiance. Oh God, they hated Ceauşescu by then, those poor people.' She stopped, her eyes huge and dark and no one spoke. 'We went out into the streets,' said Petra. 'We knew it was courting danger of the most extreme kind to go out, but it was impossible to stay indoors. We saw the crowds, and we went through the streets, the three of us holding hands so we wouldn't become separated. Everyone knew, then, that Ceauşescu and his wife would soon be deposed. No one knew how, or who would do it, but it was impossible to be in that seething mass of people and believe anything else. I remember them chanting "*Noi suntem poporul*" – "We are the people". Later they were shouting that Ceauşescu would fall. I guessed that if he did, huge numbers of political prisoners would be released. And that meant Andrei might finally find Elisabeth.'

'Did you think it would mean losing him?' said Theo.

'Yes, but it no longer mattered. I had known, almost from

the first meeting, that for Andrei, Elisabeth was more important than anything I could ever give him. Finding her was his driving passion.'

CHAPTER THIRTY-FOUR

Romania, mid-1980s

Matthew had always known his father would never be content until he found Elisabeth. He had tried to think of the cloudy-haired woman in the photo as his mother, but he could not, because he had no memory of her.

'Your father had nightmares in those first years after your mother was taken away,' Wilma said when they returned to Romania, and made a brief stay at their old house. 'He used to call out for her in his sleep. He believed she was being held in one of the old gaols. I used to hear him. It was as if he could see the stone cells and the bars at the windows. I'd go along to his bedroom to wake him up, and make him hot milk with brandy in it. But if I'd guessed you were hearing all those nightmares . . .'

'Only occasionally,' said Matthew, and because it was dear, loyal Wilma, he added a careful lie, 'I don't remember much of it.'

They left the house after one day.

'We daren't stay any longer,' Andrei's said. 'The Securitate could be watching; they'll know it's a place I'd come to.'

Matthew had no idea if the Securitate would also be watching the convent. He wondered how long they would look for a

374

escaped prisoner. He and Andrei had been in England for almost three months, but perhaps three months was not very long to the cold-eyed men of the Securitate.

They stayed at the convent for several weeks, at first not daring to go out or draw attention to themselves, grateful to Sister Teresa who brought news of what was going on in the outside world.

'It's very little different from when you left,' she said. 'Although when I go into town, I have the feeling that people are becoming restless, that something might gradually be building up under the surface. We'll pray for a peaceful outcome, for better times.'

Petra came to visit them the following year. Matthew saw that the attraction between her and his father was still very strong, but he thought it was not quite as strong as it had been in England. She's letting go, he thought. She understands he'll spend his whole life trying to find my mother if he has to, and she knows she can't be part of that.

Even so, when Petra left, she clung to Andrei for a long time.

'You'll come back, won't you?' said Andrei.

'If you want me to.'

'Yes. Oh God, yes, of course I do.'

'Then I will.'

She had returned each year, spending several weeks with Andrei in spring when Theo was at school, and often in October and November as well. Matthew had left art school by then, and taught at various schools, obtaining posts as near to Andrei as he could. But travelling was difficult – petrol was so strictly rationed it was almost impossible to obtain, and a Sunday curfew was in place. Even electricity was rationed in order to divert the supply to heavy industry, and television – for those who had a set – was reduced to two hours each day. It was whispered that phones were bugged and that one in three Romanians was an informant for the Securitate. A police state, said people, glancing nervously around to make sure they were not overheard.

Matthew managed to stay in work – education seemed to be the one thing Ceauşescu did not restrict – and he hoarded all his earnings so he could one day open his own gallery. It was his dream and his goal, but as the years went by, he wondered if it would ever become a reality.

'It could become a reality,' said Petra, when Matthew talked to her about it. 'You mustn't lose sight of it, not ever. There's a line from one of our poets – Tennyson: 'Follow the gleam.' Always do that. And something's starting to happen in this country – can't you feel it? As if the contents of a huge angry cauldron are simmering just under the surface.'

Matthew had known this for a long time. He sometimes thought it was as if something just out of sight was beating a tattoo on an invisible drum, and the sound was gradually becoming louder and more insistent. He said, 'What d'you think will happen?'

'I don't know,' she said. 'But if I'm right, everything will change. There's another line from Tennyson, as well. "The old order changeth, giving way to the new". I don't know when it will happen, that change, but I hope it's soon.'

But it was to be another two years before the bubbling cauldron of hatred and discontent finally erupted, and when it did, Petra was back in England.

Romania, December 1989

'Please stay safe both of you,' Petra said, just before Christmas. 'I think Romania's about to reach explosion point. Those people in the streets last night, the fights and the violence . . .'

'Some of the streets look like the aftermath of a war,' said Andrei, his eyes dark with anger and bitterness. 'Destruction, ash from burned cars, even blood on the pavements . . . Only this isn't a war.'

'Isn't it?' said Petra. 'Whatever it is, I think you're about to see the last act of Ceauşescu's reign, and if I could stay on to see it with you I would, but—'

'But you must be back to spend Christmas with Theo,' Andrei said. 'Of course you must. And we'll be safe. I'm a survivor. Matthew too.'

'So you are,' she said, managing a smile. 'I was forgetting that.'

So Petra went back to England, and three days later, the dam that had held in so much anger and defiance for so many years, finally burst. A great tidal wave of rebellion cascaded across the country, sweeping aside everything in the pent-up longing for freedom from a dictator's iron rule.

Matthew and his father were in the centre of Bucharest as people from all walks of life poured into the city from outlying districts. Martial law had been announced with a ban on groups larger than five people. But, incredibly, hundreds of thousands of people were gathering spontaneously, apparently prepared to brave the soldiers and tanks drafted in by Ceauşescu's henchmen.

'And helicopters,' said Matthew, looking up at the sudden whirr of machinery in the skies. 'They're dropping leaflets.'

'And d'you know what the leaflets tell us to do?' said a man next to him. 'To go home and enjoy the Christmas feast! Dear God, don't the devils know we have to queue up for hours to even get a drop of cooking oil!'

'He's coming out onto the balcony,' said someone else. 'Ceauşescu himself. There he is, the cruel greedy bastard!'

As Nicolae Ceauşescu began an impassioned speech, Matthew's father said, softly, 'He's not reaching them. Look at their faces, Matthew, look at the hatred and the anger. He's lost them, and the terrible thing is that he doesn't realize it.'

'A few people near the front are cheering him,' said Matthew, a bit doubtfully.

'It's frightened cheering. They're probably Securitate plants,' said Andrei, still keeping his voice low, mindful of eavesdroppers.

As Matthew listened to Ceauşescu reminding his audience of the achievements of the socialist revolution, about the multi-laterally developed society he had created, he knew his father was right. Ceauşescu was grasping at the vanishing remnants of power. His voice was taking on a strained, desperate note and the crowd was becoming restless. This is it, he thought. This is what Petra meant when she talked about the old order changing. It's changing now, here, in this square. Something new is struggling to be born. It won't be an easy birth and people will be hurt in the process, but if it can really happen it will be the turning point. It will sweep away the decades of dreary poverty and despair.

'I think,' said Andrei, suddenly, 'this is where we step back, Matthew. Some of the crowd are moving towards the building. Over there, look. It'll turn ugly at any minute. Let's get into one of the side streets and out of the way. I'll do a lot for Romania's freedom – I have done a lot for it – but I'm not getting caught up in mob violence and neither are you.'

They moved away as unobtrusively as possible, but as they reached the edge of the square, Matthew turned back and scanned the faces. Who were they, these people, who once had bowed their heads to the yoke of a tyrant but today were shouting their defiance of him? He stood very still, letting the extraordinary atmosphere soak into his whole being, trying to print the moment on his memory, so that one day in the future, he could look back and relive it and say, *That* was the moment when the old order changed, that was the moment when I knew the bad years were over for Romania.

Zoia had not intended to go to the central committee building that morning, but her rooms overlooked a main thoroughfare, and the shouting and running outside was impossible to ignore. She had lived in Bucharest for two years, and at first she'd liked it. She liked the feeling of being nearer to the centre of things. She tried to continue her work for the Party even though she was no longer sure if she believed in its policies and principles. She tried to ignore the feeling that her former zeal had been because of

378

Annaleise, but it was a feeling that came frequently to the surface of her mind these days. Her work in one of the city libraries was moderately interesting although not especially well paid. She hoped, as most of the staff did, that the promised national library and national museum of history would one day be completed and she could move there.

But today, just four days before Christmas, it was as if a huge fire had been ignited at Romania's heart and was spreading through the whole country, raging its way into small towns and villages, licking its greedy flames inside the houses so that people were forced outside. It forced Zoia outside. She had watched for a while, then grabbed her thick coat, and ran down the stairs to join them. As she entered the square, pushed and jostled on all sides, Ceaușescu's voice rang out over the heads of the crowds, but she could see almost at once that his words were going for nothing. He's making futile attempts to regain his authority, she thought. He's standing up there on the balcony as if he thinks he's a god, but his subjects aren't listening. They're out of his reach.

With the thought there was the sound of explosions from the outskirts of the square, and people began to run and scream. 'Bombs!' cried a woman. 'No, it's guns – the bastard's ordered the army to fire on us!' shouted a man. 'Get under cover!' Someone with a megaphone began shouting that the Securitate was firing on the people. 'It's the revolution!' bellowed the voice. The word span and bounced all round the square: *revolution, revolution . . .*

The crowd jeered and whistled, and more and more people ran into the square, turning it into a rioting, seething mass. Anti-communist chants began. 'Down with the dictator.' 'Death to the murderer.' 'Death to Nicolae Ceaușescu and the bitch Elena!'

There was a flurry of movement on the balcony, and Zoia saw Nicolae Ceaușescu, Elena at his side, scuttle back inside the building. They're afraid, she thought. They know the speech was futile, and they're slinking into cover like cowards. And these, thought Zoia, are the people for whom I spied, for whom I dealt out cruelty.

She fought her way to the side streets, and walked back to her rooms, keeping near the buildings, unnoticed, unchallenged.

The fighting continued for two more days, but Zoia remained in her rooms, not wanting – not daring – to go out.

On Christmas night she watched, on the small television she had finally managed to buy, the news that the two Ceauşescus had fled Bucharest in a helicopter. Then there was video footage of the show trial in the army schoolroom, which had been hastily converted to a makeshift courtroom. She listened to the charge of genocide against the Ceauşescu couple: genocide by starvation, lack of heating and lighting, they called it. An extraordinary charge, said the news reader. Elena appeared aloof and arrogant throughout, refusing to answer the questions put to her, refusing, as well, to acknowledge the legitimacy of her interrogators. She's not going to break, thought Zoia, leaning forward, her fists clenched, the nails digging into her palms. She'll be imperious to the end.

But Elena Ceauşescu was not imperious quite to the end. As the police made to separate her from Nicolae, intending to perform two separate executions, she rapped out an angry order. 'Together,' she said. 'We die together – together – *together* . . .' When they bound her hands behind her back she cursed and fought, saying they were breaking her arms. The police had to use force to subdue her, and Zoia's skin prickled with horror at the fury and defiance in Elena's face, this woman who had caused so much suffering and who was about to be led to her death. The cameras did not follow the two, but in her mind Zoia saw them stand against a wall in a stone yard, she saw the rifles take aim and the bullets rip into their bodies. Exactly as Zoia's mother must have looked when she stood against a wall all those years ago to be shot for a murder she had not committed – the murder Zoia herself had committed. She shivered and pushed the image away.

Back at her work in the library, she listened to the avid

discussions about the events, contributing the occasional remark. She did not say she had once met Elena – that she had travelled in a car with her and helped arrest a young woman caught making illegal broadcasts. The best thing now was to get on with her work. Life went on; bills had to be paid. You lived with your ghosts as best you could.

There was one ghost that Zoia had not expected, though.

On New Year's Day, she was crossing a street near the university, on her way to the library, when she saw three people walking across one of the squares – a woman and two men. She glanced at them incuriously, then looked again. The older man had a thin face with a small beard. He had a scholarly look about him, as if he might be a don. The younger man resembled him. But it was the woman who walked with them who drew Zoia's eyes. Once she had looked at her she could not look away.

The years and deprivations of Pitesti Gaol had stripped the flesh from Elisabeth Valk's bones, but she had been beautiful twenty years ago, and she was beautiful now, even thin and gaunt, her hair cropped short, her clothes unremarkable. She clung to the arms of the two men, as if she was afraid they might suddenly vanish, and she kept looking from one to the other. There was such deep love and gratitude in her eyes that Zoia felt something slam at the base of her throat. To feel like that, to have endured all that, and to come out and find your heart's desire still there.

None of the three saw her, but she watched them until they were out of sight. Then she turned round and went on to her work in the library as usual.

The present

'Matthew saw both his parents as heroes,' said Petra, into the quiet room. 'He saw them as idealists and even romantic. Two people who had wanted to save the world they lived in, and who had been hurt in the process.'

'But she survived,' said Theo.

'Yes. She was frail and afraid of the world. They took her to Switzerland and she had five years with them before she died.'

'And Andrei?' asked Lesley.

'He died shortly afterwards.'

'Did you meet Elisabeth?' said Theo.

'Just once. It was a curious experience. I knew so much about her: what she had done, how brave and defiant she had been. What I saw was what was left after the brutality of a Romanian gaol. And yet,' she said thoughtfully, 'there was the impression of a light still flickering somewhere. Like seeing a flame through a misted-over window.'

Theo could not think of anything to say, and it was Lesley who reached out for Petra's hand, and Guff who said, 'My dear, I'm so sorry.'

'Things heal,' she said. 'But I don't forget him.' She blinked, then said, 'Is that the doorbell?'

It was the doorbell. It was Michael Innes.

'You suggested I came back this evening,' he said, looking hesitantly at Petra's car. 'But it looks as if you've got people here, and I don't want to intrude—' He broke off, hearing sounds of crockery from the kitchen where Lesley was helping Guff find something for supper.

'Please come in,' said Theo. 'Stay to supper if you can.' Not giving Michael time to refuse, he took him into the sitting room. Michael stopped dead in the doorway, and his eyes widened.

Then Petra said in a slightly shaky voice, 'Hello, Mikhail. This is unfair, isn't it? I knew you were coming – but you didn't know I was here. Ghosts of the past gathering.'

'Petra,' he said. 'I had no idea you were here. Oh God, it's good to see you again.' He went forward and as his arms went round her. Theo, who had thought his mother was taking this meeting in her stride, saw she was crying. The two of them stood together, locked in a tight embrace. Theo had the sensation that he was

382

glimpsing a tiny fragment of the past: a fragment these two had known and were remembering.

'Sorry for the melodrama,' said Petra when she finally stepped back, still holding Michael's arm. 'Oh, Mikhail, it's been so long. I should call you Michael, shouldn't I? Can you stay to eat with us?'

'Well, if it wouldn't be—'

'It wouldn't be,' she said. 'Please stay. I still haven't heard the half of what's been going on here and I don't suppose you have, either.'

'And my great-uncle makes a mean omelette,' said Theo. 'I'll tell him to beat up another couple of eggs.' He went out, wanting to give his mother and Michael some time on their own.

Later, over the omelettes, he said to Michael, 'I understand now why you didn't seem surprised that I knew so much about Mara and Zoia and all the other things. At the time it puzzled me quite a lot, though.'

'I assumed Petra had told you, or that you remembered hearing some of it all those years ago,' said Michael, 'when Andrei and Matthew were here.' He looked back at Petra. 'Andrei and Matthew poured it all out to you, didn't they? About Jilava and the Securitate. The Black House. I remember Matthew telling me how patient and understanding you were.'

'She always is,' said Lesley and Michael glanced at her gratefully.

'But for a time it became part of my life as well as yours and theirs,' said Petra. 'Remember I was there when the rebels turned on Ceauşescu.'

'And I was safely here in England,' he said, with a trace of anger in his voice. 'I should have been there when they overthrew that evil creature.'

'You had done a lot towards it,' said Petra.

'And perhaps,' put in Guff, 'it was safer not to be there.'

'I would have gone back,' he said, 'but I was still at Queens – it

383

wasn't easy to vanish for a month or so. And there was Mara to consider.'

It was not until they were clearing the table, carrying plates to the kitchen, that Theo, keeping his voice low, said to his mother, 'I haven't asked you this yet, but you did meet Mara, I suppose?'

'I met her once, while Andrei was here. Only very briefly, though. Why?'

The others were in the kitchen – Theo could hear Lesley saying she would make coffee, and Guff asking if anyone knew where the extra cups were kept.

'I can't help wondering exactly what Mara might be capable of,' he said at last, and Petra looked at him thoughtfully.

'I don't know,' she said. 'I do know, though, that I always believed Michael would do absolutely anything to protect her.'

'From the past, d'you mean?'

'From her own particular part of the past,' said Petra.

CHAPTER THIRTY-FIVE

Mara knew that Mikhail had always tried to protect her and that he had very particularly tried to protect her from her own past. He had brought her to England, out of reach of Zoia and the Securitate, out of reach of the men in Jilava Gaol who had finally made her see – and admit – she was a murderess. After she entered St Luke's, she had tried to atone for the murder of Annaleise, but she had never been sure she had done enough. Even so, after a while she had felt safe in the convent until Theo Kendal came to Fenn House.

At first Mara had not seen Theo as a threat to her safety. She had assumed he had come to Fenn to arrange for its sale, but Sister Catherine, visiting him that day, had reported he was here for some time. This was deeply disturbing to Mara, because whatever else Theo Kendal might do in Melbray, he was bound to ask questions about Charmery's murder – questions the police had not asked, but questions that might lead to Mikhail and from Mikhail to Mara herself.

So she had watched Theo as much as she could, going stealthily down the lanes at night and stealing through the gardens of Fenn House. One night, when he was in bed, she had let herself into the house with the key she had taken four months earlier, and had switched on the laptop and read what was typed there. No one knew the quiet Sister Miriam understood computers. She had watched Sister Catherine use the convent's machine several times. There had been some library records to be transferred and she had sat next to Catherine while it was done. It did not appear difficult. Catherine had explained quite a lot of it as she went, and had later left some of her notes lying around from the computer course. Mara made her own notes from them which she studied in the privacy of her room. It was probably knowledge she would never need, but all knowledge was good, and she was even able to test it on the computer when Reverend Mother was away. No one had known about that. She had struggled a bit at first, but then realized that once you understood the basic principles, it was not so very difficult to open and type a simple document.

The laptop at Fenn House was not difficult, either, but when Mara read Theo's current work, she was appalled. He knew so much! He knew about Matthew and about Zoia and Annaleise and Elisabeth – and about Mara herself. How could he know those things? The facts were not all absolutely accurate and clearly he had made some things up, but the whole thing was so near the truth that Mara was engulfed in panic and terror. Theo Kendal was a professional writer – what he wrote was published. But if this were to be published ... Letting herself quietly out of the house and going back to St Luke's, she knew it must never be published. A way must be found to prevent it.

Gradually, a plan formed – a plan that was initially intended merely to scare him away. His vulnerable point would be his dead cousin, Charmery. Could he be persuaded that the memories of Charmery were too vivid, too painful? Could he even be brought to believe that Charmery haunted Fenn House? Men did not, in general, believe in ghosts, but it was worth trying. Mara tried it. Once when Theo was absorbed in working at the computer, once when she had lured him outside by shining a torch in the boathouse. She used two different ghost scenarios: the ticking clock, so stealthily set working while he was preparing his supper, and the dried rose left by the portrait while he investigated the light in the boathouse – the light Mara herself had created.

But either Theo did not believe in ghosts or was not easily scared, because he had remained in Melbray. Mara had suddenly seen that scaring him away was not the answer: he would write the book no matter where he was. Then the only thing to stop him writing was for him to die.

For him to die ... A second murder, so soon after Charmery's could not be risked, but how about suicide? The suicide of a man grieving so deeply for his lost love, he could not face life without her? Mara thought it was plausible. How could it be done?

In the bathroom cabinet at Fenn House had been a pack of a mild sedative: diazepam, in a 5mg strength. Mara had noted it during one of her stealthy explorations, and mentally stored it away as something that might be made use of.

The convent had a small drugs cupboard, mostly painkillers for patients recovering from major bone traumas, but there was also a supply of sedatives to help relax any patient undergoing a minor procedure. Diazepam was one of these. Mara read the dosage instructions carefully, then took four 10mg tablets. She would have preferred to use the liquid form which came in dropper bottles, but a strict check was kept on the drugs cupboard and even one missing bottle would be noticed. But tablets could be replaced by plain paracetamol which were roughly the same size and should stand up to an inspection. She effected the substitution, and back in her own room crushed the four tablets and sealed the powder in an envelope in readiness. Now it was a question of watching and being ready to act swiftly, and of making sure to always have the Fenn House key with her. It might be a long wait, of course.

But it was not. Walking in the convent grounds two days later, ostensibly absorbed in her own thoughts, she saw Theo going past St Luke's gates and into the lanes beyond. An afternoon walk, probably. Mara took a deep breath, and went quickly down the drive, praying not to meet anyone in the lane, but not really expecting to do so on such a cold afternoon. Out of sight of the convent she put on the thin surgical gloves taken from the dispensary. Even in a convent you were aware of such things as fingerprints.

Once inside Fenn House she had planned to stir the crushed pills into something he would eat or drink that same evening – beer or wine, perhaps – but a chicken casserole had been left on the kitchen table, clearly intended for that evening's meal. Absolutely ideal. Mara tipped in the contents of the envelope, waited for the powder to absorb into the liquid, then went back out. Returning to Fenn later was a bit more difficult because the convent supper was served at half past six, but she managed to slip out shortly after seven thirty, trusting he would have eaten his evening meal by then.

And so he had. He was slumped in a chair in the big sitting room. When Mara bent over him to lift one eyelid, the pupils were pinpoints. It was all right. With her heart racing, she went into the dining room, and with every nerve ending sensitive to any movement from the other room, she typed onto his computer the false confession to Charmery's murder: the confession she had so carefully composed and written out the night before.

It took barely ten minutes, and Mara stood up and pocketed the handwritten pages. On the way back to St Luke's she would tear them into tiny pieces and scatter them across the fields. But first she would take the sharpest kitchen knife she could find, and bring the blade down on each of his wrists, straight onto the veins so near the surface. She was fairly sure that if she stood behind his chair and reached down to his hands, no blood would get onto her. He would hardly know what had happened because he would be unconscious from the diazepam. And although the sedative would be found at a post mortem, it would be explained by the reference to it in the fake suicide letter.

There were several knives in the kitchen, and she chose the one that looked sharpest. Then she went back to the sitting room. But as she stood looking down at the figure in the chair, he moved, and Mara's heart lurched with panic. Had she misjudged the dose? Was he coming round? She stayed where she was, and to her horror, he half opened his eyes. One hand came up as if in defence or protest, and Mara stepped back at once, praying he had not seen her. She stood in the doorway, watching him, seeing with horror that he was definitely coming round. His eyes were partly open, although even from here they looked unfocused. He turned his head as if trying to see where he was. Could she still go through with it?

She knew she could not. Killing an unconscious man was one thing; killing a man who was in possession of his senses was vastly different and, in any case, even in this drugged state, he would easily overcome her. She went quickly across the hall, replaced the knife, and went out through the main door, closing it with the smallest whisper of sound.

Behind her, she left Theo Kendal's suicide letter on the computer.

Later, listening to him give the talk to St Luke's patients about writing books, Mara wondered what he had made of the typed confession. He seemed to have recovered from the diazepam and he appeared perfectly calm and seemed to enjoy his afternoon. But what was he really thinking? When, a few days later, he brought a cousin to see the convent's paintings, she watched him closely and even managed to talk to the cousin, but if Lesley Kendal knew what had been going on, she did not say.

Over the next twenty-four hours, Mara had the curious feeling that the threads spun all those years ago in Romania – spun by Zoia and Annaleise – were twisting together, ready to close about her. She felt oddly light-headed, as if she had fasted. As the day wore on, the light-headedness vanished. But in its place an old fear began to surface once again – the fear that the years in the

389

convent, the long hours of prayer and study, were not enough to atone for what she had done. God required something more of her if those mortal sins were to be forgiven.

After supper and prayers, she shut herself away in the library – the safe quiet room that was her own domain – and tried to work on the notes she was compiling for a study on the influence of religion on medicine. It was a project she had embarked on with Mikhail in mind. He would find it interesting, he might even make suggestions as to how it could unfold. So much of what she did was with him in mind. But tonight the words would not come and the library felt hostile. The shadows seemed to crawl nearer, exactly as the shadows in the Black House and later in Jilava had. They were watching her, those shadows and waiting to see what she did.

At half past nine – the time when the non-clinic sisters were expected to be in their own rooms – Mara went up to her bedroom. From the window she could see across to Fenn House. She could see lights in several of the windows. Was Lesley Kendal still there? She stayed at the window for a long time, staring into the darkness, hearing the ticking of her little bedside clock, like a tiny beating heart.

When ten o'clock chimed the sound startled her, and then she understood that the chimes were reminding her what she must do. She went out into the passageway, listened intently in case anyone was around, then went swiftly down the side stair to the garden door. If she was careful she might be able to get out into the lane and from there she would go into the gardens of Fenn House. Just as she had done on that afternoon four months earlier when she murdered Charmery Kendal.

It had been a long drowsy day, the kind of day when the air was scented with lilac for miles around. Mara had gone to Fenn House to find out exactly how involved Charmery Kendal was with Mikhail.

It was very quiet as she went along the drive which was overgrown and untidy. No one was around, but a car was parked near the house and windows were open, so she went round the side of the house and down the mossy steps to the main gardens. She knew that in summer, if there was no reply to a ring at the doorbell, it was acceptable to walk down to the gardens. The English liked gardens; they liked spending time in them. They were lucky to be able to do that. People in Mara's village had not had gardens and if they had, they used them to grow vegetables or even keep chickens.

Charmery Kendal was very lucky indeed. Fenn House, this nice old English home, belonged to her, and if Mikhail married her, it would belong to him as well. He deserved a nice house like this, but not if it meant Mara lost him to this pampered creature. She would consume him; she would make him her puppet. Mara could not bear to think of her beautiful sensitive brother ruined and quenched by this vain selfish girl.

She stood on the terrace, seeing the big expanse of lawn where the Kendals used to play their English games of cricket and rounders. Mara and the other sisters used to see them sometimes. There was the rose garden that had been a blaze of colour in the summer, but was now neglected and overgrown, although one or two hopeful splashes of colour still thrust through the tangles.

Charmery was stretched out on the lawn, an opened bottle of wine near her hand, and a book, lying face down by her side. She was wearing a bikini that hardly covered her body. Although Mara had thought she did not mind about Mikhail going to bed with her, seeing her like this brought a lump of angry bile into her throat.

Charmery looked slightly surprised to see Sister Miriam from St Luke's, but not unduly so. In the past, when the family were here all summer, the nuns had occasionally called, usually if there was some charity event they wanted supporting. She waved Mara to a deckchair, and offered her a glass of iced lemonade, apologizing for her awkwardness in pouring it – there was some tale about a sprained wrist.

'But Michael has strapped it up for me,' she said, holding out the slender wrist with its pink-tipped nails and crêpe bandage. 'He's so deft, isn't he? His hands have an amazing power. But they can be so gentle, as well.' She smiled slyly when she said this. Mara understood Charmery was telling her she and Mikhail had shared intimacies, and that Mikhail's hands had done a lot more than strap up her sprained wrist. Scalding jealousy flooded her body once again.

'Are you here for any special reason, Sister? A donation or something? Or were you just passing?'

The patronizing, lady-of-the-manor tone, annoyed Mara. 'There is a special reason, as it happens, Miss Kendal.'

'Charmery.'

'Charmery. It's about my brother. You do know Dr Innes is my brother?'

'Michael,' she said, as if the saying of his name claimed him as her property, the possessive bitch. 'Yes, he told me about you. We've got rather close this summer.'

'That's what I wanted to talk about. It's interesting you use the word close – there are all kinds of closeness, aren't there? All kinds of levels and depths of closeness.'

'If you're asking if we've been to bed, the answer's yes, we have,' said Charmery, 'and very pleasurably, too. I don't see what it's got to do with you.'

'I assumed you would have been to bed with him.'

'Did you? Well, you're very astute,' said Charmery. 'Michael told me how astute you are. He admires you. He looks up to you because of what happened in Romania. How you tried to protect him.'

The silence came down again. Mara had the disturbing impression that the stone statues on the lawn's edge tilted their lichen-crusted faces very slightly, so as not to miss anything.

'I always tried to keep Mikhail safe. For a lot of the time it was an unhappy, dangerous childhood. We lived under the hand of a greedy dictator.'

'I know,' said Charmery, refilling her glass from the half-empty bottle. Even from where she sat, Mara could smell the sharp fruitiness of it. 'You were in prison as well,' she said. 'That must have been a dreadful ordeal.'

So Mikhail had told her about Jilava. Again there was the sensation of something stabbing deep into Mara's vitals. No one in England knew about Jilava or Annaleise, except for Mikhail. It had been their secret, their shared past, one of the things that bound them together. But now this greedy, lacquer-nailed creature knew.

After a moment, Mara was able to say, 'Yes, it was a great ordeal. Especially since it was for something I hadn't done.'

Charmery said, 'Hadn't you? I wouldn't blame you if you had – that cruel old bitch – the Politburo woman or whatever she was – she sounds such a hag. I'd have done her in without a second thought. No, Michael didn't tell me you killed her. He said you were set up. Framed.' She drank her wine, studying Mara over the rim. 'But I have to tell you I was intrigued by the thought that you might have done it. A saintly and scholarly nun, who's really a murderess.'

'I'm not a murderess,' said Mara, forcing herself to remain calm. Charmery was not very sober by this time, Mara could see that. Probably she had not drunk an excessive amount by her own standards, but she had drunk it quickly and it was a hot afternoon.

Charmery was saying something about Fenn House, about how it was a liability. 'But my cousin Theo always loved it,' she said. 'It'll go to him if ever I die. Because of the child. It's still here, you see, that lost little thing.'

'Child?' This was something new and Mara looked at her with more attention.

'Theo's son and mine,' said Charmery, turning to look towards the faint glimmer of the river beyond the boathouse.

'You had a son with your cousin?'

'Yes, but it died,' she said, dismissively. 'Hardly anyone knew about it. It's still here, poor little thing, somewhere in the Chet. I was years ago. But d'you know, Mara, the odd thing is that since I've been here by myself, I've sometimes thought I heard it crying. Like those things from the old stories – rusalkas.'

'The souls of drowned infants,' said Mara, softly.

'Yes. My son became a rusalka,' she said. 'And he's still here. His body was never found, so I can't possibly let Fenn House go to strangers, can I? Not ever. So when I die Theo will have it. Years and years in the future, of course, but still . . .'

When I die . . . Mara felt the world snap back into focus a the words. A tremendous weight descended on her and she saw what she had to do to keep Mikhail safe for ever – and to keep him her own for ever. 'You're a bit young to be thinking of dying,' she said lightly.

'Oh, things happen to people,' said Charmery. 'Road accidents and so on. Perhaps I'll die young and it'll all be deeply tragic but everyone will remember me as young and beautiful. And Theo will have this house.'

'It's a lovely house,' said Mara conventionally.

'It's full of memories,' said Charmery. 'All the things we used to do here as children. The little rituals and traditions. The rocking chair my cousin Lesley said was a magic one – a gateway to the fantasy lands of the stories. And the old grandfather clock we used to wind up because I said it was Fenn's heart beating. We used to do that on the first night of every holiday. We said it woke up the house and the holiday couldn't begin until the clock was ticking.' She blinked and sat up straighter. 'I'm a bit drunk.'

'I think you are, a bit,' said Mara. 'Why don't we walk round the garden together – see if that clears your head.'

'All right. A walk through an English garden with a murderess,' said Charmery, getting clumsily to her feet. 'Where shall we go? Would you like to see the rose garden? My mother planted

394

Charmian roses for my tenth birthday – she was a bit of a sentimentalist. Theo used to pick a single rose and leave it on my pillow for me to find when I went to bed. Come to think of it, he was always a bit of a sentimentalist as well. In fact he was an outright romantic. I don't know what he is now. And the rose bushes are nearly all dead. Things die, Sister Miriam. My son died – Theo's son.'

Mara took a deep breath, and forcing a casualness she was not feeling, said, 'Why don't we walk down to the old boathouse?'

Afterwards it was easy to go back up the steps – pausing to snap off a couple of the Charmian roses planted all those years ago. The French windows were propped open by a large stone. She glanced back down the garden, then stepped inside the house. This was the place of all those memories. She began to walk through the rooms, touching the fold of a curtain or the back of a chair, seeing the film of dust on the tables.

The stairs were wide and uncarpeted and it was clear no one had taken polish or duster to them for a very long time. It looked as if Charmery Kendal had been a bit of a slattern. Even if Mara had allowed Mikhail to marry, she would not have let him marry such a sloven. As it was, he would remain hers, entirely and absolutely, just as he had been all their lives, until he was caught in the sticky web of this twenty-first century Messalina.

Here was the rocking chair those long-ago children had pretended would fly them to magical lands, and in the big bedroom at the front of the house was the grandfather clock they used to wind up to set Fenn's heart beating for the holidays. Mara touched the pendulum experimentally, and instantly the mechanism sprang to life and a measured ticking filled the room. It startled her because it really did sound and feel as if something had woken. She stopped the pendulum and the ticking faded.

As she went back downstairs she noticed a bunch of keys lying on a small hall table, and she paused, then picked them up. Would one of these keys fit the main door of this house? She tried one at random. It did not fit, nor did the next one, but the third one slid home and the lock turned easily. Mara checked to see if there was an identical key on the ring – surely no house of this size would have only one key – and when she found the duplicate, she removed it and pocketed it.

She went inside St Luke's, unnoticed, meeting no one. Once in her room, she wedged a chair against the door, then washed away the splashes of mud and river weed that had caught her hands and the edges of her cuffs when she held Charmery down in the river. The cuffs were carefully rinsed clean and put to dry on the windowsill, and new cuffs donned. The key to Fenn House was tucked at the back of a drawer. That left the roses. Mara considered, then laid them between the leaves of a book, and placed two heavier books on top. Later, she would press them properly, using layers of tissue paper. A reminder of what she had done.

The supper bell sounded, and, obedient to the convent's day she went downstairs to the refectory. No one would notice anything different about her, no one would suspect anything.

No one had noticed or suspected.

Charmery's murder wiped a smeary bloodied print across the uneventful life of Melbray for a time, but little by little life settled back into its uneventful pattern. The police were not seen as frequently at Fenn House. They no longer tramped around Fenn's gardens or crawled over the old boathouse with their cameras and forensic tests. If they found what Mara thought were called DNA samples that matched any of the nuns they would not think twice about it. The sisters did call at Fenn House occasionally – there was no reason to be secretive about it.

But they did not find anything that brought them to St Luke's and after a while journalists and photographers stopped haunting Melbray in the hope of finding new angles on the story.

Mara did not often see Mikhail, but when she did he seemed

quieter and thinner. He would get over it, though; he would not really have loved a woman like that – a Jezebel who had conceived a child without being married, and had let it die. It had become a rusalka, Charmery had said. The odd thing was that Mara kept remembering those words. The souls of drowned infants. It was unexpected that Charmery had known the legend, but it was fitting that she had died in the river where her son had been drowned.

Later, the news filtered through that Theo Kendal had inherited Fenn House from his cousin. So she did leave it to him, thought Mara. She had some feelings after all – feelings for the cousin she must once have loved. And feelings for the child whose body lay deep within the Chet's green mistiness.

The image of the child drowned in the Chet had remained with Mara all these months. It was with her now, as she put on her woollen cape and prepared to get out of St Luke's without being seen. At last she knew what she must do.

She silently left her room. Sister Catherine's room was nearby and twice she had heard Catherine come out and go down to the clinic wing. So it was important to be very quiet. She went down the back stair to the garden door, but before unbolting it peered through the little side window. No one was around. She had not expected anyone would be, not at this hour. She unbolted the door and stepped outside. Then, keeping well away from the main drive, she went towards the gates, and along the lane that led to Fenn House.

CHAPTER THIRTY-SIX

Catherine heard Sister Miriam go out because she was staying awake to check on a patient who had had an abscess drained that morning and would need the dressing changed. At first she did not take much notice of the sound, vaguely thinking Sister Miriam was going to the bathroom. But she did not go along the corridor to the bathroom at the far end, she came past Catherine's own door and went towards the main landing. After a moment, Catherine opened her door and looked out, wondering if anything was wrong. As she listened, she heard sounds from outside. At first she could not identify them, and thought she would just go to the main hall to make sure everything was all right. She slipped into her house shoes, reached for her cardigan, closed her own door and went quietly down the stairs.

It had begun to rain again and the strong wind was lashing the rain against the window panes, but through it Catherine heard the sound again, louder and more regular: a rhythmic clanging. She paused on the half landing, wiping away the condensation from the window to look out. The narrow window looked out over the side of the building, and through the driving rain Catherine saw that the wrought-iron gate leading out of the kitchen garden was open and swinging back and forth in the wind. The latch was an old one and had probably worked loose in the buffeting winds. It would keep banging against the garden wall all night like this, and there were a couple of patients on this side of the convent who were suffering fairly bad pain. Dr Innes had given morphine to one of them. It would be better if both of them could sleep as much as possible. It would not take a minute to slip outside and close the gate.

There was no sign of Sister Miriam, but the side door, which was usually methodically bolted with all the others, was unbolted. Surely Sister Miriam had not gone outside in this storm? But whatever she had done, the gate had better be closed. When Catherine stepped outside the coldness of the night wind made her gasp and the rain came at her like driving knives. She ran across to the gate, and was just pushing it firmly back into place when a darting movement made her turn sharply. Someone there? Catherine stood very still, scanning the darkness, wishing the wind was not quite so wild. She was just deciding the movement had been her imagination, when she glimpsed a figure like a dark shadow going between the thick bushes.

Sister Miriam.

For a moment Catherine could not think what to do. If she went back into the convent to get help, Sister Miriam would have vanished into the darkness and anything might happen to her. Catherine had no idea where Miriam was going, but she could at least go a little way after her to find out. She wrapped her cardigan round herself and went after the cloaked figure.

Her hair was flattened to her head in minutes and her thin house shoes were soaked through before she had gone a dozen paces. Sister Miriam was some way ahead, and wherever she was going it looked as if she was trying not to be seen. She was keeping off the drive, moving through the thick bushes that fringed it towards the main gates. Catherine hesitated, then saw Miriam turn left. Could she be going to the village? But it was a four-mile walk and it was ten o'clock at night. The only other place leading off this road was Fenn House. Theo! thought Catherine, remembering how someone had broken in and attacked him, and how he had told her to be careful because people were not always what they seemed. Had he meant Miriam? She glanced back at the comforting outline of St Luke's, trying to decide whether she should go back and get help. But that would take too long. If Sister Miriam really had attacked Theo two days ago for some mad, unfathomable reason, it might be too late.

Trying to ignore the lashing rain, Catherine went after her, keeping well to the shadows of the high hedges so she would not be seen. In this weather she certainly would not be heard. And if Sister Miriam really was going to Fenn House, Catherine could surely bang on the door and shout a warning to Theo.

As Mara went along the lane towards the turning to Fenn House, she had the strong feeling that something waited for her there. Was it the lost child Charmery had talked about that afternoon? The rusalka, trapped for ever in the cloudy river? Or was it Charmery herself?

Unmask the sin, Mara, they had said in Jilava. Let it into the light, see it for the evil it is, confront it and be absolved. Be absolved. Tonight Charmery was saying the same thing. Did Charmery want Mara to join her? Was the child with her – the rusalka? Yes, they were calling to her – they were saying that what she was about to do was right, it was the only way to atone.

Mara began to hurry so as not to keep them waiting.

As Catherine went into the drive, Sister Miriam was already going round the side of the house and down the path. She's not going into the house at all, she's going to the river! thought Catherine in sudden panic, and without pausing, she ran the rest of the way to the house. She half fell against the front door, banging hard on the knocker, not waiting for anyone to open it, but shouting above the rain.

'Theo – it's me – Catherine! I need help. Sister Miriam's going towards the river!'

She saw lights come on in the hall, but she was already running along the path after Miriam – along the path she had used all those years ago when Charmery called for help from the boathouse, the night David was born, the night he died. Was Charmery calling now, was that what she was hearing inside the wind and the rain? Don't be ridiculous, she thought.

Twice she slipped on the wet stones, and she could have sobbed with frustration, but each time she managed to scramble to her feet again and go forward. Behind her she could hear doors opening and voices: Theo's and a woman's voice, and another man's that sounded like Dr Innes. She half turned and shouted to them to follow her, hoping they would hear and see her in the darkness and understand. Theo's voice called out something, but the wind snatched it away. Catherine could not tell what he had said.

Here was the boathouse, dank and dismal, water dripping everywhere. Catherine stopped in the doorway, trying to see through the thick gloom. On the very edge of the landing stage, was a figure, not moving, just staring down at the black river. She's going to jump, thought Catherine in horror, and called Sister Miriam's name.

Miriam turned sharply, and although it was too dark to see her face properly, Catherine was aware of a distortion – of eyes blazing with madness.

Trying to keep her voice gentle and soothing, she said, 'Sister, what on earth are you doing out here in the rain? Let's go back to the convent.'

She moved forward, hoping to take Miriam's arm and pull her back, but Miriam put up a hand in defence.

'I'm not coming back with you,' she said, and Catherine heard with horror the spiralling madness in her voice. 'This is the only thing I can do. I have to pay for what I did, you see.'

'Sister, you haven't done anything—'

'I'm a murderess,' said Miriam. 'They said I was all those years ago, when they made me confess.'

'I don't understand. But come back with me now . . .' She edged nearer, hoping she could take Sister Miriam's arm and pull her back.

'I killed her,' cried Miriam. 'I killed Charmery Kendal! And now I have to atone.'

Her voice rose in a cry of such pain that Catherine flinched. She went forward, grabbing Miriam's arm. There was a moment when she thought she had firm hold of her, then she felt her own balance tip and realized Miriam had been about to jump and was taking Catherine with her. She fought for stability but it was already too late. The rain-swept night tilted all round her and the dark and treacherous river came up to meet her.

The icy water hit her like a massive blow and she went under almost immediately, fighting and gasping, trying to strike back to the surface, but her clothes were instantly sodden and even the flimsy shoes were dragging her down. The world became a green choking cloudiness. Catherine gasped helplessly, and felt the water go into her lungs. There was a moment when she thought; I can't die, not like this, and with the thought she was at the surface again, coughing and retching. Incredibly and blessedly, Theo was there, with Dr Innes behind him, both of them reaching out to her. Catherine felt Theo's hands, strong and safe, pulling her to the landing stage. Somehow she scrambled up onto the wooden planks, and as she fell against him his arms went round her. There was the feeling of masculinity pressed hard against her and the scent of his hair and skin. Something seemed to explode inside her mind. There was a moment of the purest mental clarity she had ever experienced – as if she was drinking light or being caressed by colour.

He released her and stepped back, looking down at her, still holding her hands. His hair was misted with rain and he looked pale although that might have been the cold night and the shock of what had just happened.

'You're safe,' he said.

'I know.' She broke off to cough and half retch, spluttering up muddy water. 'Sorry – disgusting.'

'Come back to the house,' he said. 'Lesley's fetching a blanket. But you'll be all right – you were only in the water a few minutes.'

'It felt like a lifetime,' said Catherine, still coughing up river water. 'Theo – what about Sister Miriam? Did you get to her?'

'Innes tried to reach her,' said Theo and glanced back at the dark waters behind them. 'He didn't reach her in time.'

The funeral service for Sister Miriam, once Mara Ionescu, took place in the chapel at St Luke's.

'It's semi private and it'll be very brief and unfussy,' said Michael Innes. 'But if you could bear to come.'

'We'll all come,' said Lesley. 'Of course we will.'

'Even though she confessed to killing Charmery?' Michael looked at Theo as he said this.

'Even then,' said Theo.

'The Bursar has managed to imply that her death was an accident,' said Michael. 'Suicide is very much frowned on within the Church.'

'I think I knew that in a vague way. Isn't it something to do with suicide being the product of despair, and despair being the ultimate giving up?'

'Yes. In medieval times, the monks called it *accidie*. It's still regarded as a very deadly sin, a weariness of the soul, a kind of spiritual sloth. So they're trying to avoid Mara being given that label.'

'The Church looking after its own,' said Theo, half to himself.

'It always has done,' he said.

After he had gone, Lesley said, 'What a nice man. So gentle. But you have the feeling that under the surface he might be capable of being very ungentle indeed.'

'I think he was probably quite fiery in his youth,' said Theo, glancing at her.

'I should think he's still got the capacity for being fiery now,' said Lesley quite sharply. 'And I don't know what you mean about "in his youth". He's not very much older than you.'

As she went out of the room, Theo, slightly startled, looked across at Petra, who grinned at him. 'Hadn't you seen that coming?' she said.

'No, but – there must be fifteen years between them,' said Theo.

'About that,' she agreed. 'So what?'

The funeral was as brief and unfussy as Michael had said.

Reverend Mother read the famous passage from Ecclesiastes: 'To every thing there is a season, and a time to every purpose under the heaven. A time to be born, and a time to die, a time to plant, and a time to pluck up that which is planted. A time to kill, and a time to heal. A time to break down and a time to build up . . .'

The familiar words spun round Theo's head, as he tried to visualize the child of his story: Mara who had loved and tried to protect her brother so fiercely; who had sat in the fire lit cottage and listened with absorption to the old legends and stories of her darkly romantic country; who, inside the grim sunken gaol of Jilava, had been made to believe she was a murderess, and in the end had become one. He wondered if he would ever come to terms with what Mara had done to Charmery. He wondered if he would ever understand why she had done it, or if Michael would understand. He glanced at Innes, quietly seated in the front pew, his face shuttered.

Reverend Mother was nearing the end of her reading. 'A time to love and a time to hate . . .'

Love and hate, thought Theo. I loved you, Charmery, and then for a while I hated you, he said to her memory. Every feeling I ever had for you was so intense, so exhausting. Even when you died, I couldn't free myself from your ghost. I thought you were going to stay with me for ever. But I don't think you will, not now. I think I'm letting go of you at last. And I think I'm glad, because you were burning me up.

'...a time for war and a time for peace ...'

War and peace ... Elisabeth and Andrei Valk had waged their own war; they had fought communists and believed so strongly in justice they had both endured imprisonment. But they had found some kind of peace in the end.

And what of Matthew? Had Matthew found peace?

As the mourners were ushered across the hall and into the refectory, Theo looked across at Matthew's sketches still hanging in the same place. He gave them a half nod of acknowledgement. I know you so much better now, Matthew, he thought. We're still talking about what my book will be called, but I'll stick out for *Matthew's Story*. He had not yet asked Petra or Michael where Matthew had ended up, but it had sounded as if he was still alive in the world. Theo was hoping one of them would know where. And unless it was somewhere impossible, like the far reaches of the Amazon, or the wilds of Tibet, Theo would try to meet him.

The mourners were dispersing and the sun was sinking over the fens when Catherine, who had been helping hand round cups of tea and coffee and plates of sandwiches, summoned up the courage to say, 'Theo, can we talk for a moment?'

'Of course. Here?'

'Let's go out to the garden – it's not all that cold.'

'You look fully recovered from the dousing in the Chet,' he said as they went through the side door.

'I am. It's four days ago anyway.' Catherine looked at him and, with the feeling of plunging into treacherous waters of a different kind to the Chet, said, 'Theo—'

He stopped her. 'You're staying here, aren't you?' he said.

'Yes,' said Catherine, startled. 'How did you know?'

'I think I knew when we got you out of the river that night,' he said. 'That's when you made the decision, isn't it?'

'Yes, it was. I thought I was going to drown,' said Catherine. 'And when I thought that—'

'I wasn't the one you reached for in your mind.'

'No.' She looked at him, grateful that he understood.

He made a gesture with his hands, as if he was letting go of something. 'We've sort of missed each other, haven't we?' he said. 'One of us should have been born earlier, or later, or in a different place or something.' He stood looking down at her. 'If we had met when you were eighteen . . .'

'But at eighteen I wanted something different,' said Catherine. 'And when I was eighteen, you were – I don't know how old you were, but you were probably still in love with Charmery.'

'Yes, I was.' Some strong emotion showed on his face for a moment, then he suddenly said, 'Catherine, since we're exchanging all these confidences – you met Charmery, didn't you?'

'Yes. Just once.'

'When?' And, as Catherine hesitated, he said, 'Was it nine years ago?'

'Near enough.'

'You were the one who helped Michael when David was born.'

'Yes,' said Catherine, seeing there was no way out of admitting this. 'How did you know about David?'

'Michael told me a couple of days ago,' said Theo.

'We agreed we'd never talk about it,' said Catherine. 'And I never have. But I've remembered David each year on the day of his birth.'

'Have you? Thank you.'

Catherine thought for a moment, then said, 'Charmery said

something, after it was over. I don't think she intended either of us to hear it, but I did. She looked at the baby and said, "I'm sorry, Theo . . . I loved you so much."'

For a moment he could not speak and Catherine thought she had gone too far. Then he said again, 'Thank you, Catherine.'

As they walked back towards the main doors, he was silent, but as they crossed the hall, he suddenly said, 'Shall you have any second thoughts about all this?'

'About us, d'you mean? Yes,' said Catherine, 'I'll have second thoughts, and probably third thoughts, too. But this is where I belong.'

As he left, she stood for a moment watching him walk down the drive. It's all right, she thought. I'll probably have a few bad moments thinking about what might have been, but this really is where I belong. Here in St Luke's, doing the work I studied and trained to do, seeing the years wheel by, fulfilled and deeply content.

With a brisk squaring of her shoulders to shake off any might-have-beens, she went back into the convent to help Sister Agnes with the washing-up.

Heathrow Airport was its usual seething mass of people and luggage trolleys, blared announcements in several languages and bewildering arrival and departure boards.

Theo had checked his luggage in and gone to the departure lounge. Unless there were any delays, in about ten minutes' time he would be called to board the plane and in three or four hours he would be in Switzerland. Petra had made the arrangements, and had promised that a car would meet him at Geneva.

He sat back, enjoying watching the people for these last few minutes. Who were they and where were they going? A lot of them would be holiday-makers, even at this time of year, and almost as many would be travelling on business. Some would be families going to meet up with relatives.

But none of them would be going to meet the grown-up ghost of a small boy who had haunted an old house in a remote Norfolk village.

As his flight was called, Theo smiled, picked up his hand luggage, and went to board the plane that would take him to meet Matthew.